Incognito

USA TODAY & WSJ BESTSELLING AUTHOR

SIOBHAN DAVIS

Original Paperback edition © July 2018

This Paperback edition © July 2023

ISBN-13: 978-1-959285-02-1

Editor: Kelly Hartigan (XterraWeb)

Cover design by Robin Harper

Stock imagery © Shutterstock (ballet shoes)

Stock imagery © Depositphotos (guitar & sheet music)

Musical notes are © Designed by macrovector / Freepik

Interior cover imagery © depositphotos.com

Formatted by Ciara Turley using Vellum

My dreams of attending Juilliard shattered the night tragedy struck my family.

That night, a part of me died inside.

Now, the only peace I find is in stolen moments on a rooftop where I dance to remember as much as to forget.

Until I literally stumble headfirst into Levi's life.

He's six feet two inches of ripped, hard, gorgeous temptation wrapped in a very irritating package. I swear he was sent to test me, because his hot-and-cold attitude pushes my buttons like no guy has before.

I don't know at what point I fall, but he worms his way into my heart without me noticing. One moment we are trading insults, the next we're shedding our clothes and surrendering to the searing-hot chemistry smoldering between us.

He breathes life into me again.

Before tearing me apart when I discover it's all been a lie.

He says he kept his identity a secret for my protection.

Yet I'm all alone when his enemies come for me.

Prologue

Shawn

I bolt upright in the bed, my heart hammering behind my ribcage. Blinking through sleepy eyes, I struggle to identify exactly what woke me. The black silk sheets are slightly damp underneath me, and beads of sweat cling to my brow. Pushing my longer hair back off my face, I stifle a yawn as I check the time on my cell.

An ear-shattering siren rings out, wailing painfully within the confines of my empty house, and I immediately spring into action. I jump out of bed, with my cell in my hand, and grab my wallet from the bedside table. Racing to the far corner of my master suite, I quickly punch in the code on the wall-mounted keypad. I step back as the hidden door slides open, glancing over my shoulder at the sound of approaching footfalls.

A loud crash from the hallway alerts me to the impending danger, and I falter for a split second. Anger fuels the blood flowing through my veins, and I clench and unclench my fists at my side while contemplating tackling the assholes who have broken into my house. But my manager's previous cautionary warning churns through my brain, and I know what I need to do, even if it feels cowardly to run in the opposite direction.

Emitting a frustrated sigh, I step into the darkness instead of following my instinct and rushing out to the hallway to confront the intruders. Stabbing the large red button on my right, I watch as the door glides shut, securing me behind the wall of my bedroom. Lights illuminate the darkness instantly. Wasting no time, I run, barefoot, down the narrow passageway until I meet the elevator. Adrenaline pumping, I get in, emerging a minute later in the basement of my supposedly private property, nestled deep in the Hollywood Hills.

I'm going to kick someone's ass for this. I didn't just drop over two mill installing the latest security systems to have some fucking asshole break into my house, *again*, in the middle of the night. That's assuming it's the same crew. I was out of town that time, but it shook me up enough to invoke new precautionary measures. Not that it seems to have done much good. *How the hell did they get inside the house when it's like Fort fucking Knox?* Anger mixes with frustration as I stalk forward, silently cursing every motherfucker I can think of as I run.

Still concealed behind the walls of my house, I follow the lit path to the large steel door, relieved to have made it here undetected. Pressing my thumbprint to the digital pad, I only permit myself to breathe freely once I'm safely secured behind the impenetrable door of my hidden panic room.

My fingers are curled rigidly around my cell as I drop onto the couch. Screens flicker to life on the wall in front of me, showcasing different rooms in my vast house.

My eyes scan the camera feeds, flitting from room to room as I look for signs of activity. A growl builds at the base of my throat when I spot three figures, dressed head to toe in black, scouring every inch of my bedroom. Wondering where the fuck

I am, no doubt. A smug laugh rips from my mouth. Better luck next time, dickheads.

When my cell rings, I answer without taking my eyes off the camera feed.

"The cops are on their way. Are you okay?" Luke—my manager—asks, his usual calm voice sounding ruffled.

"Yes," I say, through gritted teeth. "I'm in the panic room watching three assholes trash my bedroom." The intruders are ripping through my stuff now. Flipping my bed over, flinging furniture around the room, and dumping piles of my clothes on the hardwood floor, urgently yanking out drawers as they search for who the fuck knows what.

If they're looking for cash, they'll be sorely disappointed. I have a few hundred-dollar bills in my bedside table, but the rest of my cash is in here with me.

I learned not to leave cash lying around my house the hard way. Too often, I woke up after a night of heavy partying to discover I'd been swindled. That's what happens when you're too high and too drunk to care. When you invite every douchebag and his granny back to yours to continue the party. When you wake up beside strange girls passed out in your bed, wondering if you fucked one or all three of them or if you were too wasted to even get it up.

I promised myself never again.

I'm sick of jerks and sluts taking advantage.

And thieving assholes who have the nerve to steal into my house in the dead of night.

My head swivels to the safe on the far side of the room, and I'm grateful I decided to relocate it from my bedroom a couple months ago when this room was being built. They can trash my bedroom all they like. Hell, I hope they get distracted looking for cash and the cops get here before they have time to skip off into the sunset.

I want to find the prick determined to make my life a living hell.

The police believe the previous break-in, along with other malicious activity, is the work of one individual, someone clever who is pulling the strings in the background and doing a stellar job of hiding his tracks.

Every celebrity deals with groupies, crazies, and stalkers—it comes with the territory—but this latest crazy genuinely has me concerned. No one has ever managed to break into my house before, and now it's happened twice in as many months.

It unnerves me, has me on edge, and I could fucking do without the hassle. It's not like I don't have enough shit on my plate as it is.

"Do you know any of them?" Luke inquires, pulling me out of my mind.

"They're wearing masks, so that'd be a no," I snap.

"Just hang tight. I'm on my way, and the police should be with you shortly." He pauses momentarily. "Don't do anything stupid, Shawn. Promise me you'll stay in the sealed room."

"I'm not a fucking idiot. Just get here already." Then I hang up, tossing my cell on the couch beside me.

Man, I would fucking kill for a drink or a hit right about now. I get up and pace the room, briefly considering taking a shower to cool off before the cops get here.

The guys I hired to do the security work did a great job with this space. I have a decent-sized living area with a compact kitchen, fully stocked pantry, small bedroom, and bathroom, complete with a shower. With the rate I've been stacking up death threats, you never know how often I'll need to use this place or how long I'll be trapped here for. I wanted to make sure it had all the necessities, but, still, I think I'd go fucking crazy if I was stuck in here for any length of time.

I don't do well with confined spaces.

Reminds me too much of my brief stint in a police cell and the months I spent in rehab, and I'm trying really hard to put all that shit behind me.

My breath stalls in my chest as I scan the screen again, watching one of the guys scrawl something on my bedroom wall. The other two are hovering in the doorway, shouting at the third guy. I don't have the sound on, so I can't hear what they're saying. Figure it best to listen to it later. If they say something that incites me, I'll probably bust out of here and go after their thieving asses. But that would not be smart.

I can take care of myself; I have the height, stamina, and aggression needed to take them on. But three against one isn't good odds and only an idiot would attempt it. The last thing Mom needs is to wake up to another worrying news report.

A lump wedges in my throat, but I force all thoughts of Mom aside as I walk up to the screen, leaning in closer, eyes narrowing as I focus on the messy red message spray-painted across my bedroom wall.

As the words take on a cohesive form, all the blood turns to ice in my veins.

NOBODY PUTS BABY IN THE CORNER. VENGEANGE WILL BE MINE.

Chapter 1

Dakota

There are moments in time that are forever imprinted on your soul. When you can remember exactly where you were, who you were with, and what you were doing precisely at the point where something catastrophic occurred.

Like my dad remembers staring in shock at the TV screen, in the lobby of his accounting firm on 9/11, surrounded by his devastated employees, all horror-struck as planes hit the Twin Towers, and my mom remembers crying in the car when the radio confirmed news that Princess Diana had died in a tunnel in Paris.

I will never forget the day my life changed irrevocably.

It was exactly thirteen months ago, one sweltering-hot August night, that I received the call that shattered my world and devastated my family.

I was with my boyfriend, Cole, at his buddy Brandon's house, enjoying one of the last summer parties before we all started college. I was due to leave for New York—for Juilliard—in two weeks, and our time together was drawing to a close.

I knew it.

He knew it.

But neither one of us had mentioned it. We were going to try the whole long-distance thing, but I knew things would peter out. So, we were making every second count. Cole and I were in the middle of a highly-competitive game of beer pong with Brandon and Miley when my cell vibrated.

I ignored it. *Because who the hell answers the phone when they're smashed and in the zone?*

But it wouldn't stop. Vibrating incessantly. And a weird sensation crept over me. Cursing the intrusion, I'd grabbed my cell and answered, not stopping to check who it was.

Daddy's words penetrated my ears, but I couldn't believe them.

Couldn't hear anything over the splintering of my heart.

And the screaming.

God, the agonized screaming penetrated my soul, seeping deep, marking me for eternity.

I screamed until my throat scraped raw. Until my cries and my screams extinguished, giving way to a hazy numbness that hasn't lifted since.

Cole was concerned, and the worried expression on his face transformed to horror when he plucked the cell from my stiff fingers and listened to the news with his own ears.

The rest is a bit of a blur. Cole hugging me. Leading me comatose out of the house and into Jacob's Jeep. Jacob's mouth moving, offering condolences, no doubt, but I still couldn't hear over the relentless screaming in my head.

A shuddering breath leaves my lips as I recall that horrific moment—the moment when my world was irreparably altered.

My current surroundings come back into sharp focus as I'm pulled out of my mind, and all memories of the past, crashing headfirst into the present. I stop dancing, crumpling onto the filthy asphalt roof as crippling pain lances me on all sides.

Fuck. It's never ending. This torment.

Waves of grief crash into me.

Consuming me.

Devastating me.

Reminding me how fleeting life is.

How special those precious moments with loved ones are, and how you don't realize it until it's too late.

Demonstrating how surviving is almost more tragic than death.

Whoever said grief eases with time was a freaking liar. I'd love to punch that nameless, faceless asshole for filling grief-stricken mourners with such false hope.

I hug my arms around my waist, rocking back and forth on my knees, while I draw deep breaths, in and out, in an attempt to take back control.

Breathe, Dakota.

Live, Dakota.

Remember, Dakota.

I repeat a familiar mantra. A frantic attempt to cling to the last vestiges of myself as I drown in a sea of oblivion—my soul, my heart, my will to live, diminishing further with each passing day.

It's no wonder Cole did what he did.

I wouldn't want to be with my miserable, depressed self either.

The song changes on my cell, and Adele's husky tones swirl through the still night air. Strangely, the anguish and emotion in her voice soothes the frayed edges of my nerves. Reminding me that I'm not alone.

That other people are suffering.

And surviving.

That life must go on.

It's what she would want.

She'd hate to see me like this.

I lie flat on my back, staring up at the starry night. Wondering if she's up there. Watching me. Using that no-nonsense tone of hers to tell me to pull myself together. A small smile traverses my lips, and I haul myself to my feet, starting to dance again.

I sway to the rhythm of the music, closing my eyes and letting my body absorb the emotion of the song, using the heartbreak and sadness to dictate my movements. My limbs are loose, my feet light as I move around the empty roof of the abandoned building, twirling and flying, arching and pivoting. Dancing nonstop as successive songs tumble from my cell.

It's the only thing that helps.

The only thing that reminds me I'm still me.

That hidden inside this shell of a person somewhere lies the real Dakota Gray.

I tiptoe into my dorm room, not wanting to wake my roommate Daisy. I'm later than usual, having lost myself in the music and dance, not realizing that so much time had passed. Removing my shoes at the door, I pad to the refrigerator, grabbing a fresh bottle of water.

Most nights, I'm gone until one a.m. max, but it's much, much later than that now, and I don't want to disturb her. Especially when she's most likely happily ensconced in dreamland. No point in both of us being sleep-deprived and tired tomorrow.

I knock back the water, welcoming the icy cold liquid as it glides down my parched throat. I head toward the bathroom, frowning when I spot a thin glimmer of light creeping under the bedroom door.

"Kota? Is that you?" Daisy calls out, worry underscoring her tone.

I curse under my breath, hating that I've disturbed her in the middle of the night. Daisy is a total sweetheart, and she doesn't deserve to get dragged into my shit. Which is one of the reasons why I haven't told her about Layla or Juilliard.

I open the door to our shared bedroom, glancing sheepishly at my roommate. She's propped up in bed, surrounded by her Shawn Lucas posters, with her Kindle lying beside her. "I hope you weren't waiting up for me." I perch on the end of her bed, conscious I'm a sweaty mess and in dire need of a shower.

"You're late. I was worried." Her brows pinch together, and my heart swells at her concern.

It's been a while since anyone worried about me. Just for a second, I allow myself to feel something other than grief and guilt and despair, and it's nice. "I'm sorry I worried you. I lost track of time. You should have texted me, and I would've let you know I was okay."

Crossing her legs in front of her, she studies my eyes. Her expression is soft. "I won't pry, but I'm here if you ever need to talk about it." A heavy pressure settles on my chest, making breathing difficult. "But I really don't think it's safe for you to be going out so late at night on your own. And that abandoned building gives me the heebie-jeebies during the day. I don't know how you can go there in the pitch-dark." She visibly shivers.

"I'm not scared," I truthfully admit. "And you know I have trouble sleeping. It's better to be out there dancing than inside tossing and turning for hours."

"I don't want anything to happen to you. It's pretty isolated down by the river, and who knows what kind of weirdos use that building after dark."

"I've never seen anyone there, and this is a safe part of town." Okay, that's probably a stretch. While Iowa City doesn't have unusual rates of crime, Daisy is right—it's not safe for any woman to be roaming the city after midnight.

I'm not sure what it says about me, but that's not even a factor.

I'm not scared.

I'm the opposite.

Dancing on that rooftop every night is the only time I feel free of the crippling emotions strangling me. I make sure I'm there at twelve oh three every night. The exact time Dad's phone call came in.

And I dance.

For me.

For Layla.

For my shattered family and my lost dreams.

And I'm not frightened of the dark or unknown terrors. It's almost symbolic. Like the dark night represents my heavy soul and dancing is the only glimmer of light, a fragile spark igniting the flame. A flame that once burned so bright it almost blinded.

"There are plenty of dance classes around. Why don't you enroll in one of those instead?" she suggests, and I know her heart is in the right place.

I shake my head. "You don't understand..." My breath heaves out in choked spurts, that pressure on my chest tightening further. "I need to do it alone. And it's as much about the timing as it is the dancing and I...I need it to breathe." Averting my eyes for fear of what they'll betray, I stare at the worn beige carpet.

"Oh, Dakota." Her voice is doused in sadness, and I tip my chin up. Compassion fills her gaze, and she scoots out from under the covers, over to my side. She takes my hand in hers. "Just promise me you'll take extra precautions. And maybe you could text me when you get there and when you're leaving so I know you're safe?"

"If I wasn't so sweaty, I'd hug the shit out of you right now," I admit as tears prick my eyes. "You don't know how much it means that you care. And I pinch myself every day, so grateful I landed you as my roomie. I was terrified I was going to be paired with some nutjob."

"Me too." She smiles timidly. "I was really hoping I'd have a ready-made friend, and I couldn't be happier."

I quirk a brow. "Even if I am a reclusive weirdo who leaves you to go dancing on the roof of an abandoned building at midnight?"

"We all have our flaws," she teases, and I laugh quietly.

"Thank you. For being a good friend." Although we've only known each other three weeks, I can already tell that Daisy and I will be friends for life.

The next morning, I drag my weary body across town to the Tippie College of Business, joining the throngs of students headed toward the impressive main building. Composed of cream stone and glass, the structure has some funky architectural features that speak to the dormant creative streak in me.

But it's about the only appealing thing.

As I take a seat in one of the smaller auditoriums, I can't help wondering what I'd be doing if I was at Juilliard like I was meant to be. If I hadn't postponed my place for a year and then relinquished it.

My life would be vastly different.

A sharp ache pierces my chest cavity, but I brush it aside. It hurts to go there, and it's selfish to wish I had a different life. At least I still *have* a life. Accounting doesn't set my world on fire, and it's unlikely it ever will. I know that already, even though I've only been here a few weeks. It's about as far removed from where I thought I'd be as you can get.

Accounting was always Layla's path, not mine. She was the one destined to follow in Dad's footsteps. The one groomed to eventually take over his successful business. My dream was to dance on a world stage, but I've had to forego those notions now.

I can't disappoint my parents.

They're counting on me.

They've already lost one daughter, and they're relying on me to fill Layla's shoes. In every regard.

The only problem is, her shoes are far too big to fill.

And I already feel like I'm letting them down.

Chapter 2

Shawn

"It's a pleasure to meet you in the flesh, Mr. Lucas," Devin Morgan says, firmly shaking my hand. "Although I wish the circumstances were different." His warm smile fades, and a more serious expression washes over his features.

"You and me both," I say, flopping down, uninvited, on one of the chairs in front of his mahogany desk. "And call me Shawn. Mr. Lucas makes me sound like an old fart."

"Duly noted," he replies, fighting a smirk. "And call me Devin."

I scan the functional but plush surroundings of his office, and it's obvious this guy is doing well for himself. Morgan Security has gained a strong reputation in a short span of time, especially within celebrity circles.

In the months following the most recent home invasion, several serious death threats have been received. All messages contain similar quotes from favorite movies along with the vengeance line, and experts have confirmed it's originating from the same source. What a pity the cops showed up too late to my house *again* to apprehend the dudes. If they had, we might have the name of the person pulling the strings. While I've had my fair share of crazies and stalkers in the six years I've been in the spotlight, this feels different.

Personal.

When my dressing room was vandalized while I was performing at Summerfest, and then someone took a shot at me at the VMAs, it became deadly serious. That's when the label stepped in, demanding extra security measures be put in place. Luke found Morgan Security, and I've had a couple of chats via phone with the owner, but this is the first time I'm meeting him in person.

When I'd sat down with Luke and reps from the label to discuss the situation a couple of weeks ago, I'd been pleasantly surprised at their proposal. Not that they'd know that from my reaction. Can't give the jerks in suits any indication I'm actually loving this plan, because that would only give them more power, more control, over me. Let them think I'm pissed and frustrated when the truth is I'm excited about something for the first time in years. They think they're forcing me into hiding, for my protection, and to give me time to work on my new album, but it's in no way a hardship or inconvenience.

It didn't take anything for Luke to sell the idea to me, and I know he must've gone out on a limb to get the label to agree to it in the first place.

I'll add it to the list of stuff I owe him for.

As showbiz managers go, Luke is the shit. He refuses to take any of my crap, and I admire him for it. Not only that, he's a decent guy, and he genuinely cares about me and my career. He's not just doing this for what he can get out of it, and that's rare in this business.

I guess I should be thankful Mom found him.

But I'm still too pissed at her for bailing on me.

"Nice disguise by the way," Devin says, quickly giving me the once-over. "I doubt anyone will recognize you like that."

"I hope not. That would defeat the whole purpose." I claw my fingers through my shorter, newly dark hair. I hated having to cut my longer blond locks. I had only grown it out in recent months, in part as my latest fuck you to the label. My grungier look didn't suit the brand they've so carefully cultivated over the years, but I'm done with letting those money-grabbing power-hungry dicks dictate how I dress and how I look. It's bad enough they dictate the type of music I perform, but my hands are relatively tied there. Until my contract expires, and then they can kiss my million-dollar ass goodbye.

"The university is large enough to remain hidden, but it still has a smaller campus feel with a great sense of community," Luke proudly adds, sounding like he's personally on the University of Iowa's marketing payroll. I know the dude graduated from there, and he's got nothing but positive reports, but still. Enough is enough.

"Dude. Shut up already. I'm enrolled so you can quit with the sales pitch." I cross my legs at the ankles, leaning back in my chair. "I don't give a flying fuck about Greek life, or the Hawkeyes, or the wonderful teaching staff, or the fact it's been voted in the top five party schools in America."

"Fuck me," Luke says, startling me. He's not one to throw profanities around. "Did I just hear Shawn Lucas, bad ass popstar with a propensity for outrageous behavior and piss-poor decision-making state he doesn't care about partying?" He scrubs a hand over his smooth jaw. "I must be imagining things."

"Hardy-fucking-har. You need to watch your language. That shit is catching." I toss him a wicked smirk, and he grins back at me.

Devin clears his throat. "I have some personal business to

attend to shortly, so we'd best get started." That's a pretty blunt nod to my tardiness. We were supposed to be here over an hour ago, but punctuality has always been an issue for me.

He hands me a paper folder. "Everything is set up with the college, thanks to your manager here." He nods at Luke. "His contact smoothed things over with your last-minute application and he got you enrolled as an accounting major." Devin sits down behind his desk, staring at me with a slightly puzzled expression. "Why accounting? I thought you'd go for music."

"I'm trying to blend into the background, and choosing music is too risky. Someone might recognize my voice and put two and two together. The media will be speculating when I don't show up to the premiere next week, and it won't take them long to realize I've skipped town. They'll make it their mission to find out where I am, and I'd rather not help them by making it too easy."

"Fair point," Devin agrees.

"Besides, there's nothing these idiots can teach me. I already play three instruments, write and produce my own songs, and I was a multi-millionaire by the time I was fifteen. I'm not going to listen to some wannabe who never made it try to tell me how to succeed in the music business."

"Okay then." Devin looks amused, while Luke has a resigned look on his face.

"I've always been good at math," I continue, "and I take a keen interest in my finances. Not gonna let some shady prick steal from me. I figure, for the limited time I'm here, I might as well learn something useful."

"Smart thinking," Devin says, sliding an envelope across the desk to me. "That's your ID and bank cards in your new name, plus the keys to your penthouse and SUV. My guys have installed the necessary security measures. We'll have eyes on you at all times."

I sit up a little straighter. "How does this work?"

Devin clasps his hands in front of him as he speaks. "You'll have a bodyguard on you at all times. My guys are discreet, so you won't notice them, but rest assured they'll be there. They work on rotation, so the guys will change out every eight hours. We have secret cameras monitoring your apartment twenty-four-seven and tracking devices installed in your car and on your cell. There's an alarm button in every room of the apartment, and we built a small panic room in your closet per your instructions. It's basic but functional."

"Wow. Zero privacy. I'm so loving that." My chest tightens. I know it's for my own good, but I'm so sick of this shit. "What if I want to bring a girl home to fuck?"

Luke's face turns to stone. "Goddamn it, Shawn! Hooking up should be the last thing on your mind."

"It is. I'm only fucking with you." I smirk, and he rolls his eyes. "My sole focus is my new album. I'm done with nailing random chicks."

Truth. When I was younger, when I'd just burst onto the scene, all the pussy on tap was like manna from heaven. I overindulged like girls were going extinct. It's a wonder my dick didn't fall off from overuse. But I haven't had much action the last couple years. Initially, it was because blow and alcohol replaced the high from sex, but since I got cleaned up, I've lost interest in the girls who throw themselves at me, desperate to spend the night with a celebrity purely for the bragging rights and the opportunity to make a quick buck by sharing the deets with some sleazy scumbag journalist.

Every girl I meet, I'm wary of. They all want something from me, and I can't trust anyone. And most of the female celebrities I meet are way too into themselves to offer me anything worthwhile.

I've given up any idea of a relationship, and I'm cool with that.

This opportunity gives me the chance to be a regular guy. To walk the campus like a normal student, without the glare of the world looking at my every move, just waiting for me to fuck up again. You can't put a price on that.

When I was a kid, playing with Nick and Matt in the basement of Matt's house, we used to dream of stardom. Of cameras flashing in our faces. Of girls throwing themselves at us naked.

Now I have all that, and I wish I could go back to that basement.

Where it was solely about my two best buds and the music.

I didn't realize it back then, but those were the good times.

"The only camera inside your place is in the hallway," Devin says, dragging me back into the present. "The rest are outside in the corridor, and we have one on the balcony, so you still have privacy," he confirms just as the phone rings on his desk. As he lifts the receiver to his ear, the door swings open, and a little guy bursts eagerly into the room. "Daddy!" he shrieks, running at Devin and jumping onto his lap.

A gorgeous brunette rushes into the room after him, cradling a tiny baby in her arms. "Oh my God, I'm so sorry, Dev. He ran off before I could catch him."

"Don't fret on our behalf," Luke pipes up, always the gentleman. He stands and extends his hand to the bombshell. "I'm Luke Manning, and I'm guessing you are Mrs. Morgan?"

She nods. "I'm Angelina." Awkwardly reaching out, she shakes his hand. "But most everyone calls me Ange."

Devin stands, his son wrapped around him like a spider monkey as he rounds the desk. Leaning down, he plants a kiss on top of the sleeping baby's head before pecking his wife on the lips. "It's okay, honey. I'll be finished here in a few if you want to wait outside."

The baby wriggles within the confines of the blanket, emitting a little whimper.

Luke looks on the verge of melting into a puddle on the floor. His wife only gave birth to their firstborn a few weeks ago, and I know it's killing him being away from them right now. "How old is she?" he asks, smiling down at the baby.

"She's one month today," Ange confirms, beaming radiantly. "We're heading to her check-up shortly."

"Shut. Up." I exclaim, standing up, my eyes roaming over her lush curves in appreciation. "There's no way you just had a baby a month ago." Her tummy is flat as a board, her body slim with curves in all the right places. I've never had a thing for older women, but Ange is definitely one MILF I'd love to get my hands on.

"Are you fucking shitting me right now?" Devin glares at me, while Ange hastily covers her little boy's ears.

I smirk, taking one last lingering glance at his hot wife, purely to mess with him.

Devin steps protectively in front of her. "If you don't stop eye-fucking my wife, you and me are gonna have a big problem, *buddy*."

Ange gasps, tugging him back and shaking her head. "Devin, my God. Stop overreacting. He wasn't doing anything wrong."

Devin pins her with an incredulous look, and I pierce her with a loaded smile. One that normally melts the panties off girls and has them swooning at my feet. "Devin's right, sweetheart. I *was* mentally undressing you." I shrug, not in the least bit apologetic. "I didn't mean any disrespect, but it's not often I meet such a smoking hot momma."

Luke looks like he wants to strangle me, but Devin would definitely beat him to it.

I hold out my hand to her, brazen as you like. "Seeing as no one took the time to introduce us, I'll do the honors. I'm Shawn Lucas." She stares at me as if in a daze, and I lift her hand to my lips, planting a soft kiss on her skin.

If I wasn't a client, I'd say Devin would've punched my lights out by now.

"It's a pleasure to meet you." I wink, and her mouth hangs open.

"Control your client," Devin demands, on a growl, turning the full extent of his glare on Luke.

Luke places a restraining hand on my arm. "Shawn, knock it off. Seriously, this crap is starting to get old."

Ange gasps, finding her voice. "Shawn Lucas?" She squints, looking intently into my eyes. "You're *the* Shawn Lucas? You look really different. I'd never have recognized you."

Well, that's good to know. I mock bow, sweeping my hand out in an overly dramatic fashion—I always did have a flair for the dramatic. "The very one. In the flesh." I waggle my brows, slanting her a wide grin, and Devin gets all up in my face.

"Unless you want me to terminate our agreement right this fu—" He halts mid-word, noticing his innocent kid and the warning look on his wife's face. "Right this second, I suggest you back the hell away from my wife."

I laugh, slapping him on the shoulder. "Relax, man. I'm only messing with ya. Your wife is gorgeous, but she's yours. I get that. No need to go all caveman on me."

Devin rubs a spot between his brows, looking all tense and shit. "Ange, would you mind taking the kids and waiting outside? I won't be much longer."

Touching his arm lightly, she nods, and they share some unspoken communication as they peer into one another's eyes. It's only a subtle gesture, and there's nothing inappropriate about it, but it's wholly intimate, and a sudden pang of envy jumps up and slaps me, out of nowhere.

My Adam's apple bobs in my throat, and I sit back down in my seat, all playfulness gone.

"Vroom, vroom." A tiny hand appears at my side, and their little boy runs a toy car up and down the arm of my chair. "You like cars?" he asks, looking up at me with these big wide innocent blue eyes.

"Love 'em."

"Whaz your favrit?"

I pretend to think about it, rubbing my chin. "Hmm. Let me think. I've got a few cars," I tell him, and his eyes pop wide. "But you want to know a secret?"

He nods his head enthusiastically. "C'mere." I pat my knee and he jumps on me in a flash, narrowly avoiding elbowing me in the junk. I lower my voice and lean into his cute little face. "I have some of the best cars in the world, but my absolute favorite is this old beat-up truck my Grandpa Quinn left me after he, uh...went to heaven, because every time I sit in the cab, it reminds me of him, and every time I take it out for a drive, it reminds me of being a little boy, and I like remembering those good times."

"Can I haz a ride in your truck?" His eyes blink rapidly as he stares excitedly at me.

"Well, my truck's very far away, but maybe someday I can take you out."

"Yay!" He jumps off my lap, gripping his little car for dear life and running to his dad. "I'm gonna ride in that man's truck, Daddy."

I chuckle to hide the emotion clogging my throat.

Devin lifts him up. "That's awesome, Ayden, but now you need to say goodbye and go with your mom and sister." He pretends to whisper. "I need you to look after them for me until I'm finished with my work. Can you do that for me, buddy?"

Ayden nods agreeably. "I'll taz care of them. I'm really big now." He puffs out his chest, and damn, if that doesn't get me in the feels.

"It was nice to meet you, Shawn," Ange says, waving at me. "Even if you did bring out a side of my husband I haven't seen in a long while." She grins, ushering her boisterous son out and closing the door behind her.

"Sorry about that," Devin says, reclaiming his seat. "I thought we'd be finished by now when I made arrangements earlier."

"You are not the one who needs to apologize, Devin," Luke supplies, shooting me a stern look.

I roll my eyes. "Dude, I already apologized to the lady. Let it go." I flick my gaze to Devin. "We're good, yeah?"

"Providing you stop hitting on my wife, yeah, we're good."

"You're a lucky man," I tell him, shocking myself with my honesty.

He smiles expansively. "I am, and I never take it for granted." He looks curiously at me. "You were great with Ayden. You like kids?"

I shrug. "I have twin brothers about Ayden's age. I don't get to see them a lot, but, when I do, we have fun. They're cool little kids."

He nods in understanding, and then he's all businesslike again, hurrying through the last few items we have to cover before he brings the meeting to a close.

Devin seems to concur with the police assessment that there is one person behind this and he's not your average stalker. He explains that, most times, it's not that difficult to identify celebrity stalkers, but the person doing this to me is smarter than the norm, leaving no trail, no evidence, we can pursue. However, he assures me his team is the best, and he's positive he'll find this person and work with the authorities to bring him to justice.

The guy exudes this quiet confidence that reassures me, and I believe I'm in safe hands. I'm feeling a lot more relaxed as I leave his office, and that's a massive improvement from when I arrived.

One hour, and one massive ass-kicking from Luke, later, I'm finally standing outside my new apartment block, squinting in the faint afternoon sun as I look up at the top of the building, skimming my gaze over the large penthouse apartment that I'll call home for the next while.

There's a spring in my step as I skip into the building for the first time, and an air of anticipation swirls around me.

For the first time in years, I finally feel like I'm getting to do something for me.

Like I can properly breathe and the air is less restricting here.

Perhaps it's all in my head.

But, for now, I'm determined to make the most of this time.

To reconnect with the art of creating music.

To rediscover who I am.

Because, for the last few years, I've lost all sight of the real Shawn Lucas.

And it's time to rectify that.

Chapter 3

Dakota

"Shit!" I mumble under my breath, quickening my pace as I pound the pavements. It's not like me to sleep through my alarm, but I guess all the late nights are starting to catch up to me. Prof Jennings is a complete stickler for timekeeping, and she'll make an example of me if I'm late. I probably should've called a taxi, but we don't live that far from the business school, and I figured it would be just as quick to walk. With only five minutes to spare, I'm definitely second-guessing myself now.

Extracting my cell from the pocket of my jean skirt, I begin tapping out a quick message to Elsa, to see if she can buy me some time. I'm not watching where I'm going as I race around the corner onto the campus, slamming full-force into solid resistance. My cell flies out of my hand the same time I wobble on my feet, arms and legs flailing as I struggle to remain upright. A shriek tumbles from my mouth when I start falling. My book bag slips off my shoulder onto the ground as I grapple to maintain balance.

Large hands snake around my back, and I'm hauled against

a hard, warm, masculine chest. My face is buried in his shirt, and I'm suddenly hyper-aware of the way I'm held against him. How firmly his hands are gripping my lower back and all the ways in which we are pressed together. I swallow over the sudden ripple of electricity in the air. Notes of citrus and sandalwood tickle my nostrils, and I inhale the intoxicating masculine smell without stopping to think about it.

"Da fuck? Did you just sniff me?" Disbelief and derision are evident in his tone.

Slowly, I tip my chin up, completely embarrassed but ready to apologize, when I'm waylaid by the most gorgeous face I've ever seen. His strong jaw is peppered with a light layer of stubble, and he has full, pouty lips—currently twisted into a sneer, but I'm purposely ignoring that fact for now. His expressive green eyes are encased behind trendy black-rimmed glasses, only adding to the appeal. I've always had a thing for hot, nerdy guys in glasses, and this dude measures up even if there's nothing nerdy about him at all. With lustrous, dark hair shorn tight at the sides and worn long and effortlessly messy on top, this guy is seriously hot. Like Hollywood-level hot.

I'm already salivating.

And imagining licking every inch of his delectable body.

I jerk out of his hold as the thought lands in my mind, my cheeks flushing slightly at my barefaced visceral reaction.

"Why the fuck weren't you watching where you were going?" he demands, bending down to the ground with an irritated scowl etched across his delicious face.

I can't help ogling him as he bends over, noticing how his shirt stretches tight across his toned back, the hem riding up a few inches, exposing a strip of smooth, tan skin. My mouth is suddenly dry, my panties damp, and a foreign feeling rushes through me.

I take a step back as he straightens up, thrusting my cell and my bag at me. My eyes unashamedly roam his body from head to toe, and butterflies scatter in my chest. This guy is tall, at least over six feet, and he's built. Nicely built. Not overdone or too bulky. He's lean, with broad shoulders, abs that are clearly defined, even through the cotton of his tight shirt, and long, muscular legs that should be illegal on a guy.

He snorts out a laugh, shaking his head. "You're a real piece of work."

My eyelids flutter incessantly as I stare at him through a haze of lust.

This guy is something else.

And I'm making a total fool of myself.

I clear my throat and prepare to eat crow. I did bump into him after all, and I've been blatantly objectifying him since. "I'm so sorry. For knocking into you and for, ah..." *How exactly does one apologize for such blatant drooling?*

"Treating me like man candy?" He smirks knowingly, and the smug, condescending expression on his face raises my hackles. Arrogance is one of my pet peeves in a guy. Should've known someone who looks like this would get hit on a lot and that it'd go straight to his over-inflated head.

"You caught me unaware," I explain, holding his gaze in what I hope is a neutral but confident manner. "But I apologize for my inappropriate behavior."

He smirks again, and it shaves a layer of attractiveness off his face. He opens his mouth to speak when a ping erupts from his cell, capturing both our attention.

My nostrils flare as I spot the open game app on his phone. "Hang on here a second." I plant my hands on my hips and glare at him. "You weren't looking where you were going either!" I gesture at his cell. "You were too damned busy playing Fortnite to notice me! This is as much your fault as it is mine."

"You're just splitting hairs, Blondie." He messes the top of my head, and I see red.

"Don't call me that! It's insulting and sexist."

Cocking his head to the side, he stares incredulously at me. "And the way you were checking me out wasn't?"

Valid point.

Douchebag.

Securing the strap of my bag over my shoulder, I calm myself before issuing my parting line. "Well, I guess that makes us even then." I pierce him with a final scathing look before stepping away, walking briskly toward the entrance.

"You're welcome," he hollers after me, and I have a fleeting urge to flip him the bird, but I quell the impulse and keep my head high as I hurry toward class, composing plausible excuses to defend my tardiness in my head.

"Please, come," Elsa pleads with me from across the table in the cafeteria.

I pause, fork halfway to my mouth. "You know I would if I could, but I have to go home this weekend."

"You've gone home every weekend, Kota. Surely your parents don't expect you to keep that up indefinitely," Tabitha cuts in.

"You won't ever get freshman year back again," Elsa adds, not realizing I understand that lesson more than anyone. I've already missed out on a year, so, trust me, I don't want to waste any more time, but it's not cut and dry.

"I know, but it's complicated. My family needs me, and the main reason I chose to come to U of I was because it's only a three-hour drive back home."

Tabitha and Elsa share a look, and I stare down at my plate

of uneaten food, wishing I had a magic lamp and I could summon a genie to puff me out of here. I know I'm going to have to explain the situation to my roomie and my new classmates soon, but I need to psych myself up for the multitude of questions they'll have, and I'm not there yet.

"Hey." Tabs stretches her hand across the table, squeezing mine. "It's okay. We didn't mean to get on your back. We just want you to have fun, and there's safety in numbers at these frat parties. The last few have been wild."

An itch crawls under my skin. I've never been the type to shy away from parties. Hell, Cole and I barely missed a party our senior year. I'd love nothing more than to cut loose, to escape my problems for a few hours, but the weight of responsibility won't allow it.

"What about the following weekend?" Elsa suggests. "There's a big blowout planned at Phi Kappa Psi. Their parties are legendary and are definitely not to be missed. Do you think your parents would let you stick around Friday night and go home on Saturday instead if they knew in advance?"

I'm not surprised she has logically come to the conclusion that this is about permission. Funny thing is, I could stay here, go to the party and not go home, and Mom probably wouldn't even notice.

But Dad would.

And that's a whole other story.

"I'll ask them this weekend," I lie, hoping this puts an end to the discussion. Allowing myself to be deliberately distracted, I frown at the cracked screen of my cell. At least the phone still seems to be working, so I'll only have to pay to replace the glass.

"Oh, yay!" Elsa claps her hands. "It'll be so much fun. I really hope you can come."

"Oh my God," Tabs exclaims as we make our way to the auditorium for our income measurement class. "I totally forgot to mention this at lunch. There's this gorgeous new hottie in my business law class. Like panties-instantly-wet-hot hottie. I spent the whole class imagining all the ways I could fuck him. Had to get myself off in the bathroom after class ended."

I burst out laughing, clutching my stomach, with tears streaming out of my eyes. I laugh even harder when I spot the disgusted look on Elsa's face.

Tabs has no filter.

Like zilch.

But it's one of the things I love about her.

I was so lucky to meet both of them the day classes started and equally blessed that we all just instantly clicked. Tabs and Elsa went to the same school and they've been besties since second grade. I thought I might feel left out, but they've never made me feel anything but included. In general, everyone I've met here has been super friendly, and it's helped make the transition easier, even if I am holding so much of myself back.

"Do you have to be so crude?" Elsa asks.

"Do you have to be such a prude?" Tabs retorts.

"I'm not a prude," Elsa protests, elbowing Tabs in the ribs. "Just because I'm saving myself for my wedding night does not mean I'm a prude. I'm just exercising my right to wait."

Tabs slings her arm around Elsa's shoulder, smacking a loud kiss on her cheek. "Ah, I know that Els, and I would never criticize you for the choice you've made. I think it's great you know what you want and you have the strength to stick to your convictions. But it works both ways, you know." She gestures between them. "I've made a choice to bag as much cock as I can while I'm young, free, and single, and I'd like you to respect *my* decision."

"I do. I truly do. That doesn't mean I need to have it rubbed in my face all the time."

"Speaking of rubbing..." Tabs has a wicked glint in her eye.

Elsa slaps a palm to her forehead. "You're incorrigible. It's just as well I love you."

"You guys are so funny," I cut in. "You should start your own comedy routine."

"Nah," Tabs says, shoulder-checking me. "We're just here for *your* comedic enjoyment."

"Speaking of hotties," I say, cringing a little before the words have even left my mouth. "I crashed into this gorgeous guy this morning, and he was so fucking hot I lost all sense of reason. Made a complete spectacle of myself. Ogled him like he was a chocolate-covered strawberry dipped in champagne. I was only short of drooling, and it was so embarrassing." I shrug a little. "Until he opened his mouth and released his inner asshole, and then I didn't feel so bad."

Tabs slings her arm around me. "Ooh, I'm intrigued. Tell me more."

"It'll have to wait," Elsa says, opening the door to the auditorium. "Class is about to start."

"Rain check!" Tabs whispers as we step into the room. "We can compare notes." She waggles her brows, and I stifle a laugh.

The assistant professor starts the class, and I attempt to take notes, but my mind wanders back to the guy from this morning. Being that good-looking isn't fair on the rest of the male population. But his allure was more than just his insane hotness. He had this magnetic presence about him. This elusive power. And I felt conflicting emotions—an almost overwhelming compulsion to get to know him better and a potent urge to run a million miles in the opposite direction. Guys like him are trouble with a capital T. One second in his company and I was a messy pile of goo at his feet.

That doesn't happen to me.

Like, ever.

I kissed plenty of boys before Cole and I went steady in

tenth grade, and Cole and I got up to plenty of kinky shit, but even he didn't have that kind of power over me.

The power to render me speechless.

To have me acting like a bumbling idiot.

How does that happen with a virtual stranger?

And why did it happen?

More to the point, why have I been obsessing over him all morning?

It makes no sense, and I have no time for boys.

Dad made his feelings clear, and while a part of me feels it's irrational and unachievable, another part of me completely understands where he's coming from and why he felt the need to lay down such heavy ground rules.

"Earth to Ms. Gray," the prof barks out, and I snap out of my obsessive inner monologue.

I sit up straighter in my chair, clearing my throat as I look at the frustrated expression on his face. Shit on a brick. *What did he ask me? And why, oh why, did he choose today to pick on me?* The one day when I haven't concentrated and I'm acting like a spaced-out zombie. "Would you mind repeating the question?"

He narrows his eyes at me, and I visibly shrink in my seat. He repeats it slowly, enunciating every word clearly, as if I'm stupid or deaf or maybe he thinks I'm a mix of both.

But the worst thing of all? I haven't a clue what the answer is, so I guess I'm just going to affirm his assessment of me. Sweat trickles down the back of my neck, as I squirm uncomfortably in my seat.

"I believe the answer is EBITDA," a deep voice I recognize says from the row behind. All the tiny hairs on my arms lift in awareness, and I slink down even farther in my seat.

"If I wanted you to answer the question, Mr. Quinn, I would have asked you instead of Ms. Gray," the prof responds, determined to prolong my agony.

"Some of us are here to learn," he retorts. "Not waste half the class waiting for someone to answer something she clearly doesn't know."

"Oh my God," Elsa murmurs under her breath. "What a jerk."

"You have no idea," I mumble in reply.

"I'd like to have a word with you after class, Mr. Quinn. You too, Ms. Gray. Both of you, please stay behind."

I work hard to smother a groan. *Seriously, could this day get any worse?*

Chapter 4

Shawn/Levi

"Daydreaming and insubordination will not be tolerated in my class," the prof says as I'm standing in front of the podium facing him with the little firecracker by my side. "This is the only warning you'll get from me."

"I apologize, sir," she replies, her soft, lilting voice sending shivers down my spine and blood rushing to places it shouldn't. "I promise I'll focus one hundred percent in class from now on." If I looked over at her face, I'd bet she's giving him the puppy-dog treatment with those wide, sad, blue eyes.

He nods curtly at her. "What do you have to say for yourself, Mr. Quinn?" He tilts his head to the side, scrutinizing my face like he knows exactly my type.

It's on the tip of my tongue to tell him to screw off, but then I remember why I'm here and how important it is to keep a low profile. I can't do anything to draw unnecessary attention to myself. Summoning humility from some long-forgotten hidden place, I wet my lips and tell him what he wants to hear. "I'm sorry, sir, and I'll behave myself in the future."

His eyes narrow suspiciously before he gives me a terse nod. "Very well. I don't want any reason to call both of you out again." He jerks his head toward the door. "You're dismissed. You may leave."

Blondie doesn't need to be told twice, flying up the stairs so fast I'd swear she had wings. Pulling my ball cap out of my book bag, I ram it on my head and take the stairs two at a time, anxious to catch up with her.

Although I've honestly got no clue why.

Girls are a complication I don't want or need right now, but since she plowed into me this morning, I can't get her out of my mind. She's a conundrum my brain itches to piece together. A temptation my body wants to indulge. I should be running in the opposite direction instead of chasing her down the hall and outside the building.

I'm not surprised she's fast on her feet. She wasn't the only one inspecting the goods earlier. I was totally checking her out too, but I'm more skilled and discreet at it. No way I could miss those long, bare tan legs or the obvious muscle definition there. The girl is clearly sporty, or she works out, because she's in great shape. My hands twitch with the need to explore the smooth planes of her body, and my jeans strain against my crotch.

Cupping my hands together, I holler after her. "Hey, Blondie!" I still don't know her first name, but even if I did, I doubt I'd use it. "Wait up!"

Spinning around, she keeps walking backward, sending me a gloating smile before she blatantly flips me the bird. I come to a complete standstill, staring at her with a slack jaw. Grinning, she turns around and continues walking. I bark out a laugh, smiling to myself as I casually stroll in the same direction.

I don't know what it is about this girl, but it's refreshing.

She's a strange mix of fiery and sweet, mischievous and sad.

Keeping my head down, I walk after her. Not exactly following, but not wanting to lose her in the crowd either.

And I can't really figure out why.

Is it because she's the first girl in years to run the other way? Or is it her feistiness or the lingering sadness that surrounds her like a halo that has captured my attention? I'm not sure what it is, and I really shouldn't be entertaining any thoughts of her, but it's like she's cast me under a spell and I'm powerless to control my actions.

I follow her from a safe distance, my body warring with my mind—one part of me cautioning this is not a good idea and the other telling me to go after what I want.

She comes to a halt up ahead, facing a big guy with cropped dark hair wearing a Hawkeyes jacket. He looks like the stereotypical jock, and I'll bet he has the giant ego to match. Not that I'm in any position to criticize. I'm about as fucking stereotypical as they come.

Or, at least, I was.

As I approach, I take cover under a large tree, concealing myself in the shadows. The girl at the jock's side is a tiny thing with a mass of strawberry-blonde hair that falls in straight lines to her butt. She clings possessively to the jock's arm, glaring at my girl.

My girl? WTF?

I attempt to shake myself out of my stupor, but there's no denying the surge of protectiveness I feel toward Blondie, even if I can't fathom why or where it's come from.

Heated words are exchanged. I'm too far away to hear exactly what's being said, but, judging by the angry faces and frantic arm gestures, I'm guessing it's not an amicable conversation. I'm debating cutting in when Blondie storms off. The big guy looks a little dejected as he stares at her retreating back, but the little bitch at his side slaps his chest, shouting at him before she drags him away.

Her eyes meet mine with a flash of interest as I pass them by, and I definitely know her type. I've met enough manipulative bitches to recognize the form. Pinning the full extent of the Lucas sneer on her, I'm hugely satisfied when she visibly cowers.

Up ahead, Blondie is nowhere to be seen, so I give up the search and head back to my apartment, ignoring the stab of disappointment I feel.

After grabbing a quick bite to eat, I head into the small room at the back of the penthouse that has been remodeled into a makeshift music studio and mess around with some melodies on my guitar for a couple hours. But inspiration won't come to me, and I give up, frustrated. Heading into the living room, I sip from a bottle of water as I watch some mindless garbage on TV for a few hours.

I glance at the clock regularly.

As it approaches midnight, I grab my guitar and move over to the window seat, sitting down to watch the show.

I spotted the girl dancing on the rooftop of the old building across the way the first night I stayed here. I'm often prone to bouts of insomnia, and since the break-in and assassination attempt, I regularly have trouble sleeping so I don't tend to go to bed until I'm dead on my feet.

It was just after midnight when I first noticed her.

Moving her body with skill and finesse as she danced like an ethereal being upon the roof of the abandoned building. Now, she's the highlight of my night, and I count down the minutes until she appears.

I start strumming a few chords as I wait for her, a melody and words lingering in the hidden corners of my mind, waiting for the right moment to let loose. Checking my watch, I frown as the hand moves past midnight. She's usually here by now, and I realize how disappointed I'll be if she doesn't show.

Which only demonstrates how truly pathetic I've become. Chasing after random girls who want nothing to do with me and obsessing over some tortured soul dancing a lonesome dance at midnight.

Movement snags my attention from the corner of my eye, and I smile, like a creepy perv, as a ray of light casts dim illumination over the roof, highlighting the forlorn figure as she starts to dance. It's clear this girl has a lot of skill, and she's experienced in different forms of dance. Some nights, she's the classical ballerina pirouetting for an invisible audience. Other times, she contorts her limbs in choreographed street moves that wouldn't be out of place on my stage.

Whispers of a melody float through my mind, and I start plucking the guitar strings as an idea takes shape. I watch her, this strange, beautiful creature, and the song forms more clearly in my mind.

All this time, I've been lying to myself
That mocking face in the mirror spoke the truth
But I was too scared to see
Too afraid to fight for what I know is right
Until you broke through the haze
Lost and alone
With your beautiful, haunting moves
Silently calling out to me

She dances for longer than usual tonight, and I continue watching, and strumming, wondering what drives her there night after night.

I tell myself I'm doing nothing wrong. That it's not spying or stalking. That I'm keeping an eye on her, because it can't be safe going there alone every night. But I'm prone to addiction, and this beautiful dancer has captivated me in a way little has for years. While she's too far away to make out her features, there is something so alluring about the way she dances, something that speaks to secret pain, that calls out to me.

Like a kindred spirit.

Another tormented artist struggling to find her way in the world.

The rooftop spirals into darkness, and the girl is gone. The empty quietness echoes around me, but it's not isolating or uncomfortable. Back home in L.A., my house was constantly teeming with people and music, with laughter and noise, but it felt like the loneliest place on the planet because none of it was real.

None of those people who professed to be my friends were real.

They were all there for what they could take from me.

What a shame it took me years to figure it out.

Spent the best part of the last year making a clean sweep. And now, my house is like a mausoleum. Empty of noise and spirit. Dead, like my soul. I amble through the rooms searching for something illusive. Something to remind me I'm still alive. That there are things still worth fighting for.

But it wasn't until I came here that I truly started to believe.

My mistakes are in the past, and rehashing them won't undo them. So, I stick to the new promise I've made myself and focus on moving forward.

One step at a time.

One milestone at a time.

Yawning, I put my guitar down, smiling as I read over the lyrics scrawled across my notepad, welcoming the fire in my belly and the natural high flowing through my veins.

I knew coming here was a good idea.

It finally feels like I'm in the right space to move forward with my life.

And I think I just might have found my muse.

Another week passes, and I'm settling into a new routine. My midnight dancer has ignited a spark inside me, and I'm bristling with creativity, lyrics and tunes flowing out of me like a river.

I've thought of approaching her.

Of turning up one night on that roof.

Of seeing her up close and personal to see what the connection would be like.

But that's definitely veering into dangerous stalker territory, so I try to coax my mind into accepting the status quo and to be happy about it.

I haven't seen Blondie except during class where I make a point of hanging back until she's entered the auditorium, and then I take up position in the row behind her. I know she knows I'm there, but she refuses to acknowledge my presence, much to the delight of her friend with the curly black hair. She introduced herself to me during another class one day last week, so I know her name is Tabitha, or Tabs, as she prefers to be known.

She wasn't subtle about hitting on me, and I was as blunt as a bulldozer in turning her down flat. She took it like a champ. Or a challenge. But, meh. I don't care. Girls are not part of my agenda here.

Period.

I'm sitting in the cafeteria at dinnertime on Thursday when a strange sensation causes me to look up. From under the peak of my ball cap, I spot Blondie walking across the crowded floor, apparently headed this way. My heart pounds faster in my chest. Her eyes lock on mine, and it's as if the rest of the world ceases to exist. I'm trying to stay under the radar, so I should look away, but I can't. Her big blue eyes stare into mine, and a wave of sadness and grief rolls through me. I don't know what or who put that look in her eyes, but I have an overwhelming need to find out.

To help fix it.

She stops dead on the spot, looking at me as if she can see right through me.

As if she has the power to unlock the secrets buried deep inside.

It's unnerving and exciting at the same time.

I stand up, my chest heavy with emotion I can't decipher. I'm making my way around the table toward her when she snaps out of it, and the spell is broken. Shaking her head, she frowns. Her cheeks flush a rosy red color and she hangs her head, letting her long, wavy hair cover her face like heavy drapes as she scurries away.

I scrub a hand over my chin as I plop back down in my seat wondering what the fuck just happened.

I start loading my empty plate, silverware, and glass on the tray, getting ready to leave, when a girl drops into the seat across from me. I don't even attempt to stifle my sigh. It's like some girls see a guy sitting alone and think he's fair game. This isn't the first time I've been accosted by females while trying to mind my own business. Most times, I slink into a seat, hiding under my hoodie or my cap, trying to look inconspicuous, but that doesn't deter them. Acting like an asshole hasn't helped either. In fact, I'd say that's only added to the appeal.

Some girls get off on that shit.

Fading into the background is not as easy as I'd imagined.

"Hey," the cute redhead says, propping up on her elbows and leaning across the table at me. Her rack is on clear display in the low-cut top she's wearing, but I'm guessing that's the point.

"Did you want something?" I ask in a gruff tone, not making eye contact.

"I wanted to invite you to the frat party tomorrow night."

I lift my head, quirking a brow. Straight up. I admire that in a woman. But I'm not here to party or hook up.

Unless it's Blondie or midnight dancer, the unhelpful devil on my shoulder taunts.

Another girl slips into the seat beside me, sending me a wide smile. "Hey, Levi."

Levi is my middle name and Quinn is my mother's maiden name, so, when it came to choosing a fake identity, the choice was already made. And I kinda like that I'm incognito but still retaining an element of the real me.

Like I'm hiding in plain sight, so to speak.

"Tabitha." I stare warily at her. *What is this? A two-for-one assault?*

"Get lost, Hailey. Levi's already coming with us." Tabitha makes a shooing gesture with her hand while slanting an "I mean business" look at the redhead, and I can't help laughing. This girl redefines ballsy.

Hailey's chair scrapes loudly as she gets up, spewing liquid venom from her eyes as she glares at Tabitha. "You're such a bitch, Tabitha. Screw you." She flips her the bird before storming off.

"I don't need you to ride to the rescue," I say, amusement coloring my tone. "I'm well capable of throwing out the trash myself."

"Meow!" Tabitha claws at the empty air, smirking. "I can see that, but I'm not being altogether charitable. My invite is genuine. Come to the party."

I chuckle. "Are you always this straightforward?"

She shrugs unapologetically, throwing back her hair. "Always. You're not truly living if you don't speak your mind."

"You're preaching to the converted," I tell her. "But I'll have to decline the invite. I'm here to study. Not party."

She leans in a little closer. "If I tell you a certain gorgeous blonde, who goes by the name Dakota, will be there, would that change your mind?"

Dakota.

I like that name. It suits her.

But I've got to put an end to this shit right now. I've obviously been as subtle as a brick. Sitting up straighter, I shake my head. "Nope. Not here to hook up either."

She almost chokes on a laugh. "Yeah, right. And I'm fucking Gandhi resurrected from the grave."

My nose scrunches up. "Not a nice visual, Tabs. Actually, that's pretty gross."

"Made you smile though." She lifts her hand and we high five, as if we're ten.

"You're kinda crazy."

"I know. Everyone tells me that. Couldn't give two shits though."

I like this girl. It's nothing sexual. There's no spark of attraction between us whatsoever. But she's cool, and there's no bullshit and I like that. "Good for you." I start to gather my things, and she rises alongside me.

"I know you like her."

"I don't," I lie.

"Uh-huh." She grins knowingly. "You're as bad as she is with the denials."

Now *that* perks my interest.

She grins again. "Yup. Thought as much. We'll be at the frat house at eight. Come hang out with us. Unless you're too afraid."

I roll my eyes, determined I'm not giving in.

It doesn't matter how badly I want to.

I can't drag any girl into my world. Not with all this stalker shit hanging over my head.

Dakota is beautiful and intriguing, and I wish I could dispel the shroud of sadness she wears, but no good would come from starting something with her.

Nothing can happen.

Period.

Chapter 5

Dakota

"I look like I'm totally easy." I scowl at my reflection in the mirror.

"You look totally fuckable, and it's a perfect party dress," Tabs retaliates. "Levi won't be able to resist!" She winks suggestively, and I roll my eyes.

"How many times do I have to tell you I'm not interested? The guy is an ass."

"Keep lying to yourself if you want, but I know what I see. You're both sneaking glances at one another in class all the time. Any idiot can see the chemistry between you. And I don't think he's that bad. I'll bet he's all gooey and soft under that prickly exterior."

I roll my eyes again. "If you think he's that great, why aren't you going after him yourself?"

"Tried hitting on him," she admits, a little sheepishly, "but he's not interested in me. Besides, I know now you like him even if you won't admit it, so I'll never go there. Girl code and all."

My heart swells, and I lean in and hug her. "You're fucking awesome, girlfriend."

"I'm glad someone can appreciate my qualities," she jokes before her expression softens. "Why are you holding back?"

I want to be truthful, but I can't force the words out. "I don't date," I say instead, offering up a feeble excuse.

"Why not?"

I go with the easier truth this time. "Because my last relationship ended badly, and I swore I was never giving any guy the power to hurt me again."

"That's that Cole guy you mentioned before?" I nod, yanking the minuscule black dress up and over my head. Tabs sighs in sympathy. "He was a shit, but not every guy will let you down, and I'm not suggesting you marry Levi." Her eyes glimmer wickedly. "Just fuck him every which way to Sunday." I roar laughing as I flick through the clothes in my closet. "I'll bet he knows how to fuck like a porn star," she muses, licking her lips, and I laugh again.

"I think you're right," I agree, because there is something insanely sexual about the way Levi looks at me. Like he's stripping every layer off me and fucking me with his eyes. I'm trying to ignore him, because the few times we've interacted have ended up with me wanting to gouge his eyeballs out with a pitchfork, but the guy reels me in too, causing my hormones to overheat. A tiny part of me is grateful he's eliciting emotions and desires I'd long since buried, but the logical part of my brain tells me he's a train wreck waiting to happen, and I can't invite more trouble into my life.

Layla would laugh herself silly if she was privy to my inner thoughts. It's like we've reversed roles. If she were still alive, my sister would be the very one urging me to exercise caution. Not to throw myself headfirst into a new romance without considering the likely consequences. The old me would have shrugged, smiled, hugged her, and gone out and gotten my man without any concern for consequences.

But that's no longer me.

And I'm becoming more like my sister.

That should please me. Because it's what I've set out to do. To be that person for my parents. To give them no reason to worry or fear for my life.

So why does it feel like every day I'm dying a little more inside?

"I still can't believe you ditched the sexy black dress. You were straight fire," Tabs grumbles as we push our way into the basement of the frat house. A smoky cloud floats on top of the room, and my nostrils sniff the weed in the air with a pang of nostalgia.

"She still looks hot," Elsa loyally proclaims, looping her arm through mine. "That dress is gorgeous and sexy in an understated way that totally suits you." She skims her gaze over the flimsy material floating around me.

This dress is one of my favorites, and I wanted to feel comfortable tonight. It's been a long time since I've attended a party, and I'm a little anxious in case Cole and Mikayla are here. I wanted to look my best without it looking like I've made much of an effort. This boho-patterned, sleeveless dress ties under the bust, and the full skirt flows seductively over my hips, stopping mid-calf. When I walk, the split up the front offers a glimpse of skin without showing all the goods. The sneakers keep it casual and effortless, just how I like it.

I'm not going to apologize for refusing the traditional overtly sexy route. It's just not me. I know Tabs's heart is in the right place, but tight dresses and stiletto heels have never been my thing. I've always favored a more casual, carefree look.

"Thanks, babe." I kiss Elsa on the cheek. "And you are completely stunning, by the way. Both of you." Els is wearing a cute, flirty knee-length purple dress, and Tabs is now wearing the dress I declined. But she's a knockout in it, and she's already picking up admiring glances from several directions.

After a couple beers, I'm starting to loosen up and enjoy myself. Perhaps it wasn't such a bad idea coming here after all. Tabs and Els drag me out onto the dance floor, and I give myself over to the music, feeding my soul and dancing as if I haven't a care in the world.

"Kota," Tabs whispers in my ear. "Do you know that bitch?" She jerks her head to the side of the dance floor and I look over, ice sluicing through my veins as I spot Mikayla shooting daggers at me.

You'd swear I was the one who had betrayed her, not the other way around. "Yeah. I know her. That's Mikayla. My ex-best friend. The one Cole left me for."

"Why the fuck is she glaring at you?"

I shrug, looking away. "Don't know and don't care. After everything that went down, I realized I never really knew who she was. I feel like our whole friendship was a setup so she could dig her claws in Cole."

"Do you want to leave?" Elsa asks. She's been quietly listening the whole time.

"No way." I lift my chin defiantly. "They are not going to ruin my night. I won't let them."

Tabs nods proudly. "That's my girl." She links her arm through mine. "Let's get drunk and flirt with guys."

I don't even attempt to protest. "Lead the way."

We head to the other side of the large basement, where a makeshift bar has been set up, and grab some more red cups before moving to an empty corner of the room. I'm sipping my beer when Cole suddenly looms large in front of me. "Hi, Kotabear." He scratches the back of his neck, looking awkward. "Can we talk for a minute?"

I stare through him. "Nope. I have nothing to say to you and don't call me that. I'm not your anything anymore."

If I'm not mistaken, a flicker of anguish flares behind his eyes, but I'm beyond the point of caring. Cole was the only one I had in my corner in the aftermath of my sister's death, and he let me down in the worst possible way.

"Please." He leans in closer. "I have some stuff I need to say. It will only take a few minutes."

I slant him an incredulous look. "Why should I give you even a second of my time? After what you did?"

"I'm really sor—"

"What the fuck do you think you're doing?" Mikayla screeches, pushing her way into the space between Cole and me. She starts prodding me in the chest with her finger, as if I'm the one who sought him out. "He's not yours anymore. He's mine, and you need to stay the hell away from *My. Man*."

I remove her hand and step back. "For starters, don't touch me. And Cole came to me. Not the other way around. Seems like you might want to have a word with *your man*."

"Don't think I don't know what you're up to, you little slut."

"Kayla," Cole snaps at her. "That's enough." He takes her elbow, but she shoves him away.

"You don't want to start a war with me, Kota. Trust me, you'll lose."

I shake my head, laughing. "You're bat shit crazy if you think I want anything to do with Cole. You're both welcome to each other."

At that moment, strong arms slide around my waist from behind, and I'm hauled back against a warm body. His scent tickles my nostrils, and because I've come to recognize the smell, I instantly know it's Levi. I'm not sure what he thinks he's doing, but I'll go with the flow because the look on Cole's face right now is utterly priceless. "Hey, babe," he says, nuzzling my neck. "Sorry I'm late. What did I miss?"

"Nothing at all." I twist around in his embrace, smiling up at him like he hung the moon. Levi keeps his arms around me, tucking me in close to his side. Tabs is grinning at me like I just won the lottery, and Els's eyes are so wide it's a wonder they haven't popped clear out of her head. Smiling provocatively, I run my hand up his rock-hard abs and delectable chest.

Hey, might as well take advantage of the opportunity to feel him up while I can, because I'm pretty sure open hostilities will resume the instant Cole and Mikayla are gone.

"I'm glad you're here." I rest my head on his chest and wrap my arms around his tight waist, silently fist-pumping the air when he shivers a little from my touch.

"Why the hell are you still here?" Tabs demands to know, planting her hands on her hips as she squares up to Mikayla. "Fuck off to whatever crazy-bitch-boyfriend-stealing land you came from and never come back."

I snort-laugh. Can't help it. I hope I never end up on Tabs's shit list because she sure knows how to put someone in their place.

"Fuck you, you skank," Mikayla says, sneering at Tabs before dragging Cole away. Cole glances over his shoulder, casting me an apologetic look, but he should know it's way too late for that.

Even though I don't want to, I slide out of Levi's embrace. "You didn't have to do that, but thanks."

"It was a tough job, but someone had to do it," he says, winking.

"Ugh. Did you seriously just wink at me like some sleazy lothario?"

"Did you seriously just use the word lothario?"

I want to slap that amused grin off his face. "This from the guy who sleazy winks." I faux roll my eyes.

"Now that I've done you a solid, I think it's time you told me who that douche is." He lifts a can of soda to his mouth, and even the way his throat works as he drinks is sexy as hell.

Focus, girl. Do not let the hot-as-sin douche distract you. He may have just dug me out of a hole, but Levi is still swimming in the asshole pool. "I already thanked you, and I don't owe you an explanation."

"Well, now you're just being rude and ungrateful."

"And you're being an even bigger pain in my ass!"

Tab steps in between us. "You guys are killing me with all this sexual tension. Just fuck and be done with it already."

Elsa shakes her head in consternation. "On second thought, it's a good thing we couldn't convince Daisy to come out tonight. Her innocent ears do not need to hear this."

"Who's Daisy?" Levi asks.

"Kota's roomie," Tabs supplies. "She's a little sweetheart but completely shy and unspoiled. She'd rather stay home licking her Shawn Lucas posters than come out and sink her teeth into a real man."

Levi almost chokes on his drink, and I direct a curious look at him before refocusing on my friend. "Don't be mean, Tabs. Daisy is one of the nicest girls I've ever met."

"I'm not being mean, and I totally agree, Daisy's adorable. I'm just telling it like it is."

And that's pretty much true. Although, I haven't actually ever seen Daisy *lick* her posters—that's a complete exaggeration on Tabs's part—but she does appear to have an unnatural obsession with the troubled bad boy popstar.

Levi looks a little pale as he addresses me. "She has a thing for Shawn Lucas?"

"I know, right?!" I shake my head. "Can't figure it out myself. I mean, okay, some of his earlier stuff isn't too bad, but those last few releases were so clichéd and cheesy I wanted to vomit every time the song played on the radio."

"Me too," Tabs butts in, and I try to prepare myself for it. "But I'd still fuck him. His body was made for sin."

Levi splutters again, and my brows knit together as I stare funny at him.

"Do you always have to lower the tone?" Elsa asks.

"Do you really need an answer to that?"

"I wasn't into him when he was all prettied up," I offer, before those two get into it, "but that longer-haired look he's been sporting recently really suits him. Still, I wouldn't do him, no matter how hot he is. He's a giant bag of dicks and way more trouble than he's worth."

"I'm with you, chica," Elsa agrees, nodding. "He's a train wreck in the making. Apparently, he gets drunk and coked-up every night, and he's into threesomes and all kinds of kinky shit."

"Wow," Levi interjects. "I must write a memo to the Shawn Lucas fan club telling him never to grace these parts."

"Don't include me in your naming and shaming," Tabs, predictably, adds. "I'm totally down with threesomes and kinky shit. Shawn Lucas can come visit me anytime." She makes a suggestive gesture with her hand, and I crack up laughing.

"You're completely and utterly shameless," I tell her. "I freaking love it."

"I still want to know who that douche in the Hawks jacket is," Levi says, breaking up the light-hearted atmosphere, and blatantly changing the subject.

"It's none of your business," I say, pushing out of his way. I make a beeline for the bar. Given tonight's turn of events, I definitely need more alcohol.

He trails behind me. "I saw you outside school the other day, when they were there, and you looked upset."

I stop, turning around to face him. "Were you following me?" An anxious, fluttery feeling builds in my chest.

"What?! No!" He rubs his neck, gulping. "It wasn't like that. I was going the same direction is all."

"I'm not sure I believe you."

"Guess you'll just have to take my word for it."

"Well, that's reassuring."

"Are you always this cagey?"

"Are you always this irritating?"

A sly smirk spreads across his mouth. "Oh, Blondie." He steps into my personal space. "You have no idea how irritating I can be."

His warm breath coasts over my face, intoxicating me, and I wobble a little on my feet. He moves closer, crowding me, and heat from his body rolls over me in waves. That, combined with the intensity of the hunger on his face, has me drowning in a pool of lust, and I'm terrified I'm about to give into it. So, I blurt words I had no intention of saying. "He's my ex-boyfriend, and she's my ex-best friend."

Shock splays across his face. "What happened?"

"Why do you want to know?"

"Call it curiosity."

I sigh, moving back so I can lean against the wall. He follows, lounging alongside me and peering intently into my eyes. I feel myself falling again, so I deliberately avert my gaze, speaking with my eyes glued to the ground. "I was going through some heavy stuff last year, and I wasn't a very good girlfriend or friend, but I thought the two people closest to me would understand." My laugh is bitter. "Guess the joke was on me because they started hooking up behind my back, and they didn't even have the decency to tell me. I found them fucking in his truck, and I haven't spoken more than a few words to either of them since."

"And they go to school here." Levi states the obvious.

"Yep. Surprised you haven't heard of Cole. He's a bit of a star on the football field."

"Star dickhead more like. What do you expect with a name like Cole."

I lift my chin, smiling. "You're right. It *is* a douchey name, isn't it?"

"Keep smiling," he murmurs, leaning in closer and cupping my face.

I feel his touch all the way through to my toes. "What are you doing?" I whisper.

"Said douche is looking over here, and he doesn't look pleased."

I scoff. "I couldn't care less. If he's harboring any notions of us getting back together, he can get lost. Cheating is a hard limit for me."

Levi moves in even closer, gripping my hips and pulling me flush against his body. When he presses his hot mouth against my ear, I shiver all over. I can hear his smile when he speaks in a low tone. "Any other hard limits I should know about?" he teases, and I shudder again. His light chuckle tells me he knows it too.

"There isn't much I won't try at least once," I blurt, before mentally slapping myself up the head.

Clasping the nape of my neck, he stares straight into my eyes with lust-filled darkened pupils. "Aren't you just full of surprises, Ms. Gray."

Butterflies run amok in my chest, and my core throbs with

need. He's so close. It would only take a second to breach the tiny distance between us and kiss him.

I'm shocked by how much I want to.

Especially when I'm not even sure if I like him.

"He's still watching." He nuzzles my neck, and I smother a pleasurable whimper. My eyes close, and I clutch his waist, impatient to get closer. "I don't think he got the message."

"What message?" I rasp, and I know I'm going to bathe in embarrassment tomorrow when I think back on all this.

"The one that says you're mine."

My eyes fly open. My heart hammers wildly behind my chest. "But I'm not yours."

"He doesn't know that." He grips my hips tighter. "Do you want to make him go away for good?"

I can only nod, because my vocal cords are fried.

Along with my brain.

He rubs his thumb along my lower lip, and my knees wobble. "Just play along, okay?" His eyes seek permission, and I nod way too eagerly.

Time moves in slow motion as he bridges the gap between us and his mouth closes over mine. Surprisingly, his touch is soft, almost timid, incredibly tender. My arms encircle his neck as he flattens his hand against my lower back, holding me tight. Heat from his hand seeps into my skin through my dress, accelerating my arousal and heightening my need for him.

I take control, moving my mouth against his with needy urgency, devouring his lips and relishing the tingles zipping through my body. His touch is electric, and he tastes divine.

Like forbidden chocolate on a diet.

Or a crisp, cold beer on a hot summer's night.

He doesn't let me down, angling his head and deepening the kiss, pouring everything into his kisses until my head is swimming and my heart is all aflutter. A moan slips out of his mouth, and he pulls me even closer. His hard-on presses into my tummy, eliciting tremors of desire, and I suction my body to his, needing to get even closer. His hands roam up and down my spine, brushing dangerously close to my ass.

If he asked to take me, right here and now, I don't think I'd say no.

I don't think I could deny him a thing when he's setting my world on fire like this.

It's been so long since I've been kissed like this that I'd almost forgotten how amazing it is.

He suddenly rips his lips from mine, and I blink my eyes open, struggling to see through the fog of desire. I touch my swollen lips as I stare at his hard, furious face in confusion.

Why does he look salty AF? And so cold all of a sudden?

"I think he got the message," he snaps, jerking his head to the empty spot where Cole was standing.

"I...ah...um...thanks?" I'm uncharacteristically tongue-tied and confounded. I offer him a small, shy smile.

His eyes bore into my skull, and his scowl deepens as he turns the full extent of his mocking glare on me. "That was a one-time thing, and it *won't* be happening again."

Hurt slices across my chest, and his callous rejection heats my cheeks. *Has he forgotten who started this? That this was all his idea?* "Don't worry," I say, bitterness flooding my tone. "I got the message. And I'm not in the habit of kissing asshats, so I've zero interest in repeating the experience." Keeping my head high, I turn my back on him and return to the safety of my friends.

Chapter 6

Shawn/Levi

I hurt her. I know I did. It was written all over her face that night. And she carries it with her like an invisible load, ignoring me in class and whenever we bump into one another around campus. It's been four days since the party, since I majorly fucked up, and I haven't stopped beating myself up over it.

I should never have kissed her.

Because, fuck it, now I know what she tastes like, how good she feels pressed up against me, and I'm craving her like she's my new favorite addiction.

But it can't happen again.

It shouldn't have happened the first time.

I can tell myself I was helping her out, but that would be a lie. Yes, I wanted that douche to stop looking at her with those forlorn lovesick eyes but not as much as I wanted to lock lips with her.

She is so fucking beautiful.

So unconventional.

So unaware.

And it only makes me want her even more.

I don't know what this girl has done to me, but I can't evict her from my head. God knows, I've tried, but it's as if she's taken up residence there, and I don't know how the fuck to deal with it.

I can't risk starting anything with her, because it isn't safe, but try telling that to my selfish heart and my greedy cock. I've jerked off several times daily since Friday night, always to images of her in my mind.

The fact her roomie is, apparently, obsessed with me is another complication. Another reason to stay away. Because I can't risk discovery.

Since I failed to show up to the movie premiere, the media is speculating about where I am. They know I'm not home. That I wouldn't willingly refuse to support the song I contributed to the latest Tom Cruise movie. While we haven't released details of my stalker to the press, they have formed their own conclusions, and now the story is growing wings.

As if on cue, my cell rings, and I answer Devin's call. "Hey, man."

"Shawn, how are things?"

"Cool."

"Glad to hear it." He pauses momentarily. "Who's the girl?"

"What girl," I lie, almost like it's second nature.

"The pretty blonde you were with Friday night."

"Great," I deadpan. "It's a wonder you let me piss in private." As much as I'm impressed with their discretion—I've only noticed one of his men watching me on two occasions, and most times I forget they're even there—I don't like the fact some asshat bodyguard was probably checking Dakota out while we were kissing.

"My guys know when to afford you privacy," he assures me

before pausing again. "But I thought the plan was to stay away from girls."

"I'm trying."

"Well, try harder. Girls are a distraction you don't need right now."

"Yes, Dad." Devin's exasperated sigh filters down the line, but he ignores my teasing. "Did you just call to bust my ass over Dakota, or was there another reason?"

"I've been going through that list of names you gave me, and a couple of flags have been raised. In particular, I wanted to ask you about Matt Fairchild and Nick Montgomery."

All good humor evaporates.

Because we believe this is personal, Devin asked me to provide a list of anyone I felt might be holding a grudge as well as anyone I've come into close contact with since hitting the limelight. Luke issued him a list of everyone who works with me, past and present. It's a monster list of potential suspects—and that's even if my stalker is someone I know. It could just as easily be a crazy fan. But the real scary thing is how few of those names are people I could genuinely call friends.

Most everyone on that list has some reason to hate me.

Especially Matt and Nick.

I walk to the couch and flop down on it, closing my eyes as pressure settles on my chest. "What do you want to know?"

"How they reacted when they got dropped and whether you've had any contact with them since."

Bile travels up my throat, and shit I try to avoid thinking about swarms my mind.

Matt and Nick were my two best friends growing up. We were thick as thieves from the time we were knee-high. It was Matt's idea to start up a band in ninth grade. I could already play the guitar, drums, and keyboard by then, but as I had the best voice, it was agreed I'd take lead vocals and guitar. Nick was our drummer, and Matt played bass guitar. What started out as messing around in the garage attached to Matt's house became something more serious when we uploaded some of our videos to YouTube and became an overnight sensation.

"When we first signed with Dynamite XO Records, the initial contract was for the three of us," I start explaining. "But after the first six months, the head honcho cut the guys because he said I was the star and they were deadweight holding me back." Bitterness laces my tone. "He paid the guys off, and they went back home. Matt was pissed as all hell. Don't blame him. It was a shitty thing to do, and I was a shithead for not fighting harder for them."

"You were, what, fourteen or fifteen, at the time?"

"Yeah, but that doesn't excuse it."

"Your mom was still your manager then, right?" Devin has clearly done his homework.

"Yeah. She was even more uncomfortable with it, but she was out of her depth, and there was nothing she could do for the guys."

"And what about Nick? You said Matt was pissed. How did Nick react?"

"He was upset, but he was always the more laid-back of the three of us, and he seemed to handle it better. He said he didn't blame me but..." It doesn't need to be said. Devin knows what I mean.

"Have you had any contact with them since?"

I shake my head before remembering I'm on my cell. "No," I quietly admit. It's one of my biggest regrets. That I let the label trample all over my friend's dreams and then chickened out of keeping in touch with two guys who were more like brothers to me.

"Are they the type to bear grudges? Do you think one of them is behind this?"

I think about it carefully before answering. "I don't think so, but I don't know who they are anymore. We're not kids any longer. They're twenty-one, same age as me. Grown-ass men. Maybe they are still bitter over it. Or maybe they've moved on." I shrug, even though he can't see me.

Silence descends for a few seconds.

"Do *you* think one of them is behind this?" I ask, my voice choking a little. It would probably serve me right, but the thought that one of my ex-friends would actually try to kill me destroys me inside.

Do I deserve their wrath and their frustration?

Abso-fucking-lutely.

Do I deserve to die for my success?

I don't believe so.

I'd like to think if either of the guys still had issues with me they'd reach out and we could discuss it. But I haven't heard from either of them in over five years.

"It's too early to tell. There are a number of red flags on some of these names you've given me, but it requires a more thorough investigation."

"What will you do?"

"Dig a little deeper, and I might assign a few men to watch them for a week or two, to see if they are up to anything suspect."

"Okay. Keep me updated."

"Of course. Stay safe," he says before ending the call.

I toss my cell on the couch, rubbing my hands down my face. Bringing up the past always depresses me. I've made many mistakes on the road to fame and fortune, and there are so many things I wish I could do over.

I mope around my apartment for a few hours, on edge and aggravated. I could use a hit so badly right now. At ten p.m. I text Devin to say I need to go out for a run. He tells me to give him a few minutes to contact his guy.

I set out on foot at a quarter past ten, my bodyguard discreetly jogging behind me, slowly building my pace until I've worked up a sweat. My mind churns with shit I don't want to think about, and I push my body faster, harder, relishing the burn in my legs as I circle laps around the park.

Centered around the historic Old Capitol building, this beautiful park is a popular hangout with students who come to the Pentacrest to study or relax with friends. It's not as populated at night, so it's the perfect spot for a solitary jog.

My running top is stuck to my back, hair plastered to my forehead, as I run for miles, attempting to work off all my restlessness.

Noticing the time, I head back the way I came. Once I'm out on the main street, I stop at a store and grab a bottle of water. I walk the rest of the return journey, keeping a close eye on my watch the entire time. I want to ensure I'm home in time for my midnight dancer.

I'm crossing the street a couple blocks from my place when I spot Dakota hurrying down the lane that leads to the river.

What the hell is she doing out here by herself so late at night? She shouldn't be going down by the river all alone. It's fairly isolated there this time of night.

I'm following her before I've even processed the motion. I know she's still pissed at me, so I hang back instead of making my presence known, feeling more and more like a creepy stalker with every step. I'm sure the bodyguard following me is thinking the exact same thing.

When she reaches the abandoned building and ducks inside, my heart goes haywire in my chest.

No. Fucking. Way.

I stop and glance at my watch, my heart thud-thudding against my ribcage as I connect the dots.

Dakota is my midnight dancer?

"Sir," a deep, low voice says from behind me. "Do you mind me asking what you're doing?"

"Yes, I mind," I snap. "Stay here. Don't follow me up there. I'll be down in a while."

Decision made, I tiptoe into the old building, trailing Dakota as quietly as I can so as not to freak her out. When I reach the top floor, I stop, wondering how to do this. Cautiously, and quietly, I take the final steps to the roof. I emerge into the shadows and stay behind the small, square structure, just off to the side of where Dakota is setting up.

I should let her know I'm here, but I'm a greedy bastard.

I want to see her dance one song up close before I make myself known.

At least, that's what I promise myself.

But once she starts dancing, I'm drawn in, mesmerized by her elegant, graceful moves as she twirls and spins across the empty roof, lost in the music as she dances her heart out.

I can't take my eyes from her.

She's the most exquisite creature I've ever seen.

She pours her heart and soul into her dance, and potent emotion seeps from her bones, rippling through the air and ensnaring me in her heartbreak.

Now I see why she always seems sad behind her smile. Her heart is broken, and her dance is a plea. A desperate, wild, beautiful cry for help.

Except no one's been listening.

Even as I watched her from my window, I didn't decipher the extent of the utterly devastating heartbreak she carries in every fluid step.

How each precise, skillful movement of her body speaks the words her mouth can't, or won't, say.

I wonder if that piece of shit is responsible for this. *Did he do this to her? Were her words the other night mere bravado?*

I can't stay quiet anymore. Her pain slams into me like a thousand volts of electricity, shocking, crippling, and debilitating. As if it's my own.

It's that soul-deep agony that calls out to me as much as the chemistry between us.

We are more alike than I thought.

I step out of the shadows and wait for her to notice me.

She spins around, moving from side to side, with tears cascading down her cheeks.

The urge to envelop her in my arms is almost overpowering. I want to wipe away those tears and replace them with a smile. Then I want to hunt down the fucker who put them there and rip him to shreds.

The strength of my feelings for this girl never ceases to amaze and unnerve me. Especially when I barely know her. No girl has ever gotten under my skin in the same way.

All of a sudden, her chin jerks up and her eyes go wide as she notices me. She slams to a halt, stumbling on unsteady feet. And then an agonized, terrorized scream rings out, slicing through the air as Adele's heartfelt words swirl around us in the darkness of night.

Chapter 7

Dakota

I back away from the guy watching me from the shadows. At least, I assume it's a guy, judging by how tall and broad his shadowy form is. My heart is beating so fast I'm worried I'm on the verge of a heart attack. Blood rushes to my ears, and adrenaline floods my system.

I'm only vaguely conscious I'm screaming.

This can't be happening.

I scrabble to remember the self-defense lessons Dad made me attend last year, but I was so numb with grief that most of it didn't sink in.

The guy takes another step forward. "Dakota. It's me. Sh—Levi. I'm not here to hurt you."

Wait? What? I fight my panic, watching him closely as he takes another tentative step closer. As if on autopilot, I take another step back.

"Please, baby. Don't be frightened. I didn't mean to startle you."

"I'm...I'm not your baby," I whisper, breathing heavily as I attempt to bring my heart rate back to normal. Now that I can see his face, caught in the strip of light radiating from my portable lamp, I stop screaming. Levi's a lot of things, but I don't think he means me any harm.

Icy chills tiptoe up my spine as a new thought lands in my mind.

Is that how Layla felt? Did she believe there was no threat in the familiar too?

He moves forward, and I hold up my palm, starting to circle left toward the exit. "Don't come any closer."

He raises his hands up over his head. "I'm not here to hurt you, Dakota. I swear. I saw you when I was heading back to my apartment, and I didn't like that you were coming here all alone. It's not safe this time of night. I was going to tell you I was here, but then you started dancing and I lost all track of time."

Tears roll down my face unbidden. "This was my private sanctuary. The only place I can properly breathe, and now you've ruined it."

"I'm sorry. I didn't mean to intrude."

He almost sounds sincere, but he forgets I've seen who he really is. Someone who would kiss a girl like she's his entire world and then turn around in the next instance and crush her with nasty words and cruel looks.

"You need to let me leave."

"I'm not stopping you from leaving or doing whatever you want to do."

Taking a risk, I dash across the roof and race down the stairs, flying out of the building as he calls after me. But I can't hear over the screaming in my head and the alarm bells blaring in my ears.

I tear out of the building, running along the embankment, back out through the creepy lane and onto the brighter streets. I don't stop running until I reach my dorm. By the time I get there, I'm a sweaty, hysterical mess, and it takes Daisy almost twenty minutes to get me to calm down.

I tell her what happened in between choked sobs, and she rubs a hand up and down my back, offering much-needed comfort. A flurry of words leaves my mouth as I finally open up and tell her about Layla, so she understands this isn't a normal freak-out.

When I've finally stopped crying and shaking, she helps me into my pajamas and then into bed. I close my eyes, and even though I'm exhausted and emotionally shattered, I still can't sleep. My imagination torments me, flashing images of my sister from that night, and I curl into a fetal position, rocking back and forth in the bed, praying for the pain to end.

I drag my weary ass out of bed the next morning, almost sleepwalking to the shower. After I'm dressed, I scan the room for my bag, realizing in horror that I left all my stuff up on the roof.

Well, that's just freaking perfect.

Levi is waiting outside the entrance to the business school when I arrive. The look on his face is a mix of concern and regret. He holds my bag out for me, and I'm quick to take it. I should thank him, but my throat is dry, and words don't come easily, so I just nod before moving away.

"Dakota, wait a second." He reaches for me before quickly withdrawing his hand. "I'm really sorry about last night. I know how it must have looked, but I didn't mean to scare you or upset you." He thrusts a paper cup at me. "Peace offering?"

I consider declining, but the enticing coffee aroma is too tempting. "Thanks." I cringe at how hoarse I sound. That's what happens when you spend half your night screaming and the other half crying.

His eyes soften as he looks at me, making me uncomfortable. He's staring at me as if I'm a delicate flower. As if I might crumble into a heap if anyone says boo to me. I've had enough of those pitiful looks to last a lifetime. "I've got to go." I offer him a feeble smile as I turn around and walk off.

"Go out with me."

My eyes pop wide as I glance over my shoulder at him. "What?"

He steps up beside me. "Let's walk and talk." He doesn't wait for me to agree, falling into step on my right-hand side. "Let me take you out to dinner."

"Why?"

"Because I want to."

"Why now?"

He frowns. "What do you mean?"

"You couldn't get away from me fast enough on Friday night."

He winces. "Yeah, about that, I—"

"I'm not interested," I say, cutting him off. "I don't date, and even if I did, I would never go out with you." He looks a little crestfallen, and I feel a twinge of guilt. "And I'd appreciate it if you didn't come to the roof again."

"It's not safe for you to go there alone."

"It's none of your business!" I hiss. "I can take care of myself."

"That's not how it seemed last night. I saw the look on your face. I know something's happened to you, and maybe you're trying to prove something to yourself, but that's not the way to go about it."

Anger is like molten lava flowing through my veins. "Who are you to dictate to me? You know jack shit about me and my life, and that's the way I want to keep it." I glare at him, nostrils flaring. "Stay the hell away from me, Levi, and stay the hell away from *my* roof!"

Levi seems to have gotten my message loud and clear, and he goes out of his way to avoid me the rest of the week. Tabs tried to stage an intervention, but she gave up once she realized she was wasting her breath.

I'm still shaken over what happened on the roof.

I don't really think Levi was there to harm me, but he scared the hell out of me, and I've been on edge all week. So much so that I still haven't ventured back there.

As I head home to my parents on Friday night, my muscles are even tighter than usual, my lungs feeling more squeezed than normal. A storm is brewing inside me, and I'm wound so tight I'm on the verge of self-combustion.

Dad's car is missing as I pull into the drive, but that's no surprise. He works double the hours he worked before, anything to avoid coming home. Muriel—the lady who comes in a couple times a day to check on Mom—has left a dinner plate covered in Saran Wrap on the kitchen counter for me. My heart swells at her kind gesture. Gone are the days when I'd step foot in the house to be welcomed by tantalizing smells wafting from the kitchen.

What I wouldn't give to see Mom back at the stove she so dearly loved. My heart aches every time I think of how she's let her little bakery side business go, but, when your heart is ripped apart, and your soul is shattered, it takes enormous effort to just remember to breathe every day.

I tread up the stairs with a heavy heart, knowing what awaits me. Plastering a fake cheery smile on my face, I knock on my mother's bedroom door, waiting the obligatory few seconds before I open the door and step inside.

"Hey, Mom," I say, bending down to kiss her cheek. She's propped up in the bed, staring at the wall-mounted TV in front of her, yet I know she's seeing nothing, hearing nothing. Ignoring the sharp ache in my chest, I place the glass of water down on her bedside table and start counting out her pills. The table is littered in pill boxes of all shapes and sizes, and it kills me every time to see a woman who used to be so full of life, so full of joy, reduced to this shell of a person.

"Open up, Mom," I softly say, gently tapping her chin. Like a robot, she obeys, opening and closing her mouth as I drop a pill inside, and lift the glass to her lips, then rinse and repeat. Emotion clogs my throat, and it takes everything I have not to break down in front of her. I'm trying so hard to be strong for her, because she has always been there for me, but the longer she remains in this catatonic state, the harder it is to hold onto my strength.

I just want my mom back.

When Layla died, this family died along with her.

Then Cole left me.

And now I feel so very alone.

I'm glad I had the strength to go to college because it's the only way I'm clinging to my sanity.

But I'm already starting to resent having to come back here every weekend.

I hate myself for thinking such horrible thoughts.

Mom needs me.

And I won't let her down.

Not when I'm all she has left.

"Coffee is in the pot," I say in a detached tone the following morning when my father finally makes an appearance.

He grunts a weak "thanks," fills his mug, grabs some pancakes from the heap I made, and then trots out to the sunroom to eat his breakfast and read his paper in peace.

"College is great, Dad," I mumble to thin air. "I'm really loving my classes, and I *so* can't wait to start my internship at your offices." Sarcasm underscores my words as I continue talking to myself. I slam the skillet down in the sink and turn the faucet on. "Just think of how close we'll be with all that father-daughter bonding." I crank out a bitter laugh, seething inside as I go about cleaning up the kitchen and fixing a tray for Mom.

I count to ten outside her room, not wanting to haul my anger in with me. Drawing a deep breath, I knock and open the door. She's awake, on her side in the bed, staring off into space.

"I brought you some breakfast, Mom."

She doesn't move a muscle or acknowledge me in any way.

"We still have some of that strawberry puree I made last weekend," I tell her. "I know that's your favorite." I help her sit up, and then I start feeding her the food.

Her cotton nightgown hangs off her skeletal frame reminding me how much weight she's lost this past year. Renewed anger bubbles to the surface again. I know Muriel is here to fix lunch and dinner, so either she's slacking on the job —which I highly doubt—or Dad is the one not making her breakfast before he leaves for work or not feeding her the prepared dinner when he comes home at night.

I wonder what happened to those vows he made.

The ones that said he would love, cherish, and care for her in *sickness* and in health.

Thing is, Dad is one of those jerks who doesn't believe that mental illness is a real illness. A serious illness. Even though he can see the effect it has on his wife, he still refuses to accept it. She's here, right in front of his eyes, barely recognizable, and still he insists she's just being weak or stubborn.

I force those thoughts aside, before I start spitting blood, and concentrate on my mother.

After she's finished eating, I fill the tub and help her in, washing and drying her papery skin, and then dressing her in pants and a warm sweater. I insist on bringing her outside, to the back deck, for at least an hour a day while I'm here. Staying cooped up in her bedroom all the time isn't good for her. She's already got bedsores, and you can visibly see the muscle weakness in her limbs. The doctor encouraged me to ensure she got plenty of fresh air, so that's what I'm trying to do.

Mom is sitting on the love seat on the deck, wrapped in a heavy blanket, staring blankly out at the backyard when the doorbell chimes. I put down the book I was reading to her and peck her on the cheek. "Someone's at the front door, Mom. I'll be back in a second."

She doesn't respond. You think I'd be used to it by now, but I still hold out hope every time that she'll acknowledge me. For now, I talk to her as if she hears me. Hoping she does. Hoping she knows inside that I haven't given up on her.

Even if my father has.

Chapter 8

Shawn/Levi

Dakota hasn't returned to the roof since Tuesday night, and my muse has deserted me. I haven't been able to compose a single sentence or write any sheet music all week. I fucked up spectacularly. Now she looks at me like I'm two seconds away from attacking her with a machete.

Something has that girl spooked. I shouldn't be concerned. It's not my problem. And she's made it very clear she wants me to leave her alone. But I can't get her out of my head. She's burrowed her way in, and now she won't leave.

Which is a major problem.

Because she wants nothing to do with me.

It's Saturday morning, and I'm getting ready to drive to Devin's house when my cell rings. Padding across the hardwood floors in my bare feet, I snatch my phone from the kitchen table and groan as her name pops up on the screen. I rub a hand across my damp, bare chest, wondering if I'd get away without answering. Tucking my towel firmly around my hips, I decide to get it over and done with.

Calista redefines determination. If I don't pick up, she'll just harass the shit out of me all day.

"What?" I snap by way of greeting.

"Well, someone sure got out of the wrong side of bed today," she purrs in a voice I know she thinks is sexy, but it's just annoying as hell.

"I'm on my way out, so make it snappy." I'm being rude, but I can't help it. I've tried to fire her ass several times, but Luke insists she is one of the most efficient PAs around and that it's worth putting up with her deliberate attempts to interfere in my personal life.

"Would it kill you to act professional?"

I snort. "You mean like you do?"

Calista is the epitome of professional with everyone *but me*. I made a mistake and slept with her once about two years ago. I was spaced out, and she came on to me. I can't pretend I didn't know what I was doing, but if I'd been of sound mind, I never would've gone there. She's hot, but everyone knows not to mix business with pleasure. Now, she feels like she's earned the right to act differently around me. Like it's okay to hit on her boss, which it isn't. Especially when said boss has rejected her repeatedly and told her it's never happening again.

But it's like my words go in one ear and out the next.

"You know our relationship is more than professional."

She's just proving my point.

"I don't have time to rehash old shit, Calista. Tell me what you need or I'm hanging up."

"I have a bunch of paperwork you need to sign."

I clench my jaw in frustration as I head to my bedroom. "And this warranted a call? Just scan the stuff to me, and I'll sign and scan back. Or mail the damned stuff. Or give it to Luke next week."

"Or I could come up there and personally deliver the documents. I don't have plans for this weekend. Maybe when I'm there, I can help you unwind. You sound tense, baby. Let me take care of that for you."

I bite the inside of my cheek in frustration. This is starting to become a major problem. "I'm not interested in you like that, Calista. How many times do I have to tell you? And don't you dare attempt to come here. I'm laying low, as you well know, and your presence would *not* be welcome. Don't annoy me with this shit again." I hang up on her before she can reply.

I curse her repeatedly as I get dressed, pissed that she's ruined my good mood. Although my visit to Devin's isn't purely social, I'm looking forward to getting out of my place and hitting the open road. I haven't been out much because I don't want to tempt fate—no one has figured out my real identity, and I intend to keep it that way, but I'm starting to go a little stir-crazy cooped up in this apartment all the time.

Grabbing my keys and my jacket, I set the alarm and leave, determined to chill out before I get to Devin's house.

It takes a little over three and a half hours to reach his place, but I'm nicely chilled by the time I arrive. The weather is unseasonably warm today, and I drove with the window half down, listening to my favorite music to pass the time. Being able to do normal shit like this, and being able to walk around undetected, is even more exhilarating than I thought. The longer I'm away from my old lifestyle, the more relaxed I feel. The more I feel like I'm reconnecting with the real me.

Devin is waiting on the front porch of his house when I get out of my SUV. He shakes my hand. "Good to see you. Come on through."

He gives me a quick guided tour of his impressive home, and I wave to Ange and Ayden who are playing in the backyard. Delicious smells linger in the kitchen, tempting me. "I thought we could attend to business before dinner," Devin says, leading me to his large home office.

"What have you found?" I ask before I've even sat down. When he called a few days ago to invite me over, he implied he had discovered some stuff he wanted to discuss with me in person.

Devin removes a file from the top drawer of his desk, flipping it over. Extracting a photo, he slides it across to me. "Recognize anyone?"

The photo is crystal clear, and I immediately recognize the couple. "That's Matt and Leona."

"Doesn't it strike you as odd that your ex-best friend and your ex-girlfriend are now together? Especially considering she is from out of state."

I sit forward, propping my elbows on my knees. "She was never my girlfriend. Matt and I both fucked around with her before he left. It's not a huge stretch that he might have kept in touch with her. I always thought he had a thing for her and that it pissed him off I was sleeping with her occasionally as well."

"They only officially got together a year ago, and the timing seems a little coincidental to me."

I scrub a hand over my jaw, trying to visualize it. "I get Matt having it in for me, but I didn't do wrong by Leona. She knew it was a casual fuck-buddy arrangement, and she had no issue when I moved on, as did she."

"Perhaps he was the instigator," Devin suggests, and I shrug. Like I said before, I can't pretend to know the dude anymore.

Devin passes another photo to me. This time I don't recognize the girl. "She wasn't on the list, but she's been trying to shop intimate photos of the two of you together to the media. I've checked her finances, and she needs the cash."

"You think my stalker is a girl?" I quirk a brow, highly dubious.

He scrunches his nose. "I think it's unlikely, but I'm not ruling anything out."

"Well, I haven't a clue who she is. And who's to say the photos are genuine? They could be photoshopped," I suggest, even though it's possible they are the real deal. I lost count of the amount of times I woke up after a night of savage partying to some random naked chick in my bed, with no recollection of how she got there.

Now that I'm clean and sober, I'm not proud of my behavior, but it's a rite of passage, and if I start regretting everything I've done, I'll never properly move forward. Can't change the past. Can only make better choices from now on.

Then he hands me a picture of Nick standing outside the local gas station in my old home town, holding hands with a little dark-haired boy. I examine his face carefully, and my eyes pop wide. "Nick's a dad?"

"You didn't know?"

I shake my head. "I haven't been in contact with anyone in my old town since I left, and most of my mom's friends abandoned her after I made it. Once she remarried, she settled in L.A., so neither of us has kept up with shit in Camden."

"He's broke," Devin adds. "The ransom demand could take care of that problem for him."

"Ransom demand?" I almost choke on the words.

Devin nods. "We've just received the first one. They are demanding two mill to go away quietly."

"And if I don't pay up?"

"They are claiming the first attempt on your life was just a warning and they won't miss next time."

I rub the back of my neck. "Fuck."

"They won't get near you, Shawn. They have no clue

where you are and as long as you continue to maintain a low profile then you're safe."

My chest tightens as I struggle to digest the latest news. I don't want to think ill of my buddy, but this is my life at stake. I release a slow, agonized breath. "I really can't see Nick as my stalker, but I *can* see him doing whatever is necessary for his son." The thought he could be the one behind this doesn't sit well with me at all.

"I want you to do something." Devin tips forward in his chair. "I want you to call Matt and Nick. We're monitoring your cell, as you know, and we'll listen in. I want to see how they react."

I rub a tense spot between my brows. "Do I really need to do this? I already know it won't go well."

"You want to catch this guy and go home, don't you?"

Actually, no. I'd much rather stay leading the life of a regular guy, at least for another few months. I'm enjoying the anonymity.

"Fine." I sigh. "I'll do it."

Devin then proceeds to show me a stack of other photos, including ones with a couple of guys I used to hang with until I figured out they were freeloaders and only hanging with me for what they could get. Others are a few drunken hookups, only some I remember.

"This one concerns me," Devin says, sliding another pic to me and tapping his finger off the shiny paper.

My insides twist into knots as I'm forced to look at a face that occupied my nightmares at one time. This girl tried to claim I got her pregnant a couple years back. Looking at her face reminds me of the six months of sheer hell she put me through while I waited for her to give birth and get a paternity test. Turns out the kid wasn't mine after all. The whole experience left a bitter taste in my mouth. It was also the final straw which led to Mom permanently bailing on me, and I can't look at that girl without wanting to ram my fist through a wall.

"The douche in the picture with her is her new fiancé. The cops have been trying to pin shit on him for a couple years, but he's smart enough to leave no traceable evidence. He has history with blackmail and extortion. It's not a huge stretch to think he might have set his sights on you because of the prior connection between you and his girl, and let's not forget she tried to extort money from you before."

"I don't need to be reminded," I hiss, getting up and pacing the room. "This shit is putting me in a bad mood."

Devin stands, clamping a hand on my shoulder. "I know this isn't easy, but it has to be done. Trust me when I tell you I'll get the guy, but I need your help to do it."

Ange pops her head into the room. "I'm just about to serve dinner, and we need to eat before Kendall wakes up from her nap."

Devin walks to the door, pressing a kiss to the top of his wife's head. "We'll be right with you, hon."

He walks back to his desk, closing the file and relocking it in his desk drawer. "There's a couple more photos in there, but we can go through those after we eat. Come on." He slaps me on the back. "I hope you're hungry. Ange is an amazing cook, and she's gone a bit overboard. I think she has it in her head that you're not eating properly, and she wants to rectify that."

When we enter the dining room, an older couple are already seated at the table, along with a familiar face. "What are you doing here?" I ask my manager as he gets up from the table and comes around to greet me.

He pulls me into a bear hug. "I wanted to check-in in person. To make sure you're okay." He clasps my shoulders and gives me the once-over. "You look well. More relaxed."

"I'm chill." I clear my throat, uncomfortable with blatant

displays of affection, but I can't let Luke's gesture go without saying something. "Thanks for coming, but you didn't have to. I know you don't like being separated from your family right now."

He smiles, shoulder-checking me. "My mother-in-law is staying with us for the weekend, so it was good to have an excuse to disappear for the day." He winks, trying to shrug it off, but I know what he's doing. "I took the jet, so I'll be going home tonight, straight after dinner."

Ange breaks up our little happy reunion then, declaring dinner is ready, and I take a seat beside Luke at the table. Devin introduces me to Ange's mom Natalie and her husband Jon. Conversation flows freely around the table, and Ange's mom politely asks me questions about college. I'm guessing Devin didn't tell either of them who I really am, and I'm grateful for his discretion. Luke was also introduced as my uncle, and he could barely contain his smile. I think he fancies himself as an undercover agent or a spy or something.

Devin also wasn't kidding about Ange's cooking, and I happily accept seconds, much to her delight.

Luke and I help Devin clear away the dirty dinner plates while Ange goes to fetch Kendall from her crib. It's all so normal and it reminds me of everything I'm missing. A pang of sadness sweeps over me as I quietly rinse and stack plates in the dishwasher, trying to work out how many years it's been since I've done anything as domesticated. I've been spoiled. Having copious staff members and employees attend to my every need, my every wish, and it's made me lazy and complacent.

Luke doesn't waste the opportunity to tease me about that very fact, and I flip him the bird, while he just smiles.

Being back here, in a family environment, reminds me of all the ways I've changed. And all the things I've forgotten. Although it was only Mom and me growing up, she always insisted we eat dinner together every night, and my gramps always came to Sunday dinner. He passed away the year before I was discovered, and I used to hate that he wasn't around to see my success. He was my greatest supporter, always encouraging me to reach for the stars. Lately, I've been glad he wasn't around to witness my self-destruction. He'd have been so disappointed in me.

Somewhere along the way, I forgot my upbringing, and turned into a pretentious prick.

Ange comes into the kitchen with baby Kendall in her arms. She's exercising a fine set of lungs, bawling impressively loud for someone so small. "Someone's hungry," Ange says, laughing softly as she rubs her nose against her daughter's. "It's coming, little one." She grabs a bottle from the refrigerator, and my mouth opens before I've had time to even think about what I'm saying.

"Can I feed her?"

Devin and Ange share a look of surprise. Luke smiles proudly at me.

"I used to help Mom feed my brothers when they were babies." I feel the need to explain. "She had twins, so she needed an extra pair of hands." Not that I was around much. Luke was acting manager during Mom's maternity leave—before taking the role on full-time when she later quit—and he'd factored two weeks' vacation time into my touring schedule so I could go home and help Mom in the weeks after the babies were born. She and Steve, my new stepfather, were completely overwhelmed and grateful for the help.

I gulp over the unexpected wedge of emotion in my throat. That was one of the last happy times we had together; thinking of it now raises a whole host of feelings to the surface.

"That would be great. Thank you." Ange ushers me into the living room, and I get comfy on the couch. Then she places her daughter in my arms, and I start feeding her the bottle.

Ayden is playing with a Scalextric playset on the floor while Ange's mom and stepdad are chatting with her as they look out over the landscaped back lawn. Luke is on his cell in the corner of the room, talking in hushed tones. Devin sits down beside me, sipping a water and crossing one leg over his knee.

"You have a lovely family," I say, cradling his gorgeous little daughter in my arms. "I could run away with this little one," I surprise myself by adding. Might as well go the whole nine yards, considering I seem to have traded my balls for a pussy. "I'm sorry for how I acted that day in your office. I was being a jerk on purpose."

He chuckles. "No worries. I might have overreacted a bit." He smirks. "You know, I see a lot of myself in you." I arch a brow, and he chuckles again. "I lost myself for a while. Spent far too many years drunk and high, hooking up with random chicks from school and thinking I could outrun my problems." He slants me a knowing look. "But they always catch up to you, and I learned that no one could save me if I didn't want to save myself."

"You think I need to be saved?"

"Don't you?"

Kendall coos in my arms, and I press a kiss to her forehead, closing my eyes and soaking up her soft, newborn smell.

"Do you want kids?" he asks, tipping the bottle of water into his mouth.

"Someday, yeah."

He nods, smirking. "Maybe there's hope for you yet."

"Do you always insult your clients?" I retort.

"Only the ones I like."

I laugh, and the baby flinches in my arms. "Sorry, princess," I murmur, kissing her soft cheek.

"Hey, no falling for my other girl, or I might have to settle this with my fists."

"I could totally take you, old man, but I've already learned my lesson." I smirk back at him.

"Yet you didn't heed my warning." I stare at him in confusion. "About Dakota."

I purse my lips and glare at him. That's crossing a line. "You've been hired to consult on my safety, not my love life," I snap.

"They are not mutually exclusive. Half the names on that list are ex-girlfriends."

"Ex-hookups," I correct him. "I've never had a girlfriend."

"Well, that's a damn shame, but I don't think you should start with Dakota. Not until we've cleaned this mess up. You don't want to drag any girl into this, especially not a girl who has already been through hell."

My body locks up. "What do you mean? And how do you know?"

Luke looms large over us, temporarily halting the conversation. "I've gotta go. Don't get up," he says, as I start to straighten up, maneuvering the baby in my arms. "You look way too cute like that."

I narrow my eyes and my lips pull tight. A loud chuckle rumbles through him. "Mind yourself, and I'll talk to you soon."

"Thanks for coming, man. Later."

After Luke has left the room, I pin Devin with a serious look. "Explain what you meant by that comment about Dakota."

He straightens up. "I'm paid to keep you safe. That means I've done background checks on everyone you've met since you moved to Iowa. Especially Dakota. I've seen the pics. I can tell you're smitten." There is no teasing in his tone.

"What do you know about her?"

He shakes his head. "Nuh-uh. I'm not going to be the one to tell you."

Kendall finishes her bottle and dozes in my arms. I put the empty bottle down on the table, while I prop her carefully over my shoulder, gently rubbing her back. "I'm paying you a fucking fortune. If you've got information on her, I want it."

A muscle ticks in his jaw. "This is me doing my job. Protecting you. You know I want you to stay away from her, at least for the time being, but I'm not that old I can't remember what it's like to be wrapped up in a special girl. If you end up getting closer to her, do you really want her to know you snooped into her background before she had a chance to tell you herself?"

He pauses to let that sink in. I continue rubbing Kendall's back and she emits a loud burp which makes me proud.

"It's bad enough she doesn't know who you really are," he quietly adds, and it brings me back to the conversation about the real me Friday night. I'm fairly certain if Dakota knew I was Shawn Lucas she'd run a mile. That thought sticks in my gut.

"I thought you said to stay away from her."

"I did, but I also know you won't. That you can't. Even if you should. I've been there. It's not an easy thing to do, even if it's the right thing to do."

Putting his water down, he stands, gently lifting his daughter into his arms. She nuzzles into his chest, and he cuddles her close. "Just be careful with her, Shawn. She's been through a lot. And if you can't treat her right, you have no business going near her at all."

Chapter 9

Dakota

I answer the front door, instantly on guard when I see Muriel standing beside Dr. Nevin. "Dakota." He smiles, taking my hands in his. "It's so lovely to see you. I know this is unexpected, but we were both hoping to have a word with you."

I glance at the driveway, noticing my father's car is absent again, and I release the breath I'd been holding. "Of course." I step aside to let them enter. "Come through to the dining room. Mom is sitting out on the deck, and I want to keep my eyes on her."

Once we are all seated, with steaming hot mugs of coffee in hand, Dr. Nevin clears his throat and gets straight to the reason for his visit. "Did your father mention the conversation I had with him a couple of weeks ago?" I shake my head, and he sighs. "I thought not. I'm sorry to burden you with this, but something has to be done, and while I can take the necessary action, it would be much better coming from you."

A blanket of trepidation swathes me on all sides. "What exactly are you saying, Doctor?"

"She's getting much worse," Muriel says, confirming something I already know. "She won't eat for me, and most days she has wet the bed by the time I arrive."

"She isn't capable of looking after herself, Dakota," the doctor continues, "and her condition is deteriorating. She needs more intense treatment. She needs to be committed to a psychiatric facility, but your father is refusing to petition the court."

Of course, he is.

He doesn't believe she has serious depression and anxiety.

And he wouldn't want any of his clients or his employees to know his wife needs full-time in-patient psychiatric care.

"She eats for me," I tell him. "And she hadn't wet the bed this morning. In fact, she let me bathe and dress her."

Muriel pats my arm. "You're the only one she still responds to, but you can't be here to care for her twenty-four-seven. You've got your own life to lead."

A tsunami of guilt crashes into me. I should give up college to come back and care for her, but Dad won't allow it. Perhaps I can use that as a bargaining tool. Force him into agreeing to get her the help she needs.

But the thought of Mom in one of those places devastates me. *How can I stand by and let that happen? How can I selfishly abandon her when she needs me the most?* "I'll give up college. I'll come home and take care of her."

Dr. Nevin and Muriel exchange a look. The doctor puts his mug down and takes my hands in his. "You are, undoubtedly, one of the most devoted daughters I have ever met. Your mother is so lucky to have you. I understand you don't want this for her, but, trust me, it's in your mother's best interests. Even if you were to return home to care for her, you would only be taking care of her physical needs. She needs professional help to overcome her mental illness."

Tears roll down my face as the magnitude of what's being

said hits me square in the chest. "He will never agree," I admit, sniffling.

"He doesn't have to. You're nineteen years old, an adult in the eyes of the law. You can petition the court too."

My tears dry up as his words sink in. *I could do this, but at what cost?* Dad will disown me if I go behind his back and against his wishes.

But this isn't about what he wants. It's about what's best for Mom. "I need a little time to think it all through, and I want to speak to my father." I won't go behind his back. I'll try to reason with him, but if he doesn't agree, then I guess I'm doing it alone. Consequences be damned.

Dad only returns at nine p.m. that night, smelling of expensive whiskey and cheap perfume.

A new horror assaults my mind. *Is he cheating on Mom now?* I can't believe this is the same man I've looked up to my entire life. Yes, we had some humdinger arguments because my carefree attitude and dance plans always seemed flighty to him, but he was a good father, a good husband, and he doted on my mother.

But now he's a virtual stranger.

I see none of that man left in him.

And it's not enough to say this is grief, because I'm grieving too, but I'm not out there betraying my family. I'm doing everything I can to keep it together.

I can barely look at him as I open up the conversation we need to have. Perhaps I should've waited until tomorrow, until he's sober, but it's eating me up inside, and I can't go a second longer without getting this off my chest.

He roars at me, screaming and shouting, and I flinch at his

angry tone and furious expression. "Your mother does not need to be committed!" he yells. "She just needs a good kick in the butt to come to her senses. She isn't the only one who lost a daughter, and you don't see me moping around in bed!"

"Daddy, please. These people can help her get better. She can't stay like this."

"I'm fixing this right now," he barks, racing out of the kitchen and up the stairs.

"Leave her alone!" I screech, dashing after him, panic constricting my lungs.

I run into her room, appalled to see my father yanking my mother out of bed. She had been fast asleep when I last checked on her a half hour ago.

I grab my father's arm. "Let her go, Dad. This isn't helping." I try to pull him back, so I can get to her, but he tightens his grip on her shoulders and jostles me aside.

"This damn charade ends here." He puts his face in hers. "Do you hear me, Valerie?!" His nostrils flare when she doesn't respond, and he starts shaking her.

"Daddy, stop." I'm openly sobbing now, reaching for him. "Don't hurt her." He shakes her more violently, and I'm starting to get really concerned. "Daddy! Stop it!" I make a grab for his arm, to haul him back, but he twists around, backhanding me before I can make contact. Red-hot pain zings across my face, and I lose my balance, tumbling to the ground. Tears stream out of my eyes as I clutch my stinging cheek.

My father has never hit me before.

Never raised his hand to my sister or my mother.

So this is a complete shock, and I'm destroyed.

Dad is frozen, his hand still gripping Mom's shoulders as he stares at me. At least he seems shocked by his own action, but it doesn't erase the heartfelt hurt lancing me on all sides.

"Leave her alone," Mom whispers, staring straight ahead

without any expression on her face. "Leave my daughter alone."

Dad narrows his eyes at her before flinging her back down on the bed. Turning around, he hovers over me, anger flaring in his gaze. "See? Told you! It's all an act. A pitiful attempt to be the center of attention." He jabs his finger at Mom. "You should be ashamed of yourself, Valerie. You're a disgrace." Throwing one last glare in Mom's direction, he storms out of the room, slamming the door shut behind him.

I peer up at Mom, dazed and confused. Climbing to my feet, I walk to her side, perching on the edge of the bed. "Mom?" I reach out and touch her cheek, and she turns her head to face me. An errant sob rips from my throat as she looks me directly in the eyes for the first time in months. "Mom!" I bury my head in her chest, crying buckets when her hand lifts and gently brushes my hair.

"I'm sorry, baby. I'm so sorry," she whispers in a dry, coarse voice.

I don't know how long I stay there embracing her. She doesn't say anything else, but she doesn't need to. When I finally lift my head, she's fast asleep. Tucking the covers snugly around her, I tiptoe quietly out of the room.

All the lights are off downstairs, and I'm guessing Dad went to bed or he went out again, so I'm startled when I enter the kitchen to find him nursing a whiskey in the darkness. My heart pounds against my ribcage, and tears stab the back of my eyes, but I refuse to shed any more tears in front of him. I pour myself a glass of water, conscious he's watching me like a hawk. Garnering courage, I turn and face him. "Don't you have something to say to me?"

I want him to apologize so I know some part of the man I used to know, and respect, is still in there somewhere.

My eyes have grown accustomed to the dark, and I can see

him staring straight at me as he replies. "Your mother is not being committed and that's final." He stands, draining the rest of his drink. "And if you ever come at me like that again, you'll be sorry." He walks to me, leaning into my face. I can scarcely breathe over the lump jammed in my throat. The hostile sneer on his face terrifies me, and I'm shaking all over. "She is *my* wife, *my* responsibility, and I will handle her *my* way. If you don't like it, you know where the door is."

My lip wobbles, and tears pool in my eyes despite my previous determination. I run out of the room and straight out the front door. I don't know where I'm going, only that I need to get away from the house. From *him*.

I race across the road in front of our house without looking. The screeching of tires elevates my heart rate to coronary-inducing territory, and I stand motionless, captured in the full beam of headlights. A black SUV, with tinted windows, shudders to a standstill literally right in front of me. I stare at the dark windows for a split second before I take off, hopping the fence and running through the long grass as if my life depends on it.

Chapter 10

Shawn/Levi

The girl materializes in front of me out of nowhere, and I slam on the brakes, expletives peppering the air. Terror has a vice grip on my heart as I white-knuckle the steering wheel, pressing my foot flat to the pedal, praying I can stop in time. Noticing my car, she stops in the middle of the road as if she has a death wish. The SUV screams to a halt mere inches from her body.

Air whooshes out of my mouth in grateful relief, and I collapse over the wheel. Adrenaline floods my body, and my heart rate is off the charts. Rubbing a palm over my angst-ridden chest, I catch a fleeting glimpse of the girl before she dives over the fence into the adjoining field.

Unless my eyes are playing tricks on me, that was Dakota.

What the actual fuck?

I pull my car over to the side of the road and park. Without pausing to think about it, I jump out and take off after her.

She's stumbling her way through the long grass, veering unsteadily on her feet. When she reaches a large oak tree in the middle of the field, she drops out of sight. I run faster, only slowing down as I approach.

She's on her knees, with her arms clutched around her torso, rocking back and forth as she struggles to breathe. She looks up when she hears my approach, and I notice the dried tearstains on her face and the lost look in her panicked eyes.

I don't hesitate. Dropping down, I wrap my arms around her, pulling her into my lap. "It's okay. You're okay."

I'd like to know why the hell she was racing across the road in the pitch-dark dressed in only a flimsy dress and cardigan and in her bare feet. Debris adheres to the soles of her feet, and I reach over, carefully brushing them off.

Her breath oozes out in panicked spurts, and her chest wheezes. I run my hand up and down her back. "Breathe, Dakota. Nice and slow." I inhale and exhale deeply, encouraging her to do the same. She pins me with the saddest blue eyes, and I sweep my thumb across her cheek, caressing her soft skin. "In and out, babe. Just focus on your breathing. Draw it into your lungs and let it out nice and slow." Her breathing starts to even out, and the raspy, wheezy sound in her chest peters out.

"How are you here?" she croaks after a bit, resting her head on my chest.

I wrap my arms more tightly around her waist, keeping her close. "I was on my way back from a friend's place, and I had to pull in to get gas. You live here?"

She nods. "My whole life. My house is just over there." She points across the road.

"We have to stop meeting like this," I joke, trying to lighten the atmosphere while I toy with the long strands of her wavy blonde hair.

"One might be inclined to think you're stalking me."

I know she's only teasing, but that word causes goose

bumps to sprout all over my arms. "Or it's a complete coincidence," I say, even though I don't believe in such things.

She fists a hand in my shirt, and a delicate fragrance tickles my nostrils. She smells like sunsets and orange blossom and a million forbidden things. "The old me would have called it fate," she whispers.

I tip her chin up gently. "The old you?" The inflection in my tone hints to my curiosity.

She stares up at the bleak, starless night sky. "Do you ever feel like you're lost inside yourself?"

"All the time," I honestly admit.

"How do you find the right path back?"

"I'm still trying to figure that out." She looks into my eyes, probing the truth. I cup her face, examining her eyes for my own truth. She conveys so much with her eyes. I see the strength of her emotions, but I don't understand what's behind it. Where the hurt is coming from, and who caused it. "Why were you running across the road in the dark? And why is your cheek all red and blotchy?"

She averts her eyes and climbs out of my lap. I instantly regret pushing her. "I don't want to talk about it," she whispers, stepping away as she starts to withdraw into her shell.

I stand up and take her hand, pleased when her fingers link through mine. I'm not even sure if she realizes she's done it. "No problem," I lie, because it's not okay, but she's vulnerable right now, and I won't force her to confess if she's not ready to. "But if you ever do, you know where I am."

What the fuck am I doing?

I think I've lost my mind.

Since I left the Morgans' house, I've been thinking about what Devin said.

About keeping her safe by keeping her away from me, and here I am, only a few hours later, already making promises I shouldn't keep. It's just, when I'm with her, I get lost in her. Lost in possibility, and something I've never stopped to consider.

It's far too dangerous and risky, for both of us, but I'm not sure I know how to put a stop to it.

We walk silently, hand in hand, through the tall grass and out onto the road. I pin her to my side, looking left and right, before we cross over to the other side.

A large, well-maintained two-story cream brick house sits on an elevated position a few feet away. There's a triple garage off to one side and an outdoor seated area on the other. "I'm okay now," she says, slipping her hand out of mine. "Thank you."

"I'll walk you to the door," I insist, retaking her hand.

She has her mouth open to reply when a man with short dark blond hair appears out of nowhere on the sidewalk. "Get in the house, Dakota," he hisses, glowering at me.

"Dad."

"Now."

"No." She holds her ground, removing her hand from mine and crossing her arms over her chest. "I'm an adult and you don't get to tell me what to do."

"Don't talk back, girl, or you'll be sorry."

"I'm heading back to the city," I tell her, deliberately ignoring her prick of a father. "I'm happy to give you a ride back to your dorm."

"Over my dead body!" he roars, shoving me.

My hands ball up at my side, and it won't take much more to provoke me into using my fists. "Touch me again and *you'll* be sorry."

He snorts, grabbing Dakota roughly by the arm. She attempts to wriggle out of his grasp, but he keeps a firm hold of her. "You'd better not be messing around with this punk ass."

He sends me a derisory look. "Have you forgotten what I told you? Unless it's Cole, boys are forbidden."

Yeah, because Cole is such a stellar choice for his daughter. What a jerk.

"It's not what you're thinking. Levi is a friend and classmate."

He gives me a more thorough once-over, and I straighten my spine, narrowing my eyes as I return the favor. "My daughter is off-limits. Don't come back here."

He starts dragging her away, and I see red, sprinting after him and grabbing him by the elbow. "Your daughter can think for herself, and if you don't take your hands off her, I won't be responsible for my actions."

He shucks out of my grip, dusting his sleeves like I've just contaminated him. "Get the hell off my property or I'm calling the cops."

I cross my arms over my chest, smirking at him. "Go right ahead. I'd love you to explain the mark on her cheek."

Dakota steps in between us. "Levi, don't." Her eyes plead with me. "Please just go."

"I don't want to leave you here with him."

"I'm okay." She lightly touches my arm. "It's not how it looks."

I'm conflicted, but I can't force her hand. We're barely even friends, and I have no right to demand anything of her, but I don't like this. At all. I lower my head, whispering in her ear. "Are you sure? If you're in trouble, I can help."

"I'm sure." She nods, urging me to let this go with her eyes. "I'll talk to you Monday."

Reluctantly, I leave. As I'm pulling away from the curb, I tap in Devin's number. He answers immediately. "Text me Dakota's number and don't ask any questions. I'm not in the mood."

"Okay, but don't do anything stupid," he replies, before hanging up.

A few seconds later my cell pings, and I pull over once I'm well out of sight of her house. I tap out a quick text to her.

It's Levi. Keep my number and use it if you need to.

She replies a minute later with a simple, **Thanks.**

As I drive back to my penthouse, I fight an internal battle.

Climbing into bed, I'm no closer to a decision.

My head warns me to steer clear. That I've got enough of my own problems without getting sucked into someone else's.

But my heart can't forget my midnight dancer, and I want to be there for her in all the ways I shouldn't.

Chapter 11

Dakota

Dad spends all of Sunday attempting to lecture me about Levi. But I tune him out. It's all stuff I've heard before, and he doesn't need to warn me about strangers. I get it. And maybe I'm naïve, plain stupid, or my will to survive isn't as strong as I thought, but I don't believe Levi is a danger to me.

The way he held me last night, out by the tree, and the tender look in his eyes is not something that can be faked. And I saw something in him. Something that hints at his pain. And I can tell he gets it.

Perhaps I misjudged him.

Maybe I *should* get to know him.

Because when he was holding me, I didn't hurt so much. I didn't feel so alone.

When Dad goes to work on Monday, I swing into action. I lied and told him I didn't have any early classes, so I had an excuse for sticking around when I normally return to campus on Sunday night. Thankfully, he accepted it without interrogation.

Muriel comes to watch Mom while I go with Dr. Nevin to meet with an attorney friend of his to set everything in motion. The attorney tells me he'll draft the necessary paperwork to petition the court, and there isn't much more I can do for now.

I spend the afternoon with Mom, reluctantly leaving before Dad returns. She hasn't spoken another word since Saturday night, and the lucidity she displayed is gone too. I hate the thought of sending her to a psychiatric facility, but after my Dad's behavior Saturday night, I now know it's the safest place for her.

"So, guess who was wondering where you were yesterday?" Tabs says, waggling her brows as we sit in the auditorium, waiting for the prof to show for our taxation class on Tuesday morning.

"Please tell me it was Liam or Chris Hemsworth?" I joke.

"While I approve of the tag team, and I'm so with you, girlfriend," Tabs agrees, her eyes twinkling, "I cannot make those dreams come true. However, I can tell you that our very own resident sex god was asking where you were, and he looked seriously worried."

I don't need to ask her who she's referring to. "He didn't, ah, say anything else, did he?" I know Levi is friendly with Tabs, and I should've thought to ask him to keep what happened Saturday night to himself, but it never crossed my mind.

Her brows knit together. "Like what? Is there something I don't know?"

Damn, that girl has finely tuned antennae. "Nope. I was just curious."

She shoulder-bumps me. "Admit it. You *like* him."

"Why do you care about this so much?"

"Because I'm thinking of setting up a matchmaking business on campus and you're my practice run."

My mouth falls open. "What the what?"

She titters. "Man, you are way too easy to wind up. I'm kidding. I just want to see you happy, and you looked *really* happy Friday night when you were sucking face with him."

The prof enters the room and clears his throat, and I whisper one final comment. "He's growing on me, and that's all I'm admitting to."

By lunchtime, I'm eating my words.

"Five o'clock," Elsa says under her breath, when we're all seated in the cafeteria. "And he's coming right this way."

I jerk my head up, watching Levi stride in our direction. Butterflies swarm my chest, and my heart speeds up. I send him a shy smile as he approaches.

"Ladies." He gives us a curt nod and a tight smile before, surprisingly, continuing on his way.

My chest deflates, and I hate that.

"Where the fuck is he going?" Tabs inquires, staring curiously at Levi as he drops into a seat at an empty table behind us. Her chair scrapes as she stands.

"Sit back down," I hiss, pulling at the hem of her shirt. "You are *not* going over there."

"The hell I'm not." A new scowl paints her face.

"Leave him be. He doesn't have to sit with us if he doesn't want to."

Against my better judgment, I look over my shoulder. Levi is scrolling through his phone as he eats, ignoring everyone and everything around him. I don't understand. Especially after what he said to me Saturday night.

Having already convinced myself to let him into my life, I'm thoroughly confused.

Tabs relents, sitting back down, as I pick at my food, half-heartedly chatting with the girls over lunch. I'm wondering if I did something to upset him or maybe he's just having a bad day and needs some space. I'm sure that's it. That I'm over-reacting.

Except when I glance back over at his table sometime later, it's empty, and he's gone. He left without saying a word.

I can't properly understand why it hurts so much. But it does.

The afternoon drags, especially the last class, when I have to watch Levi ignore me again, taking a seat in the front row, instead of sitting behind me like he usually does. Deciding I need to find out if I've done something to upset him, I wait at the end of my row when class ends, hoping for an opportunity to talk to him. But he gets up and walks past me as if I don't exist.

I'm momentarily dazed, trying to figure out what the hell is going on. Chasing after him, I call out his name, but he keeps walking, his long strides seeming to pick up pace as I shout out again. But he doesn't stop or acknowledge me in any way.

My feet slow down, and I stop my forward trajectory as hurt and anger swim to the surface, forcing me to see sense. I'm sick of all this hot and cold bullshit he's pulling, so screw him. I don't need or want his kind of trouble in my life.

The next couple of days follow a similar pattern, and I'm fighting a perpetual bad mood. Levi continues to pretend like I'm invisible, so I do the same to him. He's obviously decided he wants nothing to do with me after what he witnessed on Saturday. If he's that judgmental, then I'm better off without him.

I haven't danced on the roof in over a week, and I'm sleeping even worse than normal. My body is highly strung, and by Thursday, I decide it's time to risk returning. Levi doesn't care about me, so it's stupid to continue to allow him to hold me back from the one enjoyment I have in my life. The attorney calls me that morning to tell me I'm needed in court the next afternoon, and I'm in a solemn mood the rest of the day. Once I do this, there's no going back. I'm not sure how Dad's going to react, and I'm worried about Mom, even if I know, deep down, that this is the right thing to do.

By the time I reach the roof that night, I'm considerably on edge, and I waste no time limbering up. My body rejoices as I start to move. A little stiffly at first, until I'm fully relaxed. I dance my heart out, quickly building up a sweat, throwing my body across the roof in tune to the haunting music. I twirl and twirl, my lungs filling with oxygen and my limbs reenergized. Then a familiar song plays on my cell, one I haven't heard in a long time. The memory resurrects in my mind in absolute clarity.

"You're so unbelievably talented," Layla gushes after the show, pulling me in for a hug. "I'm so proud of you, little sis. Your star shone so bright on that stage tonight."

Tears prick my eyes. My sister is the most undeniably loyal sister to have ever walked the Earth. It doesn't matter that we are like night and day, polar opposites in so many ways. Layla is always supportive. Always championing me. Always defending me when Dad questions my choices. Still they all turn up to every show, my parents included, and I know they love me, even if Dad would rather I followed Layla into accounting.

"That last song you danced was just magical," she says with a dreamy look on her face, looping her arm though mine as we make our way out to the parking lot. "The music was so evocative, and you were like an angel gliding across the stage." She looks at me with blatant admiration in her radiant blue eyes. "I wish you could see how you look when you're up on that stage. How you own it. How natural you are in the spotlight."

"Stop it. You'll give me a big head," I joke, secretly pleased at her glowing praise.

"Nah. You're not the type." She pulls me to a halt a few feet away from our parent's car. "I want you to know how good you are, Kotabear. Like seriously talented. And I want you to promise that you'll never give up your dream. That you'll always dance."

"That's easy," I say. "Because I'm not ever planning to stop dancing."

I drop to my knees, ripped apart by the memory. Grief is funny like that. It can sneak up and waylay you all over again when you're least expecting it.

God, how I wish Layla was here right now. Tears slowly roll down my face, and I give in to them. If Layla were here she'd know how to handle Dad and how best to support Mom, removing the burden of responsibility from me. She always instinctively knew what do to, and she just naturally took charge.

I was happy to let her lead, to handle all the difficult stuff, while I floated through life as if I hadn't a care in the world.

I look up at the dark sky through blurry eyes. "Why did you have to leave?" My silent tears transform to audible sobs. "I miss you so much." I rub a hand across my aching chest, rocking back and forth on the ground, my knees grazing debris on the dirty roof. A heavy weight presses down on my chest, and any relief I felt tonight has disintegrated, along with my resolve.

I don't know if I have strength to face what I need to tomorrow.

If I can step up and do what I need to do for my mother.

Clutching my arms around myself, I shed more tears. Crying for the loss of my sister, the devastation tearing my family apart, and the abandonment of my dreams.

Chapter 12

Shawn/Levi

I punch in his number with shaky hands, wishing I could've taken some liquid courage first. Tonight is the closest I've come to breaking my sobriety, and it took every ounce of willpower to avoid reaching for a bottle. I'm not sure if Matt will even accept my call, but I've got to at least try.

"Hello."

Bile floods my mouth as my ex-buddy answers the call. His voice is deeper than I remember, but it's still familiar. "Hey, Matt. It's Shawn."

Deafening silence filters through the connection.

"What the fuck do you want?" he hisses after a bit.

"To talk. I just wanted to see how you're doing."

He snorts. "You expect me to believe that? You cut me out of your life, out of the life *we* made together, ignore me for over five years, and then you just call out of the blue to *talk* for no reason?" He huffs. "What kind of idiot do you take me for?"

Nausea churns in my gut. "I'm sorry, dude. More than you could ever realize."

"Save your fucking apologies, Shawn. You're too damn late."

"If I could go back, I'd do everything different."

He snorts again. "Like what? Screw us over even more?"

"I would fight for you and Nick. I'd tell the label to go fuck themselves. That we come as a package."

"What a pity you don't have a time machine." He sneers, bitterness creeping into his tone. "Even with all your riches, there are some things money can't buy. Like forgiveness."

"If I could make it up to you, I would."

"What is this really about, Shawn? What do you want? Because I know you're not calling out of the goodness of your heart."

"Are you happy, man? I heard you're with Leona, and I hope she makes you happy."

He barks out an incredulous laugh. "This is about my *woman*? News flash, *buddy*. She can't stand you either. And she's told me everything about the life you lead now. Almost makes me glad I got out of that scene. You're a pathetic asshole, Shawn, and the music you're making is crap. I'm glad I'm no longer associated with you, and if this is some pitiful attempt to mend bridges so you can feel better about stabbing your two best buds in the back, you won't get absolution from me. I used to love you like a brother, but you're dead to me now. You died the minute you sold your soul to the devil." He pauses for a quick breath. "Don't contact me again. And stay the hell away from Leona."

The flat dial tone confirms he hung up. Dropping my cell on the couch, I get up, scrunching fistfuls of my hair as I pace my living room. "Fuckkkkkkkk!!" Frustration and rage boil my blood, and I pummel my fist into the wall, hitting it over and over until my knuckles bleed and there's a fist-sized hole in the plasterboard.

My cell vibrates, but I ignore it, resting my forehead against the wall as Matt's hurtful words penetrate deep. Everything he said was true, and I can't fault him for his anger. I deserve it. I was a shitty friend, and he deserved better. Both he and Nick did. The cell pings again, and Devin's name flashes on the screen. I snatch it up. "What?" I bellow, taking my frustration out on him.

"Are you okay?"

"What the fuck do you think?"

"I'm sorry."

"Told you it was a bad fucking idea." I start pacing again. "I need a fucking drink so bad!"

"Call your sponsor."

"No."

"Do you want me to come over? Or send my guy in to you?"

"No! I don't need a fucking babysitter! I need to drink myself into oblivion so I can't think about this shit anymore."

I need my Mom. And I don't care if that makes me sound like a pussy.

"I get it. I totally do," Devin says. "I've been teetotal since I was eighteen, and most days I still crave alcohol, especially at times of stress. Been on the brink of going there more times than I can count, but I always manage to resist, and you can too. Believe in yourself. Believe you're strong enough."

"It's easier for you. You have a lot to lose if you fall off the wagon. I've already lost everyone and everything that matters to me."

"That's fucking bullshit and you know it. The first few years I was sober were hell on earth for me. I'd lost everyone and everything that mattered to me too, but I never gave up fighting. Never stopped hoping that I'd get my life back the way I wanted it, and I sure as fuck wasn't going to achieve that constantly drunk or high." His lecture dies out, and silence engulfs us. "Take some advice from someone who's been in your shoes. Quit feeling sorry for yourself and actively do something to take back control of your life."

"What the hell do you think I'm doing in fucking Iowa!!" I roar. "This *is* me trying to take back control."

"Well, remember that the next time you feel like caving. Remember your goals and never stop fighting for them."

My anger ebbs a little. It's not him I'm mad at—it's all me.

"It definitely sounds like Matt's harboring a grudge," Devin supplies, switching the subject. "I'm going to send a couple of men to shadow him for a while, and we'll investigate further."

"Fine. Do what you need to." I don't wait for him to respond. I just hang up. Heading to the bathroom, I rub ointment on my grazed knuckles while I attempt to calm the hell down.

Man, I want to be mad at Devin for forcing me to call Matt, but I can't take my frustration out on him. Not even with the fact I still need to call Nick, and I'm probably in for more of the same. I was supposed to call them both tonight, but I'm putting the second call off until I've calmed down. I'm too scared if I call him and it goes the same way as Matt that I'll cave to my craving and drown my sorrows at the bottom of a bottle.

Instead, I take my guitar out and play some of my earlier stuff—songs that were a little immature, a little unpolished, but more real than my latest releases. Strumming the strings, I belt out the words, pouring my heart and soul into the lyrics, trying to remember a time when I still had hope, when I felt like the world was my oyster and I had my two best buddies by my side.

Now I've had time to reflect on it, everything turned to shit the minute they were gone. They were more than my best buds, my brothers. They were my connection to real life. To my sanity. Without them as my anchor, I quickly floundered.

I move to the window seat at midnight, like I still continue to do, even though my beautiful midnight dancer hasn't shown up in over a week.

Dakota must really hate my guts now.

Even though it's what I wanted, what I knew would happen when I deliberately gave her the cold shoulder, it's killing me inside. Staying away from her is like denying my body the oxygen it needs to survive, but I had to do it. I had to let her believe I'm a lying, selfish prick who says one thing and does another.

Dakota accepted it so quickly it hurts.

But there's no point crying about it after the fact.

I know I did the right thing by pushing her away because my heart is already invested, and if I didn't put a stop to it, I would've taken it all the way. I wish I could go there with her. I want to peel back her layers and discover all her hidden pieces, but I won't place her in harm's way.

Until my stalker is captured, bringing anyone new into my life is risky, especially a girl with the power to unravel me.

Doesn't mean I have to like it or that it's any easier to stomach knowing I've done a selfless thing.

I still crave her as much as I crave a high. Probably more. Which is all kinds of sick and twisted.

A flash of light across the way has me pressing my nose to the glass. A shiver dances up my spine as I spot Dakota warming up. A thrill washes over me at the sight of her, making a mockery of my inner musings. This girl is under my skin so deep I wonder if I can ever get her out.

I'm mesmerized anew as she starts moving, hooked on the way her body sways to the music. I wish I was over there so I could watch her up close and personal. So I could soak up the energy and comfort her closeness brings.

I start playing my new song, and more words surge to the forefront of my mind.

Dancing through the starry night sky
Like an angel without wings
Your pain speaks to mine, and I need this connection
To feel something I've never believed in
But I'm no good for you
Afraid I'll take you down with me
When all I want is to build you back up
To see the light shine in your blue eyes once again

I'm so caught up in the creative process that I don't notice the exact moment she falls apart. When I glance over at the roof, my breath falters in my chest at the sight of Dakota on her knees, rocking back and forth. I run to my bedroom and retrieve a set of binoculars. I don't make a habit of using these, as that's taking stalkerish tendencies to a whole, new worrying level, but I need to see her face, to know if she's okay.

She's not.

She's sobbing her heart out, and it guts me.

I can't stand by while she's wracked in pain.

Despite what I've promised myself, I know I have to go to her. I can't bear to leave her dealing with this alone. She'll probably tell me to go fuck myself, but I can deal as long as I know she's not there alone.

I fly out of the apartment and across the road, my bodyguard trailing silently behind me. Entering the abandoned building, I take the steps two at a time. Her tortured cries tickle my eardrums before I've even emerged on the roof. I walk in front of the lamp, so I don't startle her, sinking to my knees in front of her. "Dakota." I'm expecting her to fling obscenities at me, but instead she flings herself into my arms.

Not that I'm in any way complaining.

I hold her while she cries, smoothing my hand up and down her back, running my fingers through her silky hair.

"I can't do this," she whimpers after a while. "I can't do this and still know how to breathe." I don't question or interrupt her in any way, content to let her purge whatever she needs to purge. "Why did she have to die?" she whispers, fresh tears spilling out of her eyes and onto her cheeks. "Why did she have to leave me?" She looks directly into my eyes, and I wish I had the answers she seeks. "I miss her so much, and I can't stand this pain anymore. I don't know how to do it alone."

I brush damp strands of hair off her face. "You're not alone. You have friends. And you...you have me."

Fuck it.

I can't continue to lie to myself and her.

To deny how much I want and need her in my life.

She circles her arms tighter around me, burying her face in my neck. She shivers in the cool night air, and I hold her closer, pressing a kiss to the top of her head. "My apartment is only across the road. Let me take you there until you're ready to go back to your dorm. It's quiet and private, and you can take as much time as you need."

I'm expecting her to shoot me down, but, once again, she takes me by surprise, clinging to me tighter, and she whispers in my ear. "Okay."

I stand up, gently placing her on the ground while I gather up her stuff. Keeping her tucked under my arm, I steer her out of the building, and we make our way to my penthouse with my arm wrapped around her shoulder the entire time.

She wanders through the main living space, holding her arms around herself as she inspects my place.

"Can I get you anything to eat or drink?" I ask.

She spins to face me, and, at the sight of her sad, tearstained eyes, I want to rush to her side and sweep her into my arms, but I manage to restrain myself.

"Some water would be good," she murmurs, her voice hoarse from all the crying.

I grab two bottles of water and a bag of chips from the cupboard. I don't have much in the way of food, preferring to eat on campus or grab takeout on my way home. Setting the drinks and chips down on the coffee table, I walk to her side and tentatively take her hand, gently pulling her to the couch. A shiver rolls through her, and I grab a blanket from the other couch, offering it to her.

She wraps it around her slim shoulders, and I try not to ogle her formfitting yoga pants and top. "Thank you," she whispers, taking small sips of her water.

I twist around on the couch so I'm facing her, kicking off my sneakers and pulling my feet up under me. She follows my guide, and we stare shyly at one another, neither of us knowing what to say.

I want to help her, but I'm not sure how. I decide to test the waters. Clearing my throat, I take her empty hand, pleased when she curls her slender fingers through mine. "I don't want to pry or upset you, but I want you to know that I'm here for you. If you want to talk about it, then I'm all ears. Sometimes, talking helps."

"I..." She trails off and looks away.

I put my bottle of water down and gently cup her face. "I also owe you an apology." She peers into my eyes, and I see so much trust there, waiting for an opportunity to be earned. "I was ignoring you on purpose because I thought it was for the best. I've tried to stay away, because I don't want to hurt you, but I can't stay away anymore. I want to be here for you. As a friend or something more, that's up to you to decide. But I want you to know I'm sorry for pushing you away, for making you think you didn't matter, and I'm done with that now." I bring her hand to my mouth and press a kiss on her soft skin. "I'm here for you. In whatever way you need me."

She gulps, and tears pool in her eyes as she scoots forward, reaching out to run her fingers through my hair. Her touch feels so unbelievably good, and I have to smother a groan and hide the growing semi in my jeans.

"I need to get this off my chest now before I explode," she softly admits.

"You can tell me anything, and I promise it'll stay between us." I caress her cheek.

She gulps again, but a glimmer of resolve flashes in her glassy eyes. "A little over a year ago, my sister was murdered, and everything has turned to crap since then."

Chapter 13

Dakota

"Shit, I'm so sorry, Dakota. I can't even begin to imagine how awful that is." Levi's expression and his tone are nothing but sincere.

"We were completely different, in almost every conceivable way," I start explaining, "but we were so close. Always had been. Layla was only fifteen months older than me, and she was my best friend, my staunchest supporter. She always told me to follow my heart, to never give up on my dreams." I sniff, smiling as I remember all of my sister's amazing qualities.

"If I hadn't known her as well as I did, I might've thought she chose the path she did to spare me, but it wasn't like that. Layla knew her own mind and followed her own destiny. It just so happened that she was the responsible one, where I rebelled. That she *wanted* to follow in my father's footsteps and take the helm of his company, while I dreamed of dancing on the world stage. She was practical where I was impulsive. She was self-controlled where I had very little."

He smiles at me.

"What?" My brow puckers.

"You say you're rebellious, impulsive, and lacking in self-control like those are turnoffs."

I shake my head, smiling in return. "I didn't mean it like that. I was always confident in who I was, just that it was the opposite spectrum to Layla. She was the good girl to my bad girl. If anything was going to happen to one of us, it should've been me! I was the one who regularly threw caution to the wind while she was so careful, and still he found her." My voice tapers off, and I shiver all over.

He leans in and kisses my cheek, and a heady warmth spreads across my face, giving me the courage to go on. "We were all so proud of her when she scored a full ride to Stanford to study accounting and business. I cried buckets the day she left, because I knew I was going to miss her so much, but I was really happy for her because that was *her* dream."

I draw a brave breath as pain batters me from all sides.

"She loved it there. She loved her classes, she made some great friends, and she...she met a guy." I close my eyes for a brief moment. Levi starts rubbing soothing circles across the back of my hand, and it's amazingly comforting. My eyes pop open and I continue. "Ever practical, Layla had broken things off with her childhood sweetheart once she received her acceptance to Stanford. She knew the long-distance thing wouldn't work for them, so she took matters into her own hands and ended it early so that she wasn't as heartbroken by the time she left for California."

A shuddering breath leaves me, and I can feel the tenuous grip on my emotions unraveling. "She didn't date at first, but then she met this guy at the start of spring semester, and she fell head over heels for him. I couldn't wait to meet him. He sounded perfect. In hindsight, he was too perfect. I should've realized it wasn't real." I start shaking all over.

He pulls me into a hug. "You don't have to continue if it's too painful."

I hold him tight, siphoning some of his warmth and his strength. "I want to. I need to say this out loud." Although I have spoken to Daisy about it, she got the CliffsNotes version.

Without hesitation, he pulls me over into his lap and wraps his arms around me. I rest my head on his shoulder and push through my fear. "She stayed in California for summer break because she wanted to be with Gary." Knots form in my stomach and saying his name makes me want to hurl. "We don't know what caused him to flip that night, whether he had planned for her to be one of his victims all along or if it was a spur of the moment thing." I lift my head, resting my hands on his shoulders as I eyeball him. His gaze is awash with compassion. His eyes even greener without his glasses shielding them. "We only found out later that her boyfriend was Gary Knockton, the very man the police were hunting."

Awareness creeps onto his face. "I remember the news reports and how shocked everyone was that a serial killer was murdering female students on campus," he admits. I'm not overly surprised that he's aware of the case. It garnered massive national and international attention.

A messy ball of emotion builds at the back of my throat. "We were all worried for Layla when the story first broke about a serial killer, and I know my parents wanted her to come home, but it's a big campus, the police were all over it, and Layla was not the type to put herself in danger. She was always so careful, so safety conscious." I shake my head. "I still can't believe she actually dated him. That he seemed so perfect when all the time he was out raping and butchering other girls."

An intense shiver whittles through me, and I hug Levi tighter.

"I have so many unanswered questions," I admit. "They go

through my head every night, driving me crazy. I wonder did she notice anything. Any little quirks. Any things that seemed odd. Did she have any idea who the man she was sleeping with really was, or did it all come as a shock the night he turned on her? I wonder if that's how it happened. If she realized who he was, and he killed her to keep her silent, or if he was just a crazy, sick bastard who couldn't control his urge to rape and kill.

"We'll never know because he died in a shootout with police the same night he murdered my sister. She was his last victim." I swipe a tear away. "The not knowing is horrendous but not nearly as horrendous as learning how she died." Tears roll freely down my face. "He sodomized her and raped her repeatedly before slitting her throat and leaving her to bleed out."

I break down again in his arms. Sobs wrack my body, and the intense pain jackknifing through me is unbearable. I struggle to breathe. But he's there with me. Coaxing me to draw deep breaths, telling me it's going to be okay, holding me like he genuinely cares.

Eventually, the tears dry up. I notice the large damp patch on his shirt. "Sorry," I murmur. "I soaked your shirt."

"I've got more," he simply says. "You have nothing to be sorry about. My God, Dakota." He holds my face in his large, callused palms. "I am so truly sorry for your loss. No family should have to go through that."

"It's torn my family apart. Tomorrow, I have to stand before a judge and beg him to commit my mom to a psychiatric facility because my father refuses to accept she's ill, even though she has barely left her bed for over a year."

He kisses my forehead. "Baby, I'm so sorry." He sighs. "I guess now I understand where your dad's overprotectiveness is coming from and why he was so hostile toward me last weekend."

"He hit me," I blurt. "He's never hit me before. I was trying to reason with him. To get him to accept Mom needs more help than we can give her, and he went crazy."

A muscle pulses in his jaw. "I don't care what he's going through. Nothing excuses him for doing that to you. He's not going to touch you again." His voice resonates with resolve.

"It'll be a moot point after tomorrow. I'm fully expecting he's going to kick me out of the house and disown me once he discovers what I've done." I lean my head on his chest. "But I don't care. I'm doing what's best for Mom, and if he cuts me off, I'll deal. I'm only here because he wants me to step into Layla's shoes, but accounting has never been my dream. Most days, I'm bored out of my skull in class. If he does this, he'll be doing me a favor."

Don't ask me what I'll do or where I'll go, but I'll figure something out.

Right now, Mom is the priority, and that's all that matters.

"Your mom is lucky to have you."

"She spoke to me the other night for the first time in months, and I didn't realize how badly I needed her until that moment. She's all I've got left now, and I won't abandon her even if my dad has."

I close my eyes, and the steady rise and fall of his chest is comforting. We don't speak for ages, but it's not in any way awkward. I fail to stifle a yawn a while later, reluctantly lifting my head. "I'd better go," I say, fighting sleep as exhaustion finally creeps up on me.

"Stay," he whispers, brushing hair back off my face. "You can take the guest bedroom. The bed's all made up, and there's spare shit in the bathroom."

I sit up straighter, looking into his beautiful eyes. "Why are you doing this? Being nice to me?"

"I see you, Dakota," he whispers. "And I want to help." He claws a hand through his hair, and I'm envious. I want to be the one doing that. "I know I shouldn't, but I can't fight it anymore."

I should go, but I'm so tired, and if I go home now, Daisy will want to know what's wrong, and I don't want her to worry about me. Dad would freak if he knew I was staying here, and maybe that's why I agree. "Okay, thanks." I tap out a quick text to Daisy and then pad after Levi as he leads the way to the bedrooms.

I spot the acoustic guitar resting against the wall by the window as Levi steers me to the back passageway and my feet stall. "You play?" He spins around, pursing his lips as he nods. "If I wasn't so tired, I'd ask you to play me something."

He shuffles awkwardly on his feet, looking pensive. "I'll play something for you another time. I promise." He extends his hand to me. I lace my fingers in his, enjoying the warmth of his hand curled around mine. "This is the guest room," he says, opening the door and stepping aside.

The room is large and decorated in soothing shades of beige and blue. The large king bed is inviting, and I can't wait to dive under the comforter. He points to an en suite bath. "You'll find extra supplies in there. Feel free to take a shower or bath if you like, and there are towels in the cupboard." He points at the closet. "I have some shirts in there if you need something to sleep in." Shoving his hands in his pockets, he rocks back on his heels. "My room is right across the hall. If you need anything, anything at all, come get me."

"Thank you. For everything tonight."

He darts in, planting a soft kiss on my cheek. "You're welcome, and I meant everything I said tonight."

I nod, smiling as he exits the room, leaving me to my own devices. The room has been lavishly furnished with expensive walnut furniture and varnished hardwood floors. The heavy drapes are velvet, and I run my hands over the soft material, wondering who exactly Levi is and how he can afford a place like this. Something tells me there's a lot more to him than he's let me see so far, and I hope I get an opportunity to look under the hood. I want to understand this complicated man—the one who wants to hold me close and push me away at the same time.

Maybe I should be afraid, to be here with some guy I don't really know, but my gut tells me the only thing to fear with this guy is losing my heart. Something I promised myself I wouldn't do until I'm good and ready. And this isn't that time.

After grabbing one of his T-shirts—he wasn't kidding about having more, there must be forty shirts in this closet, all designer labels too—I wander into the large en suite bath, trailing my fingers along the deep tub. It's been a long while since I indulged in a bath, and I'm tempted, but I'm drained, and I just want to grab a quick shower and sleep.

Except sleep eludes me. It doesn't seem to matter that I'm dead on my feet and my brain aches with tiredness; my body refuses to cooperate.

After an hour of tossing and turning, I get up as if on autopilot, quietly walking out of my room and stopping in front of his, my hand raised in a knock. *Should I knock or just walk in?* Maybe he'll think I'm some crazy chick slipping into his bedroom at night, but I just need someone to hold me. Cole used to sneak into my bedroom sometimes, and I always loved the feel of his arms enclosing me. I've never slept better than when I was in his embrace.

Until I realized I wasn't the only one in his arms, and now all my memories are tarnished.

Shaking all thoughts of my ex from my mind, I quietly open Levi's door and slip inside. I gasp as he looks up at me, not expecting to find him awake. "Can't sleep either?" he murmurs in a deeply sexy voice, while simultaneously peeling back the covers.

"No." I shake my head, standing unsurely as I chew on the corner of my lip. "Is this okay? I'm not looking for anything. I just want to sleep in your arms."

He pats the space beside him, propping up on one elbow and yawning. "I haven't had such a delightful proposition in forever." His eyes briefly scan my body. "Come here." His voice cracks a little.

My mouth is as dry as sandpaper as I approach the bed, noticing he's bare chested. I'm trying not to stare, but it's a mammoth task. Levi is all corded, ripped muscle and lickably smooth skin. His abs are tightly rolled, and he has those awesome V-shaped indents on either side of his hips. My fingers burn with intense need, the desire to explore every hard inch of toned muscle almost knocking me off my feet. A trail of dark blond hair snakes under the covers, and I wet my lips automatically. The comforter rests over his lower half, and I'm hoping he's not naked under there, because the craving to jump his bones is already riding me hard, and I don't think I'll be able to resist if I discover he's not wearing any clothes.

He seems to understand, chuckling as he reaches out for me. "Relax, Blondie. I have boxers on. Your virtue is safe with me."

Well, damn it all to hell and back. Disappointment crests over me, but I force myself to get a grip. I didn't come in here to ride his cock. I came here seeking his comfort, and that's all he's offering.

Slipping under the covers, I roll around on my side so I'm facing him. He palms one side of my face. "I've been lying here the last hour debating whether to go get you or not." I smile at his honest admission. "You're so beautiful," he whispers, exploring my face with the tips of his fingers. "And so strong."

"I don't feel very strong," I whisper back, leaning into his touch. "I feel so out of touch with who I am, and it's scary."

"Yeah, I can relate." Placing his hands on my hips, he pulls me in closer to him. "It's late, and you've got a big day ahead of you tomorrow. You should sleep."

I wrap my arm around his waist, and he jumps a little. His skin is warm as I trace the inky patterns on his arms. I never realized he had tattoos as he always wears long-sleeved shirts. These tattoos are thick and intricate, and they tell a story. One day, I'm determined to get to the bottom of this boy's story but not now.

Now, I finally feel like I could sleep.

"Night, Levi," I murmur, my eyes automatically closing as he holds me close to his naked chest.

I barely hear his soft reply as I sink further and further into unconsciousness. "Goodnight my beautiful midnight dancer."

Chapter 14

Shawn/Levi

Dakota fell asleep almost instantly, and I just watched her, like some creepy perv, until my eyelids grew heavy, and I drifted into slumber. I thought falling asleep with her nestled in my arms was the most magical feeling ever, but I was wrong.

Waking up to find my beautiful, sweet, sad girl wrapped around me like a koala tops the year I won five Grammys in one night.

When she eased herself into my room last night, looking totally fucking gorgeous in my shirt, I knew I was a goner.

Something about this girl makes me want to bundle her up and never let her go. It's dangerous. Stupid. And completely selfish. But I'm all in now. When I first went to bed last night, I messaged Devin to request a full-time bodyguard be assigned to her asap. She won't know they're there, but it will give me peace of mind. Not that I plan on letting her out of my sight all that much, but it will depend on what this thing is between us, I guess.

I can't pressure her. Not with the stuff she confided last night. She's holding the reins, and she'll set the pace.

This will be new for me. I'm so used to getting whatever girl I want, whenever I want, and I've gotten complacent, lazy, bored.

But never with this girl.

Dakota is the furthest from predictable or boring you can get, and I'm going to enjoy getting to know her better. A pang of guilt slays me as I think about all I'm keeping hidden from her. Her comment last night about her sister not really knowing who she was sleeping with really hit home. Yes, it's not the same, but I hate that I'm concealing my true identity from her.

I console myself with the fact I'm more real with her than I've been with any other woman. And this version of myself is the truer one, the one I'm trying to reconnect to. Compartmentalizing is the only way I can do this. Dakota is getting to see the real me, and I hope, when the time comes to reveal all, that I'll be able to convince her to stay. That she'll understand my motivations were pure, and in the interests of her safety, and that Levi is the man I aspire to be in my personal life. Shawn Lucas is my profession. He's who I need to be to survive in the music industry, but that arrogant fuck of the last few years is not the real me.

Even though we're only getting started, I can already tell this girl is important. And I want to be important to her too. I pray I won't fuck this up, for both our sakes.

But, right now, I have more pressing problems. With the way she's curled around me—one leg wrapped around my hip and the other resting between my legs—there's no way she'll miss the massive hard-on prodding her stomach. I could try and maneuver out of her grip, but I don't want to let her go. I'm enjoying this far too much.

Any other time I've woken up with a girl in bed beside me,

I've been completely hungover and dying to get them the fuck out of my house before they start getting ideas. Waking up with a girl I actually like, clinging to me like I'm her everything, is a completely new feeling, and one I realize I could get used to.

"Hhmm," she murmurs in a sleepy voice, rubbing her nose against my chest. "You smell really good." I chuckle, and my chest vibrates. Slowly, she opens her eyes, yawning. Lifting her head, she peers up at me. "Morning." A stunning smile spreads across her lips, and I stop breathing.

What is this girl doing to me?

"Morning." I press a kiss to the top of her head, holding her tighter. "Did you sleep well?"

"Like a baby." Her smile widens. "Best sleep I've had since..." Her smile falters.

She doesn't need to complete the sentence for me to get it. "I know, babe. And if it helps, it's the best sleep I've had in ages too."

"You have trouble sleeping?" she asks, idly running her fingers up and down my arms. Her touch feels so good, and my dick jerks excitedly.

She notices, freezing a little. Her eyes pop wide. "Oh! Oh."

My lips tug up. "Don't worry about it. Occupational hazard if you're a guy." I wiggle my brows, hoping to break up the sudden tension. Not that it's unpleasant, but I don't want her thinking she's got to do something about it.

"It's been so long since I woke up beside a man that I'd forgotten the obligatory morning stiffy," she teases, and I laugh.

This girl is like no one I've ever met before. And it's so refreshing.

"I definitely think us men drew the short straw. Women can be fucking dripping and no one knows a thing."

She pushes off my chest, propping up on one elbow. "You did not just say that!" She playfully slaps my bare chest, and my cock aches with renewed need. "Men have it so frigging easy compared to women, and you really don't want to get me started!"

I raise my palms in surrender. "Okay, okay, you win." I twirl a lock of her hair around my finger. "You looked so damned beautiful wrapped around me this morning. There's no way I want to ruin the moment."

"Aw." She tweaks my nose. "That was really romantic. Are you a romantic, Levi?"

"I...ah...I don't really know. I've never really tried with any girl before."

"How come?" she inquires, pulling away from me to sit up.

I consider protesting, but that will only make me look needy and pathetic. I sit up beside her, leaning my back against the headboard and keeping the comforter over the evidence of my hard-on. "I've never had a proper relationship," I admit.

Her mouth gapes open. "How old are you?"

"I just turned twenty-one."

Her mouth gapes again, and I know she's mentally trying to figure it out in her head. I'm older than your average freshman. "How the hell does a guy as hot as you get to twenty-one without having a relationship?"

"You think I'm hot?" I tease, in part wanting to divert the course of this conversation. This is where shit starts getting tricky. I don't want to lie to her, but if I share too much of my life, she might figure things out, and I have to keep my identity secret to protect both of us.

She nudges me in the shoulder. "Don't act the idiot. You know you're hot."

"I guess I've just never met the right girl."

She opens her mouth to say something and then shuts it again. Tucking her messy hair behind her ears, she speaks as she stares off into space. "Relationships aren't all they're cracked up to be anyway."

I want to ask her more. About that jerkwad Cole and any others who may have come before him, but I think I've rummaged in her head enough the last twelve hours. Instead, I ask, "What time do you have to be in court?"

She rubs a hand across her chest. "Two."

"Would you like me to come with?"

She turns to face me. "What about school?"

I shrug. "Missing a few classes won't be the end of the world. I can catch up."

She nibbles on her bottom lip, and I'm jealous. What I wouldn't give to nibble her all over.

And, my raging boner is back.

"Okay. That'd be great. I could use a friend."

The friend word is all a guy needs to hear to kill a stiffy stone dead. But, I've got to remember she's been through a lot. I can't expect her to drop her panties on the spot. Not that I'd want her to. Not yet. I want to do things right with this girl. And that means letting her call the shots for now.

"Great. It's settled then. I can drive." I swing my legs out the other side of the bed, facing away from her.

Her warm, soft hands land on my shoulders. "Levi." Her dulcet tone causes a shiver to dance over my skin. She presses her luscious mouth to my ear. "Thank you."

I twist around, and there is barely a centimeter between our faces. "You don't need to keep thanking me. I'm with you because I want to be here."

Her eyes dart to my mouth, and I stop breathing again. I wonder if she's remembering our hot make out sesh in this moment like I am. Man, what I wouldn't do to taste her soft lips again.

My raging boner returns with a vengeance.

"I'm not sure I can be what you want me to be," she says, looking a little sad. "I'm pretty messed up right now."

I kiss her cheek. "I don't have any expectations," I lie. "I'm just happy to spend time with you."

Now she looks kinda disappointed, and I wonder if I said the wrong thing. I have zero experience with this stuff. This girl is bringing out a side of me I didn't know existed, and I'm walking blindfolded here.

"That's cool with me." She jumps out of the bed, and I miss her closeness already. "I'm going to head back to my dorm and get showered and changed there. I'll come back later."

I stand up and walk around the bed. "Give me a few minutes to get ready and I'll drop you at your dorm. I've got some stuff I need to do, but I can come back and get you when we need to leave."

Her gaze heads south, and her jaw slackens. Her eyes go wide, and her pupils darken as she stares at me. Oops. Forget I was only wearing boxers, and my boner is back in all its morning glory.

"Oh. Um. Holy. Wow." She glances up at me, not in the least bit embarrassed.

"See something you like, Blondie?" I flick her hair, smirking.

"Maybe." She acts all demure, but the lusty look on her face is a dead giveaway. "But I don't do the whole friends with benefits thing."

I don't do the whole friends thing. But I'm not admitting that out loud.

"Keep telling yourself that, beautiful," I whisper, winking as I walk to the door of my en suite. She's at the bedroom door when I call out to her. "By the way, you look unbelievably sexy in my clothes." I try to rein in my cocky smirk, but it's damn hard. "Now, if you'll excuse me. I have a date with my hand."

Chapter 15

Dakota

Levi is a few minutes late picking me up, and I wonder if he's blowing me off again. Until his shiny SUV comes to a screeching halt at the curb, and I chastise myself for doubting him. I know he's been hot and cold since we met, but I believed him last night. I don't understand it, but he genuinely seems to want to be my friend.

I try to dampen my disappointment, telling myself I don't have time for anything more even though I know that's a lie. But, relationships lead to complications, and I have enough on my plate as it is. For now, I'm grateful for his friendship and his support. Today is going to be difficult, and him being there with me means more than he can know.

Hopping out of the car, he takes my hand and opens the passenger door for me. My smile is authentic. "Who knew such a gent was hiding behind that prickly exterior?" I tease as I climb inside, and he laughs.

"I don't think I have much of a prickly exterior around you," he tells me, sliding behind the wheel. "You're far too difficult to resist."

His words thrill me silly. He glides easily out into the busy lunchtime traffic. "So," I say, twisting to face him. "Tell me something about yourself. You know all this heavy shit about me, and I know next to nothing about you."

It could be my imagination, but he seems to grip the steering wheel a little tighter. "What would you like to know?"

"Where did you grow up?"

He visibly relaxes. "In a small town in Knox County, Maine."

"Any brothers or sisters?"

"Growing up it was just Mom and me, but she's married now, and her and my stepfather have twin boys." He grins at me. "They are only three, but they're the coolest little kids on the planet."

His entire face lights up at the mention of his brothers, and my ovaries start a happy dance. *Who doesn't love a guy who loves his family? And a guy who clearly adores kids?* Be still my beating heart. "They must be thrilled to have a big brother."

His smile fades a little. "I don't get to see them that much." He white-knuckles the steering wheel again. "I've been working the last couple of years out of state, and my mom's been occupied with work and then with her new husband, and the twins keep them both busy."

There's a tinge of sadness in his tone. "Do you get along with your stepfather?"

"Mostly. Steve's a good guy, and he's made my mother happy, and that's all that matters. She deserves it."

"It sounds like you're close to your mom."

"She was all I had when I was a kid." His Adam's apple jumps in his throat as he steers the car out onto the highway. "And I thought she hung the moon. She sacrificed so much for me."

"She sounds amazing."

"She is."

I want to ask more, because I'm sensing there's more behind it, but I can tell he's uncomfortable discussing it, so I drop the subject. "You said you were working? Doing what?"

He drags a hand through his hair, taking a minute or two to reply. "I was working as a session musician. My mom set it up."

"Get. Out!" Color me impressed. Now the guitar makes sense. "Did you work with anyone I'd know?"

"Nah. I doubt it." He gulps, keeping his eyes on the road ahead. "It was mainly small-time stuff, but I enjoyed it. Made a good living for myself."

"I hope you don't think I'm nosy, but I *was* wondering how you could afford a place like that."

"I'm only renting it," he's quick to tell me. "But I'm fortunate I can afford to take some time off to go to college."

"Why accounting?"

He shrugs. "I wanted to study something practical, and I've always been good at math."

Is it weird that that admission kinda turns me on? There is something so sexy about a hot guy who is also intelligent and practical that gets my juices flowing. I squirm in my seat as lust simmers in my veins. At least all this is taking my mind off the impending court session. "So, your mom works in the music business?" I surmise.

"She used to, but she decided to retire a year after the twins came along."

"It's nice that she can do that. My mom was always there for me when I came home from school and practice and I loved that. She would have this gorgeous dinner made, and she'd ask me all about my day. It always made me feel so loved. I know a lot of moms need to work these days, and I would never criticize them for it, but it's really special if you can be there for your kids."

"Practice?" he asks, drilling a quick look at me. The sun decides to make a sudden appearance at that moment, bathing Levi in a bright glow. He's wearing his glasses today, but I can still make out the dilating color in his eyes, and I'm completely distracted.

"Wow, you have beautiful eyes," I tell him. "I never realized they were a green-blue color before." A muscle clenches in his jaw and he holds the steering wheel so tight I fear he's stopping all blood flow. I frown a little. "Did I say something wrong?"

Air gushes out of his mouth, and he relaxes his death-grip on the wheel. "Of course not. I'm just a little on edge today." He glances at me briefly. "I'm guessing practice was dance practice?"

I nod, deciding to let his odd reaction pass. "I've been taking dance classes since I was three."

"It shows. You're an amazing dancer."

"Thanks." His praise bolsters my fragile confidence, but it also raises questions. "How long have you been watching me dance?" I ask with a certain amount of trepidation. I'm guessing he was watching me again last night and that's how he came to my rescue.

He squirms a little in his seat before looking over at me with a sheepish look in his eyes. "I don't want to freak you out, but I want to be honest."

I grip the sides of my seat, digging my nails into the leather. If you want to freak someone out, just start a conversation with "I don't want to freak you out" and mission accomplished. "I'm freaking out already. Just tell me."

"I've seen you dancing before that night I visited the roof."

I tense up as a layer of discomfort washes over me. "You've watched me before?"

"Never on the roof, not until that night, but I can see you from my penthouse. Every night, I sat in my window and played my guitar while I watched you dance. I couldn't make out your face, it's too far away, but I was mesmerized by this incredible dancer."

"Midnight dancer," I whisper, remembering his words from last night.

He nods, and he looks a bit scared as he glances at me. "How freaked out are you?"

"I'm not sure," I answer truthfully, pulling my knees up to my chest.

"I debated saying nothing," he tells me, taking the road that leads to the courthouse. "But after what happened with your... with Layla, I didn't want to keep this from you. The last thing I want is you thinking I'm some kind of stalker."

"I appreciate that." I worry my lip between my teeth. "It's something I've thought about a lot after she died. It would be so easy to hide myself from the world, to shy away from strangers and not allow anyone to get close. To shut myself off in the name of safety, but then I wouldn't be living. My dad would prefer that. He'd rather I take that cheating douche back than fall for a stranger. Better the devil you know, etcetera."

"And what about you?" he asks, pulling into a vacant space in the parking lot of the courthouse.

"I've never been the type to compromise or fear the unknown," I admit, unbuckling my seat belt and turning to face him. "And I'm not going to start now. Cole has burnt his bridges with me. I'll never take him back, but I am more guarded, more wary, than I used to be."

"That's understandable." He takes my hand, rubbing soothing circles on my skin.

"I won't take blatant risks or chances, but I won't stop living either. I'd like to think I'm less impulsive than I was before, but I don't want to lose who I am. I can't live the rest of my life in fear. What happened to my sister is horrific, the worst thing ever, and, for as long as I live, I will never forget it, or her. But she wouldn't want me to change who I am. She'd want me to stay safe, to make informed decisions instead of rushing head first into stuff, and I'm making a conscious effort to do that, but I still want to be me."

"I think you're the bravest person I've ever met."

"I don't know about that." I offer him a sad smile, glancing nervously toward the entrance to the court. "But I'm trying."

"You make me want to be a better person," he says, and I stare inquisitively at him.

"You think you're a bad person?"

He shrugs, and when he looks at me, I see so much emotion on his face. "I've made some bad decisions in my life. Hurt people I cared about. Did stuff I shouldn't have and didn't want to."

I reach up and palm his face. "We've all done stuff we regret. It's part of growing up. The most important thing is what you learn from those experiences and how you let them shape the rest of your life and the person you want to be."

Darting forward, he pecks my lips briefly. Too briefly. Before I've had time to even acknowledge the gesture, he's pulled back. "I have never met anyone like you, and I need you in my life. I've never met anyone who has inspired me so much. Not just with my music, but in every aspect of my life. You don't just make me want to be a better person, you're already changing me. Helping me see who I could be."

His words do twisty things to my insides, but not in a bad way. Winding my fingers in his, I smile. "Sometimes, people come into our lives with the power to change us forever. Deep down, I think I recognized that when I met you, but I chose to ignore it. You're not the only one changing. You're helping me too." I look at our conjoined hands. "I feel braver, stronger, when I'm with you. Like somehow things will work out, and I don't feel as afraid." I slant him a shy smile, wondering how we're getting into the deep stuff all of a sudden. There aren't even any labels yet.

Perhaps there don't need to be.

"Maybe we were meant to meet at this juncture in our lives. To be there for each other."

He raises our joined hands, brushing his lips across the back of my knuckles. "I can't disagree, and I promise to be there for you, Dakota. For as long as you'll let me."

Chapter 16

Shawn/Levi

The session in the courthouse is difficult and emotional for Dakota, but she's keeping a brave face. I'm so proud as she gives her statement, and her love for her mother shines through. Tears glisten in her eyes when the judge sanctions the request, approving the movement of her mother to a specialist psychiatric facility. Shit will really hit the fan when her father receives notification of the court's decision. But I'll be there to help her through it.

We're back at my place, and Dakota is fast asleep on the couch, looking peaceful and angelic. Her long blonde hair fans around her face, and her small hands are curled under her cheek. She looks so young and vulnerable, even if I know she's got the inner strength of a Goliath.

She's far too good for me. I know it. But I'm a selfish bastard, and now I've made the decision to let her into my life, I'm not letting her go. I meant what I said in the car earlier. She's bringing out a different side to me, and I want to embrace that, and her.

My cell vibrates, and I take it out onto the balcony to talk to Luke. "Hey."

"How are things?" he asks.

"Good. I like it here." Casting a glance at the sleeping beauty on my couch, I know she's a large part of the reason why I do.

"You sound different."

"I feel like I'm really breathing for the first time in years."

"I'm happy to hear that, Shawn. I know this last year has been difficult for you. After rehab, I was worried you'd spiral into that dark place again, but you fought to take back control of your life, and I'm proud of you."

"Thank you."

"Your mom would be too. She misses you. You should call her."

A sharp ache pierces my chest cavity. "I miss her too, and I want to make things right with us, but I don't want to pull her into this mess either. It's good we're estranged and that it's been publicly reported. It keeps her outside the stalker's radar." Several of the messages threatened my loved ones, and I'd die if anything happened to Mom or my family because of me.

"You can still call her."

I lean over the edge of the balcony, surveying the busy street down below. "When we talk again, I want it to be face to face. The things I have to say need to be said in person, not over the phone."

"I understand."

"Just." I pause, exhaling heavily. "Just tell her I love her and the boys and I'm thinking of them always."

His voice softens. "I'll pass on the message." Silence descends for a couple seconds, until he clears his throat. "So, do you want to tell me about this midnight dancer?"

I've recorded a very rough, acoustic version of the song I

wrote for Dakota and sent it to Luke. "Not especially." He chuckles. "She's...special. Captivating and talented and just so damned real."

"You can't tell her who you are."

I sigh. "I know. Doesn't make it suck any less. What if she hates me when she finds out who I really am?"

"If she's as special as you say, she'll come around. Keep the faith."

I bark out a laugh. "Aren't you supposed to be telling me to stay away from her?"

I can hear the amusement in his tone when he replies. "Are you forgetting how well I know you? I know when you want something, and you want her. Besides, if she's the inspiration behind this song, then you need to keep her."

"You liked it?"

"Liked it? I fucking loved it."

"I need to talk to you about this cursing shit. It's becoming worrisome."

"Punk."

"Square."

He laughs. "Seriously, I'm loving this new vibe. It's raw, emotive, passionate, and although it's a departure from your other stuff, I can't imagine the label having issues with this new direction if you continue producing quality like this. And your fans love you unconditionally. They'll support you with this."

"Thanks, man." He has no idea how much I needed to hear that. I've wanted to take more of an active role with the choices being made for my next album, but the label is adamant that the formula works, and there's no need to fix something that isn't broken.

Apparently, my broken soul doesn't really count.

I have a massive following who are into my stereotypical pop music, and they lap up every release, even if it's shit. Bit by bit, it's chipped away at my soul, until I've reached a stage where I'm forcing myself into the studio and giving lackluster performances on stage.

I can't continue like that.

Which is why coming here was a blessing. It's enabling me to reconnect with my musical roots. To remember how enjoyable making music is. Reminding me how much I love performing and composing. If I can walk away from here with an album of the type of songs I want to sing, and get the label on board, then I'll be a hell of a lot happier returning to L.A.

Luke clears his voice. "So, there was another reason for my call."

An ominous silence stretches between us, and my insides coil into knots. Instantly, I know I'm not going to like this. "Just tell me." My tone reeks of resignation.

"Someone broke into our offices last night. Trashed the place and caused thousands of dollars' worth of damage." He sighs. "They left their signature message on one of the walls."

"Shit." I scrub a hand over my face. "I'm so sorry."

"It's not your fault, Shawn. You didn't ask for this."

"I fucking hate this, Luke. When is it going to end?"

"I know, Shawn, I know. But try to relax. Devin is on his way, and he's going to coordinate with the local cops. I'm guessing your stalker isn't happy you've gone into hiding, and they presumed we'd have the details of your location someplace here. I'm so glad we kept no physical or digital records and that everything was arranged verbally or via Devin's office. Knowing you are safe is a huge worry off my mind. And Devin will catch this guy. I have the utmost confidence in him."

"I do too, but I won't sleep easy at night until I know the asshole is behind bars." Luke spends another couple of minutes reassuring me, and then I end the call and head back inside just as Dakota is waking. The sight of her erases the tension from my face and my taut muscles.

Stretching her arms out over her head, she smiles when she sees me, and I want to freeze frame the moment. I also want to kiss the shit out of her, but I know I'd find it hard to stop at just that. Blood rushes south, and I'm amazed at how quickly she turns me on. But it's not just her outer beauty that attracts me. She's equally as beautiful on the inside. Her talent, intelligence, and her bravery have sucked me in as much as her gorgeous face and her alluring body.

"Hey, sleepyhead, how are you feeling?"

"Good. Surprisingly good."

"Are you hungry?" I ask as she stands.

"Starving." She rubs her flat tummy to emphasize the point.

Removing my cell from the back pocket of my jeans, I pull up the menu for my favorite takeout place. I hand it to her. "Pick what you like, and then I'll call in our order."

Shaking her head, she hands the phone back to me and skips into the kitchen. "I'll cook. It's the least I can do after today." Opening the refrigerator, she bends over to inspect the scant contents inside, waving her delectable ass at me. I smother a groan as my dick turns rock-hard in my jeans. Now, all I'm imagining is thrusting into her from behind, fucking her hard and fast as we both quickly lose control.

"Or not," she deadpans, straightening up. I quickly adjust myself and stand behind the island unit, hoping to hide the evidence of my obvious arousal. "Do you have *any* food in here?"

I shake my head. "Not much. I tend to eat out or order in."

She rolls her eyes, mumbling under her breath.

I tilt my head to the side. "What?"

"How the fuck do you look like that"—she gestures at my body—"when you don't eat properly?"

"Good genes, and I like to work out." I haven't shown her my personal gym yet, or my studio, because I'm afraid of inviting more questions I can't answer.

"How about this?" she suggests, planting her hands on her slim hips. "We walk to the store and pick up some supplies and then come back here and I'll cook."

"I don't want you to go to any trouble," I say, rounding the island now my boner has tamed. "You've had a difficult day. We can order takeout and just chill in front of the TV."

"Cooking relaxes me, and I don't mind. I'd like to cook you a meal to thank you for coming with me today."

"Well, if you insist." I give in because the prospect of a home-cooked meal is too good to turn down.

Even though it's early evening, and dusk is settling over the sky, I grab my shades and ball cap before we head out. Her eyes sparkle mischievously as we walk side by side to the local grocery store.

I really want to hold her hand, but I'm afraid to.

I have to cough over my snort of hilarity. *Who'd have thought it?* Shawn Lucas wants to hold a girl's hand, but he's too frightened to make the first move. It's fucking hilarious and so normal it's exhilarating.

"Either you're photosensitive, shy all of a sudden, or you're trying to hide," she quips. "Which is it?"

"I don't like drawing attention to myself," I murmur. She busts out laughing. "What's so funny?"

"If that's your attempt at *not* drawing attention to yourself, then you're failing. Miserably."

Huh. Valid point.

While I was self-conscious around campus when I first arrived, I've relaxed as the weeks have passed, confident that people can't tell it's me. But since a renowned celebrity blogger offered a fifty-K reward to whomever discovered where I was hiding out, I've been more paranoid than usual.

I take the shades off and pocket them but leave the ball cap on. "Better?"

"Much." She loops her arm through mine, peering up at me. "Hhm. Your eyes just look green again. Did you know your eye color changes in the light?"

Shit. I totally froze earlier when she noticed my natural eye color behind the contacts I'm wearing. I didn't realize it'd be semi-transparent in the light. Unlike earlier, I act casual this time. "Nope. Guess you learn something new about yourself every day." I smirk, and she laughs, the sound doing funny things to my insides.

"Would you eat a chicken and veggie stir fry?" she asks me as we roam the aisles in the store.

"I'm not a picky eater. I'll happily eat whatever you want to make." That earns me another earth-shattering smile, and I almost melt into a puddle of goo on the floor. I'm turning into a pussy, and it's somewhat concerning.

Dakota throws a load of stuff into my cart, way more food than we need just for dinner, but I don't protest. I plan to have her around a lot, and I want to be able to feed her more than just takeout. She tries to pay for it, and we have an argument at the register, much to the amusement of the cashier. I'd love to tell her I have more money than I know what to do with, but I can't.

"Stop pouting," I tell her as we walk back to my apartment building, laden down with bags. "You're cooking, and it's my place. It's only right I should pay for it."

"You wouldn't take gas money either today, and it doesn't sit right with me. I like to pay my way."

I could kiss her right now. Drop everything and sweep her into my arms. Most every person I've come into contact with in

L.A. has expected me to pay for everything just because I'm rich and famous. I get a lot of stuff for free—which is ridiculous when you consider how easily I can afford to pay for it—so I didn't mind paying for stuff when I was out. But, since I cleared the trash from my life, I've realized just how much those people were using me, and that stuck in my throat.

The fact this girl wants to split everything down the middle, even when her financial position is hanging in the balance, speaks volumes. Which reminds me. I need to have a word with Devin to find out if there's a way to create some kind of fake grant of which Dakota Gray is the sole recipient. If her dad cuts her off, I want to be able to cover her fees and put cash into her bank account. I know if I offered straight out, she'd turn me down and most likely be furious, so I'll have to get creative. If it comes down to it.

Dakota shoos me out of the kitchen while she cooks, and I grab my guitar and retreat to my window seat, strumming a few errant chords while I surreptitiously watch her buzzing around my kitchen. She's humming under her breath as she dances around my space, and my heart swells with some unnamed sentiment.

"This is really fucking good," I tell her after I've tasted the first mouthful.

She smiles. "It's my favorite dish. I'm glad you like it."

"Where'd you learn to cook like this?"

"Mom taught me. She's an amazing cook. She had her own little bakery business. Not a store or anything," she adds, waving her fork in the air. "She did everything from home. Mainly cakes she'd bake to order, and she also did buffets for special celebrations." Her eyes turn sad. "All that fell by the wayside when she got sick."

I put my fork down and reach across the table for her hand. "You've done the right thing. She's going to get the help she needs, and she'll be able to pick up where she left off."

"I hope so." She resumes eating, looking lost in thought.

I make her sit down while I clean up the kitchen. After, I pour her a glass of white wine and grab a can of soda for myself.

"You don't drink?" she inquires, taking a small sip of her wine.

"You noticed?"

"You were only drinking soda at the frat house, and I was curious, although it's totally cool if you don't drink by choice."

I want to be upfront with her. To tell her what I can about my past without delving into the specifics, even if opening up about this makes me want to flay the flesh from my bones. I'm also afraid of what she'll say and terrified I'll send her running. Drawing a long breath, I push through my fear and put it out there. "Alcohol and drugs are rampant in the music business, and I have a naturally addictive personality. Things got very messy, and I was totally out of control at one point. Spent some time in rehab, and I've tried to stay clean and sober since then."

She eyeballs me with a serious expression. "Thank you for telling me that, and you should be proud of yourself. I'm sure it can't be easy."

I relax into the couch. "It's not. It's a daily struggle. But I'm determined to be strong."

"Will you play for me?" she asks, gesturing over my head at my guitar. "I heard you messing around while I was cooking, and it sounded great."

I don't think she's quite ready to hear I've written a song about her yet, so I decide to play it without singing the words. She listens attentively, and our eyes are locked together the entire time. I want her to hear the words without them being sung. To listen to what she does to me.

"Wow," she admits, when the song ends, pinning me with

awestruck eyes. "That was beautiful, and it conveyed so much emotion. Like it was sad and haunting and then heartwarming and uplifting at the same time. And definitely romantic. I can imagine couples dancing to that under the moonlight. Is that one of your compositions?"

I nod, suddenly tongue-tied.

"You are hugely talented. Too talented to be a support musician."

We're getting a bit too close to the bone, and I'm starting to feel uncomfortable. "I've got some other stuff I've composed. Would you like me to play another one?"

Her eyes glow. "Please. I could listen to you play all night long."

I play another song I've written since coming here. This one is also inspired by her, but less obvious and less intimate. Closing my eyes, I belt out the words as I strum the guitar.

Resounding silence greets me when I finish, and I'm reluctant to open my eyes. When I do, I'm shocked to find Dakota staring at me in wonder with tears glistening in her eyes.

"My God, Levi. That was incredible. Your voice...it sent shivers down my spine."

I want to tell her who I am. So, so badly.

But I can't.

"Thank you. I'm glad you like it." Especially since you inspired it, I add in my head.

"I did. I really did." She stands, extending her hand to me. "And now I definitely need to dance. Besides, it's almost midnight."

"What's the significance of midnight?" I tentatively inquire, having previously speculated if there was some special reason why my midnight dancer arrived at the same time every night.

"It was three minutes past midnight when I got the call

from my dad about Layla," she quietly confirms. "And every night, at that time, I'm thinking of her. Dancing is the only thing that liberates my soul, and I need to be dancing when the pain strikes. It's the only way I survive." I nod, completely getting it. "Will you come with me? Play while I dance?"

"I would love to."

Chapter 17

Dakota

For the next two weeks, Levi comes to the roof with me every night, writing and playing music while I dance. Our joint creative spirits are feeding off one another, and my soul soars in a way it hasn't for a long time.

Which is a miracle considering my home life has reached an all-time low.

Levi came with me the first day Mom arrived at the psychiatric facility. He stayed in the car while I helped get Mom settled. He was also there that night to hold me as I sobbed into his chest. He was there again when Dad showed up the following night, screaming and roaring abuse at me. Three days later, when I got the letter from my father's attorney telling me he's cut my funding and won't be paying any more of my college fees, Levi consoled me again.

Honestly, I don't understand what he's getting out of this friendship, apart from a basket case who regularly breaks down in his arms. But I'm not looking a gift horse in the mouth. He's the only reason I'm not rocking in a corner by now. Why I feel in control, even when every part of my life is crumbling.

I've stayed at his place every night since that first night, only stopping at my dorm to pick up books and clean clothes, which is why I'm on my way to my dorm now to spend some time with Daisy. I've been neglecting my roomie, and that doesn't sit right with me.

As I round the corner to my building, I groan when I notice the familiar figure waiting by the entrance.

"Why are you here?" I hiss, glaring at Cole.

"I need to speak to you," my ex explains.

"There is nothing you have to say I want to hear. You need to leave me alone."

"Where have you been, Kotabear? I've been coming here every night this week, and you haven't been home."

I jab my finger into his chest. "Firstly, I already told you you lost the right to call me that, and secondly, it's none of your freaking business. Go back to your *girlfriend* and leave me alone."

"Are you sleeping with him? That douche from the party?"

"Screw off, Cole." I enter the building quickly, trying to slam the door in his face, but Cole always had razor-sharp reflexes. He's behind me in a flash.

"I know his type. He's a player and he's using you for sex. You'll only get hurt."

I crank out a laugh, stomping ahead, ignoring the fawning looks and curious expressions leveled Cole's way. He's starting to make a name for himself this year with the football team. Last year, as a freshman, he was on the bench, but this year they're letting him start. I'm betting Mikayla loves all the new female attention.

Not.

I hope he cheats on her. It would serve her right to get a taste of her own medicine.

"That is priceless coming from you," I spit at him over my

shoulder as I take the stairs two at a time. "Do you even hear how hypocritical you sound?" I stride down the corridor leading to my room.

Grabbing my elbow, he steers me over to the wall. "I never used you for sex, and I've never been a player."

"You cheated on me with my best friend!" I yell, not giving a shit who hears me. "While I was mourning the death of my sister!" My breathing turns erratic, and I take a brief respite to compose myself. "My sister was murdered, and I needed you, but you were too busy fucking that disloyal bitch behind my back to care." Anger is transparent in my tone, and he hears it too.

When I first discovered Cole and Mikayla were screwing, I was too numb to feel anything. But now? Now, Levi is helping to bring all my emotions to the surface, and I'm feeling all the things I should've felt at the time they betrayed me.

"I'm sorry, Dakota. I'm so, so sorry. I wish I could turn back the clock and not go there. I love you, and I never meant to hurt you."

His Adam's apple jumps in his throat, and his eyes radiate with pain. I hear the sincerity in his words but it's too late. "It's too late to make amends, Cole. You kicked me when I was already down, and that's not something I can forget."

"I miss you, baby. I miss you so much. I made a mistake. We had three great years together, and I was a fool to throw it away, but I didn't know how to help you."

"News flash!" My nostrils flare. "Fucking my best friend was not the way to help!" Hurt coasts over his face, but it's difficult to find any sympathy. He deserves to hurt for what he did to me.

"I know. I'm sorry I let you down, but I'll make it up to you. I'll get rid of her. Just say the word and she's gone."

I snort, shoving him aside so I can get past. "You are unbelievable. If you really meant what you said, you would've come here already having broken up with her. But you're hedging your bets. Not willing to let her go in case I say no. That tells me everything I need to know."

"Dakota, baby, wait." He makes a grab for me again, but I duck out of his reach.

"Don't call me baby. And don't come near me again. We're done, Cole."

I race down the hall and fly into my room, slamming the door shut before he can sneak in.

"What's going on?" Daisy asks, stopping with a fork midway to her mouth.

"My cheating slimeball of an ex is what's going on," I blurt before realizing she has a guest. "Sorry," I say. "I didn't realize you had company. I can go."

Daisy hops up. "Kota, don't go. Come say hi to Jake." Her cheeks turn fire-engine red. "He's my uh, my boyfriend."

Smiling, I walk over to the good-looking guy with the cropped dark hair. "Hi, Jake. I'm Dakota. Daisy's roomie. Nice to meet you."

"Likewise." He stands and shakes my hand. "I've heard all about you from Daise."

"Hopefully not all bad," I joke.

"On the contrary. I think you and Daise hit the roommate jackpot."

"Funny, I thought the exact same thing."

Leaning in, he kisses her briefly on the lips, and her cheeks flare up again. "I'm going to leave you two to catch up. Text me later if you want to hang out."

She circles her arms around his neck, and a twinge of envy bites me. "Will do." She kisses him quickly, and I look away, not wanting to intrude.

After he's gone, she smiles shyly at me.

I wag my finger in her face. "You've been holding out on me, missy."

"I could say the same thing," she playfully retorts. "I've been wondering if I even have a roomie anymore considering you stay every night at Levi's." While she hasn't yet met him, I have filled her in over the phone.

"I'm strictly in the friend zone," I reply. "Nothing to report there." Much to my dismay. I've slept in Levi's bed every night for two weeks, and while he holds me close, he hasn't made any moves on me. If he was interested, he would've done so by now. "He doesn't see me like that."

"And what do you want?" she asks, flopping down on the couch.

I join her. "I want more." It's the first time I've been honest with myself.

"Have you told him that?"

"No. I don't want to make a fool of myself when it's obvious he doesn't feel the same way."

She is quietly contemplative. "He knows about Layla and your mom. Isn't it possible he's holding back on purpose? Maybe he's waiting for you to make the first move."

I ruminate over her words. "I guess it's possible."

"So, what are you going to do about it?"

I grin at her. "I like this sassy side of you." She sticks her tongue out at me, and I laugh, realizing I've been doing that a lot more lately.

"I think you should put the moves on him. I'm betting he won't let you down."

"I'll consider it." I slap her knee. "But enough about me. Spill your guts, girlfriend. How did you meet Jake, and how long has it been going on?" She blushes again. "You're so cute around him. And he's gorgeous. Is he a good kisser?"

"He is. Not that I've got anything to compare him to, but he makes my toes tingle and my heart sing."

I rest my head on her shoulder. "Ah, Daise. That's so good. I'm so happy you met him. I'm glad you haven't been alone. I was feeling like the worst roomie for abandoning you."

"Don't be silly, Kota. With our different schedules, we're not here a lot at the same time anyway. And it works both ways. I know you've been through a tough time, and I'm glad you're enjoying spending time with Levi."

I lift my head, pinning her with a naughty look. "So, have you done the deed yet?"

Her cheeks turn bright red, and I bet I could warm my hands off them. "Jesus, no! I've only been with him two weeks, and it'll take a while before I'm ready to give him my virginity."

She looks a little annoyed, and I worry I've offended her. Sometimes my mouth engages before my brain kicks in. "You know time really doesn't mean anything. When you're ready, you're ready. Whether that's two days, two weeks, two months, or two years. No judgment here."

"Sorry, it's just I got teased a lot in high school over my virginity. It's a bit of a touchy subject."

"I would never criticize you for that. Elsa is openly waiting for the right guy before she gives it up, and I respect her enormously. To each their own. Speaking of, we're all heading to a frat party tomorrow night. Please come. Bring Jake. We'll have so much fun!"

She considers it for a moment. "Okay. I'll ask him."

I clap my hands like I'm five. "Yay."

She laughs before sobering up. "One thing though."

"Okay?"

"Don't mention my Shawn Lucas obsession."

My eyes pop wide. "Come again?"

"I took my posters down, because it's kinda silly at my age

to be drooling over a popstar, and I don't want Jake to think I'm some love-crazed groupie or too immature to be dating."

"Hey, no sweat. I won't breathe a word, but, you know, you shouldn't be afraid to be yourself around any guy. If he likes you, he'll have no issue with your Shawn Lucas obsession." My lips curve up at the ends as I add, "Lack of musical taste notwithstanding." I can see the attraction with the guy because he's seriously good-looking, but his musical talent leaves a lot to be desired.

"You really think so?"

I nod. "Hundo P. You shouldn't hide who you are from the person you're dating; otherwise, it's not real."

Chapter 18

Shawn/Levi

I drop my keys on the kitchen counter and open the refrigerator, smiling as my eyes roam over the evidence of Dakota's influence. Grabbing a fruit bowl and a bottle of water, I close the door with my hip and lean against the island unit. I slowly savor the fruit as I scroll through emails on my phone, groaning when I spot the number of missed calls from my assistant. It's easy to live in a bubble here. To pretend the real world in L.A. doesn't exist.

Tossing the empty container in the bin, I psych myself up before calling Calista. She answers almost immediately, as if her eyes have been glued to her cell, awaiting my call. "Hey, babe," she purrs, and my hackles are instantly raised.

"I am not your babe. I'm your boss," I snap. "But I won't be for much longer if you keep this shit up."

She's quiet for all of two seconds before giggling. "You're too funny."

Da fuck? Closing my eyes, I pray for patience I know I don't possess. "What's so urgent you had to blow up my cell?"

"The annual hospital charity visit is coming up, and the

administrator is looking to confirm the details. I didn't want to say anything until we'd spoken. Are you planning on going this year?"

"Shit." I drag a hand through my hair. "When is it?"

"The tenth of next month."

Air whooshes out of my mouth. "I don't know yet. I'll have to think about it and get back to you."

"I'll tell them we won't know until a couple days beforehand, and hopefully they'll still be okay with that."

"Thanks."

"Don't hang up!" she blurts. "There was one other thing I needed to speak to you about. My sister's getting married in three weeks, and I was hoping you'd come as my plus one."

I sigh in exasperation. "We already talked about this." Like, about a hundred times. "And I told you no. We're not dating, and you're my employee. My *employee*, Calista. I really need you to understand that." I don't know how I can be any blunter.

"But we were so good together."

I roll my eyes. "Calista. It was a meaningless, drunken fuck. We both know that. You've got to get over it. If you can't, we'll seriously have to consider your position because I'm sick of you bringing up this shit. You're a fantastic assistant, and I'd hate to lose you, but if you can't accept there'll never be anything more than a professional relationship between us, then I'll have to terminate your contract." I'm tempted to tell her I've met someone, but that would not go down well, and I could do without the additional hassle.

"I love my job and I don't want to lose it," she says quietly, and I hate that I've hurt her, but I don't know how else to get through to her. "I understand." She hangs up, and I groan.

My cell pings and I'm almost afraid to look. Expecting a text from Calista, I'm pleasantly surprised, and my whole demeanor changes, when Dakota's name pops up. I open her message, smiling like a goofball.

I left you some dinner in the microwave.

I open the microwave door, staring at the plate of lasagna covered in Saran Wrap like I must be imagining things.

Another text comes through.

And I made a salad bowl to go with. Check the refrigerator.

My breath stutters in my chest, and I'm struggling to swallow over the lump in my throat. With the exception of my mom, no one has ever cared for me this much.

Not unless they were paid to do it.

No girl has ever cooked for me before or done anything so thoughtful without seeking anything in return.

This girl slays me.

In all the best ways.

I text her back. Speaking honestly, although I know she'll think I'm messing around.

I think I'm in love.

With my lasagna?

With you. I think it but that's not what I respond. I throw out the gauntlet instead.

Of course, what else did you think I meant?

The salad is jealous.

I laugh, thinking of how long it's been since I've felt this carefree. Dakota is a fragrance I want to bottle and keep with me forever. I'm not sure how much longer I can hold off on telling her how I feel. Every night, holding her in my arms is the sweetest form of torture. I love how naturally she fits against me, but not being able to kiss her, to touch her, is killing me. I want this girl in my bed, and in my life, permanently.

At any other time, that thought would scare the fuck out of me.

But I'm only scared of it not becoming reality.

Scared she'll say no once she realizes who I am and how difficult being with me is. Bringing any girl into my kind of lifestyle is challenging but especially one as untainted as Dakota.

Still, those thoughts don't stop me from pushing things further.

Are you?

I watch with my heart in my throat as the three little dots appear, indicating she's typing her reply.

That's for me to know and you to find out.

The little minx. If she only knew how much she has me wound around her finger. I'm smiling as I heat up my lasagna, my heart bursting with emotions I haven't felt in forever.

I have a couple hours to kill while I wait for Dakota to return, so I do something I've been putting off.

I call Nick.

He doesn't answer, and I wonder if it's wise to leave a message, but I do. He returns my call about an hour later.

"Hey, man."

"Hey. I wasn't sure if you'd call me back," I respond truthfully.

"You gave me the shock of my life. Didn't think I'd ever hear from you again."

"I'm sorry it's taken me so long. There's no excuse, except that I've been a shitty friend."

We're both quiet for a bit. "We were just kids, man," he says. "Kids who thought they could play in a man's world, but we were no match for the suits."

"It doesn't exonerate me. I didn't fight for you guys, and that's my biggest regret, alongside cutting you off, but I was embarrassed and too caught up in my own shit to do anything about it. For what it's worth, I'm really fucking sorry, dude. More than you could know."

Silence fills the airwaves once again. Clearing his throat, he says, "I forgive you, Shawn. And if you're beating yourself up over the past, you shouldn't. It's over and done with, and I don't have any regrets, because that's like saying I regret the path my life has taken, and I don't. I love my son, and he's the best thing that's ever happened to me."

A layer of stress lifts off me, and I lie back on the couch, crossing my ankles. "I only just found out you had a kid. Congrats. What's his name and how old is he?"

"Reece and he's five."

"Shit, man. That must've been difficult. You were so young."

"Cheyenne told me she was pregnant three weeks after I came back from L.A., so, yeah, the timing wasn't great."

"I was wondering who the baby mama was. How is she?" I ask, purely because it's the polite, adult thing to do, but the honest truth is, I never liked her. She and Nick got together when they were fourteen, about the same time we started the band, and I was always suspicious. Nick had been chasing her for the best part of a year, and she showed no interest until suddenly she did.

"She took off eighteen months ago. We haven't seen her since."

I sit up, resting my back against the arm of the chair. "Shit. I'm sorry."

"I'm not." His sigh is laced with resignation. "She didn't take to motherhood, and she had no patience with our son. I hate to say it, but we're both better off without her."

"If you need anything, anything at all, let me know." Devin said Nick is broke, and I know he probably won't react well to this, but I'm going to offer. "I have more cash than I know what to do with, so if you need me to wire you some—"

"I don't want your fucking money, Shawn! I can take care of my son myself."

"I didn't mean to imply you couldn't. Just that I'm here, if you ever need anything."

"You don't owe me anything, dude." His voice is calmer.

"That's not how Matt sees it."

"I'm not Matt, and it's the reason we aren't in touch anymore. He's so bitter and twisted, and I don't want that negativity in my life. I know you didn't set out to screw us, Shawn. It's not your fault they wanted you and not us. If I was in your shoes, I would've done the same thing."

I hear the door click open and shut, and my smile is instant. "Thanks, buddy. I'm not sure I deserve it, but I'm grateful. I'd love to meet up again. Love to meet Reece."

"I'd like that too. It's been too long. You still in L.A.?"

"Not at the moment." I wave at Dakota as she enters the living space, gesturing at my phone.

"Where are you at? Maybe we could come visit if you're not too far away."

"I'm kinda tied up at the moment, and I've got to go. A very pretty lady has just stepped through my door demanding my attention."

Dakota raises her brows, planting her hands on her hips as she pins me with a smoldering look.

He chuckles. "I hear you, dude. Let's catch up soon, yeah?"

"Definitely. Later, man."

Tossing the cell on the couch, I get up and stride toward Dakota, grabbing her into my arms without hesitation. "I missed you," I murmur into her hair.

Sliding her arms around my waist, she rests her head on my

chest. "That's a tad melodramatic. I was only gone a few hours."

"Felt like eternity."

She snorts. "Are you turning all mushy on me, Levi?"

"Might be. They do say the way to a man's heart is through his stomach, and you leaving dinner for me is the nicest thing anyone's done for me in ages."

She looks up at me, and I want to kiss her so badly. "Well, that's really sad if it's true."

My eyes lock on her lips before I force them back up. "Thank you. It was really thoughtful."

"You're welcome, and it's not a big deal." I'm not sure she realizes her hand is trailing up my chest, but I'm not about to point that out because her touch feels too good.

"It is to me." My gaze latches onto her lips again, and my chest visibly heaves. Electricity crackles in the air, and when her eyes darken and her tongue darts out to wet her lips, I almost forget how to breathe.

"I like cooking for you," she whispers. "And I like it here with you." Now both her hands have wandered up my chest, coming to rest on my shoulders.

It would take nothing, absolutely nothing, to lean down and press my lips to hers. Nothing. But she needs to make the move. The air around us sizzles with tension, and her eyes flit to my mouth, while I'm silently encouraging her in my mind.

My pulse is throbbing in my neck, and liquid desire heats me from the inside out.

We look at one another, both of us frozen in time and space, and I know she wants this as badly as I do. It's written all over her flushed face.

But she doesn't act on it.

Stepping back, she smiles at me before dropping down into

the seat I just vacated. “What are you watching?” She picks up the remote, getting comfy on the couch.

“Whatever you want to watch,” I reply flatly, swinging around and flopping onto the couch beside her, trying to mask my disappointment.

Guess it’s another cold shower and date with my hand again tonight.

Chapter 19

Dakota

"I thought you said Daisy was coming and bringing her boy toy?" Tabs inquires the next night at the frat party.

"She'll be here. She texted earlier to confirm. They were going out for dinner first."

"Aw, that's so sweet and romantic." She thumps Levi on the arm. "That's what you should be doing. Wining and dining our girl."

"We're just friends, Tabs," I tell her for the umpteenth time, hating the words as they leave my mouth. Last night, I was so sure he was going to kiss me, but he didn't make a move, and I pulled back before he could see the hurt in my eyes. I love spending time with Levi, love sharing his living space, and I've come to rely on him in ways I probably shouldn't, but I've got to be honest and face facts. He doesn't have the same feelings for me, and that's going to be a problem, because I don't know how much longer I can deny that I want more.

But I don't want to ruin our friendship either. His support means the world to me, and I don't want to mess it up by declaring I'm falling for him if he doesn't feel the same way.

Despite the way I see him looking at me sometimes, it's increasingly looking like he wants to keep things platonic.

It's for the best.

But try telling that to my heart.

"If you say so," Tabs retorts, murmuring something that sounds suspiciously like "delusional" under her breath. She tugs on his elbow and starts whispering in his ear, and I try to ignore the envy sluicing through my veins.

"Now *they* are only friends," Elsa says, nudging in Tabs and Levi's direction. "But there is no way that guy sees you the same way. He doesn't take his eyes off you, *like ever*. Case in point." She subtly jerks her head, and, sure enough, Levi is listening to Tabs but staring straight at me.

"That's only because he's worried about me."

"I know that asshole ex of yours did a number on you, but not all guys are the same. Levi has been a rock for you with all the shit you've had on your plate recently."

I finally opened up and told Tabs and Elsa what's been going on with me. They were both wonderful and offered their support in any way they could.

"He's probably afraid of making a move when you're vulnerable," she continues, "but, trust me, I know when a guy digs a girl, and that guy has the hots for you. In a bad way."

"That's what Daisy said too."

"She's a smart cookie, that one." She squeezes my shoulders. "Annnddd here she comes right now." She waves her hands in the air like crazy, and I spin around. Sure enough, Daisy and Jake are maneuvering their way through the crowd, making a beeline for us.

"You made it!" I hug my friend and smile at Jake. "I'm so glad you're here." The party scene really isn't Daisy's thing, so I fully expected her to bail tonight. I quickly introduce Jake to Tabs and Elsa while Levi holds back, shoving his hands in his pockets and staring at the floor as if it's the most wondrous thing. I have to practically drag him over, puzzled at the momentary glint of panic flaring in his eyes. "This is Levi," I tell Daisy.

"Hey. Nice to meet you," he mumbles, barely looking at her. Tabs sends me a "what the fuck" look and I shrug. Damned if I know what's gotten into him.

"Nice to meet you too," she shyly replies. "And this is my boyfriend Jake."

Levi looks up, jerking his chin. "'Sup, man?"

They start chatting and we move aside, leaving them to it. "Wow, he's hot," Daisy blurts, before blushing beet red. "Now I see why you've barely left his side in weeks."

"If he was mine," Tabs interjects. "I'd have him handcuffed to my bed, doing all kinds of naughty shit, but this pussy, right here"—she elbows me in the ribs—"is too afraid to even kiss him. It's a damn shame. Sleeping in those arms every night and not touching him. I weep for your poor, unloved cunt." She shakes her head. "And I'm betting he has wrist strain from jerking off so much."

Elsa spits her beer all over the floor. "Jesus Christ, you'd think I'd be used to this by now, but nope. Your perverted mind still has the ability to shock me," she says, nudging her bestie with a grin.

Levi glances over Jake's shoulder again, his eyes finding mine. Our gazes lock, and my heart starts skipping a beat as he smiles. Maybe the girls are right. He's trying to be a gentleman, and I'm going to have to be the one to move us out of the friend zone.

"I'm on a roll tonight, babe," Tabs says, smacking a loud kiss on Elsa's cheek. "And I've just spotted tonight's prey. Yum. Yum." She licks her lips, zoning in on one of Cole's football buddies.

I silently groan, hoping he isn't here.

When I decided to attend U of I, I was worried about bumping into Cole and Kayla all the time, but the campus is big enough I figured I could manage to avoid them, except it hasn't quite worked out like that. Especially now that Cole seems to be actively seeking me out, if last night is any indication.

"Watch and learn, little virgin," Tabs teases Elsa, flinging her hair over her shoulder. "And don't wait up." She saunters confidently over to the football crowd, sashaying her hips seductively, and they willingly part to let her through.

"Wow." Daisy's eyes almost bug out of her head. "I wish I had a tenth of her confidence."

"She's something else," Elsa agrees. "But I wouldn't swap her for the world. There is no one more loyal than Tabs, and I love how fearless she is, how she goes after what she wants. I know I give her shit, but I admire her. She knows how to get what she wants." She pokes me in the chest. "And something tells me you do too."

The old me was totally fearless and wouldn't let anything stop her from going after what she wanted. While that girl is starting to come alive again, I'm not sure I'll ever return to the same person I was before my sister died.

I'm not sure I should either.

But Layla wouldn't want me to be a coward.

Finishing my beer, I decide I'm going to walk up to Levi and plant one on him when someone takes hold of my elbow from behind before I've had a chance to make my move.

"Kotabear." I close my eyes in frustration as Cole presses his mouth to my ear.

Levi is beside me in a flash. "Get your hands off her." I shuck out of Cole's hold, allowing Levi to tuck me protectively into the crook of his arm. "She doesn't want to talk to you, so take a hike."

"He speaks for you now?" Cole glares at Levi over my head.

"Cole, how many times do I have to say it. I told you last night. We're done, and whatever friendship we had is gone too. Just let it go."

"I did what you asked. I broke it off with her. I'm a free agent, and I want you back, baby."

Levi turns to face me, loosening his hold on me. "Wait? You *want* to get back with this loser?"

"What?! No!! Of course not."

Out of the corner of my eye, I spot Daisy looking funny at Levi.

"She wants me back. She's just afraid to hurt you in front of everyone," Cole smoothly lies, pulling me behind him. "We have history, man. You can't compete with that."

I try to move around Cole, but he misinterprets my action, plastering me to his chest. "I was her first everything, and I'll be her last, so if anyone's taking a hike, it's you, pal." He prods Levi in the chest, while I try to wriggle out of his hold, but Cole is a solid block of resistance. Before I've had time to figure out his plan, he slams his lips down on mine. Startled, I don't react for a split second. When I come to my senses, I thrust my leg up and knee him in the balls. He drops his hold on me instantly, roaring as he topples to the floor, clutching his groin.

"Don't you try that fucking shit on me again, Cole, or I'll charge you with sexual harassment. I'm not *ever* getting back with you. Not happening. You are *not* the one I want." I jerk my head up, wanting to look Levi in the eye when I tell him *he's* the one I want. Except I'm met with an empty space. "Crap. Where'd he go?"

"Out that way," Elsa points toward the back door. "Hurry

and you'll catch up to him." She gives me a gentle push, and I almost stumble on my feet.

I lean over Cole, raising my voice. "Just so there's no further misunderstanding, I don't want you. Levi is the only one I want." Pushing through the gaping crowd, I don't wait to hear Cole's response, if there is one, racing in the direction Levi disappeared.

I burst outside, climbing the steps two at a time and emerge on the dimly lit sidewalk. I spot him up ahead and call out after him, but he keeps going, walking with hunched shoulders. Thank God, I'm wearing sneakers, I think as I give chase, hollering his name the entire time. When I catch up to him, I tug on his sleeve, beseeching him to stop. "Levi. Stop. Let me explain."

"There's nothing to explain," he spits out, shoving my arm away. "I didn't take you for a pushover, but I guess I don't really know you after all."

"What the hell does that mean?" I shout, throwing my hands in the air.

He stops and spins around. "You go back to Cole, Daddy is happy, and you get to stay in school. I'm stupid for not realizing your plan sooner."

"Are you freaking kidding me right now?" I yell, incensed to the point of combustion.

"Go on, deny it. Deny that's what you've done. Deny that you chose him without even giving me a fucking chance!" he roars, and I fully expect steam to come billowing out of his ears.

Anger transforms to disappointment. "Is that genuinely what you think of me?"

"I don't need to think!" He jabs his finger in the direction of the frat house. "I just saw it with my own eyes. You kissed him right in front of me!"

"Oh, for fuck's sake, did you even look, or have you got blinders on?" I shove at his chest. "He. Kissed. Me!"

He snorts. "You didn't exactly push him away."

I rub a tense spot between my brows. "You know, for a smart guy, you sure as hell can be dumb as shit." I square up to him. "If you'd stayed around, you would've seen me knee him in the balls and tell him he wasn't the one I wanted." I shove at his chest again, thoroughly pissed at both Cole and Levi. "If you'd stayed around, you would've heard me tell the whole room how the only one I want is *you*." My chest aches painfully. "But you ran instead. You've already made up your mind about me based on the lies of my ex. Instead of thinking of all the ways in which I've shown you how much you matter to me, you just decided I'm guilty and left me."

Pain is etched across his face as he steps toward me. I step back, holding my palms up to keep him at bay. "Don't touch me. You couldn't have hurt me any more than you did tonight. You're the first guy in a long time that I've opened up to. I was vulnerable for you, because I thought you were worth it. That I could trust you. I thought you see me." I shake my head sadly. "But you don't. You don't have a clue who I really am, because if you did, you would not have reacted like that."

"Shit. Kota, baby, I'm sorry." He reaches for me again, and I take a few more steps back. "I messed up. I'm no good at this stuff, but it doesn't mean I don't see you. I *do* see you. I've always seen you."

I shake my head, starting to walk off. "It doesn't matter. Everything's ruined now. I can't do this with you."

"Please." His eyes beg for mercy. "Give me another chance. Let me make it up to you."

"It's too late. Forget it. It's better this way." I smother the pain waiting to drown me. "Goodbye, Levi."

Chapter 20

Shawn/Levi

It's been four days since I fucked everything up at the party, and I'm most definitely paying the price. My place is like a ghost town without Dakota filling it with her infectious presence. I'm back to watching her from afar. Grateful that she hasn't stopped her rooftop dancing and terrified it means she truly meant it when she said goodbye.

I want to go to her.

To drop to my knees and beg for forgiveness but I'm too afraid it won't be enough.

Besides, isn't this for the best?

Keeping her away from me and my messed-up life has always been the safest option. So what if I'm heartbroken and missing the only person gluing the fractured pieces of my heart together?

If I love her, I should stay away. Let her get on with her life without dragging her into all my shit.

The fact I didn't react appropriately, and that I still don't have a fucking clue how to handle the situation, speaks volumes. I don't know how to have a relationship, and she's better off without me.

I've purposely avoided going to class, because I don't want to see the indifference on her face. She's clearly not suffering like I am, and I don't want that rubbed in my face.

If there's one consolation, it's that this heartbreak is churning out song after song, and I've almost got a full album already. Luke is ecstatic and encouraging me to continue. So, I sit, night after night, looking at the girl I've loved and lost, frantically pouring all my feelings out onto the page.

I keep my head down in the small off-the-beat diner, perusing the menu, while waiting for Devin to make an appearance. The waitress snatches up my cup, refilling my coffee, before slapping it back down in front of me.

Someone clearly loves her job.

I snicker to myself. If she knew it was me, she'd be fawning all over the place, most likely offering me more than what's on the menu. You might think I miss that, but the honest truth is, I don't. I'm loving being a normal Joe.

"Penny for your thoughts," Devin says, sliding into the booth across from me.

"I wouldn't want to depress you," I retort, sipping the bitter liquid.

"That bad, huh?"

I shrug. "Something tells me you're about to make a bad day worse."

"Wow. Who pissed in your cornflakes?"

I shake my head, not wanting to get into it with him, but he obviously has other ideas. The sullen waitress reappears, and we both place our orders. Then he leans across the table on his elbows, pinning me with a grave look. "Is this about Dakota? Trouble in paradise?"

I groan. "Could you be any more cliché?"

He chuckles. "My men give me daily reports, and I know she hasn't been staying with you the last few nights. If you don't want to talk about it, that's fine, but I might understand a lot more than you think."

"I doubt it," I mumble.

"You don't know this, but Ange and I were neighbors growing up. We've known each other since we were two, but it took me years to get my girl, and it wasn't without its fair share of heartbreak."

"Yeah?"

He nods, lifting his cup as the waitress pours coffee in. "I had a troubled upbringing, and I tried to shield her from it by staying away. Ended up messing up more times than I could count. The one thing I've learned is that it's never a good idea to hide your feelings. If you have feelings for this girl, you should tell her."

"What if it's too late?"

"You won't know until you try."

I ponder his words for a couple minutes. "It's probably for the best. At least, this way, she's safe."

He makes a face as he tastes the coffee. "Man, this stuff is disgusting." He scrunches his nose, peering into the cup. "Is it even coffee?"

"You stop noticing after a few cups," I deadpan.

He shoves it aside. "Answer me one thing. Are you falling in love with her, or is she just someone to pass the time with while you're in town?"

A muscle clenches in my jaw at the insinuation she's a random hookup. "I love her," I blurt before I can stop myself. "I love everything about her. She's so real and down to earth, and she doesn't want anything from me but my company. She calms me and makes me remember who I used to be before all the shit got in the way. I haven't been this creatively inspired in years. She speaks to my soul, on an innate level. And I don't say this lightly, because we've only kissed one time, and she thinks that was fake." He fails to hide his smile. "Glad I amuse you." I groan, planting my head on the table. "Fuck. I've turned into a pussy. It's pathetic."

He plants a hand on my shoulder. "You're in love, and that's the way it's supposed to be."

"Why are we even talking about this?" I ask, lifting my head up. "I'm sure you didn't come here to talk about girls."

"No, but I'm always here if you need someone to talk to." His expression softens. "I didn't have a father around growing up either, and I know what it's like missing that person to turn to for advice."

"Aw, how sweet. You want to be my surrogate dad."

"Jackass," he murmurs under his breath just as the waitress reappears, practically throwing our omelets down in front of us. "Jeez," he says to her retreating back. "What's her problem?"

"I think someone pissed in her cornflakes too."

"Or maybe she's pining after some jackass who loves her but is too afraid to fight for her," he retorts, stabbing me with a knowing look.

"I'm not afraid."

"No? Then why the hell aren't you fighting for her?"

"Because she doesn't want me to."

He shakes his head. "Man, you have so much to learn."

"I'm a fucking mess without her, but I don't know if I should give her space or let her go or chase after her. My mind veers from one scenario to another."

"If you're not prepared to fight for her after hitting the first roadblock, then you're not really in love. Can you cope with never seeing her again? Never getting to touch her like you want to?"

"Ugh." I angrily cut up my food while my mind churns. "Before he passed, my gramps told me that he never remarried after my grandma's early death because he couldn't even consider holding another woman in his arms, loving another woman the way he loved her. He told me every day was like waking up and losing her all over again and that the ache in his heart never went away. I've never forgotten that conversation or how profoundly it affected me."

I swallow the messy ball of grief in my throat. "I never knew my grandma because she died when I was a baby, but I always felt like I knew her because he told me everything about her." I chew a mouthful of omelet slowly as I try to figure out my muddled thoughts. "He told me she touched his soul in a way no one else ever had, and I think...I think Dakota's touched my soul in the same way."

Devin has been quietly eating and listening as I speak. Putting his silverware down, he leans across the table. "Then you've just answered your own question."

I smile for the first time in days. "Thanks, man."

"No problem."

"It's times like this I really miss Gramps. He was the only male figure in my life growing up. The only one I could talk to about stuff, but he still wasn't my dad, you know?"

Devin nods in understanding. "I do, actually. What is the deal with your dad these days?"

I push my plate away, appetite ruined. Any mention of that man turns my stomach. I give him the synopsis. "He bailed on my mom when I was four months old and reappeared when I was fifteen, saying he wanted to get to know me and how he had all these big regrets for not being there for me. I was a douche for believing him, for letting him into my life. He used me, and I didn't even see it. Drove a bigger wedge between me and my mom at a time when she was already stressed over my shit, and we're not even speaking anymore. Mom tried to tell me, but I refused to listen to the one person who has always been there for me, and I hate myself for that. All she's ever done is try to protect me and care for me."

"She's your mother. She'll forgive you."

Tears prick the back of my eyes as I think of all the ways I've let Mom down. "I don't deserve it. And she has her new family to care for now. She doesn't need me."

"I'm sure that's not true. From all I've read and heard about your mother, I'm sure she still loves you very much and is as upset over your situation as you clearly are."

I shrug. "I want to talk to her, but not until this stalker shit is dealt with."

Devin nods. "I understand." He pauses for a second. "I listened to the taped conversation you had with Nick. While he seemed genuine, I didn't like how he subtly tried to gain confirmation of your location."

"You think that was deliberate?"

Devin nods. "There's a substantial reward on offer to the person who discovers your whereabouts and Nick is broke."

"I offered him cash, and he turned me down!"

"Because his pride wouldn't let him take it directly from you."

"But he'd have less of a guilty conscience in turning me in? I'm not buying it. I don't think Nick is behind this."

"I know you don't want to think that of him, but sometimes it's the people you least suspect who surprise you the most."

I rest my head back against the booth, totally fucking sick of this shit. "Why the hell haven't we been able to find this guy?" I demand.

"Because whoever is behind this is smart and not leaving a

trail, but they'll mess up. These people always do. And we'll be ready to take them down."

"But in the meantime, I'm to remain suspicious of every single person I come into contact with."

He shoots me a sympathetic look. "You have to be on your guard at all times. Keep your circle small and tight, and outside of that, be wary of everyone." He gestures at the waitress to bring the check. "I know it sucks, but it won't be forever. We *will* catch this guy."

As I make my way back to my apartment, I mull over Devin's words. Besides Devin, Mom, and Luke, I don't have anyone else I consider completely trustworthy. I messed things up with the one girl I know I can trust with my life.

I hope it isn't too late to prove *I'm* worthy of *her* trust.

Chapter 21

Dakota

There's a definite chill in the air these last few nights, and I shiver under my heavy sweater as I make my way through the dark, deserted alleyway toward the abandoned building. It's been five nights since I slept in Levi's arms and I miss him. Somehow, he wheedled his way into my heart, and I miss him way more than I ever missed Cole.

I'm still sick every time I think of Friday night. I can't believe Levi was so quick to judge me. Especially after everything we shared. And he hasn't made any effort to approach me. In fact, he hasn't shown up at class or the cafeteria, and I know he's purposely ignoring me.

I wish it didn't hurt as much as it did.

I obviously didn't mean that much to him if he can let me go just like that. I push into the building and trudge up the stairs. It's better I found out now before my heart was any more invested.

"What the..." My words trail off as I step out onto the roof. It's been transformed overnight. A multitude of candles rim the perimeter, casting magical shadows on the floor. Bunches of roses rest on elevated stands, scenting the air and lifting my spirits. A silver bucket with non-alcoholic champagne and two glasses rests on a small table, alongside a midnight feast of sorts.

My heart is sprinting around my chest, bursting at the seams.

Lilting music tickles my eardrums as Levi steps forward, strumming his guitar and singing.

All this time, I've been lying to myself
That mocking face in the mirror spoke the truth
But I was too scared to see
Too afraid to fight for what I know is right
Until you broke through the haze
Lost and alone
With your beautiful, haunting moves
Silently calling out to me

I'll get down on my knees
To prove I'm worthy
A girl like you deserves the world
And I want to be the one to give it to you
My beautiful midnight dancer

Dancing through the starry night sky
Like an angel without wings
Your pain speaks to mine, and I need this connection
To feel something I've never believed in
But I'm no good for you
Afraid I'll take you down with me
When all I want is to build you back up
To see the light shine in your blue eyes once again

I'll get down on my knees

To prove I'm worthy
A girl like you deserves the world
And I want to be the one to give it to you
My beautiful midnight dancer

I want to get lost in you
To drown in you
To wake up surrounded by your beauty and your goodness
You make me smile, and I don't ever wanna stop
Don't ever wanna stop
Smiling or loving you
I just wanna give you everything you're missing
And never forget how that feels

I'll get down on my knees
To prove I'm worthy
A girl like you deserves the world
And I want to be the one to give it to you
My beautiful midnight dancer

So scared, but what do you say?
To falling from the sky with me
I can't do this without you, and I need you by my side
Drowning without your kisses
Won't survive the explosion if you lose faith
But I trust in you
And I believe in us
And I know I'm ready for love

I'll get down on my knees
To prove I'm worthy
A girl like you deserves the world
And I want to be the one to give it to you

My beautiful midnight dancer

I believe in us
I believe in love
Come share my dreams, my beautiful midnight dancer

"Don't cry," he pleads when the song finishes, resting his guitar against the wall and cautiously stepping toward me.

"I didn't realize I was." My voice is choked with all I'm feeling. "That was so beautiful. You wrote words to it?"

Reaching out, he smooths my tears away. "I wrote that for you. You inspire me like no one else." He gently cups my face. "You amaze me like no one else." Leaning in, he presses his forehead to mine. "I was an ass, and I know I have no right to ask your forgiveness, but I'm begging you to give me another chance. I can't breathe without you."

His warm breath blows across my face, and the heat from his body sweeps over me, elevating my craving for him.

"I know you're finished with Cole. That you have more self-respect. I shouldn't have let him bait me like that. If you give me another chance, I promise I won't let you down again." He moves his head, peering deeply into my eyes. "I'm crazy about you, Dakota." He takes my hand and places it over his chest, right in the place where his heart thumps wildly. "You feel that?" I nod. "My heart beats only for you, and I know you said you only wanted to be friends, but I can't just be your friend." He pulls me in closer. "Not when I want so much more."

His arms wrap around my waist, and I rest my head on his chest, the frantic beating of his heart mirroring my own. Music reverberates from two speakers, and he steps back, looking expectantly at me. "Dance with me?"

I take his outstretched hand, nodding. He pulls me into his

arms as Demi Lovato's "Tell Me You Love Me" starts up, echoing in the still night air. We sway to the slightly upbeat love song, passion seeping through the lyrics and the way we move perfectly in sync. Levi is a damn good dancer, and as the song progresses, our dancing turns sexier as we grind provocatively against one another, never peeling our eyes from each other. The song ends, and another starts, but I can't tell you who or what, because I'm trapped in the hypnotic gaze of the man staring at me like I'm his everything. Levi is shielding nothing from me, and the hardness pressing against my belly tells me exactly what he wants. I'm every bit as turned on as he is. Lifting my leg, I wrap it around his hip, and he holds me there as I lean back, swaying from side to side, letting all my reservations go.

His arm slides around my lower back, and he hauls me to him, thrusting his hard-on into me, making me moan. My arms slide around his neck as he maneuvers us to the side, pressing my back flat against the wall. "Tell me you want this," he rasps, his eyes dark with lust.

I slide my fingers through his silky hair. "I want this. I want you."

His lips crash down on mine as his hand moves up and down my leg, heating me even through my leggings. My core throbs with need as we rock against one another, grabbing, clawing, greedy, and desperate. His tongue prods the seam of my mouth, and I open for him, groaning as I taste him in my mouth. Our tongues dance a wild tango as our limbs do the same. Every nerve ending in my body is on fire, and I'm consumed in the touch, taste, and feel of Levi as his mouth and his hands worship me. I rub against him, needing the friction to counteract the building need in my core. "Need you," I whimper. "Need you so bad."

I cry out when his mouth moves off mine, and he chuckles.

Nibbling on my earlobe, he starts peppering kisses up and down my neck, sending me into a tailspin. Palming his erection, I rub my hand up and down his impressive length, and he groans into my ear.

"Oh, God, Levi. I can't..."

"Tell me what you want, Kota baby, and I'll give it to you."

"I want you to fuck me. All night long," I pant. "I don't ever want you to stop."

He curses while cupping my ass and pressing against me. "See what you do to me? I'm so hard for you, baby. Have been for weeks."

I don't care that we're on a roof after midnight and that temps are plummeting. I need him inside me right now. I tug at the button on his jeans, and he chuckles, wrapping his hand around my wrist and stalling me. "Not here."

"Why the hell not?" My voice is croaky and laden with need.

"Because I want our first time to be special, and it's not going to be on a roof where anyone could see."

Okay, I suppose he has a point. If he could see me dancing from his penthouse, then chances are, others have noticed me too. But my need is such that I don't care. I'm ready to throw caution to the wind. "I don't care. I need you. I need you now."

I shriek as he scoops me up into his arms. "Tempting as that is, I'm not defiling you in public." He nips at my ear, and I squeak as he carries me down the stairs.

"Would you think I'm crazy if I told you the idea of you defiling me in public is a huge turn-on?"

He groans. "Fuck, baby. That's hot. You're so hot, and you're driving me insane."

I wriggle in his arms. "Let me down. We'll be quicker."

We hold hands while running, grinning at one another as we navigate the roads back to his apartment as fast as we can.

We crash into the elevator, and his hot mouth is on mine again. Slamming me into the side, he feasts on my lips as my hands explore his ass, squeezing his firm flesh as desire ricochets through me. His hand slips under my sweater, and I shiver when his fingers creep up my stomach and over my bra. Roughly, he kneads my breast, rubbing his thumb across my hardened nipple through the flimsy lace of my bra. I whimper into his mouth, grinding against him as my wet pussy aches with need.

The elevator pings, and he steers me out into the corridor, racing to his door. We stumble inside, our mouths fusing together again as we fumble at our clothes. Bits of clothing fly everywhere as we giggle and kiss our way to his bedroom. Lifting me up, he drops me down on his bed, crawling over me. "I have imagined this so many times, but nothing could prepare me for how gorgeous you are," he says, raking his gaze over my body. I'm only wearing my panties and bra, and he's only got his jeans on. His lips are swollen from my kisses, and his hair is all messy from my fingers. I'm betting I have the same lust-drenched look on my face. He stares down at me in awe, and I bathe in the warmth of his attention.

Bravely, I sit up, unclasping my bra and sliding it slowly down my arms. His cock jerks behind the denim as I sit up on my knees and pop the rest of the buttons on his jeans. His thumb grazes my stiff nipples as I tug his jeans down. Standing, he kicks them away and then drops his boxers, watching my expression the entire time.

I lick my lips as I reach for his long, hard length, salivating at the thought of tasting him.

"Nuh-uh." He waves his finger at me. "Not so fast, little temptress." Gently, he pushes me back and then lifts my left leg, holding it at an angle as he starts to kiss his way up my quivering flesh. When he reaches my thigh, he pushes my legs farther apart, pressing wet kisses to each thigh, moving closer and closer to where I need his mouth but never quite reaching his destination.

"Levi!" My cry is urgent, desperate, needy, and he chuckles.

"Patience, baby. I promise it'll be worth the wait." I arch my back as he kisses my pussy through my lace panties. "Fuck, you're drenched for me."

"Levi, please." I'm not beyond begging if it'll give me what I need.

He chuckles again, running his hands up and down my legs as he gazes hungrily at my chest. With deliberate intent, he reaches for my panties and draws them down my legs at an excruciatingly slow pace. My breath erupts in embarrassing puffs, but I honestly couldn't care less. He takes his time looking over my naked body, and I shiver from the intensity in his gaze.

"Jesus, Dakota. You're beautiful. So beautiful."

"Are you going to just look at me all night or actually do something?" I challenge.

He crawls over me, biting my lower lip. "I love it when you turn all bossy on me," he says, before devouring my mouth. I reach around, grabbing hold of his ass cheeks and pulling him down onto me. Laughter rumbles through him, while he peppers my face with kisses. "You're so impatient, and here I am trying to make an effort to take things slow."

"If I wanted slow I'd have asked you to make love to me," I protest. "But I asked you to fuck me for a reason. It's been over a year since I had sex, and I've spent weeks imagining this with you. Do you know how difficult it's been lying in your arms every night when I wanted so much more?"

He arches a brow. "Believe me, it was as difficult for me as it was for you. I've been walking around with a raging boner from the instant you came into my life."

"Aw, that's so romantic," I joke tweaking his nose, before my expression turns more urgent. "I can't wait a second longer. I need to feel you moving inside me. Now, Levi."

"Baby, it's been a while for me too, but I don't want to rush this. You only get one first time. I want to make it memorable."

I tenderly cup his face. "This night has already been memorable. Trust me, I won't ever forget this."

He kisses me sweetly, softly, completely at odds with the way he was just eating my face. Pulling back, he peers intently into my face. "Are you sure you want this? With me?"

I lift up and peck his lips. "Yes. I want this with you. I'm not backing out."

"Thank God," he murmurs, grinning as he starts kissing his way back down my body. He lavishes attention on my breasts, sucking one nipple, then the other, into his mouth, while molding my flesh with his deft fingers. He presses feather-soft kisses all over my stomach before lowering his mouth to my pussy. I almost stop breathing when he slowly blows across my heated flesh.

Then his mouth is there, and his tongue is going crazy, swiping up and down my folds, thrusting inside me and sucking on the taut bundles of nerves that hold the key to my bliss. I'm writhing on the bed like a wild animal, moaning and whimpering as pressure builds inside me. He plunges two fingers inside me and I scream. When his mouth suctions on my clit, I grab his head, holding him there as I crash through the wall—falling, tumbling, swirling. Swimming in an ocean of pleasure. Levi stays with me, milking every last drop before grabbing a condom from the bedside table and sheathing himself.

My hair is a mass of knots over my face, and my chest is

heaving as I come back to earth. "Holy fucking orgasm," I whisper. "That was incredible."

He shoots me a cocky smile. "I aim to please."

He winks, and I laugh, sitting up and pulling him down for a kiss, tasting myself on his lips and reveling in that fact. "Please don't make me wait any longer. I need you to fuck me."

"Baby," he says, nudging at my entrance. "You win. I'm done waiting. I need to feel you clenching around me." He thrusts into me in one hard, fast move, and I scream out again. He stalls. "You okay?"

"Oh God," I moan. "I'm more than okay. You feel so good." I start rocking my hips. "But you need to move, Levi."

"This is going to be hard and fast, baby. Can't hold back."

"Don't want you to. Fuck me hard. Do it. Do it now."

He needs no further encouragement, and he starts pounding into me, pulling out and then slamming back in. His fingers dig into my hips, and he hoists one of my legs over his shoulder, pushing deeper into me, his eyes rolling back in his head as he thrusts. Pressure is building inside me again, and I fist my hands in the sheets, arching my back and moaning. He reaches out, fondling my tits and flicking his thumb against my nipple, sending tremors of desire straight to my pussy. Sweat glides down my back as he continues to thrust into me, his movements getting more and more frantic.

"I'm going to come again," I shout, just as my orgasm hits. He roars his release, joining me in that heavenly space, both of us rocking against one another until we're fully sated. He collapses alongside me, pulling me into his sweat-slicked chest, keeping our bodies connected. I slide my leg through his and wrap my arms around him, savoring the smell and feel of him. Sex lingers in the air, and I close my eyes, committing everything to memory.

"You okay?" he softly asks, brushing tangled strands of my hair back off my face.

"Never been better," I tease, stretching up to kiss him. "That was amazing."

"I'm not sure there are adequate words in the English language to describe it," he says, pressing a fierce kiss to my forehead. "I can't lose you, Kota baby. Not now. Not ever."

I'm startled to see tears pooling at the back of his eyes. "Hey. You won't lose me. Why would you even think that?"

His face is awash with emotion as he looks at me. "Promise me that, no matter what, you'll remember this. You'll remember how good we are together. How much you mean to me."

I'm not sure where his head has gone to now, or why, but I want to reassure him, to ease whatever his worries are.

"I won't forget, Levi," I say, circling my arms around his neck and kissing him. "I promise I'll remember."

Chapter 22

Dakota

Levi and I stroll into class together on Thursday, hand in hand, and Tabs jumps up from her chair, clapping her hands like an overexcited seal. "He shoots! He scores!" she squeals, and I burst out laughing. Edging out of the row, she jumps me, hugging me to death and whispering none too quietly in my ear. "Scale of one to ten, how was it?"

"Off the scale," Levi replies, winking as he wraps his arms around me from behind, forcing Tabs to let go. "She totally rocked my world," he adds, pressing a quick kiss to my cheek.

He totally rocked mine. I'm surviving on less than three hours' sleep because Levi kept his promise, fucking me nonstop most of the night, and I loved every delicious, sexy moment of it. He physically had to drag my ass out of bed this morning.

"Judging by the "I was just fucked every which way to Sunday" look on Kota's face, I'd say you gave as good as you got." She thumps Levi on the shoulder. "Good for you, stud."

"I'd swear you were a guy in a previous lifetime," Elsa says to Tabs over her shoulder, rolling her eyes. "You've definitely got the dirty mouth to prove it."

"I'm just really happy these guys finally got it together. The sexual tension has been killing me."

Laughter tumbles out of my mouth again. "Didn't you get your fix Friday night?"

"Pft." She scoffs, her lips pulling into a disgusted line. "I thought football players knew what they were doing, but it was all wham, bam, thank you, ma'am, with that guy. And his cock was about as impressive as his fucking expertise."

"Ouch." Levi grins. "His name wasn't Cole by any chance, was it?"

I laugh, pleased that he seems to have fully put Friday night, and any jealousy concerning my ex, behind him. I take my seat as the professor walks into the room, and Levi slides in the far side of me, possessively slinging his arm around my shoulders.

Paying attention in class becomes an impossibility.

Levi doesn't miss any opportunity to slyly touch me. Brushing his lips against my cheek when he thinks no one is looking. Creeping his hand up my leg when he believes he can get away with it. Nuzzling his face into my hair and sighing when the prof turns his back to the room.

When class ends, I scan the half page of scattered notes on my pad with a smile. If I was serious about accountancy and planning on hanging around, I might be mad at him for distracting me. But my tuition is only paid to the end of the semester, and then I'm cut off. I still have no clue what I'm going to do, and I really need to start prioritizing my future.

But, right now, I want to focus on the hot guy copping a cheeky feel of my ass as I make my way out of the auditorium. We hang back behind the others as we head toward the cafeteria, sneaking sly kisses, and I just can't keep my hands off him. The feeling seems to be mutual, and he's always touching me.

"God, you two are so darn cute," Elsa says as we enter the massive hall.

"Making up for lost time," Levi quips, darting in to kiss me on the lips.

As we stand in line, he keeps his hand on my hip, whispering all the dirty stuff he plans to do to me when we get home. I lean back against him, almost pinching myself. I can't believe I have this with him. That it feels so perfect. So real. So right.

I don't miss the daggers shot my direction as we walk to our seats. Jealousy almost percolates the air. Excepting our group, Levi doesn't mix with any other students, especially girls, and I know that means I've just made a host of automatic enemies. But nothing could dampen my good mood.

We eat in a hurry and then say our goodbyes before Tabs can slip a dirty comment in. We take our time strolling the few blocks to his apartment, chatting casually as we walk. His fingers twirl in my hair and I lean up and press kisses to the underside of his jaw every so often. It's so natural being with him like this, as if I've always known him.

I shriek the minute we step foot in the penthouse when he sweeps my feet out from under me, tossing me over his shoulder. "What are you doing, you crazy ass?!" I laugh, beating my fists against his back as he strides with purpose through the living area.

"Be quiet, woman," he jokes, slapping my butt. "Trust me, you won't be complaining in a few minutes."

And he's right. He strips my clothes off, tantalizingly slow, before pushing me back on the bed and devouring every part of me with his mouth. When his head lowers to the apex of my thighs, I squirm with anticipation, shouting his name as his tongue goes to town on me. My orgasm catches me off guard, sweeping through me with urgency, and I'm shouting his name repeatedly as waves of ecstasy wash over me. Flipping me over onto my stomach, he pulls my knees up and spreads me, slapping my ass cheeks firmly, and warmth leaks from my still-quivering pussy. "Are you sore after last night baby?" he asks, as I hear the tear of a condom wrapper.

"Nope," I lie. "Give it to me hard, stud. Just how I like it."

He slams into me without warning and I scream.

"I love how enthusiastic you are," he grunts, fucking me in sharp, quick thrusts. "And I love how you shout out my name when you come. It really fucking turns me on."

"Oh, God," I moan as he plunges deep, hitting the right spot.

"Not God, baby. Just...Levi."

"Well, just Levi," I say a couple of hours later. "I think I'm well and truly fucked." I try to move but I can't. "I can't feel my legs anymore. I think you broke me."

He chuckles. "I can't feel my cock. I think you rode me to death."

Now it's my turn to giggle. "I never knew it could be this good," I murmur, curling into his side and drawing swirls on his bare chest with the tip of my finger. "I'm almost afraid to ask how you came to be this experienced."

He grumbles. "Let's not go there. The past is in the past."

"Agreed, and what you did before me doesn't bother me. I prefer to focus on the here and now because it's not like we can do anything to change what's come before."

"You're right, even if I do wish I could erase most of the women I've been with."

"I almost feel sorry for them."

"Don't." He places a gentle kiss to my temple. "None of them cared about me. It was all about what they could get out of it. How they could exploit it for personal gain."

"What do you mean?" I prop up on an elbow, looking

inquisitively at him. He throws his arm over his face, and his chest visibly rises and falls. "Levi?"

"Nothing," he says, removing his arm and letting me see his beautiful face. "Just that none of them were memorable, and I wish they hadn't happened." He smiles, but it doesn't quite meet his eyes. I get the sense there's a lot more to be said, but I decide to be magnanimous. Talking about exes is pointless anyway, so I'll give him a free pass. "What about you?"

"You don't have much to worry about. The only guy I've slept with is Cole, but he was a total horndog, and I'm pretty much open to anything, so..."

"Ugh!" He scrubs a hand over his face. "Now I really want to smash my fist in his face."

I kiss him softly. "It's in the past, and the only one I plan on sleeping with going forward is you."

Saturday arrives, and Levi comes with me to visit Mom. On all other occasions, he waited out in the car, but, now that we're together, I want Mom to meet him. Not that it will register. She's still barely coherent when I visit, but the doctors have told me her rehabilitation will take time and patience.

"Hi, Mom," I say, entering the room and kissing her cheek. She's sitting in a comfy chair by the wide window that overlooks the impressive lawn outside, staring off into space.

A loud grunt emits from the other side of the room, and Levi's eyes widen in alarm. He stares at the curtain pulled around the second bed. "That's her roomie," I murmur in a low voice. "Poor woman had a stroke at forty, and she's been in here ever since. She can't speak and she struggles to comprehend what people are saying. It's really sad. I met her daughter the second time I visited, and she broke down in tears telling me about her."

Grabbing Levi's hand, I pull him over to the small couch, and we sit down in front of Mom. She hasn't even acknowledged us yet. "Mom, I'd like you to meet someone. This is Levi." She doesn't look at him or me, and I deflate a little inside. A teeny, tiny part of me had hoped bringing someone new in to meet her might pique her interest.

He squeezes my hand. I had warned him in the car on the drive here what it'd be like. "It's very nice to meet you, Valerie. I'm Levi, Dakota's boyfriend. I brought you some orchid lilies. Dakota mentioned they were your favorite."

I lace my fingers in his as he places the vase and flowers on the windowsill beside her. We stay chatting for a half hour, but it's all one-sided. Mom doesn't respond or make any indication that she knows we're here. After a while, I can't keep the fake smile plastered on my face anymore. I glance at him. "Let's go," I mouth, and he nods.

"Bye, Momma." I lean down and kiss her cheek. "I'll be back to see you next week." My voice catches, and I squeeze my eyes shut to stall the tears.

Levi places a comforting hand on my lower back as he, too, bends over and kisses Mom on the cheek. "It was lovely to meet you, Valerie. Thank you for raising such a wonderful daughter, and I want you to know I care about her a lot."

My legs almost give way when Mom clutches his arm suddenly, eyeballing him with a lucidity I haven't seen since that awful night back at the house. I gasp when she smiles. "Look after my baby," she whispers, and tears roll down my face when he crouches down, caressing her cheek.

"I promise I will."

I grab hold of his hand and don't let go as we leave the facility. The instant we are outside, I burst into tears, and he doesn't hesitate, wrapping his arms around me. He holds me while I cry. "Sorry," I sniffle. "I just hate seeing her like that. And then, when she said that to you, it's exactly what I needed to know she *is* listening. That she does know I'm here. That some part of her is aware of what's happening."

He runs his hand up and down my back, pressing soft kisses to the top of my head. "She'll get better, babe, and this place seems to be good, although it's a shame she's not in a private room."

"Dad wouldn't sign the paperwork for the insurance to upgrade her. I know it would be more comfortable for her to be in her own room, but it's not so bad. At least she's in the right place to get the help she needs."

"Dakota." He calls my name out from behind, and a chill creeps over my spine. Slowly, I turn and face my father, securing Levi's arms around me. I can feel his body tense up.

"Dad."

"Could we talk in private, please?" He glares at Levi, and I've got no doubt Levi is returning his hostile stare.

"Whatever you need to say can be said in front of my boyfriend."

If he's shocked by the news, he doesn't show it. He gestures toward a bench at the front part of the lawn, and we walk over and sit down.

"There's no easy way to say this, so I'll just come right out with it." He has the decency to look somewhat embarrassed. "I'm divorcing your mother." I stare at him in shock, refusing to believe my ears. "I know you don't approve, and I know I've made terrible mistakes, but I need to do this because I...I'm going to be a father again."

"What?" I scramble to my feet, horrified.

He stands. "I didn't plan this, and I wouldn't have left your mother, but I can't let Monique down, and I..." He looks down at his shoes. "I can't do this anymore. I can't watch what her death has done to all of us. I just can't deal with it. It's better this way."

"So, you're just abandoning us?"

"I won't withhold your trust fund, and I won't force you to stay in U of I. I know you don't want to be there, and I think it's best if you don't come to work with me, given the circumstances. There's enough money in your fund to cover Juilliard, if they'll give you your place back. If not, it's up to you what you do with the funds. I'll assign the paperwork next week and have the documentation overnighted to you."

"I can't believe you're doing this. I can't believe you're leaving my mom. The woman you promised to love forever!" I say in a raised, angry tone of voice. Levi tightens his arms around me, and I cling to him for support.

"Things change, Dakota. Our marriage ended the night your sister died. It's too much. A constant reminder of her loss. I can't continue to live like this."

"Her name is Layla," I spit. "And we lost her too, but you don't see me walking away from my responsibilities."

He looks over his shoulder, and I notice the petite girl with the mass of black corkscrew curls leaning against the side of his car. Bile swirls in my mouth as my eyes roam over her obvious baby bump. "You brought her here?" I turn disgusted eyes on my dad. "And how old is she? She barely looks older than me."

He winces a little. "Please don't make a scene. Monique's having a difficult time with the pregnancy."

"Poor Monique," I hiss. "I guess that's what you get for screwing a married man behind his sick wife's back."

I turn around, taking Levi's hand in mine. "Can we go, please."

"Dakota." Dad's tone is pleading.

I look over my shoulder, holding my head up. "I want

nothing more to do with you. In my eyes, you died the same night Layla died. And don't come back here again. I don't want either of you upsetting Mom."

I don't wait to see his reaction, turning back to Levi and clinging to his side. I'm numb and heartbroken all over again as he helps me into his SUV.

Pulling away from the psychiatric facility, I glance at Dad one final time. He has his arms around Monique, consoling her. He doesn't attempt to look my way, and, as we drive off, anger twists and turns in my gut. Making a silent vow, I promise this is the last time I invest any more time, energy, or thought in that man.

Chapter 23

Shawn/Levi

Dakota is lost in thought when we return to the car, and I'm at a loss how to help her. "I'm so sorry. What can I do to help?" I ask after a few minutes of silence.

I want to turn my car around and pummel my fists in that asshole's face for putting the crestfallen look on my girl's face. "Talk to me about anything but that." She knots her hands in her lap. "I know I need to process what he just said, but not right now. Distract me."

"You got accepted to Juilliard?"

"Yeah. I was due to leave shortly after Layla was killed. I postponed my place because there was no way I could leave my parents, and they were terrified of me going to New York alone after what happened to my sister."

"So why didn't you go this year?" I ask, even though I've a good idea what happened.

"I couldn't leave Mom in her condition, and Dad wanted me to study accounting and eventually take over his practice." Anger burns at the back of her eyes and I feel for her.

"Couldn't you defer the place again?"

She shakes her head. "They were sympathetic, but places are limited, and they couldn't continue to keep mine open for me, especially when I couldn't tell them when or if I would definitely be taking it. I had no choice but to let it go."

"Well, that's a damn shame," I say, indicating as I move lanes to take the next exit.

She shrugs. "It is what it is. Nothing I can do about it now."

I want to ask what her plans are now, whether she is going to stay in U of I or if she has something else in mind, but I'm afraid to open that hornet's nest.

I'm supposed to be alleviating her stress, not adding to it.

"Ange used to dance." I tell her what Devin's wife told me previously. "You'll have that in common with her, and she's a great cook like you too. I think you'll really like her."

"Are you sure they know I'm coming?" she asks me again, lowering down the radio.

Devin said he needed to talk to me, and it made sense to combine the visits as they are on the same route. I told Dakota we're going to meet some of my mom's friends and they've invited us to stay for dinner. Devin assured me he'd uphold my cover, but I still hate lying to her. With every passing day, and every step closer we get, I am growing guiltier and guiltier. I hate keeping so much from her, but I don't know how to fix it. Even if I told her now, she'll be so pissed at me.

The fact she thinks Shawn Lucas is a talentless, womanizing jackass is an added complication and one that will not help my cause.

"Don't worry. They know I'm bringing you with me, and you'll love them."

Dakota carries the chocolate cake she made while I hold the flowers for Ange and candy for Ayden as we approach the front door of the Morgans' palatial home. The door is slightly ajar, and I hear raised, angry voices from inside. I share an uncomfortable look with Dakota. "Shit," she whispers. "What do we do?"

"Pretend like we haven't heard," I propose, pressing the bell and announcing our arrival.

Devin opens the door a few minutes later, and I can tell he's schooled his features into a smile to mask whatever argument we just overheard. "Levi, so good to see you again." He pulls me in for a quick hug before extending his hand to Dakota. "And it's lovely to finally meet the girl who has tamed this guy," he teases, shaking her hand.

I don't miss the quick once-over she gives him before remembering her manners. "Thank you for having me, and I hope we're not putting you out."

"Not at all." He steps aside, ushering us in. "Ange loves an opportunity to cook up a storm, and she has a soft spot for this young punk."

"I can't say that I blame her." Dakota smiles at me, and I dart in and kiss her quickly as Devin leads us into the open-plan living space. Ange is standing in the kitchen area, at the sink, looking out at the garden.

"Honey," Devin says, walking to her side and placing his hand on her lower back. Brave man. "Levi and Dakota are here."

Ange spins around, smiling warmly as she steps forward to greet my girl. "I'm Angelina, but everyone calls me Ange. It's a pleasure to meet you Dakota."

"Likewise and thank you for having us." Dakota hands the tin to her. "I hope you like chocolate cake."

Ange opens the lid and licks her lips. "This looks delicious. You didn't have to bring anything but thank you so much."

"Thanks for the invite," I say, leaning in to kiss her cheek. I hand her the flowers and candy for Ayden. "For you and the cute little guy."

She squeezes my shoulder. "That's very thoughtful. Thank you, but I'll just hide these for the moment," she adds, putting the candy away in the cupboard. "At least until Ayd has had his dinner." She puts the flowers in a vase, nestling her nose in the blooms and inhaling.

"Can I help with anything?" Dakota asks as Ange turns around.

"Not at all. Let me get you something to drink. We have water, soda, or juice."

"I'll have an apple juice if that's okay," Dakota requests.

"Coming right up," Devin says, already opening the refrigerator and pulling out a carton. He hands her a glass and pours me a soda as Ayden comes barreling into the room.

"Shawnnnnnnn!" he squeals, flinging himself at me. Panic charges through me, and Ange and Devin both freeze.

Dakota looks perplexed. "Shawn?" she mouths at me.

"It's my middle name," I lie in a low voice as I bend down to pick Ayden up. Ange glares at Devin, and Dakota still looks confused, but she lets it drop.

Crisis averted.

For now.

I pull Ayden up onto my shoulders and race around the living room with him, in the way I used to do with my little brothers. He's squealing and shrieking the entire time, clearly enjoying himself.

Dakota and I spend fifteen minutes playing with Ayden on the floor while Devin and Ange attend to dinner. When Ange brings baby Kendall in from her nap, Dakota almost melts on the spot. Happily feeding her a bottle, she looks content rocking the little one in her arms, and my stomach does a funny twist. She's a natural and I can't drag my eyes away.

Visions of her cradling our baby in her arms assault me from left field, and I hop up, terrified and strangely elated at the same time. Devin has been watching from the door, and he quietly chuckles, slapping my shoulder as if he can tell where my head's at. I walk to the bathroom feeling more than a little weirded out.

Thankfully, there are no other coronary-inducing moments during the delicious dinner, and conversation flows easily around the table. Dakota and Ange pull on their jackets and take Ayden out to the yard while Devin and I clean up. The baby is dozing in a swinging chair. "We've discovered something interesting about Matt," Devin says, as we rinse and stack the dishwasher. "He's racked up massive gambling debts and it looks like he might be about to lose his home. It also looks like his father has kicked him out of the family business."

"Shit. It must be serious if his dad has done that."

"The more I look at him, the more convinced I am he's somehow involved in this."

My chest tightens at the thought, but I can't ignore what Devin's telling me. This is what I'm paying him for after all. "Fuck." I lean back against the counter, rubbing a tense spot between my brows. "I know he's pissed at me, but to take a shot at me? To want me dead? I just can't..."

"I didn't want to tell you this over the phone." Devin pauses momentarily, shooting me a sympathetic look. "A package was sent to the record label. It was the bloody, severed head of a pig with another ransom note stuffed in its mouth."

"How much are they demanding now?"

"Three mill. The amount is increasing, and the drop-off

location changes, with each new message, along with the threat of escalation."

"But so far they haven't followed through."

"Because you going into hiding has thrown them off their game," Devin suggests. "But not for long, I'm guessing."

I exhale heavily. "So what now?"

"If it's okay with you, I'd like to keep my guys on Matt for another couple of weeks to see if we can find some evidence."

"You still think this is all on him?"

"We know whoever is behind this has a crew working for him so it's possible. Right now, we're playing all angles. It's the safest course of action until we can conclusively rule someone out."

I nod slowly. "Okay. Then do it. Whatever you need. Just add the additional cost to the invoice."

"I like Dakota," Devin adds, gesturing out the window. "I can see why you're so hung up on her."

"You'd never know she just had another bombshell dropped on her before we came here," I admit, "and that's Dakota all over. Always putting other people's needs before her own."

"I'm sorry to hear that," Devin says, wiping his hands on a towel. "Anything I can help with?"

"Actually, maybe there is something." I tell him about the psychiatric facility, and it turns out he knows one of the directors. "Is there any chance you could put in a call and see if they can upgrade Valerie to a private room? They can send the invoice to me, but I need it kept confidential. Perhaps they can come up with some plausible excuse if Dakota asks."

"I'll make the call on Monday and let you know."

"Thanks."

He smiles at me. "She's good for you. Don't fuck things up."

Devin swaps places with Ange outside, chatting to Dakota

as he pushes Ayden on the swing. Ange comes in, putting her hand on my arm as I move to step outside. "I was hoping to have a word in private with you."

"Sure."

"Let's grab some coffee and sit on the couch," she suggests, and I nod. I watch Dakota laughing and joking with Devin and chasing Ayden around the yard with a smile on my face while Ange fixes our coffee. "Someone's smitten," she teases as we move into the living area. She presses a soft kiss to baby Kendall's forehead before joining me on the couch.

"You won't hear me denying it. She's the best thing to have happened to me in years."

"Then I hope you don't mind me saying this, because she's a lovely girl, and I can tell you are both crazy about each other, so this is coming from a good place." She pauses to gather her thoughts. "I know we don't know each other all that well yet, but Devin and I both feel protective toward you, so what I'm about to say is with the best of intentions."

I nod, urging her to continue.

Her features soften, and she lowers her voice. "Keeping secrets never ends well, and I'm speaking from personal experience. How is Dakota going to feel when she finds out you've kept her in the dark, Shawn? How betrayed will she feel when she realizes she doesn't know the real you?"

I sit up straighter. "But she does know the real me," I protest. "She knows me better than most. I don't like that she doesn't know my true identity or this other side of my life, but I have to keep her safe."

"I know your intentions are honorable, but you've already exposed her by getting involved with her. You should at least consider telling her the truth now so she can decide whether she wants to accept the risk or not. Her parents have already lost a daughter, and they are probably terrified of something happening to her too."

"Jesus, Ange." I get up and start pacing. "You think I'd let anything like that happen to Dakota? I would never let her get hurt. Never!"

She stands, looking over my shoulder as the baby emits a tiny whimper. "I know you wouldn't deliberately put her in harm's way, but you've made the decision to let her into your life, and I believe she should be aware of the danger so she can be more vigilant. Maybe I'm overstepping the mark saying this, but I couldn't live with myself if anything happened and I hadn't shared my concerns with you."

Guilt has been chipping away at me since Devin's most recent revelation, but how do I tell Dakota when she's already dealing with so much? "I know you mean well, Ange, and I appreciate your honesty, but I don't want to freak Dakota out. She's been through a lot, and she needs me."

"And that's admirable, but trust me, take it from someone who kept horrible secrets from the people she loved." She shudders, looking unbearably sad for a second. "Hiding the truth and running from reality will only land you in a whole world of trouble. I'm not trying to tell you what to do, Shawn, more I'd like you to gain insight from my experiences. I made terrible choices thinking I was doing the right thing for my loved ones, but I only made things worse. I guess I just want to make sure you've considered every angle. That you've properly thought this through." She slants me a sympathetic look. "Devin will probably kill me for saying this, but if you weren't his client, I know he'd agree with me."

"That's what you were arguing about when we arrived?" I surmise.

She looks apologetic. "I'm sorry you heard that, but, yes, I don't like lying to Dakota by omission. It feels wrong."

"I shouldn't have brought her here. Shouldn't have put you in that position."

She shakes her head. "It's fine. If I didn't want her here, I wouldn't have extended the invitation. I just don't like being complicit in the deceit."

"I want to tell her, but I'm scared of losing her when I've only just found her," I admit.

Her expression softens, and she takes my elbow, stopping my frantic pacing. "Give her some credit and some space to come to terms with it, and I think she'll be fine. That girl has a good head on her shoulders, and I see the way she looks at you. This isn't casual for her either."

She stares directly into my eyes, and all I see is honest concern. "If you tell her the truth, I think you'll be pleasantly surprised."

Chapter 24

Dakota

I spend the rest of the weekend with Levi, only returning to my dorm Monday night to grab some fresh clothes. Daisy and Jake are watching TV when I come out of the bedroom, and I spend a couple of minutes shooting the shit with them. "I'm really glad you guys fixed things," she tells me.

"Me too."

"He seems like a good guy," Jake adds.

"I think so too." The fact I have a permanent smile on my face at a time when my life has turned to complete and utter shit is testament to that. I should be wallowing in despair because my family has irrevocably broken apart, and my future is lying in tatters around my feet, but I'm remarkably upbeat and that's due to Levi.

"I can't shake the feeling I've met him before or know him from somewhere," Daise says, her brows knitting together. "He looks so familiar."

"Yeah? Maybe you know him from home. He's from Knox County too."

She purses her lips, musing. "Maybe that's it. But I'm sure I wouldn't ever forget meeting him, not when he looks like that."

"Hey." Jake nudges her in the ribs. "Boyfriend sitting right here."

She blushes. "I just meant he has a memorable face," she stutters, trying to backtrack to save face.

I snort. "Sure, he does," I tease before standing. "Anyway, I think that's my cue to leave. I probably won't be back for a few days, but message or call me if you need anything." I lean down and hug her.

"Don't worry about me. I have my own boy toy to keep me company." She rests her head on Jake's shoulder, and he presses a kiss to her forehead, so I know she's in good hands.

I'm at the stove, stirring sauce for the meatballs, when Levi arrives. Sliding up behind me, he wraps his arms around my waist and presses a kiss to the throbbing pulse in my neck. "Coming home to you every day will never get old," he murmurs, planting soft kisses up and down my neck.

I lean back and twist my head, kissing him slowly, savoring every brush of our lips. "Good, because there's no getting rid of me." Turning the burner off, I spin around, circling my arms around his neck. "I love being here with you. I've never felt this comfortable with anyone before, but if you need some space, just tell me. I won't be offended if you don't want me here all the time." I've kinda unofficially moved in without us having any formal conversation. I think he's okay with it, but if he's not, that's fine too. I don't want to appear pushy or needy or outstay my welcome.

"Are you shitting me?" He hauls me flush to his chest. "I

love having you here. I was so fucking lonely until you came into my life. I'm not ever letting you leave."

I press up on my tiptoes and kiss him. "I'm falling deep for you, Levi." I peer sincerely into his eyes. "Don't let me down." A flash of remorse passes over his face, but it's gone so fast I'm not sure I didn't imagine it.

Like every other night, he insists on cleaning up after we've eaten. I'm sitting cross-legged on the couch working on an assignment when he accosts me from behind. I shriek as his hands slip under my sweater, creeping around to cup my breasts. "Hmm," he murmurs, nibbling on my ear lobe. "I think it's time for dessert."

I swat his hands away. "I've got this assignment to finish."

"What's more important," he teases, coming to kneel in front of me on the couch, removing the book from my hands and placing it on the coffee table. "Me or your homework?"

I grin wickedly at him as I lean forward, tracing my fingers over the noticeable bulge in his jeans. "Well, when you put it like that."

I don't need much convincing.

He sits down on the couch, and I pounce. Straddling his lap, I grind my pelvis against him, bending down and capturing his lips in mine. His hands go straight to my hair, and he fists my long hair around one hand, tugging my head back and stretching my neck. His lips blaze a fiery trail as he kisses a line from my chin, down my neck and over my collarbone. I shiver all over as his hands start exploring. Pulling the hem of my off-the-shoulder sweater up, he hastily removes it along with my tank top, leaving me in my lacy bra. Burying his face between my breasts, he thrusts up as we rock against one another, emitting primitive moans that cause my arousal to spike to new levels. In one swift move, he has my bra unclipped, pulling the straps down my arms and flinging it away. Then his hot mouth is on my expectant flesh, moving from one taut nipple to the other, sucking, biting and licking; working me into a frenzy in his lap.

"Baby, you are so fucking hot, and I can't get enough of you," he mumbles in between worshiping my breasts.

"The feeling is definitely mutual," I rasp, curving my back to give him more access.

I roll against him, groaning when I feel how hard he is. Jumping up, I shuck out of my jeans and panties until I'm standing naked in front of him.

"I'll never get sick of that sight," he purrs, running his hand up the inside of my thighs. "You're my every wet dream come to life, Dakota."

Laughing, I remove his hand and push him flat on his back as I get to work on his jeans. In record time, I have him stripped bare, and I'm salivating at the magnificent male specimen in front of me.

"Your body is a work of art," I admit, leaning over him as I begin to lick every delectable inch of his skin, loving how he jerks and shivers under my touch. My fingers follow the V-indents on his hips down through the trail of dark blonde hair and on to his impressive hard-on. Wrapping my hands around the base, I stroke his velvety soft length, watching his eyes roll back in his head. My tongue darts out, lapping up the precum on his tip, and he moans in pleasure. I take him into my mouth, sucking and nibbling while my hand pumps the base of his cock in measured strokes. I pick up my pace, taking more of him into my mouth and grazing my teeth against his throbbing length.

Grabbing my shoulders, he lifts me up onto his lap in one skillful move. His cock pulses beneath me, and an intense shiver rocks my body. "Ride me, baby. I want to come inside you." I grind against his erection, loving the friction of his naked flesh against mine while he reaches out, fumbling with his jeans. He hands me a condom and I roll it down over him before slowly lowering my body onto his. We both groan when I'm fully seated, staring at one another with matching heated looks. Holding onto the nape of my neck, he pulls me down for a searing hot kiss. "I'm crazy about you, my beautiful midnight dancer. Totally head over heels for you."

"I'm crazy about you too," I whisper as I start to move up and down his rock-hard length. Holding my hips, he helps set the pace, and soon the only sound in the room is flesh slapping against flesh and joint mutual groaning as we both race toward orgasm. He sits up abruptly, pulling me even closer as he thrusts up into me with more urgency. His mouth devours my lips and my breasts and pressure is building inside me. "Oh, oh, Levi. Don't stop."

He thrusts harder and faster, and my hands grip his shoulders as I ride him in sync, muscles clenching tight around his cock. We both cry out together, falling over that heavenly ledge at the same time, holding and clinging to one another, and it's one of the hottest experiences of my life.

After another round in the shower, we are back out on the couch dressed in fresh clothes. My feet are in Levi's lap and he's massaging them. "That feels so good. Your hands are like magic." And they are, even if they are callused from playing the guitar. The rough pads of his thumbs knead my feet with the right amount of pressure, and it feels like I've died and gone to heaven.

He chuckles. "I can't stop touching you. I think it's a disease."

"Well, if it is, I have it too." I grin at him.

"God, we're so nauseating, but I fucking love it." He presses kisses to my feet, and I squirm, all ticklish and giggling like a three-year-old.

"I wish we could stay here forever and never have to leave."

I sigh dreamily.

"I wish that too, babe, but reality is going to come crashing down upon us sooner rather than later."

His happy expression transforms to one of abject sorrow, and I instantly want to remove it. "Hey." I crawl over to his side, snuggling into his chest, and his arms automatically go around me. "Just because things are changing doesn't mean anything has to change with us."

An awkward silence fills the gap between us, but I don't know how to make it better. My situation has been like the unspoken elephant in the room since Dad dropped the bomb on Saturday. Levi clears his throat, holding me a little tighter. "I know you've had a lot of knockbacks lately, and I don't want to add to the pressure, but have you thought about what you want to do? Are you going to stay around here or...?"

I look up at him, hating how troubled he looks. "I'm thinking of switching my major to dance and sticking around here. With you." If anything, he looks even more tortured at that admission, and I don't understand.

"Don't do that for me. You need to make the right choices for you."

I sit up straighter, turning around so I'm facing him. "What exactly are you saying?"

He cups my cheek. "I want you in my life, Dakota. Don't doubt that. But I'm not sure how long I'm going to be here for, so I don't want you basing your decisions on me. Decide what *you* want to do, and we'll find a way to make it work."

"What do you mean? You're not planning to stay here and complete your degree?" My voice betrays my incredulity.

He exhales noisily. "I don't think so. I'll have to get back to L.A. at some point. I can't let my career fall by the wayside."

"I wasn't aware of that." *I mean, who signs up to a degree willingly knowing he doesn't have time to complete it?* It makes little sense, and not for the first time, I wonder what exactly is going on with him. My gut tells me there's a lot more to this man than he's let me see, and that's makes me uneasy. However, we're both only getting to know one another, and it's not realistic to expect him to divulge all his secrets in one go. I've got to trust he'll let me in when the time is right. Right now, I like what we have, what we're becoming, and I'm willing to give him the benefit of the doubt.

I chew on my bottom lip. "I guess I could stay here for as long as you are and then decide what I want to do. It's not like it'd be that easy to transfer mid-semester anyway, and I doubt Juilliard would let me back at such short notice." If they'll let me back at all.

He leans forward and kisses me sweetly. "The selfish part of me loves that plan because maybe you might be able to come with me, but I don't want you to hold back on my account. Do what's right for you, and I promise we'll find a way to stay together. I meant what I said, Kota baby. I don't want to lose you."

"You won't, because I don't want to lose you either."

Levi comes with me again on Saturday to visit Mom, and I'm overjoyed to find she's been moved to her own private suite. Apparently, there's some special grant she was able to avail of which enabled her to upgrade to her own room, and I could kiss the nurse for thinking to apply for it.

What's even better is the signs of improvement I see. She still doesn't talk, but she looks both of us in the eye when we speak to her, and she's smiling. When we say our goodbyes, she squeezes both our hands with tears in her eyes. I'm practically bouncing as we walk outside. I thread my arm through Levi's.

"She's starting to come around. I saw it in her eyes. Did you notice?"

"I did, babe. It's great news." He presses a kiss to my temple, and I can tell from the expression on his face that he's genuinely pleased.

"I think this calls for a celebration," he says when we are in the car en route back home. "I want to take you out to dinner. I found this cute little restaurant online that isn't too far away. What do you say, baby?" He takes my hand, lifting it quickly to his lips. "Will you have dinner with me?"

"I'd love to." I lean over the console and kiss his cheek. "Thank you for coming with me today."

"No problem. I told you I want to be in your life. To help if I can. Nothing is too much trouble for you."

God, this man. *How does he always know the right things to say?*

Back at the penthouse, I'm walking on a cloud as I head to the bathroom to take a shower while Levi calls the restaurant to make a reservation.

I stay in the shower a little longer than usual, hoping he'll join me, but after ten minutes, it's obvious he's not coming so I get out. Wrapping a fluffy towel around my body, I quickly towel dry my hair before running my fingers through it. I step out into the corridor, padding toward the kitchen to find out what time the reservation is booked for when I hear raised voices.

"Baby, please stop fighting this. You know how good we are together. Let me remind you of that."

Bile swims up my throat as they come into view, and I want to puke. A gorgeous redhead is draped all over Levi, pushing her tits into his chest and snaking her arms around his neck.

Stomping into the room, I glare at both of them. "What the hell is going on?"

Chapter 25

Shawn/Levi

Shock splays across Calista's face before she composes herself. Fucking hell! I scrunch fistfuls of my hair in frustration. This is a fucking nightmare. Removing Calista's wandering hands, I inch toward Dakota, but she holds up a hand to stop me.

"Get rid of the groupie, babe," Calista sneers, raking her gaze over Dakota in a none too charitable fashion.

"Who the fuck is she?" Dakota demands to know, hurt written all over her face as she looks to me for answers.

"No one important," I reply, stepping in front of her and forcing her gaze to mine.

"What the fuck is going on here!" Calista cries, flinging the tux at me. "Get her out of here!"

Anger simmers in my veins as I turn around. "Shut. Up. Calista. And if anyone is leaving, it's you, not my girlfriend."

She stumbles back as if slapped. "Girlfriend?" Her mouth drops open and hurt splays across her face. "You don't do girlfriends."

Dakota is looking between me and Calista trying to size up the situation. I gently cup her face, grateful when she doesn't push me away. "Dakota, I can explain everything. Just let me walk Calista out first." I plead with my eyes, almost collapsing with relief when she nods her head tersely.

"I can't believe this," Calista murmurs, looking like someone just stole her favorite Louboutins. "How could you do this to me?"

"Calista, for the umpteenth time, I am not interested in you like that. Our relationship is strictly professional, and you're lucky I don't fire your ass for this stunt. I told you over the phone that I would not be going to your sister's wedding, so you can take the tux and your interfering ass and get the hell out of here before I change my mind."

Tears gather in her eyes, and I feel like a prick even though I've done nothing wrong. "Let me call you a taxi." I pull out my cell.

"No thanks!" she hisses. "I'm well capable of making my own travel arrangements. This was a mistake," she adds, grabbing her case, purse, and coat and storming toward the door.

I snatch the tux and follow her. "Don't forget this." I thrust it at her as she opens the door. "This is your final warning," I say under my breath. "Don't make me regret this. One more stunt and you're out."

"Fine!" she snaps. "Have fun with your tramp."

I slam the door shut, leaning my forehead against the wall as I try to calm the fuck down.

"I need to know what's going on, Levi," Dakota quietly says. "Start talking."

I turn around to face her. "It's not what it looked like, I promise." She pins me with suspicious eyes, and I hate that Calista has made her doubt me. "Let's sit." Placing my hand on her lower back, I guide her to the couch.

Ange's words have weighed heavy on my mind for the last week, and I know, deep down, that she's right. That I need to confess all to Dakota, and I'm trying to pluck up the courage to go there.

I wish I could come clean with her now, but I'm too terrified of losing her. Besides, when I tell her the truth, I want to have it properly prepared. To have anticipated all her questions and objections and have an answer for everything.

I can't tell her now. Not when she's currently suspicious of me, so I have no choice but to continue to give her half-truths.

She's eyeballing me intently, waiting in expectation. I clear my throat. "Calista is my assistant. She's worked for me for years, and she has an issue with boundaries, but, I swear, nothing is going on with her. Absolutely nothing. It's all in her head."

"Your assistant?" Her brows knit together. "I didn't realize session musicians needed assistants."

"She books gigs and keeps track of my schedule and does admin and shit," I supply, digging a deeper hole for myself.

She sits with her hands in her lap, mulling over my words. "Well, if that's the truth, if she *is* your assistant, why did she have her hands on you?"

"She was all over me before I had a chance to push her away. If you'd stepped into the kitchen a few seconds later, she wouldn't have been touching me. I promise you that."

She is quietly contemplative. "Why is she delusional, Levi? Why does she think something is going on? Did something happen between you two?"

Fuck. I'm so tempted to lie, but after what she suffered at Cole's hand, I owe her this truth. I cringe as the words leave my mouth. "I made a mistake one night, and I've regretted it ever since. She was always hitting on me, but I usually just laughed her off. This time, I was too shitfaced to reject her advances, and I ended up sleeping with her. I don't even remember it. That's how fucking trashed I was. I made it clear to her straightaway that it was a mistake and it wouldn't happen again. And it hasn't. It was only that one time. Ever since then, she's acted differently with me, and I've been close to firing her so many times."

"Why didn't you?"

"Because she's actually really good at her job, and if it got out I fired her for this shit, she wouldn't work in the industry again. I don't want that on my conscience." That's only partly true. I've begged Luke to can her irritating ass on more than a couple of occasions, but he's always talked me out of it.

I'm seriously regretting that now, and I meant what I said: One more strike and she's out.

She moves my face until I'm looking her straight in the eye. "Look me in the eye and tell me that's the truth. That she doesn't mean anything to you."

I palm her face and stare solemnly into her eyes. "I swear to you that's the truth and she means nothing to me. I care about you. You're the only one I want." I want to tell her I love her, but not like this. She'll only think I'm insincere and be even more suspicious of me.

"Okay." She rests her hands on my shoulders. "I believe you, but you know I can't stand cheaters, so don't make me regret trusting you."

We cancel our dinner plans after that, neither of us in the mood, and it's something else to be pissed at Calista for.

We go to the roof as usual, and I can tell Dakota is more introspective tonight, her movements showcasing her pain even when she doesn't articulate it.

I'm sitting on the ground with my back against the wall trying to get the music right to this latest song. Dakota doesn't know it yet, but this one's inspired by her sister Layla. Closing my eyes, I start strumming my guitar, humming rather than singing as I work the melody to suit the mood.

I sense her before she speaks, as I find myself doing a lot. It's as if we're attuned to one another, and I can feel her in a room before I'm aware she's physically there.

"That's beautifully sad," she says, dropping down beside me.

"It's something new I'm working on."

"You're so talented, Levi. Too talented to be playing backup to some artist. You should be front and center stage."

This isn't the first time she's expressed that sentiment, and I don't know how I speak over the guilt pummeling my insides. "Thank you."

She places her hand on my knee, leaning forward to look at me. "I mean it. Your words touch my soul." She rubs a hand over her chest, and her eyes glisten with emotion. "Have you ever played your own stuff for anyone?"

"Yeah," I admit, averting my eyes and starting to strum the notes to her song in the hope it'll distract her. I try to avoid outright lying to her, and this is edging into dangerous territory. "Recognize this one?" I tease, pinning her with the full extent of my smile.

Her eyes glaze over in happiness. "As if I'm likely to forget. It's not every day someone writes a song for me."

I play it for her. She listens attentively, beaming at me the whole time, like she still can't believe it.

When I finish, I extend my hand and pull her up to me, wrapping my arms around her. "Are you ready to call it a night because I want to take you home and make love to you."

She slides her hand into mine. "As if I could ever refuse such a tempting offer." She pecks my lips, grinning. "Take me home, lover boy."

This time is different, and I know she's feeling it too. Every other time, we've fucked like wild animals, frantic and overly eager for one another, but not tonight. Tonight, I want to show her all the things I'm still too afraid to say. Candles flicker softly in the bedroom as I slowly undress her, removing layer after layer like I'm peeling a ripe peach. My nose grazes along the elegant column of her neck, and I savor her delicate smell. I lay her down on the bed, never taking my eyes off her as I quickly shuck out of my clothes. Then I start a slow perusal of her body, tenderly kissing every inch of her skin, worshiping her with my mouth and my hands, reveling in all the pleasurable noises she makes. She's quieter than usual as I explore her body, my hands trembling as I think about how lucky I am that she allows me to touch her like this.

When I finally push her thighs apart, I drink up her essence like it's nectar from the gods, gently licking and sucking instead of my usual thrusting, greedy approach. I leisurely pump two fingers in and out of her pussy as I suction on her clit, lavishing it with slow, swirling strokes of my tongue until she falls apart.

I move up her body, kissing her tenderly, and just take a minute to look at her. With her hair fanned out all over the pillow, her swollen lips and telltale flushed face, she looks like a goddess, an angel, a beautiful creature sent to love me and save me in all the ways I needed saving. I kiss her mouth softly. "You undo me, beautiful. In all the best ways." Her answering smile is full of adoration and much more, and my heart surges at the thought she feels it too.

This connection.

This deep passion building between us.

The start of something profound. Something permanent.

Taking my time, I roll a condom on and slowly edge inside her. Gently pinning her arms above her head, I drive into her in slow, precise, measured thrusts, whispering how beautiful she is as I tenderly make love to her. I've never taken so much care with a girl, and I've never felt the sensations coursing through my body ever before. Our eyes are locked in a heated gaze, and our moans are understated as we take our sweet time with one another.

The expression on her face mirrors how I feel inside, and I want to tell her I love her, that I want to love her forever, but I can't force those words out.

Not until she knows I'm Shawn Lucas.

Not until she can accept every part of me and all that comes with owning my heart.

After, she lies in my arms, both of us quiet but contented. "Levi," she whispers after a bit, and I look down at her.

"What, baby?"

"That was..." Tears well in her eyes and I hug her closer.

"That was everything." My voice is choked.

"It was," she whispers, pressing a kiss to my chest. "No one has ever made love to me like that. I...I'm scared."

I twist around on my side so I'm facing her. "Scared of what, beautiful?" I wind my fingers through her gorgeous hair.

"Scared of feeling too much."

I nod. "I know. I'm the same, but I think that's the way it's supposed to be." *When you're in love.* "When you've found your person," I add instead, hoping she hears the underlying message.

"I've never felt this way about anyone before," she admits, and I love how truthful she is, even when she's afraid.

"Me neither. You make me feel so much, Dakota. So, so,

much." I press a kiss to the top of her head, hauling her back in close to my chest.

"Usually I'm more of a "go with the flow" kind of girl, but I don't want to be like that with you. I want infinity with you, Levi. Never-ending moments of blissful happiness. If that's what you want too."

"It is, beautiful. That's exactly what I want." But as she sleeps peacefully in my arms, I'm terrified those blissful moments are already drawing to a close. And I know if this ends, if she can't accept what I've hidden in the interests of her safety, and she leaves me, I'll be completely and utterly destroyed.

I can't lose her. I can't lose this connection. Not when I'm finally starting to feel like me. Not when I've finally found a girl worth living for.

Reluctantly, I leave Dakota sleeping as I slip out of the bed at six a.m. to call Devin. I know he's an early riser and he'll be awake. Despite having the woman of my dreams in my arms all night, I didn't sleep well. I'm like a ticking time bomb about to explode, and I know I'm going to have to confess soon, because I can't continue like this.

I also had time to analyze a few things, and I need to discuss something with Devin.

"You're up early," he answers by way of greeting.

I'm out on the balcony, looking over a city still largely sleeping, the crisp air raising goose bumps on my bare arms. "Couldn't sleep. All this stuff is weighing on my mind, and I wanted to ask you something."

"Fire away."

"You said before you thought my stalker was a man, but you didn't exactly rule out a woman. Did you do a full check on my assistant, Calista?" I ask.

"I'm pretty sure we did, but let me just consult my file." I wait a few minutes as he walks to his home office and powers up his laptop. "Yep, we did a complete background check on her, and she came up clean. What has you reconsidering her?"

I had given him a brief rundown of my history with Calista when I handed over the list, so it doesn't take long to bring him up to speed on the latest events. "She seems to be getting clingier, and something is off about her. I can't put my finger on it. Call it a sixth sense, but could you dig a little deeper?"

"Consider it done."

The more time I spend with Dakota, the more my secrets eat away at me. It's cowardly to hold off telling her, so I promise myself on Monday that tonight's the night. "Hey," I say, as I sit with my arm around her in the cafeteria at lunchtime. "Do you want to take that rain check on dinner tonight?" I haven't had nearly enough time with her, and we haven't had any proper dates thanks to my desire to remain incognito around the town. But, if things are going to turn sour after I tell her everything tonight, I want to have many special memories to hold close to my heart.

"Sounds good. Count me in." She tweaks my nose and pecks my lips, and I can't help taking it further, holding onto her lips and drawing her into a deeper kiss.

"Some of us are trying to eat," Tabs pipes up. "So, cut that shit out. You're making me horny, and it's killing my appetite."

Dakota and I break apart, sharing grins. There is never a dull moment with Tabs around. You never know what's likely to come out of her mouth.

"You're relentlessly horny," Elsa retorts. "That's not anything new."

"Once you get a taste of cock, you'll understand," Tabs replies with a salacious wink. "Cock is my crack cocaine."

"Oh my God." Dakota busts out laughing, kissing Tabs on the cheek. "You, my friend, are one of a kind."

Tabs sends her a cheeky smile as I stand. "I've got a few things to do, but I'll come by to pick you up at seven." I tell Dakota, before pressing my mouth to her ear. "Wear something sexy."

"I will if you will." There's a naughty glint in her eye.

"Challenge accepted, Kota baby." I capture her lips in mine, kissing her passionately, uncaring we have an audience. When I break the kiss, we're both flushed and breathing erratically. Kissing this girl is like kissing a piece of heaven. I can hardly bear to leave her, but I want to get things set up for tonight. I'm only going to get one chance to do this, and I want to do it right.

I caress her cheek. "See you later, beautiful."

"Bye, babe." She blows me a kiss, and I'm still grinning by the time I reach my apartment.

A few hours later, I'm freshly showered and wearing clean jeans, standing in front of my closet wondering which shirt Dakota would find sexiest when my cell pings. Glancing at my watch, I'm tempted to ignore Devin's call, but it could be urgent.

"'Sup?" I answer, putting my cell on speaker so I can rifle through my shirts as we speak.

"We need to get to L.A. asap. I've organized a private plane for you, and my guys will escort you to the airport. How fast can you be ready?"

"Wait here a sec. What's going on? Why do I need to return to L.A. at such short notice?" The words rush out of my mouth as a horrible sense of foreboding creeps over me.

"There's no easy way to say this, Shawn, so I'm just going to lay it all out. Your stalker has struck again only this time you weren't the intended target."

Everything locks up inside me as I guess where this is going. "No!" I slump to the ground, shaking all over. "Please tell me it's not my family."

"It's your mom, Shawn. You need to come straightaway."

Chapter 26

Shawn/Levi

"Is she...is she still alive?" I force the words out of my mouth. My chest tightens to the point of pain.

"She's okay, Shawn," Devin placates me, and I release the breath I'd been holding. "She's traumatized after the experience, and medics are checking her out as we speak. I only know the basics thanks to an old police buddy of mine. He transferred to L.A. a couple of years back, and he's been assigned to the case. He called me the instant officers arrived at the scene."

I close my eyes, offering up thanks to a God I've long ignored. Then I'm on the move as I ask Devin exactly what happened, pulling on a shirt and toeing on my sneakers as I make my way out to the kitchen.

"Your stepfather had taken the boys away for the night on a camping trip, and your mother was returning alone to the house when she was ambushed at the front door by three men wearing masks. They brought her into the house, tied her up, and subjected her to a battery of questions about you. They wanted to know where you were hiding out."

"Fuck." I slam my fist into the wall as knots of guilt twist and turn in my stomach. "Is it the same three who broke into my house?"

"Looks like it."

"Shit. This is all my fault."

"This isn't on you, Shawn. You didn't ask for this." He pauses briefly. "Look, we'll talk on the plane. Just get in the car with my guys, and I'll meet you at the airport. We'll know more when we get to L.A., but your mom is okay. She's very shaken up, but she's okay," he continues to reassure me.

"Okay. See you in a bit." I kill the call, grab my wallet, keys, and jacket, and hightail it out of there.

I sit in the car with my head in my hands the entire journey. All I can think is if something serious had happened to Mom while we weren't speaking I would never ever have forgiven myself. All the shit that's gone down between us pales into insignificance in light of the situation. Tears sting my eyes as I struggle to hold it together. Images of Mom and me when I was a little kid flit through my mind, and I wish I had a magic wand and I could be there with her already, pulling her into my arms and telling her how sorry I am for all the shit I've put her through.

"How badly do you want a drink right now?" Devin asks once we're strapped into our seats on the private jet waiting to take off.

"So fucking badly I'd almost kill for it."

"I hear you, man, but it wouldn't take away the pain, and you'd feel like complete shit after."

"I know, and I'm not going to cave, but times like this are hard."

"I can relate." I know he can, and it helps having him here in more ways than one.

"Shit!" I look at my watch as the plane starts moving,

cursing again. "I fucking forgot about my date with Dakota. She's got to be wondering where I am." I pull out my cell and tap out a quick text, explaining I've had to go back to L.A. at short notice and I'll be back as soon as I can, promising I'll tell her everything and make it up to her. I repocket my cell and grip the armrests as the plane takes off into the air. "You still have someone watching over Dakota, right?"

"Twenty-four-seven," Devin confirms. "Don't worry. Nothing will happen to her while you're gone."

The three-hour plane ride seems to drag on forever, and I'm a complete basket case by the time we land in Los Angeles.

Luke is waiting at the side of the runway, lounging against a blacked-out SUV. Walking to meet me, he pulls me into a silent bear hug, squeezing me tight. We break apart and get into the car without a word. Tires squeal as the car speeds away from the airport. "How is she?" I ask, anguish lacing my tone. "Have you spoken to her?"

"Very briefly. All she did was ask for you. Repeatedly. I told her you were on your way." He pats my arm. "Your momma needs you Shawn."

"I know you're worried and on edge right now," Devin butts in, "but we have to consider this could be a trap to lure you out of hiding. I booked the jet in false names, and my police buddy will keep a team of men outside your mom's while you're there, but you need to stay inside the house and keep away from the windows."

"Whatever," I snap. "I just want to see my mom."

My nails are bitten to the bone by the time we pull up to Mom's Malibu house. My nerves are strung tight, and I clench and unclench my hands as we glide slowly up the drive. Cops guard the entrance to the house, and right now I'm so fucking grateful for Devin and his connections.

Devin throws a blanket over my head and only lets me out

of the SUV once he's conversed with his friend and checked to ensure the coast is clear. I'm bundled out of the car and into the house.

"Shawn! Shawn!" Mom's anguished cries are like a knife through my chest, but my heart soars at the same time too. It's been too long.

"Mom!" I holler, racing down the hall and into the living room. The family photos that used to line the walls in the hallway lie in broken shards on the tiled floor, and I have to weave a path around the debris to get to her. Most of the rooms are trashed, furniture overturned and drawers upended, as if an earthquake had struck. But I know this was the work of those assholes. I run into the living room, and my breath stutters in my chest.

Mom is propped up on the couch with a myriad of cushions at her back. Her legs are outstretched with a blanket thrown over her. One arm is in a sling, and her lower lip is swollen and cut, and a large purple bruise is on her right cheek. She has clearly looked better, but she is still a sight for sore eyes. I don't think I've realized quite how much I've missed her until this moment.

"Mom!" My voice is strangled, and tears sting the back of my eyes as I walk toward her.

"Shawn!" She bursts out crying, and I sink to my knees in front of her, hugging her gently, mindful of her injured arm. She sobs on my shoulder, and her whole body is wracked in pain. "I'm so glad you're here," she whimpers in between bouts of crying. "I was so afraid I wouldn't see you again. Wouldn't get to tell you how sorry I am for everything."

"Sh, Mom." I smooth a hand over her long blonde hair. "You have nothing to apologize for. I'm the one who caused all this, and I'm more sorry than you could know. If anything had happened to you or Steve or the boys, I would never have forgiven myself."

"Shawn, baby, let me look at you." Her tears dry up as she lifts her head, cupping my face. "You look so different," she says, scrutinizing my altered look, "but every bit as handsome." She kisses one cheek and then the other. "I have missed you so much. It's felt like part of my soul is missing."

"Mom." I'm trying my best to hold back tears. "I have missed you all to death. I was planning on visiting and making amends, but I wanted this crazy caught first because I didn't want to drag you into this mess." I press my forehead to hers. "I thought because we were estranged that they'd leave you alone. I'm so sorry, Mom. Please tell me you're okay." I lean back and check her face. "Did they hurt you in places I can't see?"

She shakes her head. "No, honey. It's nothing like that. They wanted to know where you were. Every time they asked me and I said I didn't know, they hit me. I'm glad you didn't tell me and that my neighbors noticed the suspicious man in my yard and called the cops, because I don't know what would've happened otherwise."

"How badly do you hurt?"

"It's not that bad, sweetheart." She takes my hand. "My shoulder is dislocated, but the medics gave me painkillers and strapped it up. My face is a little sore, but it should heal in a few days. It could've been a lot worse."

"Did they take much stuff?" I ask, looking around the strewn room.

She shakes her head. "Most of our valuables are in the safe, and they didn't find that. They took any spare cash I had lying around, but that's all."

"I hate that this happened to you, and if I ever get my hands on those responsible, they'll have me up for murder." Devin coughs very loudly, subtly motioning at the cops keeping watch in the room. His expression cautions me, and I try to rein my anger in. Luke has made himself busy in the kitchen, and he appears now, carrying a tray with coffees, offering them around.

I refocus on Mom, and it's so unbelievably good to see her. "My security guy is here with me, and he's going to assign a team to protect you and the boys in case they have plans to come back. He already sent a car to bring Steve and the twins back. They should be here soon."

Devin steps forward then, extending his hand. "I'm Devin Morgan, head of Morgan Security. It's nice to meet you, Mrs. Allen, although I wish it were under more pleasant circumstances. I'm glad you weren't seriously hurt."

"Nice to meet you too," Mom says, shaking his hand. Her cheeks flush lightly, and I have to smother a chuckle. Devin's pretty easy on the eye, and I didn't miss how Dakota had a similar reaction to him. If he was my age, I'd be jealous as hell, but he's way too old for my girl, and he's happily married, so jealousy is a pointless emotion. "You've been looking after my boy?"

Devin nods. "We have, ma'am."

"Thank you." Tears glisten in her eyes. "He's very precious to me. Please keep him safe."

"Nothing will happen to your son on my watch. You have my word."

"Thank you. That's reassuring."

"Mom, you shouldn't be worrying about me."

"I'm your mother." She squeezes my hand. "It's my job to worry. It doesn't matter how old you are, I will *always* worry about you." She swings her legs around, patting the space beside her. "Now sit up here, sweet boy, and tell me everything that's going on in your life."

I sit beside her with my arm around her waist, filling her in.

"When will I get to meet this special girl?" she asks, smiling after I've finished telling her about Dakota.

"Hopefully, when all this is over. Provided she's still by my side."

"Only a fool would let you go," Mom loyally replies.

"Only a mother would say such a thing," I tease.

"I know you're worried how she's going to react, but if she's as special as you say she is, then she'll understand."

"That's what Ange said. Devin's wife," I add before she can ask the question.

"Well, Mrs. Morgan sounds every bit as intelligent as her husband."

"Oh, she's way more intelligent than me," Devin says, not even pretending that he wasn't eavesdropping.

"Mommy!" A childish voice screams, and the pitter-patter of little feet grows louder until the twins appear in the room. "Shawn!" Noah shouts, Mom all but forgotten when he spots me. He flings himself into my arms, and I laugh, grabbing him into a fierce hug.

"Hey there, little buddy." I hug the shit out of him as he wriggles in my arms. "I missed you so much."

My other brother, Connor, wraps himself around my leg, smiling shyly at me. He's a lot more introverted than Noah, but I'm glad that both of them still remember me. I haven't seen them in person in a good while, but I've spoken with them over Skype and FaceTime because I didn't want them to forget me.

Steve has Mom enveloped in his arms, and the tormented expression on his face is good to see. Not that I've ever doubted his love for her, but it's good to know things haven't changed in my absence. That he's been taking care of them.

I swap the twins out, taking time to hug Connor too.

"Shawn." Steve clamps a hand on my shoulder. "Thank you for coming. You don't know how much your mother has missed you."

"About as much as I've missed her," I reply. "Missed all of you. For what it's worth, I'm sorry for all the pain I've caused and all that sh—stuff is a thing of the past."

"I'm very happy to hear it."

The boys are hugging Mom a little too energetically, and she winces. Steve bends down. "Boys, Mom has a sore arm, so we need to be very careful with her. Why don't you give her a kiss goodnight and you'll see her in the morning?"

"I want Shawn to bring me to bed," Noah says, pouting. Steve looks to me.

"I would love that," I confirm.

"How about I tuck you up into bed and then Shawn can come read you a story?" Steve suggests, and my brothers jump up and down.

Devin is smiling fondly at the boys, and we exchange a knowing look.

Steve leaves with the boys, and Mom turns to me. "Are you staying the night?"

I look to Devin and he nods, letting me know it's my call. "I'd like that Mom, but I'll probably have to leave by lunchtime tomorrow."

"I understand." She rests her head on my shoulder, and I carefully slide my arm around her back. "But I'm not ready to let you go just yet."

I hold her close while trying to eavesdrop on Devin's conversation with his police buddy, but they are whispering, and I can't hear what's being said. After they stop talking, I look over at Devin. "We have plenty of spare guestrooms, so you and your men can help yourselves."

"And I've just ordered some takeout," Steve says, returning to the room. "I'm sure everyone has to be hungry."

"Thank you. We appreciate it," Devin says.

"The boys are waiting for you, Shawn." Steve squeezes my shoulder, and I stand.

Luke steps forward. "I'm going to head home, Shawn, but I'll be back here first thing in the morning. Call if you need anything. Anything at all."

"Thanks, man."

He leans over to hug Mom, and I exit the room, taking the stairs to the upper floor two at a time. It's been a long time since I've helped put my brothers to bed. I can't believe how much they've grown, and I'm determined not to miss out on any more of their lives going forward.

My steps falter as I spot one of my guitars resting against the wall outside the twin's bedroom. I used to play to them when they were smaller, when Mom called on my services to help settle them at night. I've missed this.

I know Steve left it there, and it only reinforces what a good man he is. A good father and husband, and I know he'd be a good stepfather if I let him.

That's another thing I'm going to rectify.

I want to get to know Mom's husband; to form a proper relationship with him. Every time he's tried, I've kept him at arm's length. Getting to know Devin these last couple months has helped open my eyes. Since Gramps died, I've had no male role model in my life and it's good to have someone I can trust to talk to. Devin's been more like an older brother, but I know Steve would be there for me, as a father, if I asked him to.

I slide the guitar strap over my shoulder and step into the twin's room. It's been redecorated since I was last here. "Someone's a fan of the Avengers, huh?" I ask, chuckling as I count all the

Avengers-themed items in the room. Mom has a tendency to go a little overboard on things, but I know it's because we didn't have a lot when I was growing up, and it's nice that she can indulge now. Although she's never flippant or wasteful about money. Years spent counting pennies does that to a person, I guess.

I sit on the bed beside Noah and pat the other side of me for Connor. "Come over here, buddy."

"I'm gonna be Thor when I grow up," Noah says.

"And I'm gonna be The Hulk," my other brother says.

"Who will I be?" I ask.

"Duh," Noah says, chuckling. "You can't be anyone."

"Why not?"

"'Cause you're already grown up, silly."

I mess their hair, chuckling. "That's too bad. I've always seen myself as The Cap."

"Are you gonna play your guitar?" Connor asks, peering up at me with these wide innocent eyes.

"That's the plan. If you like?"

"Yes, yes." Noah jumps up, clapping his hands.

"Okay." I chuckle again. "Snuggle into me and close your eyes, and I'll play you some songs."

I close my eyes too and start playing, softly singing so as to create an ambience suitable for sleeping. Their small bodies crush into my side, and when their tiny hands rest on my chest, I feel a surge of emotion so strong my voice cracks and I mess up the words, but they don't notice because, when I open my eyes, both my brothers are already fast asleep.

I study them while they're sleeping, marveling at all the ways they've changed, and I know I'd do anything to protect these little dudes.

A gentle sob alerts me to her presence and I look up. Mom is standing in the doorway, in her pajamas, with tears in her eyes while she watches us.

Carefully extracting myself from the bed, I tuck the boys in, leaving them to sleep in the same bed, and tiptoe out of the room. I place my guitar against the wall, and then Mom pulls me into a hug, and I close my eyes, breathing her in. The only other time I've felt this deep sense of contentment is when I'm holding Dakota in my arms.

"Shit," I whisper, shucking out of Mom's embrace. "I need to check my cell. To make sure Dakota is okay."

"I put your jacket in your room. Why don't you check in with her and then come to my room? I'll have some food brought up, and we can chat some more in there."

I nod, kissing her cheek as I make my way to my old bedroom. I close the door, deliberately ignoring the pang of nostalgia as I step into the room and pull out my cell.

My heart plummets to my toes when I see the undelivered text from earlier. "Fucckk!" I flop down on the bed, groaning. We were just about to take off when I sent it to her, so it mustn't have sent before the signal died. I was too absorbed in getting to Mom on the ride from the airport to even think about checking.

Judging from the multitude of missed calls and texts, I can tell she's worried, although the last few are angrier in tone.

Fuck. I hold my head in my hands, and my heart aches. She must think I stood her up. After all that shit with Calista last weekend, this is the last thing she needed.

I check my watch, noting it's almost two a.m. back in Iowa. She might still be up. I take a chance and call her number, but there's no answer. Not wanting to leave this any longer, I send her a text.

I'm so sorry baby. Had 2 head back 2 L.A. 2 deal with emergency. Only just noticed the text I sent u didn't deliver. I'll explain everything when

I'm back. Sorry if u were worried. I'll call u l8r. Sweet dreams.

I head to Mom's room with a heavy heart, pissed that I let Dakota down so badly tonight and hoping she'll give me a chance to explain.

Mom and I stay up for another couple of hours eating pizza and talking through all the crap from the last couple of years. I tell her how sorry I am for not listening to her about my bio dad, and for letting him drive a wedge between us, and she explains how she had to resign as my manager because she couldn't watch me self-destructing anymore.

Thing is, I know she did the right thing.

And she found Luke. She ensured I was in very capable hands. Mom was never cut out to be a celebrity manager, and I know she struggled with the scene, so the fact she stuck by my side for so long tells me how much she loved me. I put her through hell with all the girls, drink, and drugs, and I pushed her away when she met Steve and had the twins, convinced she didn't need me anymore.

Now that I've come out the other side of things, I can see how selfish and immature I was.

And how very wrong.

Everything she has said and done tonight shows me how much she loves me, and, deep down, I've always known it.

It was Mom and me against the world for so long, and we have a strong bond.

One that can survive separation and cruel, harsh words that were untrue.

I'm glad we hashed it all out, that we've reconnected, and that I'll have my family back in my life again.

Devin is assigning a new team to stay here and watch over them, and as I return to Iowa the following afternoon, I know the time has arrived to come clean with Dakota. I can't continue to keep her in the dark, not when the threat has become all too real.

I'm terrified I'm going to lose her, but keeping her safe is more important than my own selfish wants and needs, and I continuously remind myself of that fact as I make my way back to her.

Chapter 27

Dakota

When Levi didn't show at seven, I wasn't all that worried. He's usually late, so I didn't sweat it. When seven thirty turned into eight, I started to become concerned. That's when I began calling him. His cell went straight to voicemail, so I texted him, over and over again. When I hadn't heard anything by nine, I walked over to his place, terrified the entire time I would find him lying unconscious or something. But his place was empty.

I checked every room, and that's when I found the recording studio, and knots formed in my stomach.

I'm the first to admit I know very little about the music industry. I've an eclectic taste in music, and I've never been obsessed with any one band or artist. In fact, I've only been to a few open-air events. But as I take in the small room with the obviously expensive technical equipment, I'm pretty sure this isn't the norm for session musicians. And he didn't mention a word to me about it, which I find weird as he plays his guitar every night while I dance, and he's shown some of his work to me. I'm not one to pry, and I thought the other closed doors were bedrooms, so this has come as a shock. *Why would he hide this from me?*

A veil of uncertainty shrouds me. I know he's been holding parts of himself back from me, but now I'm wondering if it's bigger than that. I can't put my finger on it, but something just feels off now about the whole thing.

I hang around his place for an hour, and then worry becomes rage.

He stood me up.

And he didn't even have the decency to call or text me.

It's not typical for him, and maybe I should give him the benefit of the doubt, but after that bitch showed up here last week, I've been on edge. I told him I believed him, and I do, or I did, but now I'm not so sure.

Has he been playing me all along?

All I know is something happened tonight, and whatever it was, I obviously didn't feature high enough on his list of priorities to even warrant consideration.

After Cole, I swore no guy was going to treat me like shit again.

Yet here I sit.

I get up and leave my key to his place on the counter, slamming the door shut behind me.

I'm still in a foul mood when I wake the following morning, after very little sleep. I purposely didn't answer his call at two a.m., and while his text did calm me a little, I'm not sure I believe him. *Am I so unimportant that he only thought to check his cell seven hours after he apparently sent me a text?* All I know is if I had an emergency, he'd be the first person I'd think to call. I sure as shit wouldn't forget about him for hours on end.

He's not in class, and I don't see him around the business school all day. The girls are tiptoeing around me, afraid to say the wrong thing, and I know I'm a crabby bitch, but I'm seriously pissed at myself for letting another guy pull the wool over my eyes. He's called my cell a bunch of other times, but I continue to ignore him.

Let him know what it feels like.

As if this day couldn't get any worse, Mikayla accosts me as I leave the building after my last class of the day. I have a pounding headache, and she's the last person I want to see. "Get lost," I snap before she's even opened her mouth. I stride ahead, setting off in the direction of my dorm.

She runs after me. "You stupid bitch, you couldn't leave things alone, could you?"

"If this is about Cole breaking up with you, that had nothing to do with me."

"Don't fucking lie," she yells, grabbing my elbow and stalling me.

"I'm not lying and get your filthy back-stabbing hands off me."

"Me?! What about you?" she screeches, throwing the full weight of her resting bitch face behind her words.

"If you're asking if I've been messing around with Cole behind your back, the answer is no. Why the fuck would I want your sloppy seconds?"

She snorts. "Are you really this clueless?"

I rub a tense spot between my brows. "I've had a shitty fucking day, and I'm in no mood for this, but I'm sick of you and Cole confronting me when I want nothing to do with either of you, so if you've got something to say, spit it out."

"You stole him from me in the first place!"

I look at her like she's grown ten heads. "What the hell are you talking about?"

"I told you I liked him, and you went and dated him without any consideration for my feelings!"

"Oh my God, Kayla, that was second grade! And you never mentioned Cole to me again. Seriously, you expected me to remember a passing crush when you were eight and to turn Cole down when he asked *me* out seven years later? Do you even hear how crazy you sound?"

"You could've asked me before you said yes!" she spits back, nostrils flaring.

"Like you asked me every time some guy asked you out? Get real. You are fabricating shit to try and justify the fact you betrayed me. And, guess what? I don't actually give a flying fuck anymore. You are welcome to Cole. I don't want him!" I push past her. "And I'm done with this conversation. Leave me alone, or I'll report you to security for harassment."

I am fuming the whole way home. I just want to get into my pajamas, crawl into bed with a tub of ice cream, and wallow in my heartache.

But when I step foot into my dorm, I'm shocked to find Levi sitting on the couch talking to Daisy. He doesn't usually come here, and she's only met him once. Jumping up, she looks sheepish, her cheeks turning red. "I, ah, hope you don't mind, but he was waiting out in the hall when I arrived."

I glare at her, letting her know that yes, *I do fucking mind.* I'm still furious with him and not ready to talk. Wisely, she scurries to the bedroom, shutting the door behind her.

I move to the front door and open it. "Get out. I don't want you here, and I don't want to talk to you." I'm still all fired up from my confrontation with Mikayla, and I'm in no mood for going another round with him.

"Kota, baby, pl—"

"Don't call me that!" I interrupt him. "And I don't want to hear your pathetic excuses. Just answer me this. Were you with her? The redhead? Were you fucking her and that's why you forgot I existed?"

"Jesus! No! I told you about Calista. She means nothing to me. I wasn't with her."

"I wish I could believe that."

He cautiously steps around the couch, standing in front of me. "I know you're mad, and you have every right to be, but I can explain."

"Mad?" I yell. "I am so beyond mad there isn't even a fucking word in existence that describes how I'm feeling. You weren't answering your cell, and I couldn't get a hold of you. I thought you had crashed your car or you were lying unconscious on the floor at your place! I honestly thought something horrible had happened to you because I knew you wouldn't just stand me up without telling me. Every step closer I got to your apartment building was a step closer to that night." An errant sob escapes my mouth. "I thought the worst had happened to you. I was petrified opening the door to your place. So scared I'd find you in a pool of your own blood. Do you have any idea what that did to me?"

I double over, clutching my waist as everything I felt the night I heard about Layla's murder comes flooding back.

"I'm so sorry, Dakota. I didn't even stop to think about that. I was on a plane when I sent you a text, and I didn't realize it hadn't sent until hours later. I would never intentionally stand you up. Never. Or do anything to hurt you."

"Well, you have," I hiss. "And I want you to go. I can't do this."

"Please, Dakota." He moves to touch my face, but I pull back.

"Please, go, Levi." Looking at him hurts too much right now. Everything hurts, and I need to be alone.

His eyes glimmer with sadness and regret as he nods. "I'll

go, but only because you clearly need some time. But I'll be back. And this doesn't change any of my feelings. You're still the most important person in my world."

I look down at the ground, not willing to let his face and his words take this from me. My head is a mess right now, and I need to be alone to work out how I feel.

I don't watch as he walks out, but I feel him move past me, and every ounce of my being strains toward him, but I deny my body and my heart and close the door behind him.

It feels prophetic.

The rest of the week passes by with no word from him, and that only pisses me off more. I know I told him to stay away, but I secretly wanted him to fight for me. The fact he has made no effort to call me or speak to me during class and that he acts as if I don't exist whenever we bump into each other on campus only infuriates me more. He hasn't shown up on the roof any night this week, although I've secretly hoped he's been watching me.

Ugh. I'm a complete mess, and my emotions are veering all over the place. I honestly don't know what to think or what I want.

The girls have tried talking to me, telling me to speak to him, to at least find out what he has to say, but what's the point?

If I meant anything to him, he would have tried harder.

And I hate this constant ache in my heart, and I know it only would've been worse if I'd gotten more attached. But, God, do I miss him. I miss him so much.

Now that he's not there to distract me, I've had no choice but to turn my thoughts to my future. I have no interest in accountancy, and I'm only getting up and going to class each day because otherwise the temptation to stay in bed licking my wounds is too strong. I saw how quickly Mom sank into depression, and it'd be too easy for me to do that too. But I'm not letting some guy push me over the edge, even if I had been harboring dreams of him being that special someone.

I don't know what I want to do with my life, and I don't think I've ever felt this restless, or so lost and alone.

A small crowd blocks the entrance to our building when I return home, after dark, Saturday night. Daisy and I have just been to the movies with Elsa and Tabs. They staged an intervention, ganging up on me, insisting on dragging me out for a few hours. I even surprised myself by enjoying it.

The strumming of a guitar stops me dead in my tracks. Daisy gasps when the crowd parts and Levi steps forward. Butterflies scatter in my chest, and my heart starts thumping wildly as his eyes lock on mine.

"Once upon a time, I came to Iowa and met a girl," Levi says, speaking loudly, almost as if he wants the growing crowd to hear him. "Not just any girl. A girl so unique she turned my world upside down." He steps a little closer, softly strumming the guitar. "A girl who has awoken the part of myself I thought I'd lost. A girl who made me realize all the things worth cherishing in this life, including her. I'm not always able to say the things I want to say, so I wrote her a song to show her how much she means to me."

He stops playing for a moment, reaching out and touching my face. "To make her understand she still means all that to me, even though I was an ass and I let her down in the worst way." He steps back, lovingly stroking the strings of his guitar as the melody to my song reverberates around us. His eyes drill into mine. "I sang this for you before because I needed you to hear me. Now, I'll sing it from the rooftops so everyone can hear and know how precious you are to me. Damn the fucking consequences. I want you and everyone to understand how much you mean to me, babe. You're my world, Dakota. This is for you."

Chapter 28

Shawn/Levi

This is fucking risky. Luke will kick my ass. Devin will kick my ass. Mom will kick my ass. But I don't know how else to get through to my girl. I know I told her I'd give her space, but I thought she'd come running back into my arms within a few hours, once her anger and hurt had faded, but it's been four days.

Four days that feels like four years.

I never stopped to consider how my non-appearance that night would affect her. I hate that I brought her grief to the surface, but it also proved, without a shadow of a doubt, that she loves me as much as I love her.

And I can't let that go.

Desperate times call for desperate measures.

I need to remind her how I feel about her, and I figured publicly serenading her is one way of ensuring I get through to her.

Even if the risk of discovery is greater once people hear me sing.

But I don't care about that now. I just need to get Dakota to speak to me again, so I can tell her everything.

She'll either dump my lying ass and I'll fuck off back to L.A. with a broken heart.

Or she'll stick with me and hopefully agree to come live with me in L.A.

Either way, I've decided over the course of the last few days that I'm not fucking hiding anymore.

I'm done with this asshole stalker dictating how my life plays out.

I need to be back in L.A. to be near my family, and I've got more than enough new songs to form an album which should keep the label happy.

The only thing left to work out is my relationship with Dakota.

I'm not leaving without her, I tell myself as I start singing her song. I keep my eyes locked on her beautiful face as I put my heart on the line. The crowd mushrooms in size, but I barely notice because I can't look away from the girl who has captured my heart and soul. Tears glisten in her eyes as I sing to her, pouring emotion into every word that leaves my lips.

When I'm finished, the crowd erupts into applause, but the only reaction I care about is hers.

Removing my guitar, I place it on the ground and approach her cautiously. "I'm so sorry, Dakota, but I meant everything I said to you tonight and every other night." Tears still linger in her eyes, but she's smiling. "I didn't know how else to get you to see." I cup her face, and she lifts her hand, placing it over mine. Throwing caution to the wind, I press my mouth to her ear and whisper, "I love you. I love you too much to lose you."

She sucks in a sharp breath, and I peer into her eyes.

"Do you mean that?" she whispers, pressing her body in closer to mine, sheltering our words from the nosy crowd.

"With all my heart."

With tears in her eyes, she stretches up on tiptoe and presses her lips to mine. A heady warmth invades every inch of my body, heating me from the inside. The kiss is soft and sweet and filled with so much promise. She pulls back, peering into my eyes as she whispers, "I love you too."

I gulp over the swelling of emotion in my throat, clutching her to me and hugging her fiercely. A few bystanders are shrieking and hollering, and now I wish they'd all just fade away.

"Can we get out of here?" she pleads. "As much as I loved that bold public display of affection, I need to have you to myself."

"Of course. Are you okay to come back to mine? There's lots I need to tell you."

She nods. "Let me just tell Daisy."

I pick up my guitar, watching as she hurries over to Daisy. The crowd has quickly dispersed, and most people are gone. A few girls hover around me, telling me how incredible that was and how lucky my girl is, but I barely notice them as I watch Dakota and Daisy's interaction. Daisy is staring off into space, nodding absently at whatever Dakota is saying. Then her head jerks up, and she notices me watching. Her cheeks flush red, and a look of shocked awe appears on her face.

Fuck. I think she's just figured it out.

"Let me tell her," I mouth across the gap between us, and Daisy subtly nods, gulping visibly.

"Well, that was weird," Dakota says, reappearing at my side.

"What, babe?" I ask, gratefully tucking her into my side.

"Daisy is all spaced out and acting strange, and I have no clue why."

"Was my singing that bad?" I joke.

She pokes me in the ribs as we walk out to the street where my SUV is parked. "You know that's a virtual impossibility. You sing beautifully."

I help her into the car, locking the guitar in the trunk. "Are you hungry?" I ask, as I kickstart the engine.

"Only for you."

I flash her a wide grin. "I've missed you."

"I've missed you too."

"And I'm really sorry about Monday. You've got to believe I would never intentionally stand you up or purposely ignore you. After I've explained, it will all make sense."

"It's okay. I believe you."

"You do?" I maneuver the car out into the traffic.

"Yeah. Anyone that makes such a massive public demonstration is worthy of my belief and my trust."

Shit. I really fucking hope that's true, because I want to be worthy of her trust and her forgiveness.

"Why do you look so nervous?" she asks.

"Because the things I have to tell you aren't going to be easy to hear, and I'm afraid you're going to want nothing to do with me."

She squeezes my knee. "I'm too invested and too selfish to give you up."

I pray to God that's true.

My hands are shaking as I open the door to my penthouse. The instant the door is locked, Dakota shoves me up against it, slamming her lips down on mine. Her tongue swirls into my mouth, and blood rushes straight to my dick, hardening it instantly. With huge reluctance, I break the kiss, panting as I attempt to draw a breath. Dakota grinds against me and I moan. "Baby, we need to talk."

She runs her hands up my chest, locking them behind my neck, and peers into my eyes. "I know we do. I need to hear what you have to say, and I have questions of my own, but they can wait till morning because I need something else from you right now." She rocks against my hard-on making her intentions clear.

"I need to get this off my chest, beautiful, and you're not making this easy."

"And you will," she says, stretching up to kiss me. "But not now. I need you to make love to me, Levi. Like you did the last time. I need to remember what it feels like to have your touch sear me from the inside. Please."

Aw, fuck it. I know we need to have this talk now, but how the hell can I resist her. Maybe she senses it too. That this conversation is going to change everything, and she wants to have this night to pretend like nothing is going to change.

I lift her up, and she wraps her legs around my waist as I walk us to my bedroom. She plants a trail of hot kisses on my face and neck as we move, and I drink in everything about her, committing it all to memory in case this is the last time I get to experience this with her.

My hands caress her beautiful body as I help her out of her clothes, and then it's her turn to explore as she undresses me. We don't talk. We just share silken touches and soft kisses, and then she's underneath me, writhing and moaning as I worship her all over. I watch her detonate as a powerful orgasm rockets through her body, and she's the most mesmerizing creature on the planet. Suiting up, I slide into her slowly, welcoming the way she squeezes my cock as I start to move inside her.

"I love you," I whisper in between kisses as I carefully make love to her.

Her fingers wind through my hair, and she pierces me with an intense look. "I love you too. So much it physically hurts sometimes."

Her words fill me with hope, and I capture her lips in mine, kissing her deeply. Her hands roam my body as we rock against one another, kissing and moaning as wave after wave of pleasure builds until it peaks, and we both tumble together.

After we've cleaned up, I hold her in my arms, pressing kisses to the top of her head, her cheek, her neck, wanting to kiss her forever. We don't speak. We know it's coming, but, for now, we both want to pause time, to have this one special night. I pray it's the first of many and not the last one I'll ever enjoy with her in my arms.

Sun is streaming through the open window early the next morning when Dakota's cell starts vibrating. We stir at the same time, and she reaches out for it, her hand fumbling along the top of the bedside table as she tries to focus through blurry eyes. Grabbing the phone, she holds it up to her face, squinting. Then she bolts upright, and I immediately tense up, warning bells firing on all cylinders.

"What's wrong? Is my mom okay?" she answers, panic evident in her tone.

I sit up, rubbing sleep from my eyes as I fight a yawn.

"Okay. I'll leave straightaway." Ending the call, she flings the covers off and starts picking her clothes up from the floor.

I get up, walk around the bed and place my hands on her shoulders, forcing her face up to mine. "What's going on?"

Tears well in her eyes. "My mom had a seizure, and they've taken her by ambulance to the hospital."

I pull her into my arms, hugging the shit out of her. "I'm so sorry. I'll drive you."

"Thanks." Her voice is strained as we pull apart and silently get dressed.

I'm just grabbing my keys from the kitchen counter when

my cell pings. "It's Devin," I tell her. "I just need to take this." I slip out onto the balcony and accept his call. "I can't talk now, Devin. I need to—"

"Your cover is blown," he says, cutting across me. "That stunt you pulled last night has gone viral."

"Shit!" I kick at the legs of the wicker end table in frustration. I thought I had a least twenty-four hours before I was outed. Enough time to tell Dakota the truth. But I can't rush to tell her now, and I can't hold her here, not when she needs to be with her mom. "This is the worst fucking timing ever, but there's nothing I can do about it now. I need to drive Dakota to the hospital. She just got a call that her mom had a seizure."

"I'm really sorry to hear that, but you can't drive her. Hordes of reporters have already descended on the city, and it's only a matter of time before they find you. She doesn't need that kind of attention on her or her mother."

"This is a fucking mess!" I yell.

"Calm down. I'll message my guy and get him to drive her to and from the hospital. He'll keep her safe."

I hate not going with her, but Devin is right. She doesn't need the additional worry or distraction. If someone spots me and tells her who I am before I've had a chance to tell her myself, all hell will break loose. I hope no one calls her with the news before she comes back. I guess I'll just have to take that risk. There's nothing I can do about it now. "I need to talk to her."

"Take five and call me back. We have other stuff to discuss."

I hang up without responding and walk back inside. "Baby, I'm really sorry but another emergency has popped up, and I'm not going to be able to drive you."

Hurt flickers in her eyes, and I move in, holding her face firmly. "I love you, and I want to be there for you, but I can't.

This is all tied up with what I need to tell you. I should've told you last night, but it'll have to wait until you come back. I have a guy downstairs to drive you there and back. He'll keep you safe. In the meantime, I need you to promise me something." Her sorrowful eyes meet mine. "Do not look at social media until you return. Promise me, Dakota." I press a kiss to her lips.

"You're freaking me out even more than that phone call did," she admits, breaking my heart.

"I'm sorry, but I just need you to trust me." I kiss her again. "I love you, and everything I've told you is true." I pull her hand to my chest, right over my heart. "You know the real me. You understand me better than most people. Don't forget that." She nods, and I can see her fighting to hold onto the truth in her heart. "You better go. Your mom needs you." I kiss her on the forehead. "I'll be here for you when you get back."

Chapter 29

Shawn/Levi

I walk her downstairs, and Devin's guy is waiting in the lobby. He nods at me, and I bundle Dakota up in my arms. "I wish I was going with you, baby, but you're in safe hands."

The dude steps forward, extending his hand. "I'm Tom. I'll be your escort to and from the hospital."

Dakota shakes his hand. "Thank you, Tom. I appreciate that."

She looks up at me with so many questions in her eyes. I kiss her again. "I'll tell you everything when you get back. Just don't...don't give up on me."

She stretches up on her tiptoes and kisses me. "I don't understand, but I trust you, and I love you. I'll see you later."

"Please keep her safe," I ask Tom, and he nods.

"You have my word, sir."

Dakota's brows lift but she says nothing, throwing a casual wave at me before getting into the car.

I return to my penthouse and call Devin. "Okay. Lay it on me."

"I think we've caught the stalker."

I can't believe my ears. "What? How?"

"I assigned a couple of guys to your house in the Hills, and they caught the same three intruders trying to break in again. They managed to overpower them and called the cops. They are currently under interrogation at the police station, and they're singing like canaries. Apparently, they were hired to break into your house and your mom's."

"Your theory was right," I tell him. "Do we have a name yet?"

"That's the interesting thing. The three goons say they'll give the stalker up but only to you."

"Fuck. Seriously?"

"Yes. The police need you there asap. I've chartered a plane. It leaves in ninety minutes. I've sent Mark to pick you up. I can't be there this time, but Mark will go with you, and I'll have another couple guys meet you in LAX."

"I can't leave yet, Devin. Dakota still doesn't know the truth."

"I thought you were telling her last night?"

"That was the plan, but she had other ideas, and we didn't exactly do much talking."

"Shit, Shawn. I know you don't want to leave without telling her, but this is too important to wait. If you don't show up soon, they may shut their mouths and refuse to give us the name. We need to put this guy behind bars, and that's the best way of keeping Dakota safe."

"Okay. Okay." I start frantically pacing the room. "I'll call her and let her know, but I want to return as soon as the shit is wrapped up at the station."

"Mark will organize it." He pauses for a second. "Look, I can come over and be there to talk to her when she returns, if you like."

"She doesn't even know I'm Shawn Lucas."

"She's going to find out, and most likely before you get back to tell her in person. I can help cushion the blow. Let her know you were trying to keep her safe and that you were planning on telling her everything."

"Why would you do that? It's not in your job description."

He sighs. "You're right. It's not. But you haven't been like any other client I've taken on. I don't invite people to my home, Shawn. I don't do stuff like this for them."

"Then why me?"

"Maybe it's because I see so much of myself in you or I'm just a big ole romantic at heart. Whatever it is, you're more than just a client. You're a friend, and I have your back on this if you want it."

I'm tempted to joke it off, because talking about feelings and shit doesn't come easy to me, especially not with dudes, but I can tell he's sincere, and I'm trying to turn over a new leaf, so I accept his hand of friendship. "Great, thanks, man. I know Dakota respects you, and hopefully you can keep her calm until I return."

"No problem. Now get ready and let's put this thing to bed."

I try calling Dakota several times on the way to the airport, but her cell is off. It's standard hospital policy, so I'm not that concerned. I could probably get Tom's number from Devin and call him, but if she's currently with her mom, I don't want to interrupt her. I leave her a long voicemail explaining I've been called back to L.A., but I will be back as soon as I can, and I'll tell her everything. I back it up with a text, in case anything should happen and she doesn't hear my voicemail.

I'm jumpy as hell the entire flight, and completely on edge. Wound up over the stalker and worried that I won't get to Dakota to explain in time.

Mark introduces me to two more of Devin's men when we step off the plane in L.A., and I'm shaking their hands when a horde of paparazzi rushes out of the main building. Quick as a flash, Luke appears, ushering me into the back of a waiting limo. "Fuck!" I yell, pressing my forehead into the headrest and closing my eyes in frustration.

"Good afternoon, sir," Calista formally greets me, and I jerk back in shock. Although I'm not too surprised to find her in the back seat, I *am* caught off guard by her professional tone, but in a pleasant way. Perhaps I won't have to fire her after all. I understand why she's here. I'm sure the label is freaking out over the video and is in damage control mode. I nod indifferently at her. "Calista."

"How much trouble am I in?" I ask Luke, leaning forward on my knees as the car smoothly takes off.

"Trouble?" He arches a brow. "I think you've misunderstood the situation."

"Enlighten me then."

"The label is ecstatic, Shawn. The video has over ten million views so far, and it's rapidly rising. Your fans are loving the new song, and the media speculation over the girl is crazy."

"They can't know who she is!" I drag my hands through my hair. *What the fuck was I thinking last night?* I wasn't, and that's the point. Now every asshole reporter in the country is going to be looking for my girl. And she still doesn't know I'm Shawn Lucas.

What a clusterfuck of epic proportions.

And it's all my fault for rushing into a grand gesture without properly considering the consequences. And for letting my dick rule my brain last night. I should have come clean and at least she'd be prepared. This is going to knock her off her feet, and I'm not even there to soften the blow.

"Relax, Romeo." Luke grins. "They don't want her name released. The mystery is adding to the hype."

"Until the timing is right, and then they'll want to throw her to the hounds," I snap, knowing exactly how this is going to pan out.

Luke looks sympathetic. "What did you think would happen when you serenaded her, Shawn?" He pats my knee. "It's one thing to disguise your face, but your voice isn't as easy to hide. You had to have known the risk."

"I didn't properly think it through, and I haven't even had time to come clean to her. She doesn't know I'm Shawn Lucas, and I need to get back to her as fast as possible today; otherwise, I have no chance of salvaging our relationship."

"You really care for her, don't you?"

I'm conscious of Calista typing away on her iPad but listening to every word. However, she needs to hear this too. Perhaps this will finally put an end to her delusional fantasies. "I love her, Luke. I love her like I've never loved any girl, and I plan to bring her back here with me."

If she doesn't kick me to the curb first.

He winces, and I know instantly I'm not going to like what he has to say next. "Shawn, I hate to be the one to tell you this, but you're not going back to Iowa. The label has booked tons of radio and TV appearances for you. They want to capitalize on the exposure, and they want you in the studio tomorrow. They're planning a rush release of the single, and they want to use it to build hype for the new album."

"You need to buy me a couple of days, man. Let me go back to pack up my stuff and talk to Dakota, and then I'll come back and do everything they ask."

He shakes his head sadly. "Shawn, you know I'd do anything for you, but I'm all out of favors with the label. I had to pull out all the stops to get them to agree to give you these past few months off, and I went out on a limb for your new musical direction. They gave you both, and now it's time for you to honor their faith in you. They already have everything set up."

"Fuck, no!" I bury my head in my hands as a heavy weight bears down on my chest.

"The best I can do is to schedule a day off in the next few weeks. You can return to Iowa then."

"That'll be too fucking late!" I roar, even though it's not fair to take my anger out on my manager. He's only doing his job. I'm the one who fucked everything up.

As if to rub salt in my wounds, my phone pings with a slew of new social media notifications. "Ugh!" I toss my cell at Calista. "Shut off those fucking notifications."

She takes my phone without a word and gets to work.

"I'm sorry, Shawn. None of us could have predicted this. Surely, she'll understand. It will all work out."

I want to tell him to fuck off, but I keep my lips sealed. He's only trying to help.

"And let's focus on the positives. We're going to capture the stalker, and he'll no longer be a threat. And you have the label firmly behind your new music. They are already talking about a new worldwide tour to promote it. This is what you wanted."

"I know." I flop back in the seat, staring out the window of the limo. "But I want her more."

Calista emits a little shocked gasp before hurriedly composing herself.

"Wow." Luke smiles at me. "You've fallen hard for her."

"She's everything, man. I need her by my side." Luke is grinning at me like The Joker. "What?"

"I always knew the love of a good woman was all you needed."

I flip him the bird, and he laughs. "I'm pleased for you, Shawn. You deserve to have love in your life, and I can't wait to meet her."

Chapter 30

Dakota

I'm exhausted by the time I leave the hospital that evening but grateful Mom is stable. They are running tests to find out why she had a seizure and to see if there's any permanent brain damage, but so far it looks good. Or as good as it can be, the doctor explained.

Tom waited patiently outside all day, grabbing me food and water even when I didn't ask for it. Now he's driving me back to Levi's, and I'm tempted to ask him what's going on. *Who is he and why was he deferring to Levi as sir?* My brain is too tired to try to figure it out, so I lean my head back and doze for a bit.

I didn't even have time for a shower before I left this morning and I feel gross. "Tom." I lean forward, resting my hand on the back of his seat. "Would you mind detouring to my dorm. I need to shower and grab some clean clothes."

"Of course, ma'am."

"Please, just call me Dakota."

"As you wish, Dakota." He smiles at me through the mirror, and I relax in my seat.

It's only as we're pulling up in front of my building that I realize I never gave him my address. Tiny prickles of alarm wash over me. *Who is this guy and how does he know where I live? More importantly, who exactly is Levi?*

My sense of trepidation heightens when I step into my apartment and I'm greeted by a welcoming committee. Daisy is there, along with Tabs and Elsa. They exchange looks, and I frown. "What's going on?" I drop my purse on the table and face my friends.

"How is your mom?" Daisy asks, compassion splayed across her face. I had texted her this morning to let her know what was going on.

"Stable. They are keeping her there for observation and more tests. Hopefully, they'll have some answers for me tomorrow."

"I'll go with you tomorrow, if you like," Daisy offers. "You shouldn't be there alone."

"Thanks, but Levi will probably come with."

All three trade looks again, and I throw my hands into the air. "Will someone please tell me what's going on?"

Tabs opens her mouth to speak, but Elsa clamps a hand over her lips, silencing her. Elsa clears her throat. "Have you seen social media today, Kota?"

I shake my head. "No. Why?" All the tiny hairs on the back of my neck lift. "Hang on, Levi made me promise not to look at social media today." I start to connect the dots in my head. "Because there's something he doesn't want me to see?"

Elsa nods. "What else did he say Kota?" she asks gently.

"He promised he'd explain and told me to trust him, and he said I knew the real him." I'm not telling them he told me he loves me. Not with the vibes I'm getting from the room. I have a strong feeling that whatever I'm about to discover is going to knock my socks off.

"I can't believe he didn't tell you," Daisy says.

"I can't believe you didn't realize it sooner," Tabs adds, pointing her finger at Daisy.

"For the love of all things holy, will someone please put me out of my misery?!" I shriek. "I've had a shitty day, and I know it's about to get shittier, so just hit me with it."

Elsa walks forward with her cell outstretched. "You need to see this." She presses play and a video starts. It's Levi singing to me last night outside my dorm.

"Holy shit," I exclaim when I notice how many views it has already.

"Look at the headline," Elsa prompts, and I lift my eyes to the top of the screen.

All the color drains from my face as I read the words. Then a reporter talks over the video feed, and I feel my knees going out from under me.

In breaking news today, troubled popstar Shawn Lucas has finally resurfaced after months of speculation over his whereabouts. A video uploaded by a student of the University of Iowa went viral after fans identified Lucas as the guy serenading this mystery woman. Lucas's altered appearance explains how he was able to hide in plain sight on the Iowa City campus, where college officials have confirmed he was enrolled in one of their degree programs under a pseudonym. Dynamite XO Records, Lucas's label, is reportedly delighted with the singer's new musical direction, and he is being whisked into the studio to record this song ahead of a new album and worldwide tour. But the question on everyone's lips tonight is who is Lucas's Midnight Dancer, and what exactly does she mean to him?

"Oh my God." I stumble on my feet, grabbing onto Elsa's arms to steady myself. All the missing puzzle pieces fall into place, and my mind churns with all the lies and mistruths he told me. My stomach lurches unpleasantly, and my legs turn to Jell-O as I stagger away from Elsa toward the bathroom. "I think I'm going to be sick."

Elsa holds my hair back as I empty the contents of my stomach into the toilet bowl. My heart is racing ninety miles to the hour, and voices are screaming in my head as the magnitude of my discovery plays havoc with my emotions and my body. She hands me a damp cloth, and I wipe my mouth and mop my sticky brow before falling against the side of the tub lethargically.

The others appear in the doorway, and Daisy comes forward, crouching down in front of me. "Kota? Are you okay?"

I crank out a laugh. "I don't know what the hell to think. Why would he lie to me?" My eyes beseech her for answers she doesn't have.

"We think we've figured that out, but it's not going to make things any easier," Tabs says, holding her cell out to me this time.

I don't reach for it, probing my heart to see if it can withstand another hit. I decide I might as well get all the breaking over and done with at once. With trembling fingers, I take it from her and press play. It's another video feed. This time it shows Levi getting off a private plane in LAX and climbing into a limo. A reporter appears in front of the screen with a mic in hand.

"Earlier today, multi-millionaire pop sensation Shawn Lucas returned to L.A. where he was taken immediately to the Hollywood Community Police Station to assist police with the

ongoing investigation into the stalker who has made his life a living hell for the last year. While no official police statement has been forthcoming, our sources confirm that three men were arrested in the early hours of the morning as they attempted to break into Lucas's Hollywood Hills home. It's believed these are the same group of men who broke into his home a few months ago, prompting Lucas to go into hiding, and the same team who confronted Lucas's estranged mother outside her Malibu residence only a few days ago. We expect an official statement will be issued shortly, and we'll keep you updated. Until then, this is Mira Fenargo reporting for Entertainment World Tonight."

Silence engulfs the small bathroom, but the screaming doesn't stop in my head. This is obviously the *emergency* he referred to this morning. My mind is whirling in a million different directions, and I don't know how to make it stop. "He left again?" I blurt. "He promised he would wait to explain things to me."

"Here." Tabs hands me *my* cell this time. "I didn't look at the content, but you have several new messages from him."

My hands are shaking as I pull up my messages. Pressing the speaker button on my phone, I play Levi's message for the room.

"Baby, I'm so, so sorry about this, but I've had to go back to L.A. It's another emergency, and if I could get out of it I would, but I can't. I promise to come back as soon as I can, and I will tell you everything then. I know I asked you not to look at social media, but, shit..." He sighs. "This has blown up and I may not get to you in time. I was going to tell you everything last night, but you distracted me in the best possible way."

Tabs grins at me, but I can only stare back at her in numbed awareness.

"Remember what I told you, beautiful. You know me. *And*

my feelings for you have always been honest and truthful, even if I haven't been forthcoming about every aspect of my life. There was a good reason for that, and I...shit, this is going to cut out. I love you, Dakota. Call me and we'll ta—"

The message cuts out and the room is silent. Everyone tries to gauge my mood, and they are too afraid to say anything. We all just look at one another until Tabs decides to break the ice in her own inimitable style.

"Well, fuck this depressive shit. We should be celebrating. Our girl's gone and bagged herself a sexy rock star, and we all know him. He's not the shithead the media makes him out to be. He's a good guy." She kneels in front of me. "That's what he means, sweetheart. The name he goes by is irrelevant. You know he's one of the good ones, and he's crazy about you."

"He fucking lied to me!" I holler as powerful emotion surges to the surface. "He had months to tell me the truth! Months! And he said nothing."

"He was trying to protect you," Tabs protests.

"Don't you dare fucking defend him. He made love to me when I had no clue who he really was. And he put me in harm's way by keeping me in the dark about this stalker. How could he do that to me? He knows what happened to my sister, and he should have let me make that call. Bringing me into his life could have put me in danger!" I hop up, anger fueling the adrenaline coursing through my body. "How can he say he loves me in one breath and then put me at risk in the other? And now every fucking scumbag reporter is probably looking for me."

Air is ripped from my lungs, and I bend over, wheezing. Daisy is beside me in an instant, rubbing my back and encouraging me to take deep breaths. When I can speak, I look up at her. "You're Shawn Lucas's biggest fan! How the hell didn't you figure it out?"

"I told you I thought he looked familiar, but I couldn't put my finger on it. It was only last night, when I heard him sing that I worked it out. There is no way I'd not recognize his voice."

The penny drops. "That's why you were acting all spaced out."

She nods. "He realized I'd worked it out, and he mouthed at me. He said, 'Let me tell her,' and I presumed that's why you stayed there last night. I would have told you if I knew he didn't confess. I promise."

"It's okay, Daise," I say, patting her hand. "I know you would. I trust *you*."

"I can't believe he did that last night and then didn't tell you," Elsa adds. "He must've known what would happen."

I rub a hand over my aching chest. "To be fair, he *was* trying to tell me, but I wouldn't let him. We were going to talk this morning, but then I got the call about Mom and had to leave."

"You need to give him the benefit of the doubt," Tabs says.

"I don't *need* to do fucking anything," I hiss. "I believe he was going to tell me last night, but it was already too fucking late. He's put my life at risk for months. What if that stalker had followed him here and done something to me?" I slump to the floor again. "Jesus Christ. I've been dancing on the roof of that abandoned building for months. It would've been so easy for someone to take me."

A loud knock at the door startles us all. Elsa goes off to answer it while Daisy helps me to my feet. I take a quick moment to apologize to the girls. "I'm sorry if I'm taking it out on you. It's not you I'm mad at."

"We know, babe." Tabs slants me a sympathetic look as Elsa pops her head in the door.

"There's a guy named Devin Morgan here to see you. He says Levi sent him."

Chapter 31

Dakota

Composing myself, I smooth a hand over my crumpled shirt and walk out to meet Devin. My friends stay close behind me. Devin offers me a guarded smile while standing in the middle of our living room. "Dakota. I'm sorry to barge in here like this, but I was waiting at the penthouse for you. Tom told me you asked to be brought here instead, so I took the liberty of coming to you. I hope that's okay."

Tabs is devouring Devin on sight, and it looks like she's getting ready to come out with one of her special Tabitha-isms, but I impale her with a deadly look, and she zips her lips.

"That depends on what you have to say." I gesture toward the couch, not wanting to be a bitch to the man when he welcomed me so hospitably into his home. "Please take a seat."

I sit beside him, and my friends hover in the background.

"I expect you've heard the news by now."

"You mean the fact Levi Quinn is actually Shawn Lucas or the fact he has some crazy stalker on his ass and he just made me a target? Or that every scumbag reporter in the country is trying to locate his midnight dancer a.k.a. me?" I pierce him with a serious stare. "That news?" He clears his throat, looking awkward as hell. "And now he sends you to do his dirty work for him?"

"It's not like that, Dakota. I assure you."

"Then what's it like, Devin? And don't tell me you didn't know. You did. Ange did. And neither of you said anything to me."

He has the decency to look ashamed. "Ange was furious with me for days over that, Dakota. She didn't want any part in the deception, and neither did I, but I was conflicted. Shawn is one of my clients, and it wouldn't have been professional to advise him otherwise."

"One of your clients?"

He nods, running a hand through his hair. "I own a security consultancy company called Morgan Security. Shawn hired me a few months ago to help provide personal protection while he was hiding in Iowa. I was also investigating all leads in an attempt to discover the person or persons who have been stalking him and making death threats on his life."

"He's had death threats?" I ask in a low voice, worry forming in my gut.

He nods solemnly. "Repeated threats, and he made the decision to go into hiding after someone shot at him."

"Oh my God." I clamp a hand over my chest. "That's horrible and so frightening." The thought of anyone trying to hurt Levi freaks me out, and even though I'm mad at him I can't bear the idea he could be harmed or seriously injured. And I hate he was dealing with all this alone.

"I know you are upset and angry with him right now," Devin continues, "but he was trying to keep you safe the best way he knew how."

"That's not very reassuring." He should have come clean, and we could've handled it together.

"This may upset you further, but you should know Shawn has been paying for twenty-four-seven protection for you since you came into his life. He truly cares about you, Dakota, and he would never do anything to willingly place you in danger."

"What do you mean?" I croak, butterflies somersaulting around my chest cavity.

"I have assigned bodyguards to watch over you all the time. You haven't been in danger. If anyone had come near you, they would've been dealt with immediately."

I slouch in the chair, unsure if my heart can take any more revelations today. I'm so conflicted. On the one hand, there's no denying Levi cares for me and he's taken measures to ensure I'm protected. But it still doesn't take away from the fact he has lied to me. Lied to my face. Time and time again. I don't know what to think. What to feel.

"I can't deal with this." I close my eyes and rest my head back. "It's too much."

"I'm sorry about all this. Shawn wanted to be here to tell you himself, but we think we've caught the stalker, and he had to return to help the police pin this guy down. He didn't have a choice."

That should go some way toward reassuring me, but it doesn't detract from the truth—he lied to me for months. He let me fall in love with him when I didn't have the full story. I gave him every part of me, and he didn't do the same for me. He asked me to trust him, to believe in him, in us, but how can I do that when he couldn't even share who he was with me?

Relationships that aren't built on complete honesty can't survive.

I've already experienced that reality.

"Oh my God!" Tabs shrieks unexpectedly, startling us all.

"What?" I ask, arching a brow.

"I'm just remembering our conversation from the first frat party. Remember where he kissed you the first time?"

"Oh, shit. Yeah." Despite how mad I am with him, I can't help giggling. "We totally insulted him to his face." I snort.

"Oh, this I gotta hear," Devin says, grinning.

"If I remember correctly," Elsa says, also grinning, "Kota said his music made her want to vomit and he was a giant bag of dicks."

"And you said he was a train wreck and into threesomes and kinky shit."

"And we won't even mention what Tabs said," Elsa adds, trying to smother her laughter.

Devin busts out laughing. "That is classic. I love it."

"It's a wonder he didn't hate me," I muse.

"Trust me," Devin says, having composed himself. "Shawn has a healthy ego. I'm betting those comments barely made a dent."

"And that's what I'm talking about," I supply quietly, all humor gone from my tone now. "The guy I know isn't arrogant at all. Every time he played for me, I complimented his talent, and he was almost shy about it." Of course, now I know he was only acting like that because he was lying. I shake my head. "He said I know him, but I don't know him at all."

"I don't think that's true," Devin says, drilling a look at me so I'm forced to look him straight in the eye. "He's a different man from the one I first met. I thought he'd changed, but now I realize he's just rediscovered himself. You helped get him there, and I have no doubt he showed you as much of himself as he could."

I'm so screwed up, and my head is all over the place. I honestly don't know what to think anymore. "Thank you for taking the time to see me, Devin. I do appreciate that, but I just need some time alone to think."

"Of course." He stands. Removing a card from his pocket, he hands it to me. "If you need anything, anything at all, please call me. And you don't need to be worried or scared. Until we have the stalker in custody, my men will continue protecting you."

I walk him to the door and open it. "Thank you, Devin. I'm grateful."

He turns around to face me one last time. "He's a good guy, Dakota. He may have gone about this the wrong way, but his heart was in the right place. He loves you. Let him make it up to you."

Offering him a feeble smile, I nod. He strides down the hall, and I stare blankly after him. After a bit, I close the door and lean back against it.

Tabs comes forward, snatching Devin's card from my hand. "Did you see that guy? Holy hot older guy alert. I need his number."

I snatch it back. "Quit it, Tabs. He's happily married with two kids."

"Fuck, all the sexy ones are always taken." She winks as she mock pouts, and I know she's only trying to lighten the mood. I appreciate it so much, but it'll take a lot more than that to pull me out of the funk I'm in.

"What are you going to do, Kota?" Elsa asks.

"I don't know," I admit, pushing off the door. "My head is a mess, and I have Mom to worry about, so I can't get hung up on a guy who couldn't be honest with me. He knew I was trustworthy, that I'd keep his secret, so I don't understand why he wouldn't tell me? Why he would continue to lie and deceive me like this?"

These questions and more continue to haunt me all night

long, and I spend a fretful night analyzing everything he ever said to me.

I feel so stupid for not picking up on the signs. Now everything makes sense. How he tried to keep to himself. How he never wanted to wander far from his apartment. How attached he was to his ball cap and hoodie. How he averted my questions any time I tried to get him to open up about his music.

His last words to me haven't been forgotten, but how can I trust he was telling me the truth about his feelings when it was clearly so easy for him to lie? And aren't all musicians and performers just skilled actors anyway? He asked me not to give up on him, but since the message and texts from earlier, he's made no effort to contact me. *He must know by now that I know the truth, and what? He's too chicken to call me?* That's not who I thought he was, and now I'm second-guessing everything.

Worst of all, it's brought my sister's murder to the forefront of my mind again. I can't help wondering if this is how she felt when she found out her boyfriend, the guy she'd been sleeping with, had this whole other life she knew nothing about. Yes, I know it's not a comparable situation—Levi isn't a serial killer and I know, deep down, that he wouldn't physically hurt me—but he's kept a huge part of himself hidden from me, even knowing what he did about Layla's death.

The only conclusion I can draw is that he didn't trust me enough to risk telling me the truth.

And that leads to another ugly realization.

Was I only a distraction?

Something to pass the time while he was here?

Guys like him have girls falling all over them, and he didn't earn his party-boy man-whore rep for nothing.

I can't believe I fell for all his lines. That I believed him when he said he loved me, when, all along, it was just a ploy to get me in bed.

Daisy comes with me to the hospital the next day and I'm very grateful for her company. I'm terrified to set foot outside our dorm, for fear I'll be accosted. I know it's only a matter of time before some student outs me to the media. Devin said he had someone watching over me, but he must be damned good at his job because I haven't spotted anyone shadowing me.

Either that or he lied.

I don't think Devin's that kind of guy, but my judgment is obviously not to be trusted, and he's on Levi's—*Shawn*'s—payroll, so it's not totally implausible.

Mom seems more alert today, and she's even talking. It's only a couple of sentences, but that's a massive improvement over recent months. It seems the seizure didn't just scare me.

Daisy and I are waiting in the hall outside to speak to the doctor while Mom is napping. She hasn't said one peep about Shawn so far, but I know she's just biding her time. She clears her throat. "Have you heard from him?"

I shake my head. "Nope. No new messages."

"Maybe he's waiting for you to call him."

"Hell will freeze before I call him. I'm not the one who needs to apologize."

"I know I wasn't around you guys that much, but I saw the way he looked at you at the party, and I heard the adoration in his voice the day he came to our dorm to wait for you. He really cares about you, Kota, and I know you care about him too. I don't think you should give up on him."

I snort. "Of course, you'd think that! You're his biggest fucking fan. He can do no wrong in your eyes."

"Don't be a bitch," she snaps, uncharacteristically. "I'm not talking about Shawn Lucas the popstar, I'm talking about Levi Quinn. Your boyfriend."

I pat her arm, instantly regretful. "I'm sorry. That was an unfair comment, and I know you didn't mean it like that, but he's one and the same, Daise. Levi Quinn is Shawn Lucas."

"If they are one and the same doesn't that mean you do know him?"

"I don't know." I sigh, leaning my head back. "All I know is I'm sick of thinking about it over and over. If he meant what he said, he won't give up on me. That's how I'll know."

But as the days pass, with no contact from him, I realize he didn't mean any of it. All he cares about is getting back to his life, going on TV and singing his new song—*my* song—and watching the cash pile up in his bank account as the song storms to the top of the charts.

At least Mom is out of the hospital, back at the facility, and doing much better. The seizure was caused by an adverse reaction to some of the medication she was on. Thankfully, it was only a minor seizure, and it hasn't caused any permanent damage. If anything, it's had a positive effect on her. She's more lucid and communicative than she's been in ages. I think it reminded her of her own mortality and the things she has left to live for.

I'm returning from the hospital Saturday night when I'm waylaid by a different ex. Cole is wrapped up in a Hawks scarf and a heavy black jacket as he lounges against the wall of my building.

"What are you doing here?" I ask in a weary tone when I reach him.

"I came to see how you are, and I heard about your mom. Is she okay?"

"She's doing better."

"And you?" He cups my cheek, but I take a step back, forcing his hand to drop away.

"I'm fine. Why wouldn't I be?"

He sends me a pitying look that pisses me off. "You don't have to pretend with me. I tried to tell you he was no good for you, but you wouldn't listen."

My heart hurts at his words, and I look at the ground, blinking the sudden rush of tears away.

Cole pulls me into his arms, and for a brief, fleeting second, I allow him to comfort me before I come to my senses, untangling myself from his embrace. "I'm betting you're loving this."

"What? No! Of course not. I figured the guy would slink away when I posted that video, but I didn't realize quite how spineless he is."

"Wait." Blood turns to ice in my veins. "*You* uploaded that video?"

"It was for your own good, Dakota. I didn't realize who he was when I recorded it on my phone that night, but the girlfriend of one of my football buddies was in the house when I got back, and she made the connection instantly. We spent all night comparing the guy on the video with YouTube videos of Shawn Lucas until we were in no doubt it was the same guy. I can't believe he didn't tell you who he was. What a prick. All those rock stars are interested in is getting laid. It's better you found out now."

"Screw you, Cole!"

He sends me a saucy wink, reaching for me again. "Happy to oblige anytime, babe. No one gives head like you."

"Oh. My. God. I can't believe I ever went out with you. You have turned into the biggest asshole."

"Ms. Gray?" a female voice calls out over my shoulder, capturing my attention.

I turn and watch a stick-thin blonde wearing a bright red

coat and seven-inch heels totter toward me with a microphone in hand. A big, slovenly, hairy guy with a camera hoisted over his shoulder trudges behind her.

"Oh, shit," I mumble, brushing past Cole as I make my way toward the front door.

Cole makes a grab for me. "Wait, Kotabear."

"Get lost, Cole! This is all your fault. I meant what I said before. Leave me alone."

"Ms. Gray. Is it true Shawn Lucas was in a relationship with you?" I race up the steps, blood pounding in my ears. "Dakota!" she screeches. "Are you his midnight dancer?"

I burst through the doors into the building and race up the stairs. I'm panting by the time I reach our empty dorm. Sagging to the ground, I hold my head in my hands as I attempt to recalibrate my breathing.

Renewed resolution mixes with anger inside me. Screw this shit.

I'm done with guys and their attempts to mess up my head.

It's time to take back control.

Chapter 32

Shawn

It's been a week, and Dakota is still refusing to reply to the hundreds of text messages I've sent her or return any of my calls, and I'm getting desperate. I get that she's pissed, and Devin said she needed time to work things out in her head, but nothing will get resolved if we don't communicate. I just need to talk to her. To try to get through to her. To make her realize how much I love her.

And I miss her so fucking much.

Midnight Dancer is an instant hit, my most successful release in years, and the reaction to my new direction has blown my mind. My fans and people in the industry have accepted this new side of me without question, and there's already talk of a Grammy nomination, but none of that means anything without the girl who inspired the song by my side.

All the shit with the cops this week has compounded my stress; although now they have the stalker in custody, I should be sleeping easier at night.

But I'm not.

Turns out, one of the employees of the security company I

hired to install the new system in my house was a rotten egg. He was using his position to try to steal from a few high-profile celebrities, although I was the only one he took a shot at.

Guess he just didn't care for my music.

I should be delighted the threat has been put to bed, but, to be honest, I've barely given it a passing thought. Every part of my heart and mind is consumed with the girl I love.

My insomnia has returned with a vengeance, and I spend most nights unsettled and fidgeting on crumpled sheets. I hadn't realized how much my sleeping patterns had returned to normal with Dakota curled into my side. Every single thing about her made my life better. And now I'm terrified I've lost her for good. Luke has been true to his word, and he's scheduled a day off in a couple weeks so I can fly to Iowa to speak to my baby face to face.

In the meantime, I need to up my game. Swallowing my fear, I pull up an app on my phone and order one hundred roses to be sent to Dakota. I've never sent flowers to any girl who wasn't my mom before, and usually Calista organizes such shit, but I don't trust her not to send one hundred black roses to the love of my life. Although she was professional that first day back, Calista has returned to her manipulative ways, offering me false sympathies, while attempting to paw at me, and telling me I'm better off without that gold-digger in my life.

The barrage of questions hits me like a bullet the instant I step outside the radio station after my latest appearance. Bodyguards shield me from their grabby hands, but they are less effective at shielding my ears.

"Shawn! Is it true Dakota Gray is your mystery midnight

dancer?" a reporter screams, her question reaching me across the sea of questions.

My only instinct in that moment is to protect Dakota. I turn to face the reporter, and her face lights up like a glow bug. She eagerly thrusts her mic in my face. "No, it isn't true. She isn't my midnight dancer. She's no one."

I'm still fuming by the time I reach Mom's house in Malibu a few hours later. I've decided to hang out here for a while until all the furor dies down. I'm in the gym, pounding my fists into the punching bag when Devin materializes at my side. Luke had said he needed to talk to me, but I hadn't expected him to show up in person.

He holds the bag for me, while I continue to slam my fists into it, releasing my pent-up aggression. After a while, he tosses me a towel and a bottle of water, and we wander outside, walking down toward the beach. Although it's late November, and the temps have definitely dropped, it's still pleasant. We drop down on the sand, knees elevated, watching the lapping of the waves against the shore.

"How is she?" I ask, in between swigging from the bottle.

"She seems fine. Her mom is back in the facility and she's doing well. Apart from visiting her and going to classes, she hasn't stepped foot outside her dorm."

"She won't talk to me. I think I've lost her." I'm expecting words of encouragement, but I'm met with empty space. I turn and study him. "What do you know?"

He drags a hand through his hair, sighing. "Look, she said she needed time to think, and I believed her. That's probably why she hasn't called you back, but..." He wets his lips before removing his cell from his inside pocket and handing it to me. The screen displays a new article from a well-known entertainment site, and I instantly know I'm not going to like what I read. "You know better than anyone how the press twists things, so I'm sure this isn't how it looks, but you need to see it anyway."

The headline alone sends shards of pain lancing through my heart.

"She's No One," Lucas claims as his midnight dancer cheats on him with her ex.

But it's the accompanying photo that nails the final dagger in my heart. Dakota is wrapped up in Cole's arms, and her head is resting on his chest. His smug grin makes me want to hop on a plane and do permanent damage to his face. He's wearing a Hawks scarf, and I recognize the outside of Dakota's dorm so I know the photo is recent.

"Fucking awesome." I grab tufts of my now-blond-again hair. "I just sent her one hundred roses." I stand up, striding toward the shore. Devin follows me. "I'm a fucking idiot."

"Wait up. You don't know what this is until you speak to her. Don't write her off yet."

"She won't speak to me!" I yell. "Now at least I know why."

"You just—"

"Don't. I don't want to talk about her anymore. I'm sure you didn't travel all this way to speak to me about my messed-up love life."

He rubs a hand behind the back of his neck. "Technically, you no longer require my services, so I wanted to find out how you intend to wrap things up."

"I'd like your firm to provide my personal protection going forward. I don't want any future dealings with Denning Security, not after Aaron Hunter—their *fucking employee*—was the one stalking me. I've lost all faith in them." I shove my hands in the pockets of my gym shorts as we walk by the shore. "I know you don't have a permanent operation out here, but I was hoping you might consider setting up a division in L.A. I could introduce you to tons of new clients."

"I can't pretend I haven't considered it. Are you sure you've given this enough thought?"

"I have. There isn't anyone I trust to do this but you."

"Thank you."

I nod. "Thank *you*. You helped bring this to a close, and I won't forget that."

"What about the protection on your mom and Dakota?"

"Mom hates having a bodyguard, and Dakota seems to have found a replacement, so you can pull both."

"Don't make a knee-jerk reaction you might later come to regret."

I shrug, still heartsore. "There's no need for it anymore. My stalker is out of the equation, and I'm out of her life, so she's no longer in danger. She doesn't need me or my protection anymore."

"Okay, if you're sure."

"I'm sure."

"Just one other thing. I know the police have done their job and they've found plenty of motive to justify Aaron's actions, but I'd like to continue digging a little. I'd like to find out exactly why his MO was different when it came to you. I know he had huge gambling debts and an expensive coke habit, but I'd like to finish the investigation and wrap up all the loose ends."

"Do whatever you need to do, man. You know I'm good for it."

"You seem down, honey," Mom says later on that night after I've gotten back from taping my appearance on *Jimmy Kimmel Live*.

"It's nothing," I lie.

She squeezes my shoulder. "I know it's not nothing. Talk to me. You used to tell me everything."

"When I was ten," I deadpan. "I'm not a little kid anymore."

"I know that, honey, but it doesn't mean we can't talk about the deep stuff. Is this about Dakota?" she correctly surmises.

"You want to talk about girls?" I inquire, amusement coloring my tone.

"I want to talk about *this* girl. You've never mentioned any girl to me before, so I understand the significance of you telling me about her." She sighs, looking troubled.

"What's wrong?"

She rests her head on my shoulder. "I'm so very proud of you, Shawn. I hope you know that. And not just for all you've achieved in your career, but also for the way you've matured this last year and how you've worked to refocus your life. I can't thank you enough for this life you've given me, but I worry you missed out on so much. Everything changed so fast for you, for us, and you were thrown into that lifestyle and forced to grow up. I hate that you haven't had a chance before now to meet someone special. To have a normal relationship."

She lifts her head, twisting around to face me. "And I know you. I know you're pining for her. Don't bottle up what you're feeling. Talk to me."

I don't need any further encouragement. "Dakota has gone back to her ex," I glumly tell her.

"Did she tell you that or you're assuming it based on that article?"

I shrug. "Does it matter?"

"Of course, it matters, sweetheart. You, of all people, know how the paparazzi twist things. Unless you've heard it from her mouth, you can't presume to know the truth."

I glance at my cell, for like the thousandth time tonight.

"She won't return my calls, and I sent her flowers today, and I've still heard nothing." I sigh, picking up my guitar and strumming it. "I don't need to hear it from her mouth. Actions, or inactions, in this case, speak louder than words."

Mom circles her arm around my shoulder. "If you love her, don't give up without the mother of all fights. Don't walk away until she tells you to your face that she has given up on you. All the 'what-ifs' will only torment you later." She stands, ruffling my hair like she used to when I was a kid. "True love is always worth fighting for. What have you got to lose? Either she'll tell you she still loves you or you'll get the closure you need to move on."

As I stay up into the early hours, fighting the craving for a drink, I watch my cell like a hawk while playing each and every song I wrote with her in mind on my guitar.

With every hour that ticks by, and with every second my cell remains silent, another little piece of my soul dies. But Mom's fighting spirit lingers in my DNA, and, maybe, just maybe, she was right.

I won't know unless I put her theory to the test.

Chapter 33

Dakota

The following morning, I stare at the headline on my cell with a sort of numbed awareness. My eyes float to the picture of Cole and me, and I almost puke at how deceptive it looks. I wonder if Cole is behind this too. If he sold me out to that skanky reporter to make a quick buck. Nothing he does surprises me anymore.

I sure have a habit of choosing men I end up knowing *nothing* about.

My nostrils pick up the floral scent swirling around me, and I skim my eyes over the roses adorning most every surface in the room. Daisy almost keeled over when she returned last night to find me surrounded by bunches of the stuff. My finger hovered over my cell for at least an hour while I debated with myself. It's rude not to thank Shawn for the gesture, yet, at the same time, if he thinks this lets him off the hook, he's sorely mistaken. These must have cost him a fortune, but I'd much rather have had five minutes of his time.

It's too easy to pick up the phone and ask someone to send some flowers.

Picking up the phone and giving me honest answers obviously takes more effort than he's prepared to expend.

"She's no one." That's what he told the reporter in the article when she asked about me.

If I'm no one, why is he sending me flowers? "Ugh." I slam the palm of my hand into my forehead. I'm going to give myself a brain aneurysm overthinking this stuff, and I don't do this. When Cole and I broke up, I was upset for about two seconds, but I've spent all week nursing a broken heart over Levi, or should I say Shawn, and he still occupies far too much of my head space.

Thing is, the article has totally misconstrued what happened last night with Cole, so it isn't unrealistic to believe they have manipulated Shawn's words either.

I guess there's only one way to find out. Determination races through my veins, and I don't waste any more time pondering this, pulling up his number and pressing the call button.

If he doesn't have the nerve to call me, then I'm calling him.

I refuse to spend another week mulling over all the what-ifs. I need to hear what he has to say for himself.

"Shawn's cell," a throaty female voice says as someone picks up the other line. I'm thrown off guard for a second, and I don't say anything. "I know who this is," she replies, "and you're wasting your time."

"Who is this and where is Shawn?"

"You know who I am, so don't play cute."

The voice clicks into focus. It's the redhead assistant of Shawn's who showed up at his place a couple weeks back. I wrack my brain for her name, but I can't remember it. "You're the assistant," I say, knowing it will piss her off.

"And you're the ex," she retorts, clearly gloating.

"I don't have time for this. Put Shawn on."

"I'm afraid he's a little...indisposed right now."

My stomach heaves. "What do you mean?"

"I've always been an advocate of show versus tell," she purrs down the line just as my phone pings.

I open the media attachment with shaky fingers, almost throwing up when I see the photos of Shawn in the bed, lying flat on his stomach, out for the count. He's bare from the waist up, and the sheet is twisted at a certain angle across his lower back which shows enough to confirm he's completely naked.

I can't stop the errant sob that rips from my throat.

"Aw, now don't act like that. You should know better. As if some hokey small-town girl could hold the attention of a famous rock star. I tried to warn you, but you wouldn't listen." Her tone turns nasty. "He's mine. He always has been, and he always will be. If anyone is getting a ring on her finger, it's me. So, do us all a favor and fuck off."

The drone of the dial tone greets me as she hangs up. I hold the phone in a daze, confused, upset, and feeling a million other things.

I wish Daisy was here.

I wish any of my friends were here, but they've all gone home for Thanksgiving break. I'm spending tomorrow with Mom in the psychiatric facility, but today I'm all alone, and I can't stand it a second longer.

I get up, taking each vase of flowers to the window and lining them up. Then, one at a time, I dump the roses on the ground below, before hurrying to my room and hastily packing a bag.

Ignoring the throng of reporters swarming my car, I get in and rev the engine. So help me God, but if they don't get out of my way, I'll mow each one of them down.

Fucking parasites.

But, obviously, the ferocious look on my face, and the

furious revving of the engine, has stirred their survival instincts into gear, and they all jump out of my way when I floor it, tires squealing as I head out of the parking lot and into the flow of traffic.

The farther I get from Iowa City, the more I calm down. By the time I pull into the driveway of my family home, I'm somewhat composed. I'm heartbroken but determined to wash this guy right out of my hair.

In a surprising move, Dad signed the house over to Mom a week ago—proof of a guilty conscience if I ever saw one—so I know I'm safe returning here and that I'll find the solitude I need.

The house is dark and quiet when I step foot inside. I spend the next couple of hours dusting and cleaning, trying to ignore the extra pang in my heart when I see Dad's side of the closet devoid of his belongings. With all my own personal drama, I haven't taken time to mourn the demise of my parent's marriage and the destruction of the family I used to think was unbreakable.

Slowly, I walk into Layla's room and close the door. It's exactly as she left it.

The pretty pink and purple comforter matches the drapes, and the light pastel color on the walls is a perfect complement. My sister always liked things that matched or were in an orderly fashion. I was the type of child to roll out of bed and grab mismatched clothes and odd socks while Layla looked on in abject horror as I traipsed out of the house like an eccentric without a care in the world.

I trail my fingers over the pretty comforter, smiling sadly as I take in the rest of the room. A multitude of fluffy pillows rest on the bed, alongside Snowy, one of her treasured childhood teddies. Tons of crime novels are stacked in an orderly fashion on the bookshelves over her pristine desk, alongside a neat bundle of magazines—*Forbes, Entrepreneur, Fast Company*—and a bunch of other boring titles. A massive globe rests on the other side of her shelf, and a pang of sorrow hits me square in the chest. Layla won't ever get to visit all the places she had dreamed of.

I perch on the edge of her bed, smiling at the framed photo on her bedside table. It was taken four years ago when we were in Orlando. We're both soaked after the *Jurassic Park* ride, but delightfully happy, giggling and smiling for the camera. Our arms are wrapped around one another and we look so carefree. So untroubled. A single tear rolls out of the corner of my eye. "I miss you Layla-bug," I whisper, tracing my finger over the photo. "I miss you so much, and I'm making a total mess of everything. I need you," I softly admit, lying back on her bed.

Flipping on my side, I stare at her reflection in the photo. "You always were the strong one when it came to boys. I was always the stupid one believing in true love and all that nonsense, but you had the right idea. I just wish I could harden my heart. I wish I could forget him, but he won't get out of my head." I throw an arm over my face. "What am I going to do, Layla? How do I move forward for me and Mom because it's only the two of us now and I'm not equipped to handle this."

I imagine Layla's here, and I can almost hear her voice whispering in my ear.

"Trust in yourself, Kotabear. Make the right choices for you, and make them good ones. You only get one life. Don't waste it."

A smile graces my lips as those words sink deep. Layla isn't here anymore, and I'd give anything for her to have her life over again. But that's not possible, regardless of how hard I wish for it. However, I'm still here, and she'd hate to see me like this. Floating through life uncertain, denying everything I've always dreamed of.

I owe it to my sister to live the best life I can.

In her memory. In her honor.

And for my sanity.

As I curl up in my bed that night, I feel happier than I have in weeks. I know what I want to do. Now, I just need to put things in motion.

Thanksgiving is a rather pitiful affair compared to how we usually spend it, but I don't complain. Mom is getting stronger with every passing day, and that's enough to keep my spirits up.

When I return to the house that night, I sit out on the veranda, sipping a glass of wine as I move back and forth on the veranda swing, contemplating everything I've decided to do. From now on, I'm going to honor my sister's memory by living life to the fullest and not dwelling on my mistakes.

When I return to campus, I put stage one of my plan into action. It takes several days, a myriad of interviews and auditions, and a call to Juilliard, but finally the administration in U of I allows me to switch from the accounting program to the dance program.

I reported the paps to campus security, and now a member of the security staff escorts me to and from the building each day, ensuring I'm not hassled. I ignore every other effort the paparazzi make to engage me, and after another couple of days, most of them have gone away. I feel like sending a thank you card to the disgraced politician who was caught in bed with an underage girl for diverting the attention away from me.

I'm still the subject of gossip around campus, and hushed whispers and finger-pointing follow me wherever I go, but I'm trying my best to ignore it, hopeful it'll disappear once the other students realize I'm no longer with Shawn.

Shawn is going about his business as usual in L.A., and he's clearly moved on, so I'm determined to do the same. To put the whole sorry debacle behind me. Thanks to my late transfer, I've missed a lot of classes, so I stay late most nights practicing and trying to catch up, and between my classes and Mom, I'm kept busy.

It's only at night, when I have little else to occupy my mind, that I allow myself to think about him. To miss him. I wish I could forget about him, but memories of sleeping wrapped in his strong arms refuse to go away. He made me feel safe and loved at a time when I needed it most. I can be thankful to him for that. And I'm stronger than I thought I was. I haven't fallen apart; I'm making plans for the future, and I can acknowledge the part he played in that.

On Tuesday night, I'm holed up with Tabs, Elsa, and Daisy watching some Netflix and gorging on pizza when Tabs jumps up abruptly, spilling soda all over herself. "Turn the channel," she splutters, almost choking. "Put on CBS right now!" she commands, pointing at Daisy.

Daisy blinks rapidly as she switches the channel.

I jump up as his face appears on the screen. "No. No. No. I'm not watching this."

Tabs grips my shoulders, stalling my forward projectory. "I've been skimming live tweets, and he's going to say something about you! You *have* to listen."

Part of me wants to stay, but the other part of me wants to get the hell out of Dodge. But Tabs is one stubborn bitch when she wants to be, so I give up the fight and flop back down on the couch.

Shawn is seated with his guitar propped on his lap on a small stage. Another guy with a guitar sits alongside him. They are highlighted under a spotlight, but the rest of the stage is in darkness; however, I can make out the orchestra at his back, poised and ready for some grand production. My heart flutters at the thought this might all be for me.

The camera pans to the dimly lit crowd, and their expectation is almost palpable. Shawn flicks his blond hair out of his blue eyes and smiles directly into the camera. "For weeks, everyone has been hounding me about my midnight dancer, but I've kept quiet out of respect for a girl who means the world to me. I'm breaking my silence tonight for a few reasons. For those of you who want to know, she's the best thing that's ever happened to me. She saved me when I didn't even realize how badly I needed saving. Her strength, her zest for life, her laughter, and her love have transformed my life and resurrected my joy in music."

You can almost hear the collective withholding of breath in this room. My heart is galloping around my chest like it's just won the Kentucky Derby. Shawn leans in closer as the camera zooms in on his beautiful face. There's no mistaking the sincerity on his face or the love in his eyes. "Kota baby, if you're out there watching, I love you and I miss you so much. This is for you."

I'm barely breathing as he strums his guitar and starts singing, emotion bleeding into the words as he beseeches me with his soulful lyrics and the haunting quality to his voice. Accompanied by the skillful orchestra at his rear, he is magnificent, and it's one of the most beautiful performances I've ever been privileged to hear. I'm not even aware tears are streaming down my face until the song is finished and the crowd breaks into rapturous applause, giving him a standing ovation.

"Hey," Elsa says, reaching out to wipe my tears away. "You doing okay?"

My chest heaves, and my heart literally aches for him. It's been almost a month since I've held him or talked to him, and my entire being craves him. But I still doubt my judgment. "That was sincere, right?"

"Hundo P," Tabs says.

"Kota, I know everything's messed up," Daisy says, "but there's no way he didn't mean that. He just told the whole world he loves you."

"What're you going to do?" Elsa asks.

I stand, swiping the last of my tears away. "What I should've done in the first place." I don't quite understand what's going on, but there's no way I can deny the words he just said or the obvious sentiment behind them. He told me that witch of an assistant was a manipulative bitch, and I let her play me, because I'm sure now that picture is a lie. Shawn told me he slept with her one time, but all he remembered was waking up beside her. I'm betting she took that photo then, knowing it would come in handy someday.

And I fell for it, hook, line, and sinker.

Maybe it's my delusional brain clutching onto strings, or maybe I've just nailed it.

Either way, I have to stop second-guessing everything or jumping to conclusions. I will only know the truth when I'm standing in front of him and he's speaking the words to my face.

I stand tall, and a wide smile creeps over my face. "We need to talk. If he can't come to me, then I'll go to him. Tabs"—I flick my eyes to my friend—"can you book me on the next flight to L.A. while I go pack a bag."

She gives me an approving thumbs-up as I fly out of the room to grab my stuff.

Fifteen minutes later, I'm hugging my friends as I prepare to leave.

"Give him a kiss from me." Daise almost swoons.

"But don't forget to give him hell, too," Elsa cautions. "He's still got a lot of explaining to do."

"Go reclaim your sexy rock star," Tabs grins. "And give him a—"

"Stop!" We three scream in unison, holding our hands over her mouth.

I laugh, grabbing all my friends in a group hug. "Wish me luck."

"Luck!" Tabs singsongs. "But you don't need it because that hottie lurves you!"

I'm still grinning as I make my way out of the building and start walking toward the street to call a cab. For the first time in ages, I'm completely confident in my decision. This feels like the right thing to do, and I'm just going to go with the flow. Even if I end up getting rejected, at least it will draw a line under everything.

It's late and most of the students are already tucked up in bed. I quicken my steps as an eerie sensation ghosts over me. All the tiny hairs lift on the back of my neck, and I glance behind me, suddenly on edge, but the path is clear. Telling myself I'm paranoid, I roll my eyes and will myself to calm down. As I whip my head back around, someone crashes into me from the side, knocking me off my feet.

Adrenaline courses through my body as a figure dressed all in black bends over me. I open my mouth to scream when a cloth is pressed against my mouth from behind. A strange cloying smell tickles my nostrils and clogs my throat. My legs and arms thrash about as I attempt to fight my two attackers, but my limbs turn limp so fast, and I'm struggling to keep my eyes open.

They lift me up, as if I weigh nothing, and the last thing I think before my world turns dark is that my mother won't survive this a second time.

Chapter 34

Shawn

Mom said to go big or go home, so I went all-in. Putting my heart out there in front of the nation. *The Late Late Show* is pre-recorded the day before, so the last twenty-four hours have felt like twenty-four years as I waited for it to air. Mom hugged me last night as we watched it, telling me she was proud of me. This morning, she got up at the crack of dawn to make me breakfast, hugging the shit out of me again, telling me to go get my girl.

I guess I have some things to be grateful to my stalker for—finding the girl of my dreams and reconciling with Mom.

My flight lands in Iowa shortly after ten a.m., and I waste no time getting to the business school campus. While I don't want to draw more attention to myself or Dakota, I only have today to try to make things right with her. Tugging my hood up, I lower my head as I lurk in the shadows outside the main entrance to the building, waiting for her. I know her next class is due to start soon, so I just have to wait it out. However, trying to find someone in a crowd while attempting to look inconspicuous is not without challenge.

I'm starting to get dejected after twenty minutes, especially when the crowd dwindles and I still haven't found her. Then I spot a familiar face. "Tabs!" I hiss, taking a few steps forward and beckoning her with my fingers. "Over here!"

She narrows her eyes at first, and then awareness sparks to life, and her eyes pop wide. She stalks toward me. "What are you doing *here*?"

"What do you think?" I pin her with an "are you really that stupid" look, and she slaps my arm. "Ow! That fucking hurt."

"God, you're such a pussy. If only your fans knew," she scoffs, shaking her head. Then her expression morphs into a look so dark I actually take a step back in fear. "I've got a bone to pick with you." She jabs her finger into my chest. "Actually, I have a few bones to pick with you, but we'll start with how much of chickenshit you are. I never took you for a coward, but I can't believe you didn't call her and try to fix this, instead of letting it stew for weeks."

I frown. "What the hell are you talking about? I've been calling and texting her every day. She's the one who won't speak to me."

Her eyes narrow to thin slits, and she thumps me in the arm again. "Don't fucking lie to me."

"I'm not! And quit with that shit," I demand, rubbing my arm. "You have a punch any guy would be proud of."

She smirks and then remembers what we were discussing. "If you're not lying, prove it to me." She plants her hands on her hips, leveling me with a challenging look.

Extracting my cell from the back pocket of my jeans, I pull up my call history. "Here." I thrust it at her. "Scroll down and you'll see how much I've been trying."

Her brow puckers in confusion as she flips through the list, and then a light goes off in her eyes. "Holy shit." She presses a button and curses. "This isn't Dakota's number, Shawn."

"What? Of course, it is."

She shakes her head, pulling out her own cell. "This is her number, and they don't match."

I compare the two and she's right—the number saved to my cell is *not* Dakota's. "Who the hell have I been calling then? Someone's been receiving my voice and text messages because they haven't come back undelivered." An uneasy feeling settles in my bones, and I let loose a string of expletives.

"This was deliberate," Tabs says, articulating my thoughts. She punches the number into her cell. "I'll call it and see who picks up." I hold my breath as she puts her cell on speaker, and we both listen as it goes straight to an automated voicemail. "Damn it. No personal message which confirms my suspicions."

"I think I know what's happened, but I want some verification." I dial Devin's number and he picks up on the third ring. I ask him to run a trace on the number and call me back.

"Someone wanted to break you two up," Tabs deduces, and I nod.

"I think it was my assistant. The day I landed back in L.A., I gave her my phone to turn off notifications, and I think she switched out the numbers then."

"That's not all she did." Tabs proceeds to fill me in on Dakota's call and how Calista answered and sent her an incriminating photo.

"I swear I'm not sleeping with her. It was one time, years ago, and it's never happened again. I knew she was crazy, but this is some fucked-up shit."

My phone vibrates, and I answer Devin's call, already knowing he's going to confirm Calista's involvement. Although she attempted to cover her tracks by setting the cell up with an Iowa city number, Devin has been able to trace it back to her in a matter of minutes. I hang up and call Luke immediately, giving him a quick rundown of what's happened. "I want Calista fired immediately. Revoke her security clearance and systems access and have the front desk retrieve her ID badge, laptop, cell, and anything else that is my official property." He doesn't argue this time, and a layer of stress lifts off me as I move to end the call, but Tabs holds up a palm, stalling me.

"Ask him if Kota has turned up at his offices," she says, and I lift a brow in silent question. "She took a late flight to L.A. last night. Her plan was to go to your management offices and ask to speak to your manager because she didn't trust that she'd get through to you if she called your cell," she adds.

"I heard," Luke confirms in my ear. "But she hasn't turned up here. At least not yet. I'll just double-check with security."

I shake my head at Tabs, and she frowns, glancing worriedly at the time.

"No, she hasn't made an appearance," Luke reconfirms. "I gave her name to the front desk, and I'll call you the minute she shows."

"Okay. Thanks, man."

"Shawn!" Luke's urgent tone stops me from hanging up.

"What?"

"I'm sorry about Calista. I should've listened to you. You were right about her all along."

"Just get rid of her now, Luke, and make sure she never comes back."

I hang up then, a cloud of apprehension hovering over me. "Call Dakota," I tell Tabs. "I need to know she's okay."

Tabs calls her three times in a row, but the phone goes automatically to voicemail, and my sense of apprehension multiplies.

"I don't like this," Tabs says, looking as worried as I feel.

"Me neither. Did she say what time she was planning on stopping by my management offices?"

"She had checked into a hotel at the airport and booked a cab for seven a.m. to bring her downtown. She should have been there by now. Something's wrong, Shawn." She grips my arm. "Do something."

I call Devin again and quickly update him. "Can you check to see if she got on the flight and if she checked into her hotel. I'm worried."

"Give me ten minutes, and I'll call you back."

"Let's grab a coffee," Tabs suggests, and I let her steer me to the small coffee place around the corner. I take a seat in the corner, with my back to the room and away from the window, while Tabs gets our drinks.

I drum my fingers impatiently on the tabletop, and my knee jerks up and down. I'm strung tight, and an awful sense of foreboding presses down on me, refusing to leave. Tabs hands me my black coffee, and I nod my thanks. She sits down across from me. "So." She purses her lips. "You're Shawn Lucas."

"In the flesh." I know she's just trying to distract me, but I can't even summon a smile as I reply.

"So, *are* you into it?"

I frown, and my lips pause around my coffee cup. "Into what?"

"Threesomes and kinky sex." She grins, sipping her drink like butter wouldn't melt in her mouth.

I splutter. "Want to say it louder? Those people across the street didn't hear you."

"Quit stalling, stud." She rubs her hands in glee. "Dish the dirt."

The vibration of my phone saves me from responding. I snatch it up. "Well?"

Devin's voice is solemn and littered with concern as he speaks. "She never made the flight, Shawn. She never left the city."

Nausea swamps me, and my heart is racing. "What do you mean?"

"I still have a tracker on her cell. I just traced the location. Her phone is somewhere outside her dorm."

I clamp a hand over my mouth, unable to speak over my fear. Tabs wells up when she spots the abject terror on my face.

"Take Mark and scour the grounds outside her dorm," Devin instructs. "I'm going to call my old station and campus security and see if I can get access to any camera feeds in the area. Keep in close contact with me."

"Okay." My voice is raw. My fear transparent.

"Try not to worry, Shawn. We'll find her. I promise you."

"We need to go." I stand, and Tabs follows me out of the coffee shop. I whisper the update to her, and she starts sobbing. I pull her into a quick hug. "We have to stay strong, and I'm not going to let anything happen to Dakota, I promise. Call Daisy and Elsa, just in case they've heard from her," I suggest, and she dries her eyes, pulling out her cell.

My new personal bodyguard, Mark, is waiting outside for me. We fall into step, hurrying the few blocks until we come to the side road leading to Dakota's dorm. "Let's start looking from here," he directs, slowing his gait and scanning the path as we walk.

"Neither of the girls have heard from her," Tabs says, joining us in closely examining our surroundings. We turn around the corner, stepping onto the main path that leads to the dorm. The grass is overgrown, the shrubbery untidy, in this section so we split up to scour the area. About three minutes later, Tabs yells my name, and we both race to her side. She's clutching a black bag to her chest, tears streaming down her face. "It's Kota's."

"Oh God." I squeeze my eyes shut, and a tight pain spreads across my chest.

Mark rummages in her bag, pulling out her phone which has since powered off.

I drop to the ground on my butt, resting my head on my knees while Mark checks in with Devin. Tabs is quietly crying beside me. "Who took her, Shawn? Who has her?"

I can only shake my head. *Is this sheer coincidence or has someone gone after Dakota because of what she means to me?* My most recent stalker may be behind bars, but that doesn't mean there isn't a line of crazies waiting to take his place. *Did my declaration of love provoke this?*

My cell vibrates in my pocket, and I slip it out. All the blood leaches from my face as the message loads.

It's a photo of Dakota.

She's strapped to a chair, her arms tied behind her back, her head lolling forward in a way that indicates she's unconscious.

DO AS I INSTRUCT AND SHE'LL COME TO NO HARM. IGNORE MY COMMANDS OR INVOLVE THE POLICE AND SHE DIES.

Chapter 35

Dakota

My eyes flicker open and shut, and I wet my dry lips as I slowly come to. It feels like mothballs have taken up residence in my furry mouth, and my throat is raw and aching. A coarse whimper leaves my lips involuntarily. Slowly, the room comes into focus, and I jerk wide-awake. Blood pumps furiously through my body, and my heart is beating so fast I'm scared I'm on the verge of a heart attack. My neck aches, and my arms throb, but I barely feel the pain as it all comes rushing back to me.

"Get her," a gruff voice says from behind me, raising all the tiny hairs on the back of my neck.

I scan the desolate room, noting the trash, used needles, and other debris strewn across the floor. A dirty mattress rests in one corner, and three rickety chairs line the far wall. Apart from that, the space is devoid of furniture and fittings. Paint is peeling off the walls, and some of the panes of glass are cracked in the only window in the place. It's up high on the left-hand side, and, if I had to hazard a guess, I'd say I'm in the basement of a large house or warehouse.

A door creaks open and shut behind me, and then two sets of legs appear in front of me. I lift my head, shooting daggers at the man and woman before me. The girl looks about my age, and I'd say she was pretty one time, before drugs ravaged her face and her body. She's wearing skinny jeans that are hanging off her skeletal frame, knee-high boots, and a ratty sweater that's seen better days. But it's the sunken cheeks, hollowed-out eyes and parchment-paper skin that are the telltale signs. Her hair hangs in limp strands down her back. The guy isn't much better. He's got to be at least ten or fifteen years older than she is. His hair is closely cropped to his head, and he's supporting a straggly goatee. Tattoos cover his arms and his neck, and the crazy, unfocused look in his eyes has me shivering all over.

I've never seen either of them before, and I have no clue what they want with me. Ignoring the chattering of my teeth, I try to steady my voice when I speak. "Why am I here? What do you want?"

"You're bait," the girl replies. "Provided you do as we tell you, no harm will come to you."

The guy runs his eyes over my body from head to toe, and her assurances fall flat. A heavy weight presses down on my chest as panic surges to the surface.

I think I might puke.

Thoughts of Mom threaten to unravel my composure, but I force those troubling fears aside, telling myself to keep calm and maintain focus. The best thing I can do for my mother is to get out of this alive, and I need to keep my cool and not let terror consume me.

"Why me?"

"Because you're his midnight dancer," the guy sneers, mocking me. He leans in, tracing a filthy fingernail across my cheek.

"Get your fucking hands off me!" I scream, flinching at his

touch.

He chuckles. "I don't think she's getting this," he says to the girl.

"Leave her alone, Eric," she snaps, yanking his hand back. "He won't hand over the cash if she's harmed in any way. Put your dick back in your pants and start using your brain." She prods at his temple, and he shoves her away.

"Don't fucking tell me what to do, Cheyenne. This is *my* show."

"Don't piss me off, jerk face. This was my idea, and if I hadn't come to you with it, you wouldn't be here. *I'm* calling the shots. Not you. I'm the one who knows him, not you."

Eric's whole demeanor changes in an instant. Grabbing Cheyenne to him, he demolishes her mouth while he fondles her ass. "I love it when you get all feisty. It really fucking turns me on." As if to prove his point, he directs her hand to the bulge in his pants and lets her feel.

I'm seconds away from puking. Although, watching their live porn show is far preferable to whatever Eric was dreaming up when he leered at me a few minutes ago.

"But it'll have to wait, sexy," he says, nipping at her lower lip. "I need to set things up at the drop-off point."

She rubs her palm along the length of his erection, stroking him through his jeans, while smirking. "Don't be too long."

He swats her on the butt, before sending me a sleazy look on his way out. I release the breath I'd been holding, but the sense of relief doesn't last long. Two more guys appear in the room, taking the seats at the far wall, both of them eyeballing me with the same intensity Eric displayed.

It's not in any way comforting.

But I remind myself to maintain a calm veneer, even if I'm quaking on the inside.

I know the best thing to do is to keep the kidnapper talking, so I attempt to strike up some kind of camaraderie with Cheyenne. "You know Shawn?"

"I've known him since we were kids."

"So why are you doing this?"

She drags a chair over and straddles it, facing me. "Did he tell you about Matt and Nick and how he came to find fame and fortune?"

I shake my head. I know nothing about that side of his life, but admitting that out loud probably won't help my cause.

She snorts, and a bitter look crosses her face. "Figures. Shawn's a selfish asshole who doesn't deserve his success. Nick and Matt were his best friends growing up, and they started a band when we were fourteen. Some YouTube videos of them performing went viral, and in a flash, they were whisked to L.A. by one of the biggest labels."

She starts coughing, and it's a horrid, dry, coarse sound. One of the pricks brings her a bottle of water, and she greedily knocks it back. When she's done, she tosses the bottle on the floor, grabs the guy down to her level, and plants one on him. "Thanks, baby." He grabs her boob through her sweater, and a moan flies out of her throat before she shoves him away. "Not now. Go sit down."

He saunters back to his chair, flashing me a flirty look once he has reclaimed his seat.

"Where were we?" Cheyenne says, not needing any encouragement to continue. "Yes. Nick. So, Nick was chasing me for ages, but I wasn't interested. He was cute, but nothing special, certainly not in Shawn's league." Her lips curl into a sneer. "But I wasn't good enough for that pompous dick, so I had to downgrade my options. When they started the band, and it became obvious they were onto something, I gave in to Nick. Fucking killed me to be his girlfriend, but I was in it for the long-term gain."

The longer she speaks, the more I despise her.

"I knew the guys were going to hit the big time, and I was going to get that ring on my finger, pop out a kid or two, and then divorce Nick's boring ass and walk away with a nice paycheck. Except Shawn fucking Lucas ruined everything."

She gets up, pacing the room in agitation. Venom practically seeps from her pores as she spits out the rest of her tale. "The label didn't want Nick or Matt. It was clear Shawn was the star. Instead of sticking up for his friends, he sold them out. They got a shitty payoff and were sent packing. I found out I was pregnant a couple weeks later. It wasn't a shock. I had planned it, but I didn't realize I was now tied to a loser, with his loser kid growing in my belly, but what could I do? I was fifteen and pregnant, and I knew my parents would kick me out when they heard the news."

"Man, you're a cold-hearted bitch, Cheyenne," the other guy pipes up.

"Shut up, assface, or you can forget about getting a cut of the ransom," she says, flipping him the bird.

She refocuses on her story. "So, I had the stupid kid and came up with a Plan B, but Nick is too fucking soft and too sentimental for his own good. I told him to go to Shawn and tell him we needed cash. Guilt him into it, but Nick was having none of it. He refused to blame Shawn, but I wasn't letting him off the hook that easily."

She sits back down. "Your boyfriend is a fucking asshole. He changed his number, but I got a hold of his assistant's number and called. Left messages with her for an entire week. Pleading poverty. Then I sent pictures of the snotty-nosed kid. And he just turned around and said it wasn't any of his business and he was not going to be our cash cow."

I'm betting, one hundred percent, that Shawn never got any of those messages. That bitch probably thought it was his kid, and she wanted to keep Cheyenne away from him. "His assistant never showed him the messages or the photos. I can guarantee you that. She's a fucking bitch."

Cheyenne's brows climb to her hairline, and a broad smile fixes across her face. "Interesting, and I'm tempted to ask for deets, but this isn't your story. It's mine. I want you to memorize every word I'm telling you, so you can relay it back to him later. I want him to know what he did and why it's his fault you're here today."

She tucks her greasy hair behind her ears and continues. "All he had to do was deliver the cash, and then I would have skipped off into the sunset, but he wouldn't cough it up. Nick took a job as a mechanic and spent all his payoff on a small apartment. Fucking idiot. Expected me to stay home and play mom. To stay in that deadbeat town. But Cheyenne Williams was destined for better things."

Yeah, obviously, she's come far. "Like felony kidnapping and extortion?" I blurt before I can think better of it.

The guys at the back laugh, and Cheyenne's smile withers and dies. "You don't want to make an enemy of me, girl. Trust me. I'm the only thing standing in those guys way. I just have to say the words, and they'll be inside you like that." She clicks her fingers, and I shiver as rising panic returns.

"Sorry," I whisper, hating myself for saying it, but self-preservation has kicked in. "Go on. What happened next," I encourage.

Like the flip of a coin, she smiles at me again. This girl is either doped to her eyeballs or just plain bat shit crazy. Her eyes keep rolling in her head, so I'm sure it's the former and probably the latter too. All I know is I need to keep her on my side and keep her talking.

"I left that deadbeat town and Nick behind and came to L.A."

I think she did Nick and her kid a solid by leaving, but I don't articulate that thought.

"Found my crew and dabbled in a few things until I met Eric a year ago. He was fresh out of jail and looking for his next scam. I was hellbent on revenge, so it was a match made in heaven." She throws back her head, cackling as if it's the funniest thing ever.

"And we played this so perfectly." She grins. "It was all a setup to divert attention from the real stalker, namely me. It pissed me off that Shawn went into hiding, but we adjusted our plans accordingly, knowing it would draw him out. Discovering you was the icing on the cake."

"So, are you saying the stalker the police have in custody is innocent?"

She laughs, slapping her thighs. "Hardly! It was all part of the plan. We hired those three idiots to do all the donkey work and sent them to Shawn's house the second time knowing they would get caught. Eric's brother, Aaron, agreed to take the fall for a bigger share of the pot. He hasn't done time before, so the sentence will be more lenient. And when he gets out, he'll have all that lovely money waiting for him."

She presses her mouth to my ear. "Or so he thinks," she whispers, winking conspiratorially as if I'm in this with her.

She sits back down in her chair. "We knew Shawn would call off the bodyguards once he believed his stalker was no longer a threat, so we bided our time until we could get to you. And now here we are," she says, just as the door creaks open behind me. "About to be rich beyond our wildest dreams. You can tell Shawn he could have spared you this, spared himself all the shit we did to him in the last year, if he'd just paid up in the first place." She straightens up, slanting me a superior look. "No one messes with Cheyenne Williams and gets away unscathed."

Chapter 36

Shawn

We dropped Tabs off at her place before heading to the bank and then on to my penthouse. Devin is here, plugged into his cell as he taps away on his laptop. A couple of other guys from his team are also in the apartment, heads focused on their laptops and screens as they converse in hushed tones. The place is a hive of activity, but it does little to quell the brewing storm in my head. Devin ends his call and comes up to me as I step foot in the room. He slaps me on the back. "How are you holding up?"

"I'm not." I draw exaggerated mouthfuls of air into my lungs. "This is all my fault. If I hadn't gotten jealous, I never would've taken the bodyguard off her and she wouldn't have been taken."

Mark and Tom drop the duffel bags by the door and stand guard.

"You don't know that, Shawn," Devin replies. "Besides, there didn't seem to be a legitimate reason to continue protection."

"That's neither here nor there now. We need to focus on finding her. Any updates?"

Devin sits back down, nodding at the empty chair beside him, and I sink into it. "They are using an untraceable cell to send you messages so that's a dead end. However, we might have another lead." I lean forward on my elbows. "The rendezvous point is interesting." A second text had come in a little while ago with a set time and place to meet along with a demand for five million dollars.

We haven't notified the police because Devin is an ex-cop, and he has this in hand. It needs to look like we're cooperating, hence why the guys are guarding my five mill in the two duffel bags. I thought the bank manager might keel over when I made the demand, but he came through with the cash in record time.

"You remember I said I wanted to tie up loose ends with Aaron Hunter?" I nod. "A few things were niggling at me, and I've uncovered something interesting. Aaron is half-brother to a guy named Eric Spencer. You ever heard of him?" I rack my brains and shake my head. "Eric is an ex-cop. He was dirty to the core, and an addict to boot. Was involved in tons of illegal shit until he was caught and put away for five years. Guess who he did time with?"

"Santa Claus?" I snap, having no patience for this. Not when my girl is out there being held by these assholes.

Devin ignores my little outburst. "The three hired guns who gave up Aaron."

"Hang on. I'm getting confused." I try to sort this out in my head. "So, Eric is a dirty cop who was in jail with the three assholes who broke into my house and tied up my mom and he's the brother of the guy who worked for the security company who turned out to be my stalker?"

"Correct. Except I don't think Aaron Hunter was the mastermind."

"Eric is."

"Exactly. Aaron was the fall guy."

"Shit. You think Eric is behind this now? He's the one who has Dakota?"

"I'm hoping he does, because we just got a lock on Eric's cell and it's only a couple miles from the drop-off location."

I hop up out of my seat. "So what the hell are we waiting for?" I yell.

"For this," he says as another guy enters the room carrying a large black sports bag. He drops it on the counter and unzips it. Devin hands out guns and bulletproof vests. I don't bother mounting a protest when he refuses to give me a gun. I've never handled one before, and I'd probably just shoot myself in the foot or something. I'll leave that to the experts and focus on getting my girl the hell out of there before things turn nasty.

The ten of us set off in two blacked-out SUVs. I ride beside Devin, holding my head in my hands as I offer up prayers to every deity known to mankind. I promise God I'll do anything once Dakota gets out of this alive and unharmed.

There is nothing like a hostage situation to focus the mind. To make me realize how deeply I love this girl. If anything happens to her today, I'll die.

"Why did this guy have me in his sights?" I ask Devin when we're only a few miles out. I need to talk before I lose my mind.

"That I don't know. It might not be anything personal. It could be he deemed you an easier target than other celebrities. Maybe his brother was the one identifying the targets based on the intel he had at his fingertips." He leans forward, pressing his elbows into his knees. "We'll get to the bottom of it, but, right now, finding Dakota and getting her to safety is our priority."

The SUVs come to a halt behind an abandoned building, a

few miles off the beaten track, ten minutes later. We've only got forty minutes until we're due at the official drop-off point, so I hope Devin's hunch is right.

"I think you were right, boss," a burly dude with thickset glasses says, handing an iPad to Devin. "There are five heat signatures in the basement of the adjoining building, and the cell location is locked on. Eric is in there, along with four others."

"The building has been derelict for years," another guy pipes up from behind us. "Whatever is going on in there is definitely not legit."

"Okay." Devin hands back the iPad, holding his men's attention. "We'll take the rear entrance, and beta unit will cover the front. Arm your weapons and follow my lead. You know the drill. Keep your wits about you. Cover all the bases. Don't open fire unless they are threatening Dakota or it's self-defense. Let's play this safe." He turns to the guy with the glasses. "Gunner, I want you to stay here. When I have visual confirmation, I'll give you the signal and you radio the cops then."

"Understood, sir."

"Right. Let's do this. Shawn, you stay put."

"Over my dead body. That's my girl in there, and there's no way I'm sitting in this car like a fucking pussy. Don't make me pull rank, Devin, because I fucking will."

I detect a slight smirk, but he hides it quickly. "Fine, but no heroics. You let us do our job. If shit hits the fan, and you have a clear path to Dakota, take it. Otherwise, you stay the hell back."

"Agreed," I lie.

We scramble out of our vehicle, keeping our backs flat to the wall as we make our way, covertly, from one building to the next. If this wasn't a life or death scenario, I'd be high on all this Jason Bourne shit, but I'm too freaking worried to take any pleasure in this moment.

We slip into the building through an open crack in the wall, walking slowly and quietly across the floor, careful to sidestep any debris which would make noise and give us away. My heart is in my throat as we descend the stairs to the lower level. Devin holds up a hand as the sound of voices reaches our ears. Adrenaline is flooding my system, and I wipe my sweaty palms along the back of my jeans. We inch forward, excruciatingly slowly, and the voices grow louder. It's coming from a room at the very end of the corridor. The door is shut and Devin frowns. I can almost see the wheels churning in his head as he contemplates how to approach this. The guys are having the weirdest nonverbal conversation as they mouth and gesture wildly with their hands.

A piercing cry rings out, and I don't stop to think. Devin's eyes widen in horror as I run to the door and open it, racing inside. Some bastard with a nasty glint in his eye has his hands wrapped around Dakota's hair, yanking her head back at a painful angle. She's still strapped to the chair, in the center of the room, arms and legs bound.

Two guys at the back of the room hop up, producing guns and pointing them at me, but I don't care. They won't get any money if I'm dead, so I'm betting no one's planning on shooting me.

Not yet anyway.

I stalk toward the bastard hurting my girl and shove him. The clicking of weapons brings me back to reality, and I freeze as one of the men prods the butt of his gun in my temple and the second one holds his weapon to the back of Dakota's head. Then my eyes wander to the other female in the room, and my mouth hangs open.

"Cheyenne?"

"Hello, Shawn." She spits out my name like it's poison.

"What the fuck?" I stare at her like she's sprouted horns or wings or some shit. "You're behind this?"

"Surprise."

Her crazy eyes and weird pallor give her away. She's high as a kite, and that makes her completely unpredictable. "Why?"

She steps toward me, running her hand over my cheek and I flinch. I always thought this chick was manipulative and self-centered, but Nick was besotted with her, and he couldn't see what Matt and I could see. "For the money, honey."

"Chey. We need to regroup," the bastard on the floor says, climbing to his feet and instantly punching me in the gut. "You're lucky you don't have a bullet in your skull, but try that again, and I won't hesitate to end you." Collapsing to my knees, I groan, thinking now would be a great time for Devin and his men to make an appearance, but I hear nothing from the corridor, and I've got no clue what they're up to.

Cheyenne and the scary prick, who I'm assuming is Eric, converse in a corner of the room while the other two keep their guns trained on us.

I turn my attention to Dakota, glancing up at her, relief mixing with longing and fear as I set eyes on her for the first time in weeks. "Are you okay?" I ask her. "Did they hurt you?" I don't see any obvious signs of injury to her person or clothing, but that doesn't mean she isn't hurt.

"No," she whispers, before adding, "I can't believe you're here." Her eyes search mine, and I try to convey that it's fine, that I'm not alone.

Cheyenne and the prick are arguing now. No doubt, Eric is figuring things out, and me showing up here unexpectedly has thwarted their plans. If he's an ex-cop, then he should know the score. But judging by the way his eyes are darting all over the place, I'm betting he's juiced up too, so perhaps he's not thinking clearly.

A loud pop emits from the corridor outside, and the three men race to the door, communicating with their eyes as they point their weapons and indiscriminately start firing blind. Cheyenne shrieks, backing into a wall and covering her ears with her hands.

The next couple minutes shave a few years off my life.

Gunfire is still being traded out in the corridor as the ceiling implodes in parts, raining clouds of dust and debris on us. Devin's men start dropping from wires through the ceiling into the room. Jumping up, I drag Dakota's chair over to the wall and bend over her, shielding her with my body as shots ring out behind us. Cheyenne starts screaming, and we both look sideways at her. She's sitting on the ground with her knees pulled into her chest, her hands still covering her ears as she screams and cries. I doubt she expected things to turn out like this. She always was too single-minded.

Dakota's trembling underneath me, but she's holding it together. I drink her in, trying to block out the shit going on around us. We stare at one another, emotion and electricity crackling in the space between us, as if we aren't in this situation. My heart kicks off, careening around my chest. Existing without Dakota is not something I'd ever survive. She's as vital to me as breathing. "I love you."

"I love you too," she says, and even though it's messed up, I can't help smiling.

"Clear." Devin's voice rings out, and the gunfire stops. Now, the only sound in the room is Cheyenne's hysterical screaming. Devin clamps a hand on my shoulder. "It's okay. You're safe. They're dead."

I straighten up. "Thank you."

"Yes," Dakota adds, and I'm proud of how strong her voice sounds. "Thank you for saving me." She's no longer looking at Devin.

Kneeling down, I untie the binds around her feet while Devin works to free her hands. Then I'm pulling her up into my arms and hugging the shit out of her. Sirens wail in the distance, and relief consumes me. Dakota circles her arms around my waist, resting her head on my chest, and, in the midst of this bloody nightmare, I find my everlasting peace.

Chapter 37

Shawn

I go with Dakota in the ambulance to the hospital. Even though she insists she's uninjured, it's standard protocol after what she's been through. I hold her hand the entire time, and we don't move our eyes from one another.

Devin shows up with his police buddy friend just as she's being discharged. We both give initial statements and agree to go to the station in the morning to make our formal reports. Then Devin drives us back to the penthouse. I keep my arms around Dakota the whole time, and I'm so grateful she made it through this physically unscathed. Mentally, I'm not so sure. She's been quiet, and we haven't said more than a few words to one another, but I'm letting her dictate this.

I run her a bath while she calls her friends to let them know she's safe. I'm testing the water, when I feel her behind me. I stand and walk toward her. She looks a million miles away. "Hey." I gently cup her beautiful face. "Are you doing all right?"

She lifts her chin, peering into my eyes. "I always knew there was something weird about your eyes." Raising her hand, she gently explores my face and then runs her fingers through my hair. "I'm not sure which I prefer. Dark or blond. You look good with both."

"I'm sorry I didn't tell you. I thought I was protecting you and…" A shuddering breath leaves my lips. "I was scared you wouldn't want me if you knew."

She looks intently at me. "Take a bath with me?"

Her words startle me, but it's not an unpleasant surprise. I tug my shirt up over my head, tossing it to the ground. We quietly undress and then I get into the bath first, resting my back against the end of the tub. Dakota steps in front of me, sliding down between my legs. I wrap my arms around her, propping my chin on her shoulder as ripples of warm water wash over us.

"I can understand your fear," she says after a couple minutes. "But you still should've told me. Especially when you found out about Layla."

"I know," I whisper, squeezing her tight. "I fucked up, but I want to make it up to you, if you'll let me."

"Everything feels like a lie," she whispers.

I twist her around until she's straddling me, and I eyeball her with as much sincerity as I can muster. "It wasn't a lie. It was more real than anything I've experienced in years." I grip the nape of her neck. "I meant everything I said to you. I love you. I love you very much. I have never had these feelings for any other woman, ever." I rub my thumb along the side of her neck as I talk. "I tried to stay away from you at the start, to not drag you into this, but I couldn't stay away. As I fell deeper, the guilt increased, and I wanted to come clean, but you weren't exactly my biggest fan, and my lifestyle is crazy and not an easy sell. I was too selfish, but you should know I gave you as much of the truth as I could. I tried not to lie, because I didn't want to do that to you." I lean in and press a kiss to the underside of her jaw. "I've shared things with you that no one else knows. Please say it's not too late. That I haven't completely screwed everything up."

She's quiet for a minute. Then she caresses my cheek, and there isn't a part of me her touch doesn't ignite.

If this is the end for us, I don't think I'll ever get over it.

"Tell me everything I need to know," she says, and I do.

We stay in the bath until the water turns cold as we talk it out. I tell her about Calista and her efforts to ruin things for us, what Devin and I discovered about Eric, and she relays the conversation she had with Cheyenne.

We dry each other off and dress in fluffy robes, eating takeout in front of the fire as we continue talking. She's peppering me with questions, and I answer each one with brutal honesty, until she seems to run out of things to ask me. It's past midnight, and I'm exhausted but unwilling to let this night end. Especially if it's the last one I get to share with her. She isn't giving much away, and I don't know where her head's at, so it's time to make my intentions clear.

I scoot in closer to her on the couch, taking her hands in mine. "Dakota. I love you, and I want you as my girlfriend. Move to L.A. Share my life with me." My heart is thumping in my chest as I await her reply.

She leans in and kisses me softly, just once, but it's everything. I've missed the feel of her mouth against mine. "I want to, but I can't."

I'm devastated, but I try to keep a brave face. "I understand."

She touches my face, keeping her eyes trained on mine. "I changed my major, and I'm studying dance now although that's not really a big deal. I'm sure I could transfer to a college in L.A."

Damn straight. I'm not against using my celebrity leverage

to help my loved ones, and it wouldn't take much to get her into whatever program she wanted. But that isn't the issue. "Your mom," I say, and she nods.

"I can't leave her. Not until she's well, and even then..."

"It's okay. I completely understand, and you wouldn't be the girl I fell in love with if you didn't want to be here for her."

She cups one side of my face. "You've been honest with me tonight, so I want to be the same. There is another reason." A pained expression crosses her eyes. "I'd be lying if I said what went down hasn't shaken my faith in you, because it has. I can tell you're sincere, and I want to trust you, but—"

"It's going to take time to earn back your trust," I finish for her.

She nods. "I also don't know if I can handle your lifestyle and all those girls..."

"Babe." I peer into her eyes. "There's been a lot less girls than you'd think and no one in ages. You know I've never been in a relationship before you. I've only ever had one-night stands. You're the first girl I've done this with. The only one I want to continue doing it with."

"What about Alannah Fields? Wasn't she your girlfriend one time?"

My lips tug up at the corners. "I think someone's been Googling me."

"Guilty as charged," she readily admits. "Now fess up."

I tweak her nose. "You're cute when you're jealous, but you have nothing to worry about. It was all fake. She'd just signed to my label, and they wanted her to gain exposure before her single debuted. I didn't so much as kiss her in the three months we were parading around the place as boyfriend and girlfriend."

"Hmm." She looks wary.

"You don't believe me?"

"I do, it's just hard to believe. I mean, she's stunning. And you were, what, seventeen at the time? I know how horny seventeen-year-old guys are."

Now I have a renewed interest in kicking the shit out of her ex. "Don't fucking remind me. I still owe that asshole Cole a punch or two for sniffing around you after I left."

"By the way, that photo was completely misleading. I didn't do anything with him, or anyone, since you left. You should also know he was the one who uploaded the video."

"I'll add it to the ever-growing list of reasons why I hate that fucker." She snickers, and it brings a smile to my face. "To answer your earlier question, Alannah isn't my type."

She arches a brow. "You have a type?"

I grin as I wrap my arms around her waist and haul her into my lap. "Yeah. Just one. The beautiful blonde who dances like an angel." I nuzzle into her neck. "You're the only one I want for keeps, Dakota. It's only ever you."

Chapter 38

Dakota

I melt into his arms, unable to deny my feelings any more. It hurts that he kept so much from me, but after talking it out for hours, I understand his motivations more clearly, and I know he did it out of concern for me. The fact he asked me to move to L.A. with him shows how serious he is about this. If I was doubting his love before, I'm not doubting it now. But I meant what I said—I can't leave Mom when she's so fragile, and he needs to earn back my trust before I make such a bold step.

I think Layla would be proud of me.

The old me would've followed him to L.A. and worried about the consequences later. Perhaps it's the result of all that's happened to me since she died, or I've just finally grown up. But I get it now.

The sense of responsibility that comes from doing the right thing, but it no longer feels like a burden.

"Can I ask you something else," Shawn says, and I lift my head from his shoulder. I'm still sitting in his lap, trying to ignore the semi he's sporting under his robe.

"Of course. We're an open book now, you and I." I grace him with a genuine smile, and his answering one is breath stealing. I thought he was gorgeous before with his dark hair and green eyes, but this blond-haired blue-eyed version floors me every time he looks at me. Shawn is beautiful. Inside and out.

"Moving to L.A. is clearly a non-runner, but what does that mean for us? Do you still want an us?" The vulnerability in his gaze almost undoes me.

"Yes, I still want an us."

He buries his face in my shoulder. "Thank fuck."

"How will this work?"

He lifts his head. "We're not that far away from one another, and I have a private plane." He winks, and I roll my eyes. "I'll come to you when I have time off, or you can travel to me?"

I like that he's posed it as a question. That he's including me in the decision. "I'd like that, and perhaps it will help ease me into the lifestyle."

"Maybe your first trip could be Christmas? I know it's only a couple weeks away, but my mom has invited you and your mom to come spend the holidays with us. I can organize all the travel arrangements, and we have plenty of guest rooms. Please say you'll come?"

"You told your mom about me?"

He nods. "I've been staying at her house since I returned to L.A. and we're reconnecting."

He had told me before that he wasn't really speaking to his mom although he hadn't gone into details. I run my fingers around the back of his neck. "I'm really pleased you've patched things up with her. Family is important."

"*So* important," he agrees. "Will you come? Pretty please?"

I laugh. "I will if you promise to never say that again. Especially not in public."

"Your wish is my command." His lips tug up at the corners.

"Mom is doing better, but she's still uncommunicative at times. I don't want things to be awkward."

He grips the nape of my neck. "My mom knows everything, and she's sympathetic. She just wants to meet you both."

Stress flitters off my shoulders. "I can't wait to meet her. Thank you. I was kinda dreading the holidays."

"You're so strong, Dakota. So brave. Are you really okay after everything today?"

I nod. "I am. I mean, I was terrified, but, somehow, I just knew it would be okay and that helped keep me calm. I can't properly explain it, but I wasn't freaking out like I probably should have. I...I just knew you wouldn't let anything happen to me." I wrap my arms around his neck. "I haven't thanked you for saving me. You're my hero."

He shakes his head. "I'm not the hero. Devin was amazing. He just took control and kept me sane at the same time. I think I owe that guy a bonus or something."

"You're still a hero to me," I whisper. "You burst into that room without any consideration for your own wellbeing."

He pushes my hair back off my face. "I heard you cry out and I didn't hesitate. If anything had happened to you..." He shivers, and I hug him tight, before climbing off his lap and extending my hand to him.

"I'm here. You're here. We're both alive and well," I tell him, as he gets up. I rise on tiptoes and kiss him properly for the first time in weeks. His arms sweep around my back, and he pulls me up. I wrap my legs around his waist, and he locks his arms under my butt. "I say we should celebrate life," I whisper over his mouth.

"What did you have in mind?" His voice is gruff and needy.

"I want my boyfriend to make love to me," I softly reply. "I want him to remind me why it's fantastic to be alive."

Shawn carries me to his bedroom, sprinkling kisses all over my face and neck as we walk. We strip out of our robes and fall on the bed in a pile of tangled limbs. Our kisses quickly grow hot and heavy as weeks of pent-up longing explodes in a mesh of sexual frenzy. I push him flat on his back and straddle him. Leaning down, I nip at his lips, biting and sucking as I grind against his lap. He emits these sexy sounds as I toy with him, heating my blood to boiling point. I sit up abruptly. "I want to feel you inside me with no barrier. I'm on the pill and I'm clean."

"Me too. I've always used condoms."

"As have I." Cole went through a phase of begging me to ride him bareback, but I always held back. "I was saving this for you."

I lower myself slowly on top of him, and we both groan as our heat mingles and our bodies start moving against one another. I ride him slowly and sensually, dipping down to kiss him, stroking his tongue with mine as he thrusts up into me. Then he takes control, sitting up while holding me in his lap, and we rock against each other as his hands and mouth explore every inch of my body. We climax together, clinging to one another as we ride wave after euphoric wave. Then we collapse in a sweaty heap on the bed, and he pulls me to him, spooning me from behind. "I want to do this with you every day for the rest of my life," he tells me, and I inwardly swoon.

"You're quite the romantic for a bad boy," I tease.

"Well, I do write love songs for a living."

I laugh, holding his arms more tightly around me. "You got me there." I sigh contentedly. "And I take it back. I don't hate your music. I love your music and your voice, and I love watching you play. Your words inspire me."

"You inspire me. Every day, and in every way."

My heart swells to bursting point. "My God, Shawn.

You're ruining me for eternity." My voice is choked with emotion.

"Good, because I plan to keep on ruining you for as long as you'll let me." He kisses my temple. "I love you, my beautiful midnight dancer."

"And I love you, my sweet, sexy rock star," I reply in a breathy voice just before sleep claims me.

Epilogue

Six Months Later - Dakota

"Are you sure you'll be okay? I can wait another few weeks or—"

"Sweetheart," Mom says, cutting across me. "I'll be fine. Your Aunt Hilda is here now and I'm much better." She holds my hands and squeezes. "Thanks to you, my beautiful sweet girl. I love you so much."

Tears sting my eyes as they have done regularly in the four months since Mom returned home. She still attends the outpatient clinic and she's still on medication, and she most likely will be for the rest of her life. The doctors are delighted with her progress, and with every passing day, I see more and more of the mother I used to know.

She won't ever be the same.

Neither will I.

No one could be after the tragedy we've endured, but we're both surviving and finally moving forward with our lives. "I love you too, Mom, and I'll phone every day."

She laughs, grabbing me into a hug. "Now I know you're

lying. You'll be having too much fun on tour to be thinking of me."

"I could never forget you, Mom. You're too much a part of me."

She tweaks my nose. "I know that, silly, but I need you to promise me something."

"Anything."

"Live your life and stop worrying about me. You are finally getting to live your dream, and you have that gorgeous man, who adores you, by your side. Have fun. Explore the world. Enjoy being in love. And when you come back to visit, I'll be waiting to hear all about it."

"Thanks, Mom." I kiss her cheek. "Remember I'm only at the end of the phone if you need me for anything."

"Take care, darling." We kiss and hug one final time before I walk down the steps, away from my family home, and into the car waiting for me.

The driver closes my door and I get settled, rolling down the window and waving to Mom and Aunt Hilda as the car glides away. I send a quick text to Shawn to let him know I'm en route to the airport.

As the landscape passes by in a blur, I take a moment to recall the whirlwind that has been the last six months of my life. Shawn and I have spent every spare moment together, splitting our time between Iowa and L.A. We even found the time at Easter to travel to Hawaii for a mini vacay. Mom had been home six weeks by then and she was doing well. Aunt Hilda visited to look after her in my absence, and she never left. My aunt is eight years older than Mom, and she never married, so she has no ties. The arrangement worked out well.

Mom and Dad were officially divorced two weeks before he became a father for the third time. He has since married Monique, and they live in the city with their new daughter.

Mom has taken it far better than I expected, but we don't talk about him much, so I'm not sure if that's just a front for me or if she's genuinely okay with it.

I have yet to meet my new half-sister, but I want to. Dad invited me to visit after she was born, but I'm not ready yet. I know she's innocent, and what happened to my family isn't her fault, but I'm still processing all my feelings, and I can't enter her life until I'm in the right place. I'm not sure I'll ever be welcoming of Monique, but I guess if I want to attempt to repair the relationship with Dad, then I'm going to have to try.

For now, I'm moving on with other aspects of my life and focusing on me.

At least things with L.A.'s hottest, sexiest, most-in-demand rock star are going well. Better than well. I'm head over heels in love with my man and excited to move things forward in our relationship.

Shawn's L.A. lifestyle took some time to adjust to, and if I'm being brutally honest with myself, I'm still not all the way there. It's a whole other ball game, and the fake people, the greed, and materialism aren't something I'll ever get used to, but I'm prepared to make the sacrifice for the man I love.

Besides, he's the one making all my dreams come true.

In a week's time, I'll begin rehearsals for his world tour which kicks off in the U.K. in three months, and I'm in that excited-nervous space. The tour is a year-long one, so we won't be back until this time next year. Then we'll have the summer together before I take up my place in Juilliard. I'm extremely lucky that they've given me another opportunity, and I'm really looking forward to fulfilling my childhood ambition. Shawn is planning on relocating to New York with me, although he will have to travel a lot, but I have faith we'll make it work. We love each other too much to let what we have go.

Getting to dance on a worldwide stage is another childhood

ambition, and I still have to pinch myself to realize this is happening. Although Shawn offered me an instant contract, I refused to be given preferential treatment, and I auditioned in front of his dance director and head choreographer like every other dancer.

I wanted to earn this on my own merit and not because I'm the star's girlfriend, even if that's what everyone else assumes.

I've gotten a lot of flak from his fans and the media in the last few months, but I'm riding the storm. Shelly, his PR person, has been very helpful, coaching me and providing tips before every public event. The first time I appeared at an official event as his girlfriend was one of the most nerve wracking experiences of my life, but Shawn never left my side, and, gradually I've learned to relax. Dealing with the fans and groupies is something I'm still struggling with, but it's part of being in a relationship with one of the most famous men on the planet.

The fan reaction to our relationship has been extreme. Either they hate me and blow up social media criticizing every little thing about me or they love me and the effect I've had on their boy. I've had girls stop me in the street asking for *my* autograph. I've also had girls shout horrific abuse and spit at me when I've been out. I have a full-time personal bodyguard now —Shawn was insistent after everything that went down—and it's taken some getting used to.

But the tradeoff is worth it.

Shawn is everything I never realized I wanted or needed. He brightens my world in so many ways, and he goes out of his way to make me feel cherished and loved, never failing to call me on a daily basis, regardless of how hectic his schedule is.

For a guy who hadn't the first clue about relationships when we first met, my man sure has done me proud.

He always has my back, no matter what, and he refuses to

clip my wings, constantly supporting and encouraging me, making me believe I can achieve anything I set my mind to.

I didn't think it was possible to love a guy as much as I love him, but every day I fall more and more in love with him, and I'm excited for this next phase of our relationship.

I send him a quick text as I strap myself into the seat on his private jet, accepting the glass of champagne from the hostess with a grateful smile.

Shawn

I stand on the shoreline of my private beach in Malibu, basking under the warmth of the sun, contemplating how much my life has changed in the last year. I still feel like pinching myself to be living this life. The one I always imagined when I was a punk ass kid strumming my guitar in the garage of Matt's house.

I've tried reaching out to Matt several times in the last year, but he wants nothing to do with me, and I have to respect his wishes.

Maybe some friendships just weren't built to last.

"Uncle Shawn!" Reece, Nick's son, screeches, barreling toward me on his short legs. "Look what I made for Kota."

I crouch down, ruffling his hair as I examine the colorful mess on the page. "Wow. You made her an awesome card. She's going to love it, buddy. Thank you." I hold out my fist and we knuckle touch. My brothers come racing out onto the sand, and Reece thrusts the card at me before running to meet them. I grin as I watch the three of them chase one another around, laughing gleefully.

"Here, man. Figure you could use one of these." Nick hands me a cold bottle of water as I carefully slide the card into the back pocket of my shorts.

"Thanks, bud."

"Has she landed yet?" he asks, watching the boys as he sips a beer.

"Thirty minutes ago. She should be here soon."

"Good stuff." He clamps a hand on my shoulder. "You've got yourself a good one, Shawn. Hold onto her."

"I plan to." I rub a hand over my jaw, unsure how to bring this up but wanting to get it out of the way before Dakota arrives. "I'm sorry about Cheyenne, man." His ex, and Reece's mother, was sent to jail for ten years last month for the part she played in Dakota's kidnapping and the earlier attempt on my life.

Dakota and I both had to testify, and we made a plea for leniency for Reece's sake. Even if we both feel she's a bad influence, she's still his mother, and we didn't want this for him.

Nick and I have grown really close again, and I'm trying to persuade him to join my band on tour. The money is great, and he could bring his son, but he still seems reluctant. I'm hoping Dakota might be able to get through to him where I've failed.

"Shawn!" Mum hollers from the patio, waving her hands frantically at me.

"I better see what she wants. Keep an eye on the little monsters."

Nick nods. "Sure. I'll coax them back in a few."

"Sup?" I ask Mom, dragging my hands through my longer hair. Dakota loves my hair like this, so I have no desire to cut it. I swear I almost come in my pants every time she runs her fingers through it.

"I forgot the damned shrimp."

I place my hands on her shoulders, chuckling. "Mom, relax. It's only Dakota. She's not going to care if we have shrimp or not."

"But it's her favorite."

I gesture at the table laden down with food. "Mom. You have enough food to feed an army. Chill. And you know Kota's laid-back. She wouldn't want you fussing."

Mom messes up my hair. "I just want everything to be perfect for you. This is a big step. You bought a house together, and I know it's serious between you."

"You can't mention that in front of her. You know she's a bit weird about money, and I haven't told her I put her name on the deeds yet. I want it to be a surprise, and I need to time it right."

She makes a zipping motion with her finger. "These lips are sealed." She smacks a kiss to my cheek. "I'm just so happy you're happy and that you've found a lovely, sweet, genuine girl who loves you for you."

Nick comes up behind us, chuckling when the boys rush past us, squealing and shouting as they head for the playroom. "Boys! Stop running in the house," Mom says, chasing after them.

"I wouldn't be surprised if your mom already has your wedding all mapped out," he says, grinning. "She can't stop gushing about Dakota."

"I wouldn't be surprised either, and if I have my way, she'll get the chance to implement her ideas."

"Hot damn. I knew it was the real deal, but I didn't know it was that serious already."

I shrug, like it's no biggie, but Nick knows me better than most. "It is, but it's not like I'll be going there anytime soon. Kota's only twenty and we've still got plenty of things to squeeze in before marriage and babies."

"She's here!" Mom calls from inside the house, and I all but sprint to the front door.

I rush outside as Dakota emerges from the car. She's wearing a summery white dress that stops at her knees and flip-flops. Her long wavy hair is loose, blowing in the gentle breeze, and her gorgeous skin is bare of makeup. My breath stutters in my chest, as it always does whenever I see her. She has no idea how completely stunning she is, or the full extent of the effect she has on me. With every passing day, I love her deeper and stronger. No amount of time with her will ever be enough. Closing the gap between us, I sweep her into my arms, swinging her around. She giggles, pressing down on my shoulders. "Put me down, you idiot!" she chastises, but she's smiling.

"I'm excited you're finally here. Sue me if I'm overly enthusiastic." I place her feet on the ground and smash my lips to hers. It's been two weeks since we last saw one another and I've missed my girl. She wraps her arms around my neck and presses her hot body against mine, kissing me back with the same intensity, uncaring that Mom and Nick are standing at the door watching our amorous display.

"Get a room!" Nick hollers, and I reluctantly drag my lips away.

"Welcome home, baby," I whisper, holding her in a tight hug.

She beams up at me, before shucking out of my embrace and moving over to hug Mom and Nick.

I help the driver unload her cases and then take her hand, leading her through the house.

"I can't believe how much you've done already." Her face glows with happiness and pride. "I hope you left something for me to do."

"I was just following your plans, baby," I wrap my arms around her from behind as we step into the large kitchen, nuzzling my nose in her neck. "And I only did the main living spaces because I knew everyone was coming today. The rest of the house is a blank canvas for you to do whatever you want with."

The decision to sell my Hollywood Hills home and move closer to Mom was the best idea I'd had in ages, but I wouldn't have made the move if Dakota hadn't been in agreement. We house hunted together and we both fell in love with this beach-side two-story seven-bedroom property on three acres of land. It's in a private secluded part of Malibu, and only a few miles from Mom's house. I moved in ten days ago and I've been crazy busy putting the finishing touches to my new album and furnishing the house before this weekend. But my special project was my main focus, and I can't wait a minute longer to show her.

"Mom, I'm gonna show Dakota her surprise now. Can you hold dinner for ten minutes?"

Mom grins before giving me a thumbs-up.

Dakota twists around in my arms, looking up at me. "What are you up to, Lev—Shawn."

I laugh. She still forgets sometimes and calls me Levi. Not that I mind in the slightest. Once she's a permanent fixture at my side she can call me whatever the hell she wants. "Come with me and I'll show you." Lacing my fingers in hers, I pull her to the far side of the house. We have a gym, home theater and game room over on this side of the house, along with the room I've just renovated especially for her. I stop in front of the closed door, pulling her into my arms. "I'm so glad you're here. I couldn't sleep last night I was so excited."

She laughs. "You're like a giddy ten-year-old right now, and I couldn't love you more." She smiles adoringly at me, and my heart trips over itself. "This feels like a new start, and I am so happy to be doing this here with you."

I place a searing hot kiss on her lips, and I'm instantly hard. I rock against her, and she moans. Running her hand down between our bodies, she gently palms my hard-on. "I can't wait to have sex on tap," she murmurs, rubbing her hand up and down my now straining length. "And I can't wait to fuck you in every room of our new house."

"Stop being so damn perfect," I tease, nipping at her lower lip. "Or at least hold that thought for later when we're alone."

"Deal." She steps away, grinning. "Now show me my surprise."

I open the door to her new dance studio and watch every emotion imaginable flit across her face as she slowly steps into the room, twirling around and taking it all in. Then she flings herself at me, jumping into my arms and I have to react fast to avoid losing my balance. "Oh my God! You are unbelievably amazing, and I love you so much."

She's kissing me all over and her enthusiasm is infectious. "You can thank me properly later."

"Oh, I plan to thank you, and love you, for a long, long time." Her adoring smile does funny things to my insides.

I kiss the end of her nose. "I love the sound of that."

And as I take her hand and lead her back to my family, I intend to make sure that's our new reality.

Want to read Ange and Devin's backstory? Check out ***Inseparable*** available now in ebook, paperback, and audiobook format.

Gritty, Angsty, Stand-alone New Adult Contemporary Romance

A childhood promise. An unbreakable bond. One tragic event that shatters everything.

It all started with the boys next door...

Devin and Ayden were my best friends. We were practically joined at the hip since age two. When we were kids, we thought we were invincible, inseparable, that nothing or no one could come between us.

But we were wrong.

Everything turned to crap our senior year of high school.

Devin was turning into a clone of his deadbeat lowlife father—fighting, getting wasted, and screwing his way through every girl in town. I'd been hiding a secret crush on him for years. Afraid to tell him how I felt in case I ruined everything. So, I kept quiet and slowly watched him self-destruct with a constant ache in my heart.

Where Devin was all brooding darkness, Ayden was the shining light. Our star quarterback with the bright future whom everyone loved. But something wasn't right. He was so guarded, and he wouldn't let me in.

When Devin publicly shamed me, Ayden took my side, and our awesome-threesome bond was severed. The split was devastating. The heartbreak inevitable.

Ayden and I moved on with our lives, but the pain never lessened, and Devin was never far from our thoughts.

Until it all came to a head in college, and one eventful night changed everything.

Now, I've lost the two people who matter more to me than life itself. Nothing will ever be the same again.

***Inseparable* is available now in ebook, paperback, and audiobook format.**

About the Author

Siobhan Davis is a *USA Today, Wall Street Journal*, and Amazon Top 5 bestselling romance author. **Siobhan** writes emotionally intense stories with swoon-worthy romance, complex characters, and tons of unexpected plot twists and turns that will have you flipping the pages beyond bedtime! She has sold over 2 million books, and her titles are translated into several languages.

Prior to becoming a full-time writer, Siobhan forged a successful corporate career in human resource management.

She lives in the Garden County of Ireland with her husband and two sons.

You can connect with Siobhan in the following ways:

Website: www.siobhandavis.com
Facebook: AuthorSiobhanDavis
Instagram: @siobhandavisauthor
Tiktok: @siobhandavisauthor
Email: siobhan@siobhandavis.com

Books by Siobhan Davis

KENNEDY BOYS SERIES

Upper Young Adult/New Adult Contemporary Romance

Finding Kyler

Losing Kyler

Keeping Kyler

The Irish Getaway

Loving Kalvin

Saving Brad

Seducing Kaden

Forgiving Keven

Summer in Nantucket

Releasing Keanu

Adoring Keaton

Reforming Kent

Moonlight in Massachusetts

STAND-ALONES

New Adult Contemporary Romance

Inseparable

Incognito

When Forever Changes

No Feelings Involved

Still Falling for You

Second Chances Box Set

Holding on to Forever

Always Meant to Be

Tell It to My Heart

The One I Want

Reverse Harem Romance

Surviving Amber Springs

Dark Mafia Romance

Vengeance of a Mafia Quee

RYDEVILLE ELITE SERIES

Dark High School Romance

Cruel Intentions

Twisted Betrayal

Sweet Retribution

Charlie

Jackson

Sawyer

*The Hate I Feel^*

Drew

MAZZONE MAFIA SERIES

Dark Mafia Romance

Condemned to Love

Forbidden to Love

Scared to Love

Mazzone Mafia: The Complete Series

THE ACCARDI TWINS

Dark Mafia Romance

CKONY #1^

CKONY #2^

THE SAINTHOOD (BOYS OF LOWELL HIGH)

Dark HS Reverse Harem Romance

Resurrection

Rebellion

Reign

Revere

The Sainthood: The Complete Series

DIRTY CRAZY BAD DUET

Dark College Reverse Harem Romance

Dirty Crazy Bad - A Prequel Short Story

Dirty Crazy Bad # 1

Dirty Crazy Bad #2

ALL OF ME DUET

Angsty New Adult Romance

Say I'm The One

Let Me Love You

Hold Me Close

All of Me: The Complete Series

ALINTHIA SERIES

Upper YA/NA Paranormal Romance/Reverse Harem

The Lost Savior

The Secret Heir

The Warrior Princess

The Chosen One

The Rightful Queen^

SAVEN SERIES

Young Adult Science Fiction/Paranormal Romance

Saven Deception

Logan

Saven Disclosure

Saven Denial

Saven Defiance

Axton

Saven Deliverance

Saven: The Complete Series

^Release date to be confirmed